SUCH STUFF AS DREAMS

Thomas Garlinghouse

OPEN
BOOKS

Published by Open Books

Interior design by Siva Ram Maganti

Cover image © Ninell shutterstock.com/g/ninell

To my mom, Barbara M. Garlinghouse
Artist, painter and beautiful soul

"We are such stuff as dreams are made on, and our
little life is rounded with a sleep."

–William Shakespeare, *The Tempest*, Act 4, Scene 1

CHAPTER 1

Los Angeles, 1936

THE FURIOUS *CLACK, CLACK, clack* of a typewriter reverberated against the thin walls of the small beach cottage as, outside, the sun began to set over the Pacific Ocean. Had Joe Holliday been looking up at that moment his eyes would have feasted on a vivid tableau of colors—oranges, reds, and purples—splashed across the sky through the window.

But he wasn't looking up. He sat hunched over his Remington, his brow furrowed in concentration, his fingers pounding out a steady rhythm on the keys. His attention—indeed, his sole focus—was on finishing the last few sentences of a screenplay that had been his entire *raison d'être* for the past few months. He was oblivious to everything else.

Called *One Step Away from Heaven*, it was the culmination of many weeks of concentrated effort—of sweat, anguish, toil, and countless false starts. It was his first original screenplay for Apex Studios, and he had treated it differently from the hack work—the "potboilers"—he'd been contracted to write for the last four years. This screenplay was different; it was original, dealt with timeless, universal themes, had complex characters, and a gripping storyline. It was a tale of political corruption, ambition, greed, and individual redemption set during the Teapot Dome scandal of the Harding Administration. In short, he considered it his...well, if not his masterpiece, then at least a story of which he could be eminently proud.

1

He pounded out the last few words, his fingers punching the keys with authority. Then all at once, as the final key slapped out the final letter, it was over.

He stared at the page for a moment, as if unable to believe the thing was done. After all that torture and strife, the beast was slain. He read the last few lines of dialogue to himself and then grinned, satisfied.

Leaning forward, he yanked the page out of the Remington and, with a flourish, slapped it face down on the stack of loose pages that constituted his screenplay.

There was a tumbler of scotch sitting by the typewriter. He'd poured it hours ago but hadn't touched it because he'd been so engrossed in writing. Now, as he reached for it, his eyes darted up. The sun was already down but the sky was still ablaze with brilliant color. His gaze lingered over the scene. It had been one of those picture-perfect days in southern California, filled with vivid blue vistas, sunshine, and citrus-laced breezes. And now the day was about to cash in on all that beauty by staging one final burst of brilliance before settling into night.

He sipped his scotch, grimacing at the harshness of the alcohol as it hit his throat. He felt something brush against his leg and looked down. His cat, Desdemona, was staring up at him with huge green eyes, her tail swishing back and forth.

He smiled. "Where have you been hiding, Dez?"

The cat hopped up onto his lap. She meowed once, turned in a half circle, and then settled down. She purred as Joe sipped his drink and gently stroked her soft fur.

He began to feel loose and relaxed as the alcohol suffused through him. The languid sounds of evening drifted about, and he let out a contented yawn.

All at once, he tossed back the rest of his drink in a single swallow and set the glass on the table. He put the cat down and pushed away from his typewriter, impulsively standing up. His lower back was sore; he reached around and kneaded the area with his fingers.

Desdemona twined herself between his legs and meowed plaintively.

"You're not going to leave me alone, are you?" he said.

He scooped her up and, cradling her in his arms like a baby, stepped out onto the small patio that fronted the beach. A balmy breeze rustled his hair. It was the first wisp of wind in more than a week, and it felt pleasingly cool against his cheeks. The air smelled of salt and he could hear the lap of the waves on the sand down by the water. He stood and gazed up at the sky.

The final vestiges of sunset were fading into inky night. Stars began to appear, tiny pinpricks of light, first one, then another. Soon, he knew, the immense vault of the sky would be awash with stars and a full moon would rise above the San Gabriel Mountains to the east.

"Whattaya think, Dez?" Joe said softly, continuing to stare up at the sky, a dreamy look on his face.

Desdemona meowed, and Joe chuckled.

"You said it, sister," he replied, nodding slowly. "You said it."

———————

The next morning Joe awoke early. He showered, shaved, and, wearing boxer shorts and a clean white undershirt, combed through his sparse wardrobe looking for something decent—and, importantly, clean—to wear. He was scheduled to meet with the studio head, C.J. Greenwood, sharply at ten o'clock to discuss his screenplay, and didn't want to look like a bum. He dug into his chest of drawers and pulled out all the clothes he thought were the most presentable. These he laid out on the top of his bed. He stood lingering over them for a while, scratching his chin in contemplation. He finally opted for a pair of tan pleated trousers, a button-down dress shirt, and his old, but still sturdy, two-toned Oxfords. Hastily knotting a tie, he placed his manuscript in a leather satchel and, tossing on a well-used but still presentable two-button, Herringbone jacket, left the cottage.

He took the Red Car trolley up Santa Monica Boulevard as the morning sun glinted off shop windows and the polished chrome of cars parked along the street. Although it was still early, the streets were beginning to get crowded as people scurried to work, popped in and out of shops, and hurried along the sidewalk. Despite this being the seventh year of the Depression, Los Angeles—and southern California, in general—was doing well compared to the rest of the nation. While economic failure after economic failure characterized much of the country, southern California, buoyed by its film industry, was managing not only to keep its head above water but also to thrive. Hollywood played a psychological role, as well. Joe knew that people flocked to the movies to escape the drudgery, pessimism, and hardships that had become the norm over the past several years. Hence the fact that most of Joe's screenplays contained happy endings, where right prevailed over might, the "little guy" ended up besting the bully, and most importantly, the guy always got the girl.

Joe exited the trolley at Wilshire Boulevard, just a few blocks from Apex Studios and walked the rest of the way on foot. Consulting his watch, he saw he was early for his meeting and figured there was no need to hurry. He slowed his pace to a stroll.

He was still feeling elated from having finished his screenplay. All the long hours, the numerous revisions, and the meticulous research he'd done had paid off. He felt it was the finest work he had yet produced. Even if he spent the rest of his career doing hack work, this one screenplay—this one burst of creative brilliance—would give him a lifetime of satisfaction.

When he reached the main gate, he waved at the security guard—a man named Woodrow "Woody" Davis—who occupied the kiosk. Woody was a permanent fixture, having manned the gate for the last twenty years. He waved Joe through the immense, arch-like gate, and soon Joe was striding along the brick walkway that cut across the main grounds of the studio. To his right were the large, hangar-like sound stages where most movie interiors were shot, and to his left, appearing like the buildings of some sedate Midwestern college, were the offices of the studio executives. Beyond them was the backlot, where a host of buildings that contained dressing rooms, storage facilities, sets, and the writers' cottages were housed.

He arrived at the executive offices a good fifteen minutes early for his meeting and strode through the main hall to the elevator, which he took up to the top floor. The bell rang and the doors slid open. Exiting, he stood for a moment on the well-polished parquet floor. At the end of the hallway loomed Greenwood's office. Some of his fellow writers called it the "gateway to hell." Dante's line from *The Inferno* flashed in his mind, "Abandon all hope, ye who enter here," as he contemplated the imposing green doors. He closed his eyes and took a deep breath.

He always felt a little nervous when meeting with Greenwood and debated whether to barge in now or wait a few minutes before entering. The famous producer was notoriously mercurial, governed by constantly changing mood swings that kept his various assistants in a perpetual state of anxiety. Trying to anticipate which way his pendulum-like mood would swing at any given moment was a task that ensured a revolving door of new assistants.

Opening his eyes, he screwed up his courage. There was no time like the present, he told himself. He smoothed his hair and proceeded down the hallway, his shoes clicking smartly against the floor. He gave the door a few smart raps.

"Come in," a voice he recognized as Marjorie Hayden's—with its clipped and precise diction—echoed from inside the office. She was Greenwood's personal secretary and the only person who had ever managed to stay with the producer for any length of time.

He opened the door and took a tentative step inside.

Ms. Hayden, who was sitting at her desk, looked up, scrutinizing Joe over the rim of her half glasses. "Ah, Mr. Holliday. Come in." She glanced at her watch. "You're early."

She was an impeccably dressed woman in her forties with an attractive figure and green eyes.

"Yes, I am a little bit. Sorry." He closed the door behind him with a soft click.

"Not a problem." She pressed an intercom button on her desk with a well-manicured finger.

"Yes, Ms. Hayden?" crackled a voice in response.

"Mr. Holliday is here to see you, sir."

"Send him in."

Marjorie gave him an encouraging smile. "You heard the man."

Thrusting his shoulders back in an unconscious effort to buoy his confidence, Joe strode into Greenwood's office, feeling as if he'd entered a lion's den.

C.J. Greenwood, the "absolute ruler" of Apex Studios, sat behind his heavy oak desk at the far end of the room, a telephone crammed against his ear. When he saw Joe, he put his hand over the receiver and impatiently motioned the writer to the seat opposite his desk. Then he turned his attention back to the phone and his face darkened.

"Goddamn it," he growled into the mouthpiece, the tone of his voice rising with each word uttered, "I don't give a rat's ass what you think about it, I pay the bills around here! And I want those sets done by next Monday! What the hell do I pay you for?"

Joe sat down and placed his satchel on his lap. He stared across at Greenwood as the man launched into a full-blown tongue-lashing of the poor bastard on the other end of the line.

"If those sets aren't up and running by that date, it's your ass in a sling!" He screamed into the phone. "Do I make myself clear?!"

Despite instilling fear in everyone in the studio, the producer wasn't much to look at. He was short and overweight with a receding hairline and heavy, dark eyebrows. He wore wire-framed spectacles that were constantly sliding down his nose so that he was always pushing them back up with his short, fat fingers.

Though Joe would never say it out loud, he thought there was something almost comical about the way Greenwood lorded it over his studio kingdom, sort of like a Napoleon haranguing his underlings. In fact, one nickname—among many—he had acquired was Bonaparte, though no one dared to utter it in his presence. The one redeeming physical quality he had were dark, piercing eyes. They were eyes that, once focused on something, penetrated with the power of a laser beam.

Perhaps as a means of drawing attention away from his less than impressive physical attributes, Greenwood's clothes always reflected the latest in men's fashion. And this morning was no exception. He was wearing a double-breasted, charcoal suit over a white shirt and brilliantly red silk tie. A matching silk handkerchief, impeccably folded, protruded from his breast pocket.

"This conversation is over!" Greenwood roared. "Just remember what I said!" He slammed the phone down on its receiver with a bang. He sat quietly for a moment, calming himself. His glasses slid down his nose and he pushed them back up. Then he glanced across the table and focused those dark eyes on Joe.

"You're early," he said.

Joe blinked. Greenwood had made the comment in such an ambiguous tone, Joe didn't know whether the producer was pleased or irritated.

"Sorry," Joe said, guessing that Greenwood was probably irritated.

"Why are you apologizing?" Greenwood demanded. It was now obvious that he had meant it as a compliment.

Joe cleared his throat. "Anyway," he said, "I've finished it."

"You have?" Greenwood drew his eyebrows together into a hard line. "What have you finished?"

"The screenplay."

"What screenplay, for Christ's sake?"

"*One Step Away from Heaven.*"

Greenwood looked at him for a moment and then nodded. "Oh, that. Is that why I scheduled this meeting?"

Joe hesitated. "Well, yes," he said, "at least that was what I was led to believe."

Greenwood let out an irritated sigh and gestured impatiently. "Well, let's see it, then."

Joe unbuckled the straps of the satchel and extracted the

manuscript. He handed it over to the producer.

Greenwood thumped it down on his desk, licked a finger, and began to flip through it, page by page.

"Has the editorial department looked at this yet?" Greenwood asked, glancing up.

"No," Joe shook his head. "You said you wanted to see it first thing when it was done."

Greenwood nodded. He drew his eyebrows together and glanced at his wristwatch before adjusting his glasses and returning his gaze to the script.

Joe sat quietly, but his heart was racing. He stared at Greenwood, noting the man's furrowed brow as he studied the document. Was it a frown of disapproval or simply concentration? Anxiety shot through him like an electric current. What if Greenwood didn't like it? What if, after all that work, Greenwood decided he didn't want to make it? Such a thing was not out of the realm of possibility. He picked at a callus on his finger and tried to calm himself.

Greenwood continued to read for several long minutes. Joe took the downtime to glance around the room. Greenwood's office was plush, modern, and spacious. The walls were heavily paneled and covered with expensive paintings. There was luxurious carpeting on the floor and a big antique cabinet that served as a wet bar standing up against one wall.

Finally, Greenwood glanced up and adjusted his glasses. "Impressive. You've really outdone yourself here."

Joe let out a sigh of relief and grinned.

"But, unfortunately," Greenwood announced with a deflating abruptness, "we can't use it."

Joe's face dropped, his grin immediately evaporating. "What? Why?"

"Because I've got a new project in mind."

Joe just stared at him, stunned into silence.

Greenwood gave Joe one of his rare sympathetic looks. "Look, kid, this is good. Really good, but we have to go with what's hot."

Joe remained silent, not knowing what to say.

"And do you know what's hot right now?" Greenwood asked.

Joe broke out of his paralysis. He shook his head.

"Shakespeare."

"Shakespeare?"

Greenwood looked at Joe as if he were a dullard. "Don't you know who he is? You of all people."

"Yes, of course I do," Joe nodded, flustered. "But I mean—"

Before Joe could finish, Greenwood continued. "Ever heard of this guy Welles?"

"Who?"

"Orson Welles."

Joe had to think for a moment, but then it hit him. Welles was the guy who was doing some innovative stage productions in New York City. At only twenty-one, he was already an accomplished stage director, so much so that the east coast press had dubbed him a "wunderkind."

"I met him once," Greenwood said. "He's a colossal SOB, but a talented SOB. His production of *Macbeth* with all those Negroes was a huge hit earlier this year. The press went crackers over it."

Joe recalled reading a blurb about the production a while back in *Variety*. Welles had used an entire Negro cast and set the play on a fictional Caribbean island made to resemble Haiti. He had turned the requisite Scottish witches into Voodoo practitioners. The production had been a huge success, consistently playing before sold-out crowds. The press had christened it the "Voodoo Macbeth."

"Anyway," Greenwood said, "I want to do something similar."

Joe gave Greenwood a blank stare. "You want to do a 'Voodoo Macbeth?'"

"I didn't say the same," Greenwood snapped. "I said something similar."

Joe nodded, beginning to understand where this might be headed.

Greenwood suddenly stood up and strode around to the front of the desk. He leaned his rear against the edge and folded his arms across his chest.

"I know this might sound strange coming from me because

Apex Studios has made its reputation as a place that makes B pictures. That's not something I'm going to apologize for, by the way. Those pictures have been our stock and trade from day one. They've put bread on the table and made Apex what it is. And yet—" He paused and unfolded his arms, placing his hands palm-down on the edge of the desk. He nodded gravely. "I sometimes think that we can do more. Create some real art."

"I sympathize," Joe said, "that's why—"

Before Joe could finish, Greenwood pushed away from the desk and began to pace the room as if possessed by restless energy that needed an outlet. Joe swiveled in his seat to follow him.

"I want to do a modern production of a Shakespeare play," Greenwood said.

"What do you mean 'modern'?"

"I want to put one of his plays in a contemporary setting. Like right here in LA, or New York. Hell, or even Peoria, Illinois."

Joe nodded. "Which play were you thinking of doing?"

"I don't know. I'll leave that for you to figure out."

"*Hamlet? Othello? A Midsummer Night's Dream?*"

Greenwood waved him off, continuing to pace. "I don't care. But we still have to make allowances for popular taste. For example, we have to make sure the heroine is pretty." He paused to shake his head. "And I don't want to use all that flowery language. Nobody understands it."

Joe raised an eyebrow. "Don't use his verse? But that's what makes him Shakespeare. With all due respect, sir, without that—"

"I said it'll be in modern English," Greenwood retorted. "No 'thees' or 'thous,' or all that fancy language. As I said, we have to make allowances for popular taste."

"Well, sir," Joe interjected, "not all of Shakespeare's stuff is highbrow by any means. He peppered his plays with quite a lot of bawdy—"

"Yes, Holliday, I know you have a master's in English literature," Greenwood said irritably. "You don't need to parade your learning."

"I'm not sir, I'm merely pointing out—"

"Don't contradict me, for Christ's sake."

Joe fell silent.

"The point I'm trying to make," Greenwood went on, "is we have to walk a fine line between highbrow and popular appeal. Too highbrow and we lose the masses, and too lowbrow we lose the critics. And I want both. I want the public's money and the critics' praise. You get my drift?"

Joe nodded but remained silent, his head swirling. He was trying to comprehend all these sudden changes.

"And by the way," Greenwood said, "we have to move on this. Strike while the iron's hot. I have a number of investors already lined up, so I'll need a finished draft by the end of May."

"May?" Joe's face dropped for the second time today. "But that's less than two months away."

Greenwood stopped pacing and stared at Joe. "Come on, Holliday. If you can't do this, just tell me now, for Christ's sake. There are other writers on the lot. I picked you because I thought you could do it." His eyes narrowed. "But if I'm mistaken, I'd like to know."

"No, no," Joe said quickly. "I can do it. But—"

Greenwood adjusted his eyeglasses and frowned at his young writer, waiting for him to continue. "But what?"

"It's nothing," Joe said. He cleared his throat and adjusted himself on his chair, sitting up straight. "I'll be happy to take it on, sir. But are you sure you don't have any idea what play you want to do?"

"Good God, man," Greenwood growled, "I told you, that's something for you to figure out!"

"Yes, sir."

Greenwood walked back around his desk and sat down in his chair, his bulk noticeably thumping against the seat. "Let's meet again on Monday. That'll give you the whole weekend to digest all this. You can bring me a treatment and we can discuss it further."

Joe nodded.

"Wait a second," Greenwood said with characteristic fickleness. He shook his head. "Monday's no good. I'm meeting with those crybabies from the goddamned contractor's union. That's sure to spoil my day. We'll have to meet on Tuesday instead. That'll give you an extra day to think about all this." He grinned and looked at Joe slyly. "And, Christ, if you can't come up with an idea in three days, we'll have to renegotiate your contract."

Greenwood had uttered that last statement flippantly, but Joe knew that the producer was only half-joking. As if to confirm this, the sly amusement in Greenwood's eyes gave way to a more pointed look. "Be here at ten o'clock sharp on Tuesday morning. I expect a finished treatment. And I expect it to be good."

Joe was silent for a long moment, his head swirling, trying to digest all this. Finally, he nodded.

CHAPTER 2

JOE LEFT GREENWOOD'S OFFICE smoldering with indignation. He took the elevator down to the ground floor, and when the doors slid open, stalked down the hallway, his footsteps echoing like rifle shots against the well-swept surface. He came outside and stood for a moment, gazing out at the bright sunshine and drooping palm trees set over an immaculately cut lawn. The air was scented with the pleasant odor of roses and lilies. There was a languid, unhurried quality to the day. It was yet another perfect day in southern California.

But Joe wasn't in the mood to notice the day's beauty. He felt like he'd been buffeted by a whirlwind. Or sucker-punched in the stomach.

He couldn't believe his screenplay had been dismissed with such rapidity, with such little regard to how much effort he'd put into it. Greenwood had been the one to encourage him in the first place. He'd told Joe he wanted an original screenplay, something different from the typical B movie bilge they normally cranked out.

And what was this about not using Shakespeare's language? It was ludicrous. What would be the point, for Christ's sake? He frowned. Still, he'd agreed to do it, and Apex Studios was his employer, for better or for worse.

Shaking his head with disgust, he thrust both hands into his pockets and clamped his satchel under his arm. He descended the steps and proceeded down the path with heavy strides, kicking at the few stray rocks on the path.

Eventually, near Sound Stage number twelve, he came to a bench set under a large, spreading palm tree. He sat down, placing his satchel on the space next to him.

He glanced at his watch. It was only a little after eleven o'clock. He had a full hour before his girlfriend, Betsy Parker, was let out for lunch. She was filming *The Queen's Cavalier*, a swashbuckler set during the great social and political upheaval of the French Revolution.

He reached into his shirt pocket and pulled out a fresh package of Lucky Strike cigarettes, which he smacked against his palm. Extracting a cigarette, he stuck it in the corner of his mouth and lit it with a metal lighter. He leaned back, gazed into the distance, and blew out a puff of smoke.

The distant San Gabriels framed the horizon. For several minutes, he watched wisps of cloud float above the summits like tattered bits of gauze against the sheer blue of the sky. Lowering his gaze, his eyes traveled around the sculptured lawn. The studio was quiet. There were few people out, mostly technicians and messengers, scurrying back and forth from the executive offices and the sound stages, carrying memos and directives.

Joe dropped the stub of his cigarette on the ground and crushed it out on the gravel with the sole of his shoe. He glanced down at his watch again, bored.

When he looked back up, he noticed a tall man striding toward him from across the lawn. His arms swung loosely as he walked, his stride self-assured and easy.

Joe put up his hand and squinted into the sun to get a better look. The man had dark hair and a well-groomed mustache. To his surprise, it dawned on him he was looking at Clark Gable, one of the up-and-coming actors on the lot. As he neared, Joe was again reminded of just how large and broad-shouldered Gable actually was. Physically, he was everything central casting was looking for in a star. He had the chest of a heavyweight boxer, the engaging eyes of a wistful poet, and the sharp, lantern-like jawline of General Pershing. And there was no doubt the man's star was on the rise. He had recently finished filming a romantic comedy with Myrna Loy. *Variety* and *The Hollywood Reporter* had given the film high marks and tapped Gable as an "up-and-coming" actor to watch. He was currently in production for a picture based on a Jack London novel. And yet, though Joe couldn't say why, he had always felt that Gable seemed somewhat uncomfortable in the role of "movie star." He sensed that the actor would be much more contented out in the woods, chopping trees or paddling a canoe.

Before Joe knew it, Gable was standing next to him. The man's bulk cast Joe in shadow. "This seat taken, chief?" he asked, gesturing down at the spot next to Joe.

Joe looked up at the broad-shouldered actor, surprised that the man had addressed him so casually. He moved his satchel. "Uh, no, I—"

Gable sat down with a thump. He was quiet for a moment but then burst out. "Christ on a stick! You know anything about dames?"

"Me? No, not really." Joe hesitated and shrugged. "Well, I mean, maybe a little."

"Wish to God I did. I don't understand them at all. They can be so damned..." He scratched his head and frowned, trying to think of the appropriate word.

"Infuriating?" Joe offered.

"That's the word." He looked over at Joe with sudden interest, his pale blue eyes appraising. "Hey, you an actor?"

"No, I'm a writer."

"Thought that might be the case." He scrutinized Joe for a moment longer. "You don't look like an actor."

Joe raised an eyebrow, not sure how to take the man's comment. "Oh."

"No offense, though."

"No, none taken."

Gable leaned back and gazed up at the distant mountains, raising his hand to shade his eyes. "Damned nice day, huh? Another day in Paradise. Sure beats the hell out of Ohio."

Joe nodded and looked toward the horizon. The San Gabriels were clear and stark above the Los Angeles basin.

Gable leaned forward, putting his elbows on the tops of his knees. "You know what gets me? I'll tell you. The way they get so…Christ, there I go again, I can't even think of the word."

"Indignant?"

"Yeah, that's it." He looked at Joe appraisingly and thrust a finger at him. "Hey, chief, you're good." Without missing a beat, Gable continued. "I keep telling her I'm a guy, for Christ's sake. I like to do guy things. I like to fish and hunt. So sue me." He looked over at Joe. "You're a guy, right? So you know what I'm talking about."

Joe nodded. "Yeah, sure, I like to do 'guy' things. I like to fish."

Gable winked. "Thought you might. I can always tell. This town has too many…"

Joe kept silent this time, just listening.

"Over the weekend," Gable said, "I go on a fishing trip out to Catalina. So, yeah, okay, it goes a little longer than I'd originally planned, and I get back late. Too late for some soiree in Beverly Hills that she's been hounding me about all week. But that's no reason…"

"To get bent out of shape?"

"Bingo. I mean, it seems like there's some stupid soiree every damn weekend. What's the big deal in missing one? Why's this one so special?"

Joe opened his mouth to speak but suddenly clamped it shut and fell silent. He knew the questions were rhetorical, but it was as if Gable's magnetic presence almost demanded an answer from him.

Gable put out his hand. "I'm Clark, by the way."

Joe nodded. "Yeah, I know who you are." He shook Gable's hand. "I'm Joe."

Gable just nodded and grunted.

They sat in silence for a time.

Gable slapped the top of his thighs with his hands and jumped to his feet. "Well," he said, "I should get back. Gotta meet with

Bonaparte in fifteen minutes. Good to meet you, chief." With a wink and a smile that displayed brilliantly white teeth, he sauntered off.

———————

On Sound Stage number twelve, meanwhile, there was a flurry of activity. Technicians and stagehands were rushing about, hauling cables, adjusting lights, tinkering with delicate sound equipment, and putting the finishing touches on anything—and everything— that needed it. Oblivious to all the furor, the director was sitting in his chair poring over the script, going over details with his screenwriter and his assistant director. On the floor next to him was his bullhorn, standing vertical like a traffic cone.

The main set, made to resemble the French court of Louis XVI, was ground zero. Like minor celestial bodies held in orbit by a larger force, everyone seemed to be revolving around, and making particular allowances for, the two people in the center of the set—the star actor and actress, Roger Powell and Lillian Russell. Both were wearing costumes befitting nobles of the French court. Surrounding them was a gaggle of makeup artists, daubing makeup and applying highlights to cheeks and foreheads.

More than anything else, Roger Powell seemed annoyed as one of the makeup artists tried to powder his cheeks. He was tall, dark-haired and strikingly handsome, with chiseled features and icy blue eyes. He was dressed in the long coat and fashionable wig of an eighteenth-century French nobleman. A long rapier was sheathed at his side and he wore long, knee-high boots. The actress, an attractive blonde, was wearing a high wig and billowing dress made of satin and silk.

Two extras stood near the back of the set, out of the glare of the main lights and partially obscured by shadows. They were both dressed as fashionable women of the court, faces heavy with pancake makeup and wearing high, "Fontange" style powdered wigs. One was short and pretty, a brunette with large brown eyes, attractive dimples, and a small, pert nose. The other was her exact opposite. She was tall, leggy, and blonde, pretty, but with well-defined eyebrows that gave her face a perpetually sardonic cast.

The tall blonde, Elsa Zabrowski, glanced at Roger and then leaned over and nudged her shorter companion with an elbow. "Think he'll get it right this time?" she whispered, her voice flavored by a heavy Bronx accent.

The shorter actress, Betsy Parker, rolled her eyes. "I hope so because I'm starving." She directed her gaze at the director. "Mr. Leighton needs to put his foot down this time."

The taller actress smirked. "Don't hold your breath."

Both actresses watched as, finally, everything was ready for the scene to be shot. The makeup artists scurried away, and the camera was rolled into place. The heavy stage lights snapped on, illuminating the set with brilliant light. At a sign from the director, the sound technician flipped a switch.

"Places everyone!" Leighton shouted through his bullhorn. "We're rolling!"

A technician darted in front of the camera holding a black slate clapboard. "*The Queen's Cavalier*, scene four, take twelve," he droned monotonously, snapping the clapboard shut with a quick motion and ducking out of the way of the camera.

"Action!" Leighton bellowed.

Roger strode forward, his shoulders thrown back and his chest out, his heavy boots ringing against the sound stage floor. With one hand on the hilt of his sword, he reached out with the other and took Lillian's hand. He helped her to her feet. For a moment they stood face to face, their lips mere inches from each other. The camera continued to roll as a palpable hush fell over everyone. Lillian's eyes were expectant as she gazed at her fellow actor. Roger took a deep breath and then delivered his lines, this time flawlessly.

"Cut!" Leighton shouted. "That's a take!"

A collective sigh of relief went up from the cast and crew.

"Okay, people," Leighton said, "let's break for lunch. Meet back here in half an hour."

Betsy took off her wig, scratched her scalp, and made a move to leave.

Elsa leaned close to Betsy's elbow. Out of the corner of her mouth, she whispered, "Twenty's the charm."

Betsy chuckled and rolled her eyes. "See you later." She headed for the door.

Roger materialized in front of her. He impulsively grabbed her hand and, bowing forward, kissed it with a grand flourish.

"Mademoiselle," he said, affecting a French accent, "you look exquisite today."

She pulled her hand away and gazed at him with one eyebrow arched. "What are you doing, Roger?"

"Kissing your hand," he said.

"I can see that. Why?"

He grinned. "When I see such a beautiful maiden, I can't help myself. I must kiss her hand."

"I already said no, Roger."

His grin faltered, and he dropped his accent. "C'mon Betsy, why do you have to be so hard on me?"

"I'm not being hard on you. I'm just not interested."

Roger put up his hands in a pleading gesture. "For Christ's sake, Betsy, what's one cup of coffee?"

"It's coffee now, is it? Yesterday you were proposing dinner."

"Why won't you go out with me?"

"How many times do I have to tell you?" Betsy said. "I have a boyfriend."

Roger paused for the briefest of moments, his lip curling in a smirk. "The writer?"

She glared at him. "Yes, the writer."

––––––––

Joe looked up and saw Betsy emerge from the front door of the sound stage, still in her eighteenth-century dress but without her wig. He stood up and waved. Her face broke into a dimpled smile

19

when she saw him, and she waved back.

The sight of her always managed to put a smile on his face, no matter how depressed or frustrated he felt. She was sweet, vivacious, and always seemed so positive—a trait he wished he possessed in greater amounts. Lifting her dress a few inches off the ground, she made toward him.

"How long have you been waiting?" she asked, coming up and sitting down on the bench. She proceeded to take a ham sandwich out of a paper bag.

"An hour."

"An hour?" She looked at him, squinting up into the sun. "But I thought you had a meeting with Greenwood this morning."

"I did."

"How'd it go?"

"Not too well."

She stared at him in surprise. "Why? What happened?"

"He rejected my script."

"*One Step Away from Heaven?*"

He nodded.

"But I don't understand?" Her large eyes focused on him with a puzzled look. "Weren't you under contract to write that?"

Joe nodded again.

Betsy patted the empty space on the bench next to her. "Have a seat."

Joe thrust his hands into his pockets and sat down with a disgruntled sigh.

"So why does he suddenly not want it?" she asked, beginning to eat her sandwich.

Joe sat back, took his hands out of his pockets and folded them across his chest. He shrugged and stared gloomily into the distance. "He's on to another project."

"Another script?"

He nodded.

Betsy munched thoughtfully for a moment, and then looked at him. "What is it?"

"The script?"

She nodded.

"He wants to do a modern version of a Shakespeare play. He wants me to write it."

She lowered her sandwich, looking at him. "But that's good," she said quickly. "You love Shakespeare!"

"Yes, I do. Every writer worth his salt does. But that's not the point."

"What's the point, then?" Betsy asked.

"He just completely dismissed my script," Joe said angrily. "God, I've been sweating over *One Step* for months. And he barely looked at it. It's a really good script. I poured my guts into it." He paused, looking at Betsy. "When I was writing it, I really felt like I was creating something. Something good and lasting. Something creative and original. Something I could be proud of."

Betsy was silent. She continued to eat her sandwich. After a moment, she looked over. "What play does he want to do?"

"He's leaving that up to me, apparently."

"Then that means you have more leeway to be creative. Isn't that what you're always kvetching about, anyway? The studio never lets you be creative. Well, this is your chance."

"But I was creative with *One Step*. That's the whole point."

"Well then, you'll just have to be as creative with this new script." She continued to munch her sandwich. In between bites she said, "What does he mean by a modern version, anyway?"

"It means he wants to put the story in a modern, contemporary setting. Like setting *Much Ado About Nothing* in Grand Central Park, or something. Or make Macbeth a bonds salesman."

"A bonds salesman?" Betsy said, looking at him with a frown.

"I'm being facetious," Joe said.

After that, he fell silent and stared sullenly up at the mountains.

Betsy reached out and rested her hand on his arm, giving him a sympathetic smile. "At least he didn't fire you, Joe. At least you still have a job. And if he wants you to work on this script that means he still has faith in you. He still thinks you're a good writer."

Despite himself, Joe managed to crack a smile. "Always the optimist, aren't you?"

Betsy gave him a serene smile, revealing attractively dimpled cheeks. "Not much point in being anything else, is there?"

CHAPTER 3

JOE SAT IN FRONT of his Remington and stared at a blank sheet of paper. For a moment it seemed like he was in a catatonic trance, mesmerized by the whiteness of the page. But a second later his shoulders slumped, and he sighed. He sat back and scratched his head.

He'd been sitting now for the last twenty minutes, completely devoid of ideas. He couldn't seem to get in gear this morning. After spending most of the night mulling over what Betsy had said—about transferring his creativity into the new project— he'd resolved to get over his huge disappointment about *One Step Away from Heaven*, lick his wounds, and do exactly as she'd counseled: throw himself into the Shakespeare project with vigor. She had been right about another thing as well: he'd long been a great admirer of the Bard, constantly amazed how Shakespeare could shift so effortlessly from tragedy and pathos to comedy and epic drama. He'd spent many hours in college poring over the man's plays and poems, analyzing his style, pondering his imagery, and envying his creative use of language and metaphor. The man was a true literary genius.

But now, as he sat down to write a scenario, his mind had gone blank. It was as if he'd been drained of all creative juices. He couldn't figure out what to write, didn't have the inkling of an idea—at least none that sparked any enthusiasm. Should he set *Othello* in the modern American military? What if he made Hamlet the scion of a wealthy industrialist? Or the son of a famous opera singer? Perhaps Castle Elsinore could be a grand opera house? What about setting *Romeo and Juliet* on a south sea island? Or on the mean streets of New York?

Frustrated, he pushed away from his desk and got to his feet. He began to pace back and forth across the floor, stopping occasionally to glare at his Remington—as if the machine was somehow the cause of his writer's block. Finally, he stopped and turned to stare out the window. The morning sun sparkled on the water like a thousand diamonds, and the skies above were bright blue, hung here and there with wispy traces of cloud. A swell was rolling in and each wave broke against the sandbar with a thumping crash of whitewater, reverberating through his feet. A flock of seagulls stood on the wet sand at the water's edge.

Something brushed against him and he looked down. Desdemona was winding herself sinuously between his legs and purring. It was one of her purrs that signaled she wanted something from him. He looked down at her with a puzzled expression but soon realized what she wanted. With his mind so focused on trying to come up with a workable scenario, he'd forgotten to feed her this morning.

He scooped her up and carried her into the kitchen, setting her down next to her food bowl. She looked up at him and meowed as he took a tin of sardines from the cabinet.

"Hold your horses, Dez," he said. He opened the tin and spooned its contents into her bowl. Desdemona fell on the food hungrily. He reached down and gave the cat a pet. She arched her back against his hand but went on eating.

"I'll take that as a thank you," he said, chuckling. He stepped back and put his hands on his hips, watching the cat tear into her food without any sense of decorum. At least someone was content, he thought. He turned and marched back into the living room. This time he was determined to get something on paper. He sat down and, methodically, rolled up both sleeves. He sat for several long minutes, staring at the Remington with fierce concentration. A minute elapsed, and then another. Frustrated, he tapped his fingers against the tabletop and continued to glare at the typewriter, this time even harder. Finally, his shoulders slumped, and he let out a disgruntled little sigh. He ran a hand through his hair. He wasn't getting anywhere this morning. Sitting back, he lit a cigarette and took several long drags, blowing the smoke upward in a thin line, watching the swirling patterns gently bump against the ceiling and dissipate.

Setting his cigarette down on the edge of the ashtray, he stood up again. What on God's green earth did it take to get the Muse to descend? Did he have to sacrifice a virgin at the altar? Burn incense? Why was he having difficulty coming up with a viable concept?

He went over to a cabinet and opened the top drawer. Inside was a cardboard box. He reached in and carefully took it out, setting it on top of the cabinet. It was a standard nine by twelve manuscript box, though tattered and old. He lifted off the lid. Inside was a thick manuscript, the typewritten pages dog-eared and stained. It was all six hundred pages of his novel *All That Glitters*. In a combination of inspiration and mad frenzy, he had written it after college when he had lived a few short years in New York City. It was finished but he'd never been satisfied with the last few chapters and always considered it in a perpetual state of rewrite. As a consequence, its pages were marred by numerous pencil marks, notes, crossed out sentences, countless additions and omissions, and even coffee stains. He had never been able to get it published, despite sending it out to numerous publishers, though he still held out hope that one day he would. He still had dreams that one day he'd be a published novelist.

Moistening his index finger, he lifted the title page and thumbed through the manuscript page by page. He read sentences at random and snatches of dialogue, some he remembered and some he'd forgotten. After several minutes, he sighed, replaced the pages, and put the lid back on the box. He shoved the whole thing back into the drawer, which he closed with a slam.

He'd vowed to himself that he would get it published but it

had been several years since he had even looked at it. But it was a vow he intended to keep, despite most of his time during the last several years devoted to screenwriting.

Stepping away from the cabinet, he continued pacing.

Suddenly it hit him. What if he set *Richard III* in a contemporary Hollywood movie studio? Greenwood would make a great Richard III, Joe thought. He began to picture scenes and soon the seeds of an idea grew. He sat back down, took a final drag of his cigarette, and then stubbed it out. Cracking his knuckles, he immediately started typing.

He was at it for a good fifteen minutes when, all at once, he stopped typing. It was like he'd come out of a trance. He glanced at what he had written, silently reading back the sentences, his mouth moving over the words. A furrow came to his brow. As he read on, the furrow only increased until his features turned into a distinct scowl. He sat back and shook his head disgustedly. What he'd written was drivel. Pure, unadulterated drivel. And there was no way Greenwood would allow a caricature of himself. He yanked out the sheet, crumpled it up into a ball, and hurled it across the room.

Impulsively, he stood up. He glanced at his wristwatch and noticed the time: eleven forty-two. He'd been at it all morning and had nothing—absolutely nothing—to show for his exertions. He was done with writing for the day. It was pointless. He wasn't getting anything done, and he felt he could barely string two coherent sentences together.

He rolled down his sleeves and buttoned them up. Then he grabbed his coat, flung open the door, and stalked outside.

Joe found a pay phone at the end of the street across from a liquor store. He deposited a nickel and hastily dialed Betsy's number. He was soon connected with Betsy's boarding house where he heard the deep Irish brogue of Mrs. Kendall, the landlady.

"May I ask who's calling please?"

"This is Joe Holliday."

"Oh, good day, Mr. Holliday. You'll be wanting Ms. Parker, then?"

"Yes. Is she in, please?"

"One moment."

Joe tapped the toe of his shoe against the pavement, waiting. He glanced across the street, his eyes locking on a wino seated on the curb outside the liquor store. The man was guzzling sloppily from a bottle. Soon Betsy's dulcet voice came on the line.

"Hiya Joe."

"Hi, Betsy."

"What's cooking?"

"Not me, that's for sure."

"What do you mean? Aren't you supposed to be writing today?"

"That's what I mean," Joe said. "I'm supposed to be, but I've got a huge case of writer's block."

"Poor boy." Betsy's voice shifted to a soothing tone. "Is there anything I can do?"

"You can meet me for dinner. How does the Brown Derby sound?"

"What time were you thinking?"

"Five o'clock."

"Could we make it six o'clock instead?" she said. "I'm meeting with Madam Petrova later this afternoon."

"Who?"

"You know who," Betsy said, irritated. "My spiritual advisor. I have a 'reading' this afternoon."

Joe paused. "Oh, her. Right."

"Can you pick me up right after? I'll be done by six."

"Yeah, okay."

"You can sound a little more enthusiastic, Joe," she said. "You know how much my spiritual growth means to me. Madam Petrova tells me she might be able to contact my grandfather."

Joe was silent.

"Isn't that exciting?"

"I suppose so," Joe mumbled.

"C'mon, Joe, don't be a stick in the mud."

"I'm sorry. It's just that—" He paused, falling into silence.

"Just what?"

"Nothing," he said. "I'll see you at six."

Joe hung up the phone. He stood motionless for a moment, gazing across the street at the wino. The man had passed out and was lying face down on the curb, snoring away, the bottle empty at his side. He watched as a patron exited the liquor store, stepped over the wino, and proceeded down the street. Joe gazed at the scene one last time and then turned and headed back to the house.

———————

Joe felt a tingling of impatient irritation as he stood on the pavement outside Madam Petrova's house in Brentwood and waited. The shades were drawn so he couldn't see inside but he knew they were in the kitchen, sitting around a table, communing with the spirits. It was something Betsy did on a regular basis, usually once a month, sometimes twice when she was feeling particularly distressed or had a burning question. She was a great believer in the spirit world, in reincarnation, and such things as auras, chakras, and the power of the mind. Madam Petrova—for a fee— would go into trance and contact Betsy's "spirit guides" who would advise her on matters of life, love, and happiness. The session lasted about an hour.

Betsy had tried on several occasions to get Joe interested in attending a reading or one of the larger séances she occasionally took part in, but Joe had always dragged his feet or made up some excuse as to why he couldn't attend. The thing that most frustrated Betsy was Joe's reluctance even to discuss the matter. He seemed inordinately tight-lipped about the whole subject.

There was a reason, of course, but Joe didn't discuss it with anyone. Not even Betsy. It was something deep inside him, deep within his psyche. It was his great secret and not anything he'd ever think of divulging. But now, as he lit up a cigarette and gazed at the house, contemplating what Betsy might be discussing, his mind began to drift back. To a time many, many years ago.

The young boy was lost in his own world. He sat in the sandbox outside the house, happily shoveling sand into a pail. The sun hung low in the sky, burnishing the clouds with orange.

Across from the boy stood a tall, slim man nattily attired in a pinstripe suit and green waistcoat. He wore a bowler hat and a gold watch chain dangled from his waistcoat pocket, glinting brilliantly as it caught the last few rays of the setting sun. He came over and knelt in front of the boy.

"Good evening, young Master Joseph," he said cheerily, his blue eyes sparkling. "Having fun? What are we doing today?"

Joe looked up and smiled back. "I'm making a castle," he said.

"A castle? How grand!"

Joe nodded and continued to shovel sand.

"Who lives there?" the man asked.

"A king, a prince, and a princess."

"What about a duke?"

Joe squinted up at his companion. "What's that?"

"A duke is a member of the nobility. Usually, he's just below the king in importance."

Joe paused, but a second later said, "He can live here, too, I guess."

"It might get crowded," the man observed. "How are you going to fit everyone inside?"

Joe thought for a moment, and then he said, "I'll make a bigger castle."

"That's an excellent idea, Joseph. I wish I'd thought of that."

Joe looked up at the older man and grinned.

They continued to chat, Joe explaining how he intended to make the castle bigger as the man asked further questions.

A shadow fell over Joe and, surprised, he looked up. He saw his mother standing at the edge of the sandbox, her hands on her hips. The sun was behind her so that her outline was silhouetted. "Who are you talking to, Joe?" she asked.

"Hi, mother!" Joe said.

"I asked you who you were talking to," his mother said. Her voice was stern.

Joe pointed at the man in front of him. "My friend."

Joe's mother squinted to where Joe had pointed. She stared for a moment, her expression blank, and then looked back at Joe. "There's no one there, Joe."

"Yes, there is," Joe insisted. He continued to point at the nattily attired man who was standing and listening attentively. "My friend is there."

This time, she didn't deign to look where Joe was pointing, but simply glared at her son and strode into the sandbox. "Come here," she said, grabbing him by the ear and pulling him to his feet.

"Ouch!" he exclaimed, dropping his shovel. Tears began to fill his eyes.

She marched him back to the house where Joe was unceremoniously plopped down on the sofa in the living room.

"Stay there!" his mother demanded. She left the room.

Joe wiped his nose with the back of his hand and dangled his feet over the edge of the sofa. His mother was gone for several long minutes and he looked down at his toes. Gradually, his tears subsided, and he glanced out the window. His well-dressed friend was standing in the sandbox, holding his bowler and looking back at the house. Even from the distance that separated them, Joe could tell that the man was concerned.

Heavy footfalls sounded. Joe spun around. His father came to a stop in the center of the room, glaring at his son through thick spectacles. He was holding a rolled-up newspaper.

"He's doing it again, Fred," Joe's mother said, wringing her hands. She began to pace back and forth behind her husband in nervous agitation.

Joe's father set the newspaper down on the coffee table. He straightened and folded his arms across his chest.

"Joe, you must stop doing this," he said. "These people you see aren't real."

"But they are," Joe insisted.

"No, they're not."

"They are!"

The older man's face darkened, and he scowled. "Don't talk back to me, young man! And, no, they are not real. They're simply in your imagination.

You will stop talking to them. You will never talk to them again."

"I won't!"

"Go to your room this instant!" his father shouted.

Joe looked down at his palms for a moment. "But they're my friends," he said, tears beginning to well up again. He looked back up, his voice almost pleading, "They're my friends."

"Go to your room!"

Joe remained sitting, his heart thumping in his chest.

"I said go to your room!"

This time, Joe bowed his head and hopped off the sofa. He began to ascend the staircase. He was halfway up when his father's voice stopped him. "Joe."

He turned around. His father was standing at the foot of the stairs. His demeanor was stern, uncompromising. His arms remained folded across his chest.

"These people do not exist, Joe," his father said. "Repeat after me, 'they do not exist.'"

Joe was silent. He stared down at the ground. His throat burned.

"Repeat after me, Joe," his father demanded.

Joe continued to remain silent. Tears streamed down his cheeks. His lips trembled.

"You will repeat after me! 'They do not exist!'"

Joe mumbled, the words escaping his lips like an act of betrayal. "They do not exist."

CHAPTER 4

THE ROOM WAS DARK except for a single candle that sent flickering shadows across the walls.

Madam Petrova sat at her kitchen table. Her eyes were closed, and her brow was furrowed in deep concentration. She was as still as a statue with the candle set on the table in front of her, its flame highlighting her cheekbones and casting the hollows beneath them in shadow. An older but still attractive woman, she had long dark hair, which was streaked with gray and fell to her shoulders.

Betsy sat across the table, her eyes riveted on the medium's face. She scarcely dared to breathe. Betsy knew not to disturb Madam Petrova when she was in a trance. But tonight she was anxious, impatient, and fidgety, and doing everything in her power to sit as still as possible.

Madam Petrova took a deep breath and seemed to relax a little, though her eyes remained closed. "An entity has stepped forward," she said.

Betsy tensed, both excited and nervous. "Who is it?"

"A man," Madam Petrova replied.

Betsy felt her excitement rise. "Is it my grandfather?"

Madam Petrova shook her head. "No."

Betsy frowned and her shoulders slumped, disappointed. She was about to ask another question when Madam Petrova spoke up again.

"He will not completely show himself to me," she said. "I cannot see his face because it is obscured. He is rather thin and dressed in black." She paused, knitting her eyebrows together. "But there is something—"

Betsy was silent, listening, hanging on to her every word.

Madam Petrova wrinkled her brow and continued. "There is something oddly familiar about him." She cocked her head, as if listening. Silence descended on the room as Madam Petrova remained quiet for several moments.

"He says he has a message for your friend," she said finally.

Betsy raised her eyebrows in surprise. "My friend?"

Madam Petrova nodded. "The entity says that your friend will soon embark upon a very significant, life-altering project. Part of this project will involve remembering things he has long forgotten."

"What friend of mine is he referring to?" Betsy asked. She was bursting with curiosity.

"He is very eager to make himself known to your friend when the time is right."

"But my friend. Who is—"

Madam Petrova held up her hand as if to silence Betsy. "He wants to make it clear that your friend trusts the process as it unfolds. This is very important to its success. He must not fear or doubt. He must have complete faith."

Betsy was silent, perplexed. She shifted in her seat. She still didn't know to what "friend" the entity was referring. But she didn't press it; she tried a different tack.

"What kind of project is it?"

"The entity says it is a writing project."

———————

"Well," Betsy said, staring at Joe from across the table, "what do you think?" Her eyes were fastened on Joe's face.

Joe scratched his chin, his expression pensive. "I don't know." He took a drink of his Coca-Cola, mulling over everything she had just told him.

They were seated at an oversized booth in the Brown Derby. It was a busy night and a swirl of conversation filled the air, mixed with the clink of utensils and the mad shuffling of feet as waitresses scurried back and forth from the kitchen and the dining room. A jukebox was playing Jackie Cooper's "Me and My Girl," but it was nearly drowned out by all the chatter and boisterous laughter in the room.

"It has to be you," Betsy insisted. Her eyes were bright and animated.

"You think so?"

She nodded. "The spirit mentioned a writing project. And you're the only writer I know."

Joe paused and shrugged. "It sounds pretty general to me."

"General? I think it sounds pretty specific."

"Why didn't he just come out and say what this whole thing is about, and who the message was meant for? Why does he have to be so obscure?"

"I don't know," Betsy said. "I'm not a ghost."

He paused for a moment. "She said it would be life-altering?"

Betsy nodded. "She called it a 'life-altering project.' Those were her exact words."

"Did she say how?"

"You mean how it would alter your life?"

Joe nodded.

"No," Betsy said, shaking her head. "Just that it would."

Joe was silent. He carefully set his Coke back down on the table and glanced at Betsy. "Madam Petrova knows I'm a writer, right? So, she would obviously know that—"

"We're not going to have this argument again, are we?" Betsy said, a frown darkening her brow.

"I'm just saying you should be careful. There are a lot of charlatans out there."

Blood rose to Betsy's cheeks. "Madam Petrova is not a charlatan!"

"Calm down, Betsy, I'm not saying she is, but—"

"Then why even bring that up?"

Joe sighed. "I'm sorry. I just don't want you to get hurt."

Betsy continued to glare at him for a moment longer, but then calmed. She reached across the table and placed her hand on Joe's wrist. "I'm a big girl, Joe. I can handle myself."

He smiled at her. "I know you can. I'm sorry. It's just that sometimes I get concerned. I mean, this world is a crazy place. And sometimes you can be so—"

She raised an eyebrow, blood beginning to rise to her cheeks again. "I can be so what?"

He stopped. "I'm digging the hole deeper, aren't I?"

She nodded.

Their dinner soon arrived. Joe was hungrier than he realized and wasted no time digging into his chicken fried steak and potatoes. Betsy, by contrast, seemed much more circumspect and picked at her lamb chops and boiled vegetables.

They ate for a moment in silence.

"What are you doing tomorrow?" Betsy asked at length.

"Going to the library to do some research," Joe said, in between bites. "Greenwood wants a treatment by Tuesday. And I don't have a clue about how to start. I'm hoping to get inspiration."

They continued eating. Talk swirled about them. They talked aimlessly for a while as they ate but eventually circled back to the topic at hand.

"Look," Betsy said, lowering her fork. "I know I can sometimes be a Pollyanna. But it's my nature. I can't help it." She paused for a moment and then sitting up straight, her head held high, she continued, "But I'm stronger than you think. I'm much stronger."

Joe stopped eating and looked up at her. The words had been uttered with a forcefulness that surprised him. He gazed into Betsy's eyes, saw a fierce determination there, saw the way her chin jutted with a certain defiant cast and knew her words weren't simply the idle boasts of someone trying to convince themselves of something. It suddenly dawned on him that it was this determination—this strong willfulness—though wrapped in the outward appearance of an ingénue, that had allowed a young and poor farm girl from Minnesota to leave her home and travel to California, get a job in the film industry, and carve out a life for herself.

"I know I'm small and I'm pretty, and because of that people don't think I'm of much consequence," Betsy continued. "But they're wrong."

"I don't think that," Joe said, shaking his head. "I don't think that at all."

"I know you don't, but I don't want you to worry about me so much. I can take care of myself."

"I know you can," he said. "I'm sorry about what I said earlier. I didn't mean it."

For a moment Betsy seemed about to speak. But then she looked away, chewing on her bottom lip.

He noticed the gesture. "What's wrong?"

"It's nothing," she said.

Joe put down his fork and sat back. He gave her a pointed look and folded his arms across his chest. "What's wrong?"

"I've never told you this before," Betsy said, "because I don't want to relive it, but once when my father—"

She stopped, and Joe saw that her lip was trembling slightly. She took a deep breath, steeled herself, and went on. "Once when my father was hitting my mother, I stepped in between them. And he began to hit me instead. But I got him to stop. I got him to stop beating my mother."

Joe was stunned into silence. He'd never heard this story, had no inkling anything like that had ever happened to Betsy. She'd once mentioned that her father was a "difficult man," but he'd had no clue about what that had exactly meant.

"How old were you?" he asked.

"I was twelve."

He stared at her for a long moment, imagining her at that age. He tried to picture a tender young girl standing up to a grown man engulfed in a violent rage.

"Were you hurt?"

She nodded and gave a sardonic grin. "Two black eyes, a split lip, and a broken nose."

"He broke your nose?" Joe was appalled and angered. "Christ, how can a grown man even think—"

"Because he was a drunk," she said. "Because he was a low-down, surly drunk."

Joe shook his head, at a loss for words.

Betsy sat up straight and pointed at her face. "Look at my nose straight on," she said. "Notice anything?"

He leaned forward and squinted. He noticed that the bridge of her nose did not form a straight line. "It curves slightly to the side." He blinked. "I never noticed that before."

"Courtesy of my father," she said with cold humor.

"Still," he added, sitting back, "it doesn't look that bad. In fact, it doesn't look bad at all. I don't think I would've noticed if you hadn't told me."

"That's only because I was lucky enough to have it set."

"And your mother? Was she—"

Her face hardened and she was silent for a moment. "I got him to stop," she said simply, repeating her earlier statement.

A short silence settled between them.

"I'm not telling you any of this to upset you," Betsy said after a moment, trying to give him a reassuring smile. "I guess what I'm trying to say is you can't always judge a book by its cover. And you can't shield me from everything, Joe. Like I said, I'm stronger than I look. I may bend a little, but I won't break."

He reached across the table and gave her hand a gentle squeeze. She looked at him, her eyes filled with emotion. He stared back, engulfed by a deep admiration for her, and suddenly felt closer to her than he'd ever felt.

———————

After dinner, they strolled arm-in-arm along Wilshire Avenue. A dry Santa Ana breeze was blowing from the east, and the air was warm, smelling of desert landscapes—of sage and mesquite.

"You haven't said a word since we left the restaurant," Betsy said. "Are you all right?"

"I'm fine," Joe said. "Just thinking."

"About what?"

"About that story you told me earlier. About your father."

She stopped and put her hand on his arm. "Should I not have told you?"

"No," he said, shaking his head quickly. "I'm just sorry you had to go through that."

"I don't want anyone to feel sorry for me," Betsy said, "least of all you. I don't want anyone thinking I'm some poor helpless waif. Because I'm not. And I'm not the only person who had a violent drunk for a father. That episode in my life is over. It's in the past."

"But you still think about it?"

"Sure, every once in a while," she said, nodding. "Like tonight. And, yes, it makes me sad and angry and even vulnerable. But I refuse to be defined by it. My life is here now. With you and with my acting. That's what matters."

He smiled down at her. "You never cease to amaze me, you know that?"

"Me amaze you?" She turned her head to look up at him, an expression of genuine surprise etching her features. "You're the one who amazes me. You're so well-educated and sophisticated, and I'm—"

"Don't even say it," Joe intervened.

"You don't know what I was going to say."

"Maybe not the exact words," he said. "But I don't want you to talk like that, Betsy. You've overcome a lot. I'm not sure many people could bounce back from what you've gone through."

She shrugged. "It's just that sometimes I feel so inadequate next to you."

"Why on earth do you say that?"

"Because you're so smart and educated." She shrugged and sighed audibly. "It's just that I want to do so much. I want to see so much. I'd love to travel. I haven't been anywhere. If I ever become a successful actress, I'm going to travel."

"Where do you want to go?"

"All over. Spain, Italy, France. But I'd really love to see the castles of England. I've always been drawn to them."

"Really?" He was surprised. "You never told me that."

"Oh, yes," she said, nodding emphatically. "Growing up, I had this picture book of the castles of England. It was so romantic. I used to gaze at it for hours, imagining I was a princess."

Joe chuckled. They continued walking.

"And anyway," Joe said, "a fat lot my education has done for me. You're looking at a guy whose best screenplay just got rejected. Heck, you're looking at a guy who can't even get his book published."

"You mean your novel?"

He nodded and broke into a sarcastic chuckle. "There must be some strange inverse correlation at work here."

"What do you mean?" Betsy asked.

"The harder I work at something the less likely it is that it'll get published or produced. Whether it's a screenplay or my novel." He shrugged irritably, thrust both hands into his pockets, and walked a few paces in front of Betsy. "Sometimes I don't know why I even bother. Maybe I should get a different job. Something that is at least useful, like bricking a wall or digging a ditch."

She caught up to him and squeezed his arm. "Oh, but you will. I know you will. You're going to be a famous writer."

"Maybe posthumously," he said.

She looked at him with a quizzical expression.

"I mean after I die," he explained.

"There's no need to be morbid," Betsy said.

"I'm sorry," he said, "you're right." He sighed and gazed across the street where two disheveled looking men were huddled over a trashcan, digging around for scraps. One of them pulled out a chicken bone and began to gnaw on it ravenously.

"I guess I should count my blessings," Joe said. "Some fellas can't even find work and here I am, gainfully employed but bitching about my unpublished novel. I guess I don't really have a lot to complain about, do I?"

"Just because you have a good job doesn't mean you have to give up on your dreams," Betsy said. "Our dreams are the things that help define us. They're the things that motivate us to forge ahead."

They walked in silence for a time. Betsy sidled closer to Joe and he put his arm around her waist. The stars were barely visible because of the bright city lights but the moon was full, shining brilliantly above the buildings.

Joe yawned and glanced at his watch. It was a few minutes after midnight. He'd been sprawled on the couch reading a copy of the *Atlantic Monthly* for the last few hours—ever since he'd returned from his dinner with Betsy. Dropping the magazine on the floor, he pushed up from the couch and tottered across the floor to the light switch. As he snapped off the living room lights, he glanced out the window. The moon hung over the Pacific Ocean like a giant white pearl, casting its pale radiance on the surface of the water. He yawned again and rubbed his eyes. Turning back, he plopped down on the couch. Desdemona rushed over and curled up between his legs.

He readjusted his position on the sofa, turning first on his side and then on his back. Desdemona meowed at the sudden movement. Finally comfortable, he lifted his forearm and laid it across his eyes. It wasn't long before he drifted off, a dream taking shape within the depths of his mind.

The square tower of St. Paul's Cathedral loomed over the city of London. Silhouetted against the sky, it caught the last rays of the afternoon sun and glinted like a jewel.

As the city fell into shadow, a heavy fog, cold and damp, began rolling in off the Thames. It saturated the air, veiling everything in gray, falling on the cobblestones and drifting forward in a vaporous cloud, branching off and snaking down narrow alleyways between closely spaced buildings.

The heavy clomp of boots rang out as a man rounded the corner of an apothecary's shop. Striding forward, he gradually emerged from the mist. Dressed all in black, he wore a wide-brimmed black hat, pulled low over his forehead, a plain black doublet, black breeches, and black leather boots. Even his cloak, which he wrapped around him to ward off the chill, was black.

He was young, in his early twenties, and had the look of a Puritan, and yet there were a number of subtle differences that marked him as standing outside the purified faith. The two most obvious were his shoulder-length brown hair and the wispy Van Dyke beard that jutted from his chin. It was well known that members of these radical Protestant sects eschewed all forms of unnecessary bodily adornment, long hair and beards prominent among them. The other difference, however, was much more nuanced. There was a certain sardonic cast to his eyes that was hard to imagine a Puritan possessing. The man's eyes seemed to peer out at the world with what might be described as a facetious stare.

He proceeded down the cobblestones with purposeful strides, ignoring the beggars and whores that lined both sides of the street, the former beseeching with palms open, the latter gesticulating with animated catcalls, shaking hips and bosoms.

The young man drew his cloak tighter about himself and brushed past them all without so much as a sideways glance. The hard set of his mouth suggested neither pity for the mendicants nor interest in the harlots. He was wholly intent on his destination.

The district through which he passed was a bewildering network of streets, alleyways, and narrow passages. A mismatched collection of shops, stalls, taverns, and ordinaries—all seemingly thrown together without any thought of organization—lined both sides. With the failing light, torches were being lit all along the street, and shops and stalls were closing. The taverns and ordinaries, however, were just now opening for business.

Indeed, despite the hour, the streets were beginning to get crowded. But this time, rather than the merchants and traders, the buyers and sellers, the housewives, maids, and servants typical of daylight hours, the thoroughfares and alleyways of the city were given over to a different brand of denizen. Buyers and sellers of a decidedly different order: The philanderers, the libertines, the cutpurses, the thieves, the murderers.

He heard men singing lustily in a tavern up ahead. Gathering his cloak, he strode up to the entrance and, lingering at the threshold for a moment, peered inside. Immediately his nostrils were assaulted by the smell of sweat, ale, urine, and boiled meat. The singing was coming from several well-dressed young men gathered around a table. With tankards raised aloft and faces flushed, they belted out a tune, which, the young man noted, was flavored liberally with bawdy references. He looked past them, scanning the room briefly, his gaze finally coming to rest on a man who was seated alone at a table near the far wall. His back was to the door and he was hunched over his ale, oblivious to everything that transpired around him. Or so it seemed.

The young man produced some rolled up parchment from underneath his cloak, doffed his hat, and strode through the door. He made his way toward the man sitting alone.

Approaching footfalls made the man at the table look up. He was an older man with a weathered face—blunt nose, heavy eyebrows, and ruddy cheeks. A momentary look of surprise was replaced by one of recognition, and he grinned.

The two men exchanged words of greeting. The seated man gestured at the table and the young man sat down. He swept his cloak aside and brought forth the parchment. He glanced over his shoulder at the gallants who were still singing and frowned. If anything, their voices were louder, more boisterous.

"How canst we conduct business with such caterwauling?" he said.

"Pay no heed to those fools," the other replied. He cast them a contemptuous stare. "Gallants from the Inns of Court no doubt. Strutting popinjays out to display their feathers. Pay them no heed." He pointed at the parchment and rubbed his hands eagerly.

"'Tis finished?" he asked.

"Aye."

"Pray, let us have a look."

42

The young man handed over the parchment. The older man undid the bit of twine that kept it rolled up and laid it flat on the table, smoothing the document with the flat of his hand. He wet his index finger and flipped through the pages for a moment, scanning the text. Then he flipped back to the beginning and, brow furrowed in concentration, spent several minutes reading.

The young man glanced around the tavern as the man read. The singers had quieted down, though loud talk still filled the room, and laughter broke out periodically in bursts. In one corner of the room, several men sat around smoking tobacco from clay pipes, blue haze swirling about their heads.

The older man finally looked up. "'Tis wondrous good," he said, grinning. He grabbed the young man's hand and shook it vigorously.

The young man, who had until then been so serious, finally broke into his own self-satisfied grin.

Chapter 5

THE MORNING SUN FLOODED in through the window, tossing an oblique column of light on the floor and the sofa. Joe stirred. He removed his forearm from his eyes and opened them slowly, blinking as he focused on the ceiling. He lay there for a long moment, not exactly sure where he was—in Elizabethan England or Los Angeles. The dream images were still fresh in his mind, still vivid. The fog-shrouded streets of London, the wood-framed houses, the beggars, the whores, and the tavern denizens—all these lingered in his consciousness. He'd never had such a realistic dream. It had almost felt as if he'd been there, witnessing everything—the sights, sounds, and smells, even the chill of the fog.

He rubbed his eyes and sat up on his elbows. He looked around to make sure he wasn't still dreaming. The familiar confines of his living room stared back at him.

He swung his legs over the edge of the sofa, planted them on the floor, and sat up. Running a hand through his tousled hair, he yawned and glanced around the room, looking for Desdemona. But the cat was nowhere to be found. He stood up, rubbed his eyes one final time, and padded into the kitchen.

Joe filled a kettle with tap water and set it on the stove to boil. He took down a tin of coffee from the cabinet and took off the lid. As he prepared a cup, he gazed out the window.

Morning haze was beginning to burn off as the sun rose higher. Above the water, seagulls swooped and dived. Joe watched them as the coffee brewed. When it was ready, he poured himself a mug.

Desdemona suddenly appeared as if conjured from thin air. The cat sidled up against Joe's legs.

"Good morning," Joe said, leaning down and gently scratching her head. "I was wondering where you'd gone."

The cat looked up at him, her eyes unblinking and expectant.

He walked over to the kitchen table and sat down. The cat followed him and hopped onto his lap.

He continued to stare out at the beach as he sipped his coffee. The dream lingered in his mind. Unlike so many dreams, which faded into obscurity with the light of morning, this one remained stark in his memory—indelibly etched in his consciousness. He tried to remember if he'd ever experienced anything like it. At least not recently. As a child, he used to have very lifelike dreams, though he didn't remember them well now. What he did remember was waking up and, in his youthful mind, trying to figure out what was more real, the dream or the waking state. No doubt all his recent focus on Elizabethan drama had set his mind to flights of fancy. Still, there was something about the dream that he couldn't dismiss as mere fantasy. It had felt as if he had watched some genuine slice of life; that he had been allowed to experience some glimpse of the past.

He shook his head, bringing himself back to reality. He needed to buckle down today and get some work done, he told himself. He needed to come up with a workable treatment for Greenwood by Tuesday. He didn't have time to ponder dreams—no matter how lifelike or intriguing.

———

Later that morning, Joe was deep in the bowels of the Los Angeles Public Library, ensconced in the Elizabethan drama section. His attention was focused on the book in his hands, an Oxford Great Books copy of *Macbeth*, while clamped under his left elbow was a copy of *Hamlet*. He flipped through the play until he came to Act five, Scene five, his favorite. He smoothed the spine and began to read.

> Tomorrow, and tomorrow, and tomorrow,
> Creeps in this petty pace from day to day
> To the last syllable of recorded time,
> And all our yesterdays have lighted fools
> The way to dusty death. Out, out, brief candle!
> Life's but a walking shadow, a poor player
> That struts and frets his hour upon the stage
> And then is heard no more. It is a tale
> Told by an idiot, full of sound and fury,
> Signifying nothing.

Joe never tired of reading that passage. The language was like nothing else he'd ever read. It was worded in such a way that the reader almost forgot that it was an image of futility and death, and that, in it, Macbeth was soon to die in battle. It was elegant yet simple, evidence of a wordsmith at the height of his powers. In short, it was brilliant, and he wished someday to write something as lasting and profound. He continued flipping through the book, reading snatches of dialogue here and there.

There was a sudden loud thump behind him. Startled, he looked over his shoulder. A large tome had fallen from the shelf behind him and now lay open on the ground. A small cloud of dust hung suspended above the book before settling back down again.

Puzzled, he stood looking around for a second, trying to figure out how the book might have fallen. But there wasn't anyone about. It must have tumbled off the shelf of its own accord, he guessed. He set *Macbeth* and *Hamlet* on the shelf and knelt to pick up the book. It lay open to a play called *The Apple Orchard* by William Shakespeare and Thomas Middleton. His brow furrowed. He'd never heard of a play by Shakespeare called *The Apple Orchard*. Nor had he heard of Thomas Middleton. Curious, he picked up the book, which weighed several pounds, and closed it, glancing at the cover. *Shakespeare's Apocrypha: A Critical Study of the Bard's Lost and Unfinished Plays.*

Hefting it, he shoved the book back into the spot from which it had tumbled. He turned back and picked up the copy of *Macbeth* and flipped it open, trying to find where he'd left off.

There was another loud thump behind him. Startled, he jumped again. When he turned around, he saw that the same book had fallen from the shelf. He leaned over to retrieve it again and was surprised to see that it lay open to the same section: *The Apple Orchard.*

He stood up slowly and glanced around. But, yet again, there was no one in sight. He inspected the empty spot on the shelf to see if there was some obstruction that had caused the book to fall. But it was empty.

He felt his spine tingle.

Kneeling, he picked up the book and put it under his arm. Standing back up, he turned and walked down the length of the book-lined aisle and emerged into a small reading room with chairs and tables. He sat down at a table near the window, thumped the book down, and switched on one of the reading lamps.

He opened the book, flipping past the title page, the frontispiece, the table of contents, and the dedication, until he came to the introduction. He smoothed the spine and started reading.

William Shakespeare (1564-1616) is considered the world's greatest playwright. His works have been translated into some eighty languages and have helped shape the very language we speak today by introducing numerous words, phrases, and figures of speech. His plays are known around the world for their universal themes and insight into the human condition. During his lifetime he is believed to have written at least thirty-six plays, divided into comedies, histories, and tragedies. Shakespeare's colleagues, John Heminges and Henry Condell, collected his plays and published them in the 1623 First

Folio. It is possible that few of Shakespeare's works would have survived had not the two men put the Folio together.

Scholars have long debated whether Shakespeare wrote additional plays that were not collected in the First Folio. Together, these are known as Shakespeare's apocrypha, and consist of plays that are attributed to him, but the attribution is either disputed or simply unclear. The exact number, of course, is not known and it is suspected that many of these have perhaps been lost. Nevertheless, a scattered remnant has survived, mostly "foul" texts that were either unfinished or, with the passage of years, attributed to other authors. Still other plays are mentioned in the works and scattered correspondence of other writers.

Joe finished the introduction and thumbed through the book until he came to the chapter on *The Apple Orchard.*

In the year before Shakespeare's death in 1616, there is some evidence that he and fellow playwright Thomas Middleton, a younger contemporary, were collaborating on a play called *The Apple Orchard.* It is not at all strange that Shakespeare would have collaborated with a younger colleague, like Middleton. In his later years it was well known that he collaborated with the playwright John Fletcher on *The Two Noble Kinsmen* and *Henry VIII.* It is also suspected that *Timon of Athens*, which was likely written in 1607, was an earlier collaborative effort between Shakespeare and Middleton.

Very little is known about *The Apple Orchard* as no finished copies have ever survived, and scholars speculate that it was unfinished at the time of Shakespeare's death. The play is first mentioned in a note Richard Burbage, who co-owned the Globe Theater, wrote in the margins of his receipt book for December 1615. He writes that Shakespeare and Middleton's play, *The Apple Orchard*, was "stille in constructyon [sic]" but expressed pessimism, based on his knowledge of Shakespeare's prolonged illness, that it would ever be finished.

Tangible evidence of the play's existence first came to light in 1854 when a manuscript was discovered among the private archives of Lord Percival Haulton, the 3rd Earl of Chelmsford. It was unearthed by his son after the Earl's death. The son, Edward Haulton, attempted to sell the manuscript, though he met with little success because his asking price was considered exorbitant by potential buyers. Finally, a collector named Henry Rutledge, who was a man of considerable private means and an amateur Shakespeare scholar, purchased the manuscript for an undisclosed sum. Instead of squirreling it away in his private papers, Rutledge brought it to the attention of the leading Shakespeare scholar of the day, Alexander Dyce. After a thorough textual analysis, Dyce determined that the manuscript was an original, written in approximately 1615.

The manuscript, in quarto form, contains the beginning of a play called *The Apple Orchard*, which, on its title page, is attributed to "W. Shakespeare and T. Middleton, Gents." It tells the story of Prince Nicholas of Bohemia, a naive young man who has no interest in political matters. He wants to be a poet rather than a ruler. But his father, the ailing but still manly ruler of Bohemia, has other plans, and attempts to force his son to accept his birthright. He also believes the young prince is too innocent and inexperienced, and endeavors to "harden" the young man. Only Act One was apparently written, though this contains three scenes. Scene One takes place in the eponymous apple orchard, which is the sanctuary of the prince. It is a place where he often composes his poetry and muses on the state of the world. This scene opens with a long soliloquy, which functions as a kind of prologue in which Prince Nicholas takes the audience into his confidence. He begins by lamenting his lot in life. Although he has been reared in the lap of luxury, he is restless and feels unfulfilled and trapped. He longs to see the world, experience life, beauty, and love.

Act One, Scene Two, shifts to inside the palace where Nicholas's father, King Leopold, tells his trusted advisor, Lord Claudio, of his plans to force Nicholas to marry. He believes such a move will oblige the young man to assume greater responsibility. It will also ensure succession of Leopold's line. Lord Claudio has picked out just the bride for Nicholas, a young woman named Beatrice who Lord Claudio claims is a minor German princess but is in actuality the royal advisor's niece. In an aside to the audience, Claudio tells of his plan to poison the King and manipulate the young Prince through his control of Beatrice.

Act One, Scene Three opens with Nicholas confessing to his manservant, Theodore, of his father's desire to toughen him up and remake him into a feared ruler. Theodore, knowing of the Prince's true desires, lends a sympathetic ear. They are interrupted by the entrance of Duchess Livia, Nicholas's stepmother. It is obvious through the dialogue between Nicholas and Livia that the young man is wholly smitten with his stepmother.

Here the play abruptly ends—in the middle of Act One, Scene Three. Scholars have long debated whether…

Joe stopped reading. He thumped the book closed and turned to stare out the window, watching cars pass back and forth on the street below.

What he'd just read was fascinating; he had never heard any of this little-known literary history. Not even during his graduate work at Dartmouth. He stood up, tucked the book under his arm, and headed for the check-out counter.

———————

With *Shakespeare's Apocrypha* under his arm, Joe left the library, crossed a busy intersection, and made his way west along Wilshire Boulevard. It was midday and the city bustled with activity. Cars zipped back and forth along the street and pedestrians crowded the sidewalks, jostling each other as they pursued their various destinations.

He stopped at the newsstand on the corner of Wilshire and Highland, one of the city's busiest intersections. To his surprise, several people were gathered around the stand with newspapers in their hands. They were all chattering away in excited tones. He wedged himself in between two patrons to get a better look at what headlines were causing the commotion. Immediately his eyes were drawn to the front page of the *Los Angeles Times*.

"Germany Reoccupies the Rhineland!" the headline screamed.

He noticed the other papers' headlines: "Hitler Invasion of the Rhineland called 'Act of War' by France" and "Paris Demands League Send Troops to Rhine."

He bought a copy of the *Times* and read the story as he walked.

On Saturday, March 7, German Chancellor Adolph Hitler sent 25,000 troops into the Rhineland in direct violation of the Treaty of Versailles. The troops entered on bicycles, and no effort was made to stop the incursion despite the Rhineland being declared a permanent demilitarized zone. It was the first time since the end of the Great War in 1918 that German troops had been in the region.

The reaction of European leaders was swift and immediate, with France expressing the loudest condemnation. The French Prime Minister, Léon Blum declared that France stood ready, supported by her allies, to force

Germany to abandon the Rhineland. However, Blum made it clear that all peaceful methods under the League of Nations would be exhausted first before any possibility of a military response.

Joe lowered the paper, stunned. He slowed to a stop, allowing the news to sink in. He felt people brush by him as they walked past. The situation in Europe was getting worse and worse. And nobody was doing anything about it. Hitler was getting away with murder and making all the other European leaders look like inept, impotent fools.

He folded the paper and stuffed it in his back pocket. Taking a deep breath, he readjusted the book to a better position under his arm and strode down the street, his shoes snapping a sharp staccato on the pavement.

The long walk combined with the sun's warmth soothed him, and for a while at least, he forgot about the headlines. For some inexplicable reason, his thoughts drifted back to his days at Dartmouth. He had done his master's there—on the influence of Stoic philosophy on the novels of Henry James—and had contemplated staying to get his doctorate in literature. He loved the subject and wanted to explore it in even greater detail, perhaps even embark on a teaching career. But the lure of writing fiction—of artistic creation—got the better of him. For a while after college he lived in New York and supported himself by writing articles for magazines as he worked on his novel. But after only a few years of living a bohemian hand-to-mouth existence and acquiring a small mountain of rejection slips for his novel, he decided there must be a better way to earn a living. He got a position as a journalist at one of the city's newspapers—*The Brooklyn Daily Eagle*. But he didn't stay there long. When a friend mentioned that Hollywood was looking for talented screenwriters, he thought "what the heck" and decided to give it a shot. He quit the paper and moved west.

His first job in Hollywood had been at the small Troy Studios in Culver City where he had worked as a script "reader," in charge of assessing, and offering opinions on, the viability of potential scripts. It required he summarize novels and plays and evaluate their potential for the screen. The job hadn't been particularly illuminating because most of the scripts he read had been profoundly bad, but it had been a great way to study the art of scriptwriting. The job had lasted a year before Troy went bankrupt at the beginning of the Depression and Joe was hired by Apex Studios. Almost immediately, Greenwood had seen potential in the Dartmouth-educated, almost-literature professor, and hired him as a full-fledged screenwriter.

Joe discovered a fondness for the work that surprised him. In fact, he had to admit that one of the most satisfying things in those early days was looking up and seeing SCREENPLAY BY JOSEPH L. HOLLIDAY emblazoned across the screen in big, bold letters. It always gave him a mad rush of excitement. Most importantly, though, he was good at it. He was a quick learner, and before long, was cranking out a ceaseless stream of the one—and two-reel films the studio invariably assigned to him—costume dramas, Westerns, swashbucklers, or tales of knights, British Victorian soldiers, or Roman legionnaires. He thus fell into the pleasant life of a Hollywood screenwriter. A steady paycheck didn't hurt either. But, little by little, he grew increasingly bored by the formulaic dramas—each one a carbon copy of the one before—he was paid to write. He felt the tug of trying his hand at something with lasting literary merit. Consequently, many months ago when Greenwood asked him to write an original drama, he had jumped at the chance.

Too bad that hadn't worked out.

And then there was the constant siren call of his novel. He vowed to finish it one of these days—if he could only find the time.

Still, in the meantime, there was only one task that need concern him now. He simply had to get a treatment to Greenwood. He needed to figure out how to give one of Shakespeare's tales a modern twist. But which one? And how? He thought back on all the scenarios he'd earlier posed. There was *Othello* in a modern military setting. Romeo and Juliet as south sea islanders. *Richard III* set in modern Hollywood. Hamlet as the scion of a wealthy industrialist.

The last one seemed to have the most promise. He could picture Hamlet as a young man home from university, his father recently murdered, and his uncle installed as head of the company. The philosophically inclined young man suspects foul play. And when his father appears, in the form of a ghost, Hamlet is galvanized, all the while battling his own emotional ups and downs, altering between despondency, misanthropy, anger, fear, and a righteous desire for vengeance.

The challenge, of course, was to make Hamlet resonate with a modern audience. He had to strike a chord between "highbrow and lowbrow," as Greenwood had put it. Perhaps he could model Hamlet on one of those "swing kids" that were becoming increasingly visible on the streets of towns and cities.

All this mulled in Joe's mind as he made his way back to his cottage. By the time he reached the front door, the seeds of an idea had been planted and he was eager to get it all down on paper.

CHAPTER 6

WITH THE TREATMENT UNDER his arm, Joe arrived at Greenwood's office on Tuesday morning. He was surprised to find a small crowd. Several men—six in number, Joe counted—were standing around the producer's desk, all dressed in well-pressed business suits and silk ties. Many were smoking cigarettes and chatting. The air was tinged with pomade and aftershave. Greenwood sat tilted back in his chair, talking with two of the men. From their precise, clipped accents, Joe could tell they were British.

He stood at the threshold for a moment, confused, trying to decide whether he'd barged in on a meeting or this was, in fact, the meeting he'd been told to attend. He glanced down at his wristwatch to check the time. It was exactly ten o'clock.

When Greenwood saw Joe, he sprang from his chair. "Here's our writer now," he announced.

The buzz of conversation ceased, and everyone turned in Joe's direction. For a moment he stared back, not knowing what to say as he felt the concentrated force of their gaze on him. But, snapping out of his paralysis, he cleared his throat, took a tentative step inside, and opened his mouth to speak.

"Joe," Greenwood intervened, "I'd like you to meet our investors. I've been telling them about you." He turned back to the assembled throng. "Gentleman, I'd like you to meet Mr. Joe Holliday, one of our distinguished screenwriters. He'll be the main writer working on the script."

Joe was immediately the center of attention as the investors crowded around him. Introductions were made and Joe found himself shaking hands and trying to remember everyone's name.

When the tumult had quieted down, Greenwood stepped forward, taking over the reins yet again.

"Joe," he said, "everyone is very eager to hear about the script." He rubbed his hands together. "What have you got for us?"

Joe cleared his throat again and watched as the investors grew silent, listening. With everyone's eyes trained on him and a hushed, expectant silence filling the office, he felt like a caged animal on display. But he plowed forward.

"Well," he began, "I decided to do a modern retelling of *Hamlet.*"

He noticed several heads nodding in approval and spontaneous grins breaking out on otherwise staid faces. With that subtle sign of encouragement, Joe continued. He launched into his treatment, explaining how he'd structured the basic story to fit in with modern times while at the same time striving to stay true to the original. He spoke for about ten minutes, and when he had finished, there was applause. He glanced at Greenwood. The producer was beaming, like a proud father. He came over and shook Joe's hand and then turned to the investors, still holding Joe's hand.

"What did I tell you, gentlemen?" he said. "Do we have the best writers in Hollywood, or what?"

There was an enthusiastic nod of agreement and, like a dam bursting, the six men crowded around Joe, competing to shake his hand, slapping him on the back with exaggerated *bonhomie* and peppering him with questions and comments, which came simultaneously and from all directions.

"Good show, old chap!"

"Who's going to play Hamlet?"

"When do you think the script will be finished?"

"Who's going to play Ophelia?"

Joe heard Greenwood's voice above the din. "Everything will be answered in due course, gentlemen. In the meantime, this calls for a celebration, don't you think? I know it's early, but I think I'd like a drink. Anyone care to join me?"

The crowd shifted over to the wet bar where, to his surprise, Joe noticed two servers from the studio commissary. They were decked out in white tuxedos and sported white gloves. They must've slipped in during the last few minutes when Joe was fielding all the questions. They immediately set about mixing martinis.

One of the investors, however, stayed behind to chat. He introduced himself as Archie Duncan-Jones. He was a short, overweight man with a shock of bright red hair and green eyes lit by a humorous twinkle. Unlike the others, who were dressed impeccably, Duncan-Jones presented a somewhat disheveled appearance. Although his clothes were expensive, he wore them with a casualness that bespoke a certain amount of carelessness, as if he didn't pay attention to his appearance. His tie was askew and his hair in need of both a trim and a comb.

"I must say," Duncan-Jones said, "I'm very excited about this project." Despite his appearance, his accent was precise and upper crust.

Joe chuckled. "Yes, I gathered that."

The man laughed along with Joe, a booming infectious laugh. "I'm afraid we came on rather like a herd of thundering elephants," he said. "Awfully sorry about that."

"No need to apologize. I understand the enthusiasm."

"I really do think this is a splendid idea."

"I'm glad you think so," Joe said.

"By the way," Duncan-Jones added with a sly wink, "we were all hoping you'd pick *Hamlet*."

"What if I hadn't?" Joe asked.

The man gave a subtle grin. "I think we might have been able to persuade you. Anyway, I'll be quite excited to see the finished script. Placing *Hamlet* in a modern setting should make for an interesting picture. It sounds positively avant-garde, doesn't it?"

"Well, I'll do my best. I haven't actually started yet. But the treatment is finished. That's a start, at least."

"What did Sir Francis Drake say? 'There must be a beginning of any great matter, but the continuing unto the end until it be thoroughly finished yields the true glory.'"

Joe warmed to the short, garrulous Englishman as they continued to chat. He was lively and eager and seemed genuinely interested in the screenwriting process. Joe learned that Duncan-Jones had for years run his father's textile business in Coventry. The business had been so wildly successful that he had been able to retire a multimillionaire and could now indulge his whims. One of these was the motion picture business. He was content now to invest in pictures but expressed interest in one day perhaps owning his own movie studio.

"I must confess," Duncan-Jones said, "I have great admiration for writers. I don't understand how the deuce you're able to pull it off."

"Pull what off?

"Writing day in and day out. I once had dreams of being a writer when I was younger, but I'm afraid I just didn't quite have the knack. Or the discipline." Duncan-Jones grinned. "I still don't. I'm much better with figures. My old dad, God rest his soul, was the same way. Must run in the family."

"What did Mark Twain say? 'Writing is easy. All you have to do is cross out the wrong words.'"

Duncan-Jones chuckled. "Ah, yes, your inimitable American humorist. A true man of letters. Anyway," he said, "I may not be much of a writer, but I do consider myself a bit of an amateur Shakespeare scholar. And since you mentioned Mr. Twain, where do you stand on the 'Shakespeare authorship question?'"

"You mean, whether such a person actually existed?"

Duncan-Jones nodded. "And whether he wrote the plays attributed to him, or whether it was someone else. Your Mr. Twain seemed to think he was a fraud."

"To be perfectly honest," Joe said, "I've never thought too deeply about it."

"Really?" Duncan-Jones raised an eyebrow, surprised. "You've never considered it?"

"No, not really," Joe said, shaking his head. "I know the

controversy, of course, but I've never put much stock in it."

"You've never thought that maybe the Earl of Oxford or Christopher Marlowe was the real author?"

"No, I pretty much have always assumed that Shakespeare was Shakespeare. And as to whether he wrote all his plays, well," Joe shrugged, "I guess if push came to shove, I'd say he probably wrote most of them, though he certainly collaborated on a few. In fact, that reminds me, I was just reading *Shakespeare's Apocrypha*—"

"*A Critical Study of the Bard's Lost and Unfinished Plays?*"

Joe nodded, surprised. "Yes, that's the one. You've heard of it?"

"Excellent work," Duncan-Jones said. "I have a copy myself. The author takes your position, though. He believes Shakespeare, except for a few collaborations, wrote all the plays attributed to him."

"I take it, then, you don't think he wrote them."

"I wouldn't go that far, but I do think the jury's still out. I have too many unanswered questions to form a definitive opinion just yet."

"What questions?"

"Perhaps that is something we might discuss at a later date," Duncan-Jones said. "The point is, we're all very excited to see this thing come off." He winked at Joe and, with a breezy smile, said, "Whether Shakespeare was a fraud or not."

When everyone had left, Greenwood grinned broadly and lit up a cigar. His eyes beamed with satisfaction as he turned to Joe. "Excellent, Holliday, just excellent. What we need to do now is get started on the script. We still have a tight deadline. I'd like you to get cracking."

Joe nodded.

The intercom buzzed. Greenwood took his cigar from his mouth and leaned over the desk, pressing the button. "Yes, Ms. Hayden?"

"Mr. Gable has arrived."

Greenwood's demeanor changed and he frowned. "For Christ's sake," he mumbled under his breath. Then he spoke into the intercom, "Send him in."

In seconds, Clark Gable angled his shoulders through the door and sauntered into the office, hands in his pockets, a facetious grin on his face. "Hiya, Charles Jacob," he said, "am I late?"

Greenwood stuck his cigar in his mouth and glared at the actor. "You're an hour late. You missed the entire meeting."

Gable feigned disappointment. "Darn." He glanced over and saw Joe. "Oh hey, chief," he said, surprised. "Didn't know you were tangled up in all this."

"He's writing the screenplay," Greenwood said.

Gable momentarily brightened. "Well, good, at least that's—"

"Is it possible for you to arrive on time for a meeting once in your life?" Greenwood intervened, removing his cigar.

"Sorry," Gable said, grinning, "But I got detained." He glanced around the office and saw all the empty martini glasses. He directed his gaze back at Greenwood and grinned slyly. "Looks like the meeting went well."

Greenwood continued to glare at him. He adjusted his glasses and turned to Joe. "Will you try to convince this dumb ox that Shakespeare would be good for his career, for Christ's sake?"

Before Joe could answer, Gable chimed in. "I don't know how many times we have to argue this," he said. "I don't like it."

"I don't care if you don't like it," Greenwood replied, scowling, his voice sharp and stinging. "I hold your contract and unless you want to break it, I suggest you do as I say. I own you, goddamn it!"

The producer's tone had its intended effect. Gable's manner changed abruptly. Gone was the tone of mockery and facetiousness. He folded his arms across his chest and scowled right back at the producer. "If you think prancing around in tights would be good for my career, then you're as mad as a hatter."

"How many times do I have to pound it into your thick skull? This picture is going to be set in modern times. You're not going to be wearing tights." Greenwood looked over at Joe. "Tell him, for Christ's sake,"

"Well, yes," Joe said, clearing his throat. His reply was slow and cautious. "That's true. We're going to put the play in a modern setting. So, I'm assuming the style of dress will be contemporary."

"It *will* be contemporary, for crying out loud!" Greenwood hollered.

Gable looked over at Greenwood, his eyes skeptical. "You're assuring me I won't have to wear tights?"

"Good God," Greenwood said, "yes, you won't have to wear tights! Do I have to put it in writing?"

"Just promise me."

Greenwood rolled his eyes. "I promise. There, you happy?"

Gable continued to look skeptical, though there was now a hint of resignation. "But I still have to deliver those lines, don't I? It's the most ridiculous stuff I've ever heard." He gave a fey snap of the wrist and spoke in a high-pitched, nasally voice. "'Oh, Titus, thou hast wronged me!'"

Greenwood shook his head, disgusted. "Jesus H. Christ," he said. "If you act it like that it *will* ruin your career."

Before Gable could reply, Greenwood turned to Joe. "By the way," he said, "that reminds me. I've had a change of heart. I've decided to use Shakespeare's language."

Joe looked at him, surprised. "You mean—"

"Yes, yes," Greenwood said, irritated, "we go with the language."

"For Christ's sake," Gable muttered, shaking his head.

Joe approached the writer's cottage. It was a single-story stucco building with a red tile roof, made up to look like a Spanish ranch-style house. Two immense eucalyptus trees towered overhead, affording ample shade and suffusing the air with a pungent smell. Next to it was a second building, also in the ranch-style but much larger. It was the new writer's cottage that Greenwood was building. It was nearly finished, and Greenwood had promised to unveil it soon.

The door to the original writer's cottage was ajar and Joe pushed it all the way open. He peered around, surprised to see that it was deserted except for a single occupant who was seated at one of the writer's stations, his back to the door. He was smoking a cigarette, his feet up on his desk. It didn't look like he was working particularly hard.

Joe stepped inside. At the sound of Joe's footsteps, the man swung his feet off the desk and spun around, his swivel chair squeaking from the sudden movement. It was David Levy, a fellow writer and friend. The man lowered his cigarette and squinted at Joe from across the room. Immediately he reached for his wire-rimmed glasses and put them on, hooking the curved sides behind his ears. His face was thin and hawk-like with a sharp, jutting chin and crowned by thick black hair. Seeing Joe, his dark eyes widened in surprise, and he said, "Well, well, well, I'll be damned. The prodigal has returned. Where the hell have you been?"

"Working from home."

David arched an eyebrow sardonically. "No longer mingling with the proles, huh? What are we, chopped liver?"

Joe grinned.

"And anyway," David went on, "don't you know Greenlog frowns on that sort of thing?" His voice took on the mock accent of a Prussian officer. "The commandant wants all his lieutenants at their posts!"

Joe shrugged. "I figure what he doesn't know won't hurt him."

"I wouldn't be banking on that notion if I were you." David grinned. "You know how extensive his spy network is. I'm told it's more notorious than the Bolshevik secret police."

"You're certainly qualified to make that comparison."

David laughed dryly.

Joe wandered over to his desk and dropped the treatment down with a thump. He pulled his chair out and gazed around the room, taking in the empty chairs. "Where is everyone, by the way?"

"At some meeting."

"What meeting?"

"I don't know, it was all very hush, hush." David winked conspiratorially. "Probably some commie thing."

"Then why aren't you attending?" Joe asked, sitting down. "Aren't you our resident dialectical materialist?"

"Haven't you heard the news?"

"How would I?" Joe grinned, keeping the banter going. "I don't read *Pravda*. That's your bailiwick."

David took a long drag on his cigarette and gave a look of mock nonchalance. "I am apparently no longer in the good graces of the Party." He shrugged. "I suppose I like my paycheck too much. That, and I'm not very disciplined. Certainly not disciplined enough to make a good Marxist-Leninist." He grinned and looked at Joe. "Anyway, I'm joking. There is no meeting."

"I figured as much."

"They all went out to get a drink."

Joe looked at his watch. "At this hour? The sun isn't even close to the yardarm, let alone over it."

"They finished a final draft of *Guns of the Khyber* and were in the mood to celebrate. They left me here to hold the fort."

"Let the inmate run the asylum, huh?"

David chuckled. "Something like that."

Joe grabbed a clean sheet of paper and inserted it into the typewriter, scrolling it into place. He looked over at David, who had kicked up his feet again and was continuing to smoke his cigarette, blowing smoke rings at the ceiling in slow deliberate breaths.

The smell of tobacco gave Joe a craving and he reached inside his shirt pocket, but it was empty. He fumbled around in his trouser pockets. But they were empty, too. "Damn it," he muttered.

David tossed him a pack of Chesterfield cigarettes.

Joe caught it in mid-air. "Thanks." He extracted a cigarette, put it between his lips, and as he was lighting it asked, "You still working on—" he paused. "What was it called again?"

"The *Song of Solomon*. And, yes, I'm still working on it, though

I don't think 'working' is precisely the word I'd use today. To be honest, I haven't written a single goddamned word all day."

"What *have* you been doing?"

"You're pretty much looking at it," David said. "Smoking a raft of cigarettes and lamenting the state of the world."

"Very productive."

"Never underestimate the power of idleness," David said. He cleared his throat and quoted in his best didactic manner: "'Far from idleness being the root of all evil, it is rather the only true good.'"

"Kierkegaard," Joe said out of the corner of his mouth.

"Damn," David replied, frowning, "I can't stump you at all, can I?" He sat for several more minutes, puffing thoughtfully on his cigarette. Joe worked away on his typewriter. But after a moment David looked across at Joe, and said, "You been reading the papers?"

Joe looked up and saw an expression of sober reflection on his fellow writer's face. He nodded, knowing exactly what David was talking about.

"Someone's got to stop that son-of-a-bitch," David muttered.

"I agree, but it looks as if that isn't going to happen any time soon."

"This is just a precursor to war, mark my words."

They were both silent. Joe knew that David had relatives in Germany and had been trying to get them extradited to the United States for the last year but had only met with bureaucratic red tape. He had long denounced Hitler as a demagogue and dangerous anti-Semite who would lead the world into war. At first, Joe had dismissed David's diatribes as overblown, believing that the world community would not want to rush into a second war, especially because the first one had been so devastating. But now it was obvious David's fulminations against Hitler had not been hyperbole. As each day brought some new outrage perpetrated by Hitler and his thugs, it did indeed seem like the world was poised for war.

"By the way," David said, breaking the silence, "I heard."

Joe looked up. "What did you hear?"

"About *One Step Away from Heaven.*" His expression was genuinely sympathetic. "I'm sorry. I know you put a lot of work into that."

Joe shrugged and tried to stifle the irritation that still rankled him. "Life rolls on." He paused. "Speaking of Kierkegaard, 'life can only be understood backwards, but it must be lived forwards.'"

David picked up on his body language. "Greenlog can be a bastard sometimes."

Joe shrugged again and took a long drag. They were both silent for a moment until Joe scooted his chair closer to his desk. He started typing again.

"So," David said, glancing at the treatment on Joe's desk, "by the fact you're carrying around something about *Hamlet,* I take it the rumor is true?"

Joe stopped typing and looked over at him. "The rumor?"

"You're working on Greenwood's vaunted Shakespeare script?"

Joe nodded. "I'm the anointed one."

"That's funny," David said, squinting at him with mock seriousness. "I never pegged you as the Messiah type."

"What do you know? You Jews don't believe in a Messiah."

"Yes we do, we just don't believe he's arrived yet."

"I stand corrected."

"Yet again."

Joe chuckled.

"So, how's it going, by the way?" David asked.

"The Shakespeare script?"

David nodded.

"Just getting started on it."

"Just getting started!" David exclaimed, mimicking Greenwood. "You should've finished that thing weeks ago! What the hell have you been doing, diddling yourself?"

CHAPTER 7

THAT EVENING, JOE CALLED Betsy from the pay phone across the street from the liquor store. "They liked it," he said. "*Hamlet* got the green light."

"I heard. Congratulations."

He was surprised and somewhat crestfallen. "You already heard?"

"News travels fast on the lot."

"I guess so," he chuckled, recovering. "What you didn't hear was that C.J. wants Gable to play the lead. But that's not settled, so keep it under your hat." He paused. "Anyway, I guess this means your illustrious Madam Petrova was right."

"You mean about the writing project?"

"Yes."

Betsy was silent for a moment. "I'm not sure this was what she was talking about."

"What do you mean?"

"I don't know, but I got the impression it was something else."

"Like what?"

"Some other writing project. Something of a more personal nature."

Joe was confused. "Why do you think that?"

"It's just a gut feeling."

Joe chuckled again. "Well, I don't think I'll have any time for something like that. At least not right now."

"Why not?"

"Because I'll be absorbed with working on *Hamlet*. I won't have time for anything else. Greenwood wants a draft by May."

"May?" She was stunned. "You're kidding, right?"

"No, that's the deal, I'm afraid."

"But that's impossible! He can't expect you to write a whole script in two months."

"That's what C.J. wants."

"Do you think you can do it?" she asked.

"I'm going to have to. I have no choice."

She paused. "So, what's it about anyway?"

"What's what about?"

"*Hamlet.*"

Joe was surprised. "You've never read it?"

"No, Joe, I haven't," she said, irritation in her voice. "I know I'm supposed to be the girlfriend of a writer, but—"

"I'm sorry," Joe said. "I didn't mean it like that. I'm just surprised."

"Why?"

"Because it's maybe the most important work of Western literature." He paused. "I guess I just assumed everybody has at least a basic familiarity with the story."

"We all haven't had the educational opportunities you've had, Joe."

"Yes, yes, I know. I'm sorry."

"So, what's it about?" she asked again.

Joe chuckled. "That's kind of a loaded question."

"What do you mean?"

"It's just that people have asked that question for ages and everyone seems to have a different answer."

"That doesn't help me understand it, Joe," Betsy said. "All I know is that it's about a Danish prince who is really sad and depressed. And there's a ghost, and a sword fight, but that's about it."

Joe chuckled again. "Well," he said, "I was going to say it's about revenge and the consequences of revenge. And the mystery of death. And justice. And filial duty versus doing what's right. And the uncertainty of life. But I'm guessing you just want to hear the story."

"Yes, why don't we just start with the basic plot?"

Joe's voice became animated. "It starts out with a death. Prince

Hamlet's father, the king of Denmark, is killed and he suspects his uncle Claudius, but can't prove anything. In the meantime, his mother has married Claudius."

"She was married to the guy who got killed?"

Joe nodded. "Yes, the king. But now Claudius is the king. Anyway, one night Hamlet sees his father's ghost. It tells him—"

"What's her name?"

Joe came to a halt. "Who?"

"Hamlet's mother."

"Gertrude." Joe continued, "The ghost tells him to seek revenge. But Hamlet at first doesn't know what to think. Is the ghost really his father? Or a demon leading him astray?"

"What do you think?"

"We can talk about that later. Right now, I'll just tell you the basic story."

"Okay."

"Hamlet is torn by indecision, not knowing what course of action he should take, so he falls into a deep depression. He begins to act like a madman so as to try to find out the truth behind the murder. I'm leaving a lot out but that's okay. So, anyway, when a troupe of actors arrives at the castle, Hamlet persuades them to act out his play, which is about the murder of a king."

"Clever," Betsy said.

"The plan works and during the murder scene Claudius storms out. Hamlet is now utterly convinced and seeks his uncle's murder. He catches up with the king, but Claudius is praying so Hamlet can't kill him."

"Why not?"

"He believes he will go directly to heaven, and he wants his uncle to suffer. So he kills Polonius instead."

"Who?" she asked.

"I didn't mention him, did I?"

"No."

"He's the lord chamberlain."

"What's a chamberlain?"

"A kind of court official," Joe said. "He's in charge of protocol. Hamlet kills him by accident. He stabs him while Polonius is standing behind a curtain."

Betsy was silent, listening, but suddenly interjected. "Isn't there a love interest in this?" she asked. "I thought Hamlet had a beloved."

"Yes, he does. Ophelia."

"How come you didn't mention her?"

"She's Polonius's daughter."

"He killed her father? Boy, this guy is really messing up, isn't he?"

"It gets worse. She goes mad and commits suicide."

"She dies, too?"

He nodded. "Well, it is a tragedy."

Joe went on to explain that Claudius tries to have Hamlet killed when the prince is in England. But the plot fails. When Hamlet returns to Denmark, Polonius's son Laertes, angered by the death of his father and sister, challenges the prince to a duel. But the odds are far from even. Claudius persuades Laertes to poison the tip of his sword. He also poisons a glass of wine in case Hamlet comes away from the duel unscathed. The two men fight and Hamlet scores two hits on Laertes.

"Gertrude is excited for her son and toasts him by drinking the poisoned wine," Joe said. "Of course, Claudius tries to stop her but fails. In the ensuing chaos, Laertes manages to slash Hamlet with his poisoned blade, but Hamlet wrestles the sword from him and wounds Laertes with his own poisoned sword. Hamlet then kills Claudius."

"And Laertes dies, too?"

"Yes, he dies, too. They all die."

Betsy was silent for a moment. "Boy, I didn't realize it was so depressing."

"It's not," Joe said quickly. "I mean, it kind of is. But it's a brilliant play."

Betsy was silent for a moment. "Are you going to be at the studio tomorrow?"

"Yes, I'll be in. I have to meet with C.J. again. Then I'm going to spend the rest of the day writing. By the way, don't you have your big scene tomorrow? Your speaking scene?"

"I do."

"Nervous?"

"A little," she admitted.

"Don't worry, you'll do great."

"You think so?"

"Yes, of course," he said.

"I hope so."

"You will." He hung up the phone and turned toward the coast. A stiff breeze had sprung up off the water. It carried the heavy smell of salt. Joe threw up the collar of his jacket and quickened his steps toward the cottage.

———————————

A cool sea breeze drifted in through the open window, stirring the curtains.

Seated in front of his Remington, Joe shivered. He lit a cigarette and took a long drag. Turning his head but keeping his eyes on the typewriter, he blew out a ring of smoke. It was carried away by the breeze that swept through the room.

He carefully laid his cigarette down on the edge of the ashtray, scratched his cheek, and started typing again. A copy of *Hamlet* was at his elbow, open to Act One, Scene One—the first appearance of the ghost of Hamlet's father. Next to it was *Shakespeare's Apocrypha*, unopened.

Joe shivered as a stronger puff of wind gusted in through the window. This time the curtains billowed back and forth. He stared at them and listened to the wind as it whistled around the eaves of the house outside. He pushed his chair back and stood up. Crossing the room, he closed the window with a slam.

When he returned to his desk, he noticed that *Hamlet* was closed, and the *Apocrypha* was opened—to *The Apple Orchard*.

He blinked. This was becoming a habit and for a moment he just stared at the book. Then he lifted his head and slowly glanced around the room. But everything was still and quiet. Aside from the occasional gust of wind outside and the normal creaks and groans of the cottage, he didn't notice anything out of the ordinary.

He closed the *Apocrypha* with a thump and reopened *Hamlet*, flipping forward to Act One. Sitting down, he started typing again. He'd been at it for several minutes, engrossed in the work, when another chilly breeze swept into the room.

He looked up with a puzzled frown. *Where had that gust come from?* he wondered. Had he closed all the windows? He glanced around the room but noticed that all the windows in the living room were closed. What about the kitchen window? He must have left that open, he told himself. Standing up, he walked down the short hallway to the kitchen. But the kitchen window was shut, too. He scratched his head and stood for a moment, glancing around the room. Again, everything seemed normal, nothing was out of place. Then he angled back to the living room. He was about to sit back down when he noticed, yet again, *Hamlet* was closed—and the *Apocrypha* was flipped open to *The Apple Orchard.*

Joe stood completely still, his spine tingling. The silence was palpable. The only thing he heard was the slow ticking of the clock on the wall. It was as if for a moment the world lay in some sort of suspended animation, hovering on the brink of—he wasn't sure what. Tentatively, he looked around the room, as if seeing it for the first time, noticing certain imperfections—on the walls and furniture—that he had never noticed before. He closed his eyes, feeling his heart thump hard in his chest. When he opened them, he directed his gaze down at *The Apple Orchard.*

"Is this it?" he said aloud, his voice sounding strangely loud in the silence of the house. "Is this what you want me to do?"

His questions were met with silence, but he felt a strange sensation as if two hands rested gently on his shoulders.

———————

Later that night, Joe tossed and turned in bed, unable to sleep. More than once, he sat up and glanced at the clock, to see what time it was. But each time only a few minutes had elapsed. He lay down on his back and stared up at the ceiling. He stayed in that position for a long time, thinking about the events of the night, trying to process whether what he'd experienced was legitimate rather than his own mind playing tricks on him.

Finally, his eyes grew heavy and he began to drift off. The last thing he remembered, before sliding off into dreams, was the presence of a shadowy figure at the foot of his bed, watching him.

A candle flickered, throwing pale light into a dimly lit room. The low ceiling, blunt crossbeams, and crudely timbered walls suggested the upper loft of a multistory building.

At the far end of the room, near the window, a man sat hunched over a small oak table. He was huddled against the chill in his padded doublet. The only sound was the quill in the man's hand as it scratched along the thick vellum paper. He stopped to dip the quill into the inkhorn before continuing to write.

Outside, the sounds of London drifted upward—the grating squeak of wheeled carts as they rumbled over cobbled streets, the clop of hooves, occasional shouted voices, and barking dogs.

The man stopped writing and looked up, gazing for a moment out the window, his expression thoughtful. Brown hair framed his face and fell to his collar. A neat Van Dyke beard clustered on his chin. He carefully put down the quill and stared at the paper for a long moment, flexing tired, cold fingers.

"What is it, Thomas?" a voice behind him asked. "What ails thee?"

The man glanced over his shoulder at his companion, who sat on a stool at the opposite end of the room. His face was partially obscured by shadows, though the light from the candle gleamed on a single gold earring in his left earlobe. He was looking at Thomas with a quizzical expression, a large tome open on his lap.

Thomas furrowed his brow and gestured down at the paper. "This character, Nicholas. Methinks he needs fleshing out."

"Fleshing out?"

"Aye," Thomas nodded. "His affections seem swayed more by base sentiment than by the lofty strains of singing angels. He seems less a poet and more a churlish peacock."

"Then flesh away, good Thomas. But make haste. Henslowe is not a patient man. We must finish by two days' time, as thou well know."

Thomas nodded and picked up the quill, which he dipped into the inkwell. He scratched out a few more sentences but then, abruptly, put the quill down again. He blew on the page where the ink was still wet. He sighed and sat back, massaging his writing hand.

"By my troth," he said, "if only the Muse might descend. My brain has turned to clotted cream."

His companion chuckled. "And mine to gooseberry preserve." He paused for a moment, and then closed the book with an authoritative thump. "The devil take Henslowe! Enough for tonight. Let's away to the Boar's Head for a tankard."

Thomas grinned. He reached down to pat the shillings in his coin pouch. His companion stood up, straightened his doublet, and broke into verse:

"Man was not made solely for toil and sweat,
But for ale and wine and good friends well met."

Thomas, buttoning his doublet, added his own:

"Let not these many days through our fingers slip,
Whilst my kisses might drown some maiden's cherry lip."

"That's good, Thomas," the man said. "Thou should write such down."

"'Tis only doggerel," Thomas replied.

"Aye, but good doggerel."

"Is there such a thing?"

"Aye, 'tis an old and underappreciated form," the man said. "Chaucer was its master."

"'Dog'-gerel and its 'master.'" Thomas grinned. "I believe thou maketh a pun. Did the good Sir Geoffrey lead his 'dog-gerel' about upon a leash?"

"Nay, methinks he was more apt to unleash his 'dog-erel' and set it with biting fangs upon the written page."

Laughing, both men strode toward the doorway, their boots pounding against the wooden floorboards.

CHAPTER 8

BETSY SAT AT A table in the studio commissary, poring over a script of *The Queen's Cavalier*. She was ramrod straight, holding the script in front of her as if it were holy writ. Despite the chatter of voices that surrounded her, her concentration was focused and unflappable. Her "big" scene was coming up and she wanted to be prepared. It was the first time the studio had given her lines to speak—and though it was only four words, "Here you are, milady"—she didn't want to botch it. She wanted to deliver them with believability and crispness. For a moment the thought of actually speaking lines in a Hollywood movie, albeit a run-of-the-mill costume drama, almost made her giddy. After plodding her way as an extra through a dozen or more movies, the long-awaited day had arrived. She couldn't describe the thrill of delivering dialogue, of getting billing in the credits. Of seeing her name on the screen. It was the culmination of a dream.

"Rehearsing?"

Surprised, Betsy looked up.

Roger Powell was standing over her, his smile even broader—and oilier—than usual. He wasn't filming any scenes today, so he was dressed casually, in a white bush shirt, pleated trousers, and two-toned Oxfords.

She sighed and lowered the script. "What do you want this time, Roger?"

"My, my," he said, "are you always so touchy?"

"Only when you're around to bother me."

"Look," Roger said, his voice taking on a wounded tone, "I didn't come here to badger you. I just wanted to wish you luck. I know today is your big scene."

She sighed again, but this time it wasn't one of exasperation. "I'm sorry I snapped at you," she said. "I guess I'm just a little tense. I want to do well."

His smile reappeared. "And so you shall."

"You think so?"

"Of course. You're a natural. I can tell."

"Thanks, Roger. I appreciate it."

He lingered at the table, thrusting his hands into his pockets. He swung his gaze around the commissary for a moment before directing it back on Betsy. "So, how's your boyfriend?"

"Busy. He's working on the *Hamlet* script."

Roger nodded and fell quiet, continuing to linger. It was obvious something was on his mind.

"I really have to study, Roger. Is there something you want?"

"Look," he said, "I meant what I said, about you being a natural. But I wanted to give you some advice."

She raised an eyebrow, studying him with a skeptical gaze. She wasn't entirely sure she wanted to hear any advice from Roger and was tempted to say so, but she stayed quiet.

"It takes more than just talent to succeed in this business," he said.

She continued to listen but felt a little bit unsure where this conversation might be headed.

"What I mean is," Roger went on, "you should set your sights higher."

"What's that mean?" Betsy replied.

"I'm just saying the sky's the limit to an attractive and talented young woman like yourself. You don't have to be an extra the rest of your life." He paused, giving her a pointed look. "You want to be a real actress, don't you?"

"Of course I do. That's why I got into this business."

"Well, then, there are ways of achieving that, if you play your cards right."

She regarded him with narrowed eyes. "What do you mean, 'if I play my cards right'?"

"Look," he said, "if you just allow yourself to be a little more— what's the word?—flexible, a little more obliging, you might—"

"Obliging to whom? You?" She cut him off. "Quit talking in circles. Why don't you just say what's on your mind, Roger."

He paused for a moment before blurting out, "Why are you tying yourself down to that hack writer? With his salary, he's barely able to pay the rent. I could take you to real restaurants, to nightclubs. I have my own table at the Cocoanut Grove. I could buy you furs and jewels. I could open up a whole new world for you."

"You just won't let it go, will you?"

"Because I think you're making a mistake."

"I'm so glad to hear you know my mind better than I do," Betsy said sarcastically.

"Look, I'm not saying that. I'm just saying—"

"I'm not going to be one of your many conquests, Roger," Betsy said, angry now. "If that's what you mean by being 'more flexible' than count me out. And Joe is not a hack. He's a great writer!"

"Writers are a dime a dozen in this business. They're like cheap suits, if you don't like one, you toss it and get another. Better yet, they're like cigars. You burn through one and grab another." He paused. "And if your boyfriend is such a great writer, why is he working here, cranking out hackneyed westerns and formulaic costume dramas?"

"I could ask you the same question. If you're such a big movie star, why are *you* here?"

"Because, my dear," Roger said, effecting an air of bored insouciance, "Apex Studios is only a momentary stepping stone. I'll squeeze it for all its worth and move on to bigger and better things."

"What 'bigger and better' things?"

He gave a smug little smile. "Let's just say I have a number of irons in the fire at the moment."

"I wouldn't say that too loudly, Greenwood might be in earshot."

Roger waved a dismissive hand. "Greenwood's a pussycat."

"Oh really? That's the first I've heard of it."

"I've got him wrapped around my finger. He knows I'm the biggest star he's got. He's not about to muddy the waters."

"What about Gable?" Betsy said.

Roger frowned. "What about him?"

"He's starting to get some choice roles. Sounds like he might be nipping at your heels."

"Gable couldn't act his way out of a box."

"Why don't you tell that to Greenwood?" Betsy said. "I think he disagrees with you."

"What do you mean?"

"If you and Greenwood are so tight, then I can only guess he must've forgotten to mention who he's casting as Hamlet."

Roger's expression faltered and his face stiffened. He stared at Betsy with narrowed eyes. "What do you mean? What have you heard?"

"Exactly that," Betsy said. "He has someone else in mind to play Hamlet."

"Who?"

This time, Betsy felt obliged to give her own smug little smile. "Wouldn't you like to know?"

Roger's hand shot out and seized her arm. "Who?"

"Ow!" Betsy grimaced, surprised. "Hey, let go! What's the big idea?"

"Tell me who," Roger hissed, his grip on her arm like an iron vise.

"Let go!" She tried to pull her arm away, but he only tightened his grasp, his fingers digging into her arm.

"Tell me!"

"Who do you think?" she said. "The rumor is Hamlet is going to Gable."

Roger's eyes widened in surprise and he scowled. "Gable? That big, dumb—"

"Let go, will you!" Betsy jerked her arm, trying to pull away. Roger released his grip.

Betsy sat massaging her arm and glared at him. "The next

time you do that, buster—"

Before Betsy could finish her sentence, Roger spun on his heel and stomped off, muttering to himself.

Betsy watched him go, continuing to massage her arm.

———————

Greenwood struck a match and lit a cigar. He drew on it for a long moment so that the end glowed red and then blew out a ring of smoke, which drifted lazily up toward the ceiling.

"Like I said, Holliday, we gotta move on this. Those limey investors want a draft by the end of the month."

Joe was sitting across from the producer, staring fixedly out the window. His mind was preoccupied with the events of last night, and he wasn't paying attention to Greenwood. Instead, his eyes were focused on the pale morning light that gleamed on the pavement below Greenwood's office.

When he didn't answer, Greenwood erupted. "Damn it, Holliday, are you listening to me?!"

Joe spun back around. His gaze came back from the depths of space and fastened on Greenwood. "I'm sorry, sir. What did you say?"

Greenwood glared at him. "For Christ's sake, man, have you heard anything I've said?"

"I'm sorry. You were talking about the script?"

"Of course I was talking about the script!" Greenwood snarled. "What did you think I was talking about? Greta Garbo's legs!"

"Sorry, sir. It's just that—" He paused.

"What?"

Joe shook his head. "It's nothing, sir, sorry."

Greenwood glared at him for a moment longer, then continued. "I said we gotta move on the script. We need a draft by the end of the month."

Joe came out of his fog. "The end of the month?" He blinked dully. "I thought you said by the end of May?"

"Things change," Greenwood offered by way of explanation. He tapped ash into an ashtray on his desk. "The investors want a draft sooner rather than later, so I told them they'll get one by the end of the month."

"That doesn't give us a lot of time."

"That's exactly my point!" Greenwood bellowed angrily. "That's why we have to move on it!" He stared at Joe with a scrutinizing gaze. "What's gotten into you today, Holliday? I can't tell if you're going deaf or senile. Pay attention, for Christ's sake."

"Sorry, sir." It was the fifth time he'd uttered "sorry" in the last few minutes. "I guess I was drifting."

"I'll say." Greenwood took a long drag on his cigar, seemingly to calm himself. "To make matters worse, I just this morning learned Hal Levinsky over at Palm Studios is set to make *Romeo and Juliet*. He's got that swishy Brit actor Leslie Howard lined up to play Romeo. That son-of-a-bitch is trying to steal my thunder. I'll bet he's doing it deliberately."

Joe knew that Levinsky was Greenwood's biggest rival. The two men detested one another with a vehemence that was the talk of Hollywood.

"Well, sir, I don't think that should be too—"

"Don't even try to defend that cheap son-of-a-bitch!" Greenwood hissed. He leaned forward, his gaze boring into Joe. "Do you know what Levinsky did before he got into the movie business?"

Joe had heard this exact rant before, but he saw no point in bringing that up. He shook his head, feigning ignorance.

"He sold carpets, for crying out loud! He was a goddamned carpet salesman. You ask me he's still a lousy, no-good carpet salesman."

Joe was silent. It was pointless to comment. He knew that adding anything to the present conversation would set Greenwood off on another harangue.

But Greenwood was over his tirade. He sat back and took another drag on his cigar. His eyes narrowed as he continued to gaze at Joe. "Now," he said, changing gears, "can you do it?"

"You mean—"

"I mean have a finished copy by the end of the month."

Joe paused, fidgeting. The request was unreasonable. But there was nothing he could do. He'd learned that sometimes in this business you just had to grin and bear it. He sat up straight and nodded. "Yes, of course, sir."

"Good. I want you camped out in the writer's cottage. By the way, there's a rumor you haven't been seen there recently." His gaze was accusatory. "Why not?"

"I sometimes find it easier to write at home, sir." He shrugged. "It's just my habit."

"Then break it. You can write at home in the evenings but you're to use the cottage during the day. I didn't pay for the damn place so you could avoid using it. Is that clear?"

"Yes, sir, I understand."

Greenwood leaned back in his chair, blew out another ring of smoke and gazed at Joe with a cold, probing stare. "So, how far have you gotten?"

"On the script?"

Greenwood gave an exasperated shake of his head. "Christ, you're dense today, Holliday." He nodded aggressively. "Yes, the script."

"Not far. I've only just started."

"But you have *something* written, right?"

"Just a few pages."

Greenwood grunted and drew on his cigar again. He blew out smoke and pushed his glasses up the bridge of his nose. He gazed at the burning tip of his cigar for a moment, as if mulling something over. But then, seemingly reaching a conclusion, he nodded and looked directly at Joe. "I suppose that's okay. But we can't waste time."

Joe just nodded.

Joe left Greenwood's office and wandered through the studio grounds in a daze. Everything seemed to be happening so fast it made his head spin. A month seemed like a long time, but Joe knew the complexities of screenwriting often required rewrite after rewrite, a process that could drag on indefinitely. The typical amount of time it took to write a screenplay was about three months, but most screenplays often took even longer—because the producer or director invariably wanted to change this or that scene, expand or delete dialogue, or add an additional character. In short, the process was frequently a task that required time, patience and, above all, a thick skin.

But all of that seemed to pale in comparison to the mysterious happenings he'd recently experienced. Why did it seem as if something—or someone—was trying to sabotage the *Hamlet* script or at least divert his attention to *The Apple Orchard?* What was the significance of this play? Why did it seem as if every time he turned around *The Apple Orchard* was staring him in the face?

He wondered what Betsy would think of all this. She would no doubt want him to talk to Madam Petrova.

He stopped walking and scratched his chin. Maybe that wasn't such a bad idea, he told himself. If she was legitimate, she might be able to tell him what this was all about.

He glanced at his watch. It was a few minutes before ten. Betsy would be taking her Union-mandated fifteen minute break then. He decided to confide in her, tell her about the odd occurrences that had been happening to him. She was all the way across the studio but if he hurried now, he'd probably be able to catch her. He turned and headed towards the sound stages.

As he walked across the studio, it was as if he had entered another world. He passed men and women dressed in all manner of different costumes. Joe passed pirates, Roman senators, chorus girls, medieval knights, and British Victorian soldiers. Occasionally, someone with a cowboy hat and sporting six-guns trotted by on a horse.

He was walking so swiftly and buried in his own thoughts he almost didn't hear the deep voice behind him. "Hey, kid!"

Joe turned around and standing behind him was Clark Gable.

The tall, well-built actor had a surprisingly candid look on his face.

"Hi, Clark."

"Got a minute?"

Joe glanced at his watch again, hesitant. "I'm kind of in a hurry."

"Should only take a couple minutes," Gable said.

"All right," Joe conceded with a sigh.

Gable gestured at the nearest studio door. "Mind if we go in there to talk?"

Joe gazed at the closed door. "You want to talk on a sound stage?"

"Yeah, you mind?"

"I guess not," Joe said, shrugging, though he was curious why Gable would choose such a venue. He wondered if he was about to be on the receiving end of some sort of joke. Gable was well known among the other actors as an inveterate prankster. But the sober look on Gable's face made it clear that the tall actor was serious.

Joe followed as Gable opened the stage door and entered. It was dark and deserted inside, with a curious mothball-like smell, as if the building hadn't been used in a while. Gable closed the door with a clang and switched on the lights. The sounds reverberated through the building, magnified by the stage's unique acoustics.

"Sorry about all the cloak and dagger," Gable said, turning back around. "But I've got a bit of a problem and I don't want anyone else to hear."

Joe nodded hesitantly. He wasn't sure whether to be honored or put upon by Gable's confession. "Is it a woman again?" he asked.

"No, nothing like that. I'm actually doing pretty well in the woman department," Gable grinned but then grew serious again. "It's got to do with Shakespeare."

"Shakespeare?" Joe studied him and suddenly nodded in understanding. "Oh, you mean you still don't want to do Hamlet? I'm not sure I can help. If you're really dead set against the picture, you'll just have to tell Greenwood. He can't force you to be in it."

"Yes, he can. But that's not my problem. I already agreed to do it."

"Oh, I see." Joe was surprised, and he fell silent.

Gable took a long time coming to the point. He looked at the floor and scratched his ear, a pained expression on his face. Then he glanced up and looked straight at Joe.

"You're a writer, so you probably went to college, right?"

"Yes, I went to college."

"And you have a master's degree or something, right?"

Joe nodded. He still wasn't sure where this conversation was headed, and he gave Gable a questioning look.

"Anyway," Gable continued, "I picked up a copy of the play last night."

"Hamlet?"

Gable nodded. "Thought I'd do a little reading in preparation. And, for the life of me, I couldn't understand a single damn word. It's like Greek. If I'm going to deliver those lines, I have to know what the hell I'm saying, otherwise I'm sunk. You understand?"

Joe nodded. "Yeah, I get it. But what do you want me to do?"

"Coach me."

"Coach you?" Joe was puzzled. "I don't understand. You mean—"

"I mean help me understand his writing. And what the hell the play's about. The whole thing doesn't make any sense to me." Gable paused. "Look, I know you're busy, but this would be hugely helpful."

Joe scratched his chin; Gable was right, he was in fact pretty damn busy right now.

Gable noted his reluctance. "Look," he said, "we don't have to meet all the time, just a few times would work, at least until I understand it. And I could make it worth your while."

"No, no," Joe said, waving his hand dismissively. "I couldn't take your money. That wouldn't be right." After a moment he said, "But sure, yeah, I'll help you."

Gable's face broke into a wide grin and he grabbed Joe's hand, pumping it vigorously. "Thanks, chief, you're a saint. But if you don't mind, I'd like to keep all this on the QT."

"I understand."

———————————

Breathless, Joe caught up with Betsy as she was going back into the sound stage. She was dressed in her "lady of the court" attire and her powdered wig. Her face was heavily made up with a surfeit of face powder.

"What are you doing here?" she asked, surprised to see him. "I thought you were writing today."

"I am, but I have to talk to you."

"I can't right now, Joe, I'm about to shoot my scene."

"It'll just take a second, I promise."

She sighed in exasperation and put her hands on her hips, "Okay, but make it quick."

"When are you going to see Madam Petrova next?"

She cocked her head in surprise and stared at him. "Tomorrow night. Why?"

"I need to talk to her."

"You want to talk to her?" Her eyes widened in surprise.

"Yes. Can I tag along?"

"Of course you can." She paused. "But why the sudden interest?"

"I'll explain later. Let's meet at Duke's this evening."

"Okay."

He gave her a peck on the cheek. "Now go in there and break a leg."

CHAPTER 9

"BREAK A LEG, BREAK a leg..." Betsy repeated the phrase over and over to herself like a mantra.

She adjusted her wig and took a deep breath, hoping to quell the butterflies that roiled her stomach. She stared at the sound stage door, watching the line of actors and actresses begin to file inside. Then, with sudden determination, she lifted the hem of her dress just above her ankles and joined the line. As she stepped through the threshold, she heard a loud metallic clang followed by the buzz of electricity. Immediately the room was filled with brilliant light.

Shielding her eyes against the glare, she looked around. Leighton was standing at the edge of the set with his cameraman, his sound technician, and his script supervisor. They were huddled around a copy of the script, deep in conversation. Other technicians were organizing the set for the next scene, darting back and forth.

Betsy noticed Lillian Russell chatting with another actor, a man named Harry Beaumont who was playing Cardinal de Brienne. He was dressed in a long scarlet cassock, a matching skullcap, and sported an elaborate crucifix around his neck. With his tall, stooped bearing, hollow cheeks, and taciturn eyes, he looked as if he'd stepped out of a painting by El Greco.

Betsy hesitated for a moment and then approached them cautiously. At the sound of her footsteps, Lillian looked around. "Hiya, kid," she said, smiling, "you ready?"

"You bet," Betsy said, trying her best to mask her anxiety.

"You ain't nervous, are you?"

Betsy shook her head. "No, not at all," she lied.

"Good," Lillian said, "'cause this thing will be a cinch."

"If you say so."

Lillian looked at her with a little smile. "I thought you weren't nervous?"

"No, no," Betsy said quickly, "I'm not, I just want to do well."

Lillian chuckled. "In my book 'just wanting to do well' means you're nervous."

Betsy was about to protest but stopped herself. She nodded sheepishly. "Maybe a little."

"Don't worry," Lillian said, "just relax, it'll be fine."

"All right, everyone!" Leighton called out, bellowing through his bullhorn. "Five minutes until we shoot. Let's get organized, people!"

Lillian reached out and grabbed Betsy's hand. "C'mon," she said. She led the young actress over to the set, which was made to resemble the inside of an eighteenth-century French chapel. A huge, ornate stained-glass window adorned one wall and below it was an altar with a gold crucifix.

Make-up artists seemed to materialize around them, and before Betsy knew what was happening, they were applying last minute dabs of make-up on her face. Lillian took it in stride, but Betsy found it a bit disconcerting; almost as if she were nothing more than a prop that required paint.

"Just remember to hit all your marks," Lillian said through the side of her mouth, trying to avoid the tiny puffballs aimed at her face. "That's the thing Leighton really hates. People missing their marks. You've heard him rant and rave when people don't."

Betsy nodded. She knew all too well.

"Actors to the set and everyone in their places!" Leighton yelled.

Lillian glanced over at Betsy. "Remember kid, this'll be a cinch."

Betsy nodded again, hoping the older actress was right.

Every table at Duke's was occupied. Joe was lucky to have arrived when he had; otherwise, he wouldn't have been able to find a seat. He glanced around. It was thronged with couples, mostly young people, many of whom had just gotten off work. Joe recognized a few faces from the studio, but most were strangers, men and women from the nearby commercial district.

Joe blew smoke from his nostrils and stubbed out his cigarette in an ashtray on the table. Impatiently he looked at his watch. It was already a quarter past six. He wondered what was keeping Betsy. She was a good fifteen minutes late.

Joe watched as a young woman wearing a powder blue sweater, bobby socks, and saddle shoes walked up to the jukebox and deposited a coin. Soon the diner was flooded with the honeyed strains of Benny Goodman's "Stardust."

Betsy finally came through the door. She was wearing a long coat over a plain red dress. A red beret framed her face, enhancing her large, brown eyes. Her complexion was flushed as if she had hurried the last several blocks.

"Sorry I'm late," she said. She took off her coat, draped it over the back of her chair, and sat down across from Joe.

"I was beginning to wonder," he said. "What happened to you?"

She caught her breath, took a moment to adjust her beret, and then began to speak excitedly, the words gushing out of her in a torrent. "You're not going to believe it," she said, "my scene took only two takes, and that was only because a light blew out on the first take. I hit my mark perfectly. Both times."

"So you nailed it," Joe said, grinning. "I knew you would. You're a natural."

She laughed. "You sound just like Roger Powell."

Joe furrowed his brow and looked at her. "What do you mean?"

"Never mind," she said, waving her hand dismissively. "The less said about that guy the better. Anyway, let me tell you about it. I was nervous at first but when Leighton yelled 'action'

I went into autopilot. And it was much easier than I thought." She reached across the table and grabbed his hand, giving it an excited squeeze. "Joe, this is it! This is what I want to do the rest of my life. The whole thing just reaffirms why I got into acting in the first place. I can't describe how exciting it is! It makes me feel so alive. God, I'd be acting even if they didn't pay me."

Joe was amused at her enthusiasm, and he grinned. "Then it's a good thing they're paying you."

She gave a self-conscious smile. "That makes me sound silly, doesn't it?"

"Not at all," he said, "never apologize for your passions."

"Do you feel that way about your writing?"

He paused. "It's more of a compulsion," he said after a moment.

"What do you mean?"

"It's something I can't control. I suppose I have to write, or I couldn't live with myself."

"But don't you get any enjoyment out of it?"

He shrugged. "It's work."

She gazed at him with a keen eye. "I don't believe that."

He suddenly realized how ridiculous he had sounded. He shook his head as if clearing his mind of the thought. "You're right," he said, "I'm being stupid. Yes, I get tremendous enjoyment out of it. I get as much pleasure out of it as you get out of acting. I'm kidding myself to think otherwise." He grinned. "But it's still work."

A waitress came to their table and they ordered Cokes.

"Madam Petrova once told me that if I worked hard, I'd succeed at my acting. But she said my success would come in a very unexpected way." She paused and looked at him with big round eyes. "What do you suppose she meant?"

Joe shrugged. "I don't know. What do you think?"

"I haven't the foggiest." She stopped and looked at him curiously. "That reminds me. Why on earth are you suddenly so hot to see Madam Petrova? I thought you said she was a fraud."

"I didn't exactly say she was a fraud," Joe said defensively.

"Could've fooled me."

"All I said was—" He stopped and shook his head, exasperated. "It doesn't matter. Anyway, I've been having a lot of weird experiences recently, and I want to see if she can help me."

Interest flared in Betsy's eyes. "What kind of experiences?"

He told her about his dreams and his discovery of *Shakespeare's Apocrypha* and the strange experiences surrounding that book. He mentioned how *Shakespeare's Apocrypha* kept flipping open to *The Apple Orchard* as if by magic.

"That can't be a coincidence," Betsy chimed in.

"Well, there was a breeze," Joe replied.

"Don't be silly. It wasn't that breezy. And each time to the same page?"

"Yeah, I know, that doesn't make a lot of sense."

"I think it was a ghost," Betsy said decisively. "They were trying to communicate with you."

Joe was quiet. He shrugged.

"I'm sure Madam Petrova will be able to find out who it was, and what they were trying to tell you."

Their Cokes soon arrived. Betsy was quiet for a moment, sipping her drink through a straw. She placed the glass down on the table and glanced across at Joe, her face thoughtful.

"Want to know what else I think?" she said. "I think this is the writing project Madam Petrova was talking about that day. Remember?"

"That did cross my mind," Joe acknowledged.

"It has to be," she insisted. "It makes perfect sense." She nodded with sudden certainty. "*The Apple Orchard* is the writing project."

Joe took a sip of his Coke. "Maybe you're right. But the problem is, I can't do it right now. I have to work on the *Hamlet* script." He shook his head. "I can't do both."

"Why not?"

"Betsy, script writing takes a lot of time and effort. I can't just shift willy-nilly from one to the other. And the studio is paying me for the script. I can't afford to spend time on anything else right now, especially since we have such a tight deadline."

"So, write the play after you finish *Hamlet*."

Joe paused. "That's the weird thing. Every time I start work on *Hamlet*, it's like something tries to prevent me."

"What do you mean?"

"Exactly that," he said. "It's like something—or someone—doesn't want me to write *Hamlet*."

———————

Later that evening, after dropping Betsy at her boarding house, Joe hopped on the Red Car and rode it west to Santa Monica. He got out at the last stop, which was only a few blocks away from his cottage.

The night was cool, and a thick fog had settled over everything, carrying with it the heavy smell of salt. Overhead, the streetlights appeared as fuzzy orange orbs. He threw up the collar of his jacket and thrust both hands into his pockets.

His thoughts lingered on the events of the last few days. Not only was he dealing with a mercurial producer who was apt to change his mind at the drop of a hat, but his discovery of *The Apple Orchard* had re-opened a chapter in his life he thought he had closed many, many years ago. And he wasn't sure he wanted it re-opened. He had made a fine life for himself without his "ability" and he didn't see the benefit in trying to get it back, even if that were possible. But now things were different. It was as if those secrets he'd buried so long ago were now coming back to torment him.

Still, despite all this, he couldn't help but find his mind awash in memories. One memory, in particular, came back again and again.

The young boy sat at the foot of his bed, his legs and feet dangling over the side. He stared across the room at four individuals who stood shoulder to shoulder in front of the window. They were as different from one another as could possibly be imagined. A large, broad-shouldered

Viking warrior stood farthest to the right, towering over the others. He was dressed in chainmail armor and wore an iron helmet, from which long blond hair streamed down and fell over his shoulders. Next to him was a slightly built Asian man, with a shaved head and dark, compassionate eyes. He wore the saffron robe of a Buddhist monk; it was draped over his frame and attached to one shoulder like a Roman toga. Flanking him was a Native American, his face painted in red and black, his ears pierced, and hair adorned in colorful eagle feathers. Farthest to the left was Joe's nattily dressed sandbox playmate.

"You all have to go," the boy said, his face red and puffy from tears. "I can't see you anymore."

The nattily dressed man stepped forward. His gaze rested on the young boy with a tenderness that was almost fatherly.

"We are saddened, Joseph," he said, "but we understand."

Tears began to fill Joe's eyes, and he dropped his head.

The man came over and knelt in front of Joe.

"I want to tell you something, Joseph," he said, his voice soft and reassuring. Joe sniffed and looked up. But his eyes were blurry and unfocused. "Are you listening?"

Joe wiped his nose and nodded. This time his eyes focused on his friend.

"When we're gone you won't be able to see or hear us anymore, but we want you to know that we love you, and we will be with you." He paused, keeping his eyes focused on Joe. "Do you understand?

Joe nodded, his chin trembling. "Will I ever see you again?"

"Who knows what the future will bring," the apparition said, "but you can always dream. And when you do, look carefully. You might see us." He smiled gently and stood up. "Now we will vanish and melt into air—into thin air."

Joe looked at him, beginning to feel his eyes tear up again.

The ghost didn't say any more. He stepped back and fell into line with the others. The four entities stood together for several moments, all standing parallel as if captured in a snapshot, saying nothing. Then, all at once, they began to fade. The process was slow at first but gathered momentum with each passing second. Joe watched as their images grew fuzzy, their outlines hazy and indistinct. In seconds all that was left was a gauzy wisp of rapidly disappearing fog that marked where they had stood. Soon the room was empty. The four individuals had disappeared—as if they had never been there at all.

Joe dropped his head in his hands and sobbed.

Joe unlocked the front door of his cottage and stepped inside. He switched on lights and took off his jacket. Desdemona came slinking down the hallway, meowing. The cat rubbed up against him and he reached down and patted her head.

"Sorry I'm late, Dez," he said. "Let's go get you some food."

They went into the kitchen where Joe doled out sardines into Desdemona's bowl.

As the cat ate, he poured himself a splash of scotch and gazed out the window. The fog was still thick, and he couldn't see very far, less than ten feet. In the distance, he heard the crash of surf. He'd lived in this house now for the past four years and the sound was both a comfort and an inspiration. In fact, to him, it was almost like music. He liked nothing better than falling asleep to the metronome-like sound of the waves as they washed back and forth up the beach.

Turning away from the window, he held up his glass and stared meditatively at the rich amber liquid. He swirled the contents for a moment but then threw back the scotch in one gulp, placing the empty glass down on the counter. It clinked lightly against the top. He turned and retraced his steps into the living room. He switched on the radio and listened to the tail end of *Amos 'n' Andy*. When that was finished, he wandered about the house, restless.

He stood for a moment, looking around. The room was still and quiet; the only sound he heard was the distant crack of the waves outside. When he was a child, he used to close his eyes, remain quiet for a few seconds, and invariably one of his friends would appear.

Could he do the same thing now, he wondered? After all these years, could he still communicate with the spirits?

He continued to gaze around the room, torn between closing

his eyes and keeping them open. Then, with sudden determination, he clamped them shut. For several seconds he felt nothing. He was about to reopen his eyes, figuring nothing was going to happen when he perceived a vague presence, almost a heaviness in the air. The feeling was strange yet familiar. It felt apart from him but also close, as if hovering over his shoulder. The feeling began to grow in intensity—strong and solid—as if something, or someone, was beginning to form, to grow out of the ether.

His eyes flashed open, and the feeling vanished. He took a deep breath to steady himself and looked around the room. Nobody was there, and he almost felt relieved. He wasn't ready, he told himself; he simply wasn't ready. He gave a shuddering shake of his head—as if to banish the episode from his mind—and began to pace the room. He wasn't ready to dredge up the past. Or was it fear?

CHAPTER 10

JOE DROPPED HIS CIGARETTE on the curb and took a deliberate moment to ground it out with the toe of his shoe, leaving a blackened smear on the concrete.

Betsy, who was several paces ahead, stopped and glanced over her shoulder. "You coming?"

Joe gave a curt nod and ambled forward, following her up to the front door of Madam Petrova's house.

"Are you ready?" Betsy asked as they stood at the door.

Joe frowned at her. "Yes," he growled irritably. "How many times are you going to ask me that?"

"I'm sorry, but you seem nervous."

"I'm fine," he said without looking at her. But truth be told, he wasn't fine. His little experiment last night was weighing on him. He had felt a presence—he knew somebody had been there—but had stopped short of trying to communicate. Did he really know what he was getting himself into? What would this lead to? Did he want to bring this all back up again? Would all the pain of his childhood come flooding back, as well?

"What's wrong?" she asked.

"Nothing," he grunted. "I said I'm fine."

"No, you're not," she said, "you're acting like a pill."

"I said I'm fine," he repeated testily.

"Don't get snotty with me," Betsy snapped, irritation beginning to creep into her own voice.

"I'm not getting snotty."

"Yes, you are," she said, glaring at him. "You're the one who wanted to 'tag along,' remember?" She paused, her eyes suddenly sympathetic. "I thought you wanted to do this."

Joe sighed and nodded. He shoved his hands into his pockets. "You're right, Betsy. I'm sorry. I am acting like a pill."

She looked at him for a moment, then grinned, her normal, happy disposition returning. She rang the doorbell.

After several moments, the door swung open, revealing a tall, amply built woman with an enormous jutting bosom. Joe had never seen Madam Petrova before so was somewhat surprised by her imposing stature. She was nearly as tall as he was, an elegant woman with large brown eyes and long dark hair streaked with grey. She was dressed in a house dress over which she had thrown a multi-colored shawl. All in all, she gave off a distinct air of bohemianism—as if she had just stepped out of a Greenwich Village salon.

"Betsy," she said in greeting. Her voice was flavored with a strong Russian accent. Smiling, she leaned forward and embraced the young actress.

When she had pulled away, Betsy said, "This is my friend, Joe."

"Of course," Madam Petrova said, nodding and eyeing Joe with a sly smile, "the writer." She straightened, drew an air of formality about her, and extended her hand. Her wrist was encircled with numerous bracelets that tinkled musically with the sudden movement.

Joe reached out and took her hand. As they touched, he saw her expression change. A look of surprise replaced the sardonic amusement she had cultivated up till then.

She was silent for a moment and her brow furrowed, staring at him. "That's interesting," she said as if mulling something over. She held his hand a moment longer and continued to gaze deeply into his eyes. There was an awkwardness in the moment that followed, and Joe wasn't sure what to do. But before he could ask what "interesting" meant, Madam Petrova gestured to both. "Come in, come in."

She led them into the foyer, down a narrow hallway lined

with photographs, and into the kitchen. It was dimly lit, and Joe noticed that the windows had been drawn and deliberately shaded with dark curtains. There was a round kitchen table at the far end on which was set an unlit candle.

Betsy made her way over to the table and sat down. She gestured for Joe to join her. He sauntered over and slumped down.

Madam Petrova continued past them and walked over to the stove.

Joe was quiet as he surveyed the room. He leaned over and whispered in Betsy's ear, "What do we do now?"

"Just wait," Betsy said.

"I shall be there in a moment," Madam Petrova announced as if overhearing their whispered conversation. She stood by the stove and extracted a single match from a matchbox, which she deftly struck. A small flame jumped up and she flicked off the lights. She carried the match over to the table, her hand cupped around it as she walked. Leaning forward, she lit the candle, blew out the match, and settled herself across from them. She adjusted her shawl, took a deep breath and said, "Okay, my children, let's see what the spirits tell us."

Joe watched as Madam Petrova gazed into the flame, her eyes steady and unblinking. The candlelight flickered over her face. Then she closed her eyes. She took a deep breath and was quiet for several long minutes.

Joe watched her in the ensuing silence, waiting for something to happen. But she remained silent, breathing slowly in and out. Joe fidgeted in his seat and cleared his throat. Betsy nudged him with her elbow. "Shhh," she whispered, giving him a sharp sidelong glance.

Madam Petrova finally spoke up, "An entity has come forward."

Joe felt a presence at his right shoulder. It was strong and solid, identical to the presence he had felt the previous night.

"He is standing next to Joe," Madam Petrova said, confirming Joe's impression. "It is the same entity we conversed with previously."

"Is he showing his face this time?" Betsy asked.

Madam Petrova shook her head. "No, his face is still obscured."

Betsy gave a frustrated sigh. "Well, will he at least—"

Madam Petrova put up her hand for silence. Inclining her head, she listened for a moment, and then, with a surprised look on her face, turned to Joe. "The spirit says he is a friend of yours."

Joe raised an eyebrow. "Of mine?"

Madam Petrova nodded.

"Who is he?" Joe asked.

"He says he will reveal himself later tonight. He says there is much he would like to discuss with you. He says he wants to finish something you and he started long ago."

"Something we started?" Joe was confused.

"That is what he said."

"What is it?"

"He says that in time you will remember."

Joe was silent. He stared at the flame, letting all this information sink in.

"There is something else that he would like to tell you," Madam Petrova added.

Joe looked up. "Yes?"

"The entity says that you have not lost your ability. You have only suppressed it. It is there for you to use any time you wish. It is just a matter of stepping through the portal."

———

"Are you sure you don't want me to come inside with you?" Betsy asked. She was standing with Joe outside the door of the beach cottage.

"No," Joe said, shaking his head and fumbling in his pocket for his keys. "I'll be fine." He glanced back at the curb where the taxi was waiting, its engine idling. "You'd better get back before he leaves without you."

Betsy leaned over and kissed him goodnight. She turned and started down the path; she had walked several paces when she stopped and pivoted back around, a curious look on her face.

"What did Madam Petrova mean when she mentioned that thing about your 'ability?'"

"I don't know," he mumbled.

"Yes, you do."

"It's late," Joe said, irritation in his voice. "And I'm tired."

"I want to know."

"Betsy, your cab is waiting."

"He can wait," Betsy said. She gave him a challenging stare and planted both hands on her hips. She tapped her toe. "She said something about stepping through a portal."

Joe sighed. He knew Betsy wasn't going to leave until she had an answer. "You really want to know?"

She nodded.

"I've never told this to anyone."

"You can tell me," she said.

"Okay," he replied, "here goes: when I was little I had the ability to see and communicate with spirits."

Her eyes widened in astonishment. "You saw ghosts?"

He nodded.

"That's amazing," she said.

"I didn't think it was amazing at all. In fact, I thought everyone could do it. The spirits were my friends, my playmates. It was only later I learned what I was doing was different, and that not everyone could do it. Anyway, my parents were upset. They forced me to give it all up, so I told the spirits to go away. I never saw them again."

Betsy was speechless but finally she said, "How old were you?"

"When I told them to go away?"

She nodded.

"Ten or eleven. Something like that."

"How come you never told me this?"

He shrugged. "I don't know. I guess it was too painful. I didn't want to relive all that again. I mean, I spent most of my childhood thinking I was abnormal."

"But you are abnormal," Betsy said with a wry smile.

Joe raised an eyebrow.

Betsy's face broke into a wide grin and she laughed. "In a good way, I mean."

Before Joe could reply, Betsy ran up to him, threw her arms around his neck, and gave him a hard, fierce kiss. He was stunned, but before he could say anything, she released her grip, turned, and ran back to the taxi. She scrambled inside and slammed the door. The taxi zoomed away amid a plume of exhaust.

Joe watched the vehicle disappear down the street. Then he turned and unlocked the door. But instead of stepping in right away he lingered on the threshold and peered inside, feeling a vague sense of apprehension. The cottage was still and quiet and, with the lights off adding a sense of disquiet to the atmosphere, the dwelling suddenly seemed somehow less a home and more a place harboring mysterious secrets. Madam Petrova's words rang in his ears, "He will reveal himself later tonight."

Taking a deep breath, Joe went inside. He switched on the lights and proceeded down the hallway, his footsteps echoing on the hardwood floor. He came into the living room and shucked off his jacket, draped it over the back of a chair, and emptied the contents of his pockets—some coins and his keys—onto a table.

As he looked around the room, he felt his weariness dissipate but the sense of apprehension only grew more intense. In fact, if anything, he was feeling restless—restless and anxious. It was times like these he craved a cigarette, but he didn't want one now. He thought about having a splash of scotch to steady his nerves but, strangely, that didn't appeal either.

He glanced around, searching for Desdemona, but didn't see her anywhere. He finally spied her on top of a cabinet. She was lying next to his prized Tiffany lamp, one of the few items in his house that was actually worth something. The cat was sprawled across the top, one paw dangling idly over the side. He was surprised to see her there. She rarely ventured to such a lofty height, preferring to curl up on a chair or the couch. He went over and stroked her soft fur. She purred and gazed at him through half-closed eyes.

"We're supposed to have a visitor tonight," he told her.

The cat simply went on purring, oblivious.

He wandered over to the couch and slumped down, still feeling restless. His gaze roamed about the room, his eyes and ears alert. But the house was quiet. Nothing seemed out of the ordinary.

On the small coffee table in front of him was a copy of James Hilton's novel, *Lost Horizon*, about the mythical Shangri-La, the utopian lamasery hidden high in the mountains of Tibet. He'd been reading it on and off for the last week and was halfway through it. The book had struck a nerve with the general public and had become a best seller. Word had it that Frank Capra over at Columbia Pictures was involved in bringing it to the screen. Joe knew the screenwriter, Bob Riskin, who was rumored to be working with Capra on the screenplay. They had worked together at Troy Studios before Joe left for Apex and Riskin for Columbia.

Joe reached over and picked up the novel. Sitting back, he flipped it open and started reading. Soon he was engrossed in a world of enigmatic Tibetan lamas, snow-clad mountain peaks, and ancient and mysterious secrets. His immediate surroundings began to fade as the magic of the book took hold.

Suddenly there was a loud crash.

Joe jumped, and the book tumbled from his hands. He sprang to his feet and looked around, his heart in his throat.

The lamp was lying on the floor beside the cabinet, and Desdemona was up and alert. He stared at the lamp for a moment and then at the cat. *Desdemona must have knocked it off*, he thought to himself. He sighed in relief and went over to pick it up. Luckily it wasn't damaged, and he set it back on the cabinet. Putting his hands on his hips, he glared at the cat. "You scared the bejesus out of me, Dez."

The cat meowed, but it was a meow that was far from content. An arched ridge of hair stood up on her back, and her eyes were big and round.

"You all right, Dez?"

The cat meowed again, and Joe reached out to stroke her fur. Soon, after a few moments, the cat had calmed down and was purring again.

Joe returned to the couch and bent down to pick up the book. It was then a strange feeling came over him, stopping him in his tracks. He hesitated, left the book on the ground, and straightened back up, rising to his full height. He gazed around, feeling the hair on his arms and neck standing up. The atmosphere in the room had changed. There was now a heaviness in the air that was unmistakable. It was as if an unseen presence was watching him. His eyes were drawn to the far hallway.

At the end, half obscured in shadows, a figure began to form. It was a silhouette at first but gradually took on substance and clarity. Joe tensed, scarcely daring to breathe as its head and shoulders materialized. This was followed by its torso and legs. Soon a man stood in the shadows, and Joe's jaw gaped open. The light was dim so Joe couldn't make out specific details, but he noticed that the man was of medium height and slender, with longish hair that fell about his shoulders.

Joe's heart thumped, and to his shock and bewilderment, the man strode forward, emerging from the shadows like a dream come to life, an apparition taking flesh. A thousand incoherent thoughts raced through his mind as he watched the figure advance toward him with a confident tread. Soon they stood face to face. For a moment there was an acute silence, and in that moment, Joe felt a sensation akin to timelessness, as if he was standing on some threshold, some doorway that led to a world beyond his wildest imaginations. Joe studied the man as if gazing at the inhabitant of another planet. He looked to be in his late thirties or early forties and was dressed in what appeared to be Elizabethan garb. Over a white linen shirt with a flared collar was a black padded doublet with gold buttons running vertically down the front. Loose fitting breeches reached down to his knees and were tucked into high leather boots.

Joe's gaze fixed on the man's face. He had a high, broad

forehead and dark, intelligent eyes. His hair, a dark brown, was worn long and reached his shoulders. He had a mustache and a neat, well-trimmed beard that extended to a sharp point. From his left ear gleamed a circular gold earring.

Joe stared, blinked, and stared again; he was speechless. He had seen the famous portrait before, of course, but to see the man in person—to behold the face of the immortal Bard, William Shakespeare—was an entirely different matter. He stared in utter amazement.

The silence was broken by the apparition's voice. "Good greetings upon thee, Thomas," he said, his features breaking into a warm-hearted grin. "How art thee?"

The voice was strangely accented; it didn't sound like a contemporary British accent, nor did it sound like what he had assumed Elizabethan English to sound like—mellifluous and grandiose. It was much earthier than he had expected. At the same time, there was a musical quality to it, a lightness that he found pleasant to the ear. It was altogether unusual, and he was at pains to categorize it.

The visitor continued to smile as if waiting for a reply.

But all Joe could do was continue to stare, unable to find his voice. He finally broke out of his paralysis. "You…you're William Shakespeare," he stammered.

The man nodded and bowed in elaborate greeting, extending his right leg in front of him and bending forward at the waist. As he straightened, he said, "Thomas, we hath been a long time apart. Thou art well?"

"Yes, I'm well," Joe replied. "Thank you." He hesitated and stared intently at the ghost. "We…we know each other?"

"Aye, verily," Shakespeare said. "We were peers." His grin grew broader and his eyes glittered. "By my troth, the times we had, Thomas. If only thou couldst but remember."

"Why do you call me Thomas?"

"My humblest pardon. Forsooth, thy name is indeed Joseph in this life, but in that life, the life we didst share, I knew thee as

Thomas. Thou were a fellow playwright—and my stalwart friend."

Joe was silent, trying to make sense of all that was happening. "I don't know what to say," he said finally.

"Thou might simply greet an old friend."

"You must forgive me," Joe said, "I'm still a little shaken by all this. Everything has happened...so suddenly. It's been such a long time since—" He left the sentence unfinished.

"'Tis only natural," Shakespeare replied, nodding in sympathy. "Take whatever time thou needs."

"Do you mind if I sit down?"

"Nay, indeed."

Joe fell back onto the couch with a thump.

Shakespeare remained standing. He folded his arms and glanced around the room with a cool appraisal, his eyes narrowed and discerning. "These modern dwellings are much an improvement over the lodgings we once frequented." He paused and tugged lightly at his beard. "Still, methinks there is a certain something missing. A certain 'coziness,' to use thy modern word, that such structures lack."

"You said we shared a life together?" Joe asked abruptly.

"Aye, that we did."

"And I was a playwright?"

Shakespeare nodded. "And a poet."

Joe paused and furrowed his brow. "I was...Thomas Middleton?"

Shakespeare nodded again. "Doth that surprise thee?"

"I'm not sure," Joe said. He thought for a moment. "What I mean is, I know nothing about him. I discovered his existence only recently."

"Indeed," Shakespeare said, "thou hast forgotten much, but in time things will be revealed and thou shalt remember many things thou hast forgotten."

"Tell me something about him," Joe said.

"What wouldst thou like to know?"

"What kind of man was he?"

"A most admirable gentleman and a gifted wordsmith. He

was possessed of a keen understanding of human motivation, a quality that aided him in his playwriting. To use thy modern phraseology, he was akin to a psychologist in his understanding of human nature."

"The dreams I've had recently," Joe said. "They were—"

"Glimpses of the past," Shakespeare told him. "Brief vignettes of that life."

"Those things actually happened?"

"Aye."

Joe was quiet for a moment. He was still trying to process all that was occurring. He was amazed by how quickly he had fallen back into his old "ability." But he was even more amazed by the revelations Shakespeare was telling him.

"And this play," he said finally, "*The Apple Orchard*. We collaborated on it? Is it the reason you've contacted me?"

Shakespeare gave an enigmatic smile.

Joe scratched his ear and grimaced. "The thing is," he said, "I'd like to work on it, of course, but I'm already working on a screenplay. And that's going to take up all my time, I'm afraid."

"Aye, indeed," Shakespeare said, nodding. "'Tis *Hamlet* thou work upon."

"Yes, and I've committed to that."

"Thomas, Thomas," Shakespeare said, shaking his head slowly, "that work is finished. 'Twas finished long ago and to my eminent satisfaction. There is naught to be added nor subtracted from it. Let us embark upon this new endeavor."

"I'd like to," Joe said, "but I can't."

"Doth thou not trust me?"

Joe looked at him. He felt the sincerity of the man's words run through him like an electric current. It wasn't just a question, he realized; it was a statement, one way of saying "you can indeed trust me." He sat quietly for a long moment, his gaze aimed at the floor. When he at last looked up, he saw that Shakespeare was smiling at him, but it was a soft, comforting smile.

"Let us finish what we started so long ago," the ghost said.

CHAPTER 11

JOE AWOKE WITH A start. He sat up in bed and looked around the room, momentarily confused. Desdemona was curled in a tight ball at his feet. She glanced up at the sudden movement, her eyes appearing fluorescent yellow in the dim light of morning. He stared at her, and as their eyes locked, everything came flooding back.

He and Shakespeare had worked long into the night. Joe had done the typing while Shakespeare had paced the room or hovered over his shoulder, drawing heavily on his clay pipe, a cloud of smoke following him about the room. Through a combination of brainstorming, free association, agreement, disagreement, and all the other mysteries that constituted the creative process, they had banged out several pages of *The Apple Orchard*.

Pushing back the covers, Joe swung his legs over the bed and sat on the edge of the mattress. He scratched his scalp and for a moment wondered if he had dreamt the whole thing. There had been a surreal aspect to the night that was undeniable. But, by the same token, once he'd recovered from his initial shock, he had enjoyed the proceedings, carried along by Shakespeare's enthusiasm.

He rose, put on a shirt, and wandered into the living room. It was redolent of unemptied ashtrays and stale cigarette smoke. Next to the typewriter was a small stack of pages, the fruit of last night's labor. He flipped through the manuscript, marveling at what they'd accomplished. Lifting his eyes, he looked around, half-expecting to see Shakespeare standing in the room, but there was no one. Nor did he sense anyone. The only thing he noticed was a very impatient Desdemona standing at the entrance to the kitchen, meowing at him, awaiting her breakfast.

Joe shifted the weight of the Remington from his left arm to his right and watched as Greenwood inserted a key into the door of the newly renovated writer's cottage. As the studio head fumbled with the lock, Joe glanced over at Marjorie Hayden who had accompanied Greenwood from the executive offices. She stood rigid and erect and, as always, was dressed in a conservative two-piece suit of dark beige. Her hair was done up in a severe bun and her glasses sat perfectly level on her nose. She was holding her ever present notepad, an accessory that accompanied her every-where. When she saw his glance, she nodded, and a faint smile played on her lips.

Greenwood unlocked the door and pushed it open. He stepped inside and motioned for Joe to follow, his gesture a mixture of impatience and excitement.

"Come in, come in," he urged.

Joe waited for Marjorie to step forward, but she waved him off. "You go first," she said.

"What are you waiting for?" Greenwood demanded, looking over his shoulder.

Joe dutifully stepped inside and Marjorie followed. Green-wood flipped on the lights and the room was illuminated. The immaculately scrubbed floor reflected the overhead glare, and all the furnishings sparkled like jewels. Everything was so brilliant Joe blinked.

"What do you think?" Greenwood said, sweeping his arm in a grand gesture as if he were a French king showing off the Pal-ace of Versailles. "Pretty swanky, huh?" His voice was animated and impassioned. He was in one of his rare jovial moods, and Joe wondered whether it was a Benzedrine-fueled mood. It was rumored that Greenwood occasionally partook of the drug. But the man's eyes were clear.

After his eyes had adjusted to the brightness, Joe looked around in wonder. There were the typical writer's stations, but these were more spacious than those in the older cottage. At the far end was a cozy sitting area, ringed by chairs and couches. Near one of the windows was a telephone and next to it, on a nearby table, sat a Silex vacuum coffee maker—the latest and most sophisticated design in coffee makers. "It's Xanadu," Joe said, continuing to gaze around.

"I have no clue what that means," Greenwood said, "but I'll assume it's a compliment." His eyes focused on the typewriter Joe had been lugging around. "For God's sake, put that down," he said, showing a flash of his old, dictatorial self.

Joe deposited the heavy typewriter on the nearest desk and massaged his sore arm.

Immediately Greenwood shifted to a more congenial tone. "It's got all the latest conveniences," he said. He pointed to the sitting area. "I know how all you writers like to bounce ideas off each other, so I had that area constructed. Now you can gab to your heart's content."

"It's all so amazing," Joe said. "I'm stunned."

"Do I know how to treat my writers well, or don't I?" Greenwood said, grinning.

Joe grinned back at him, but it was an ironic grin. In fact, it was rare when Greenwood did anything remotely nice for his studio writers. Mostly he just berated them, imposed unrealistic expectations, paid them a pittance, and ordered them about, like everyone else who worked for him. But as Joe continued to gaze around the room, at the expensive and elaborate furnishings, he began to wonder if Greenwood was suddenly turning over a new leaf.

"I know I've put you under a lot of pressure recently," Greenwood said. "So, I want to make it up to you."

Joe was stunned at the admission, but he remained quiet.

"I want this to be your office—and your office alone—for the remainder of the time you work on *Hamlet*," Greenwood went on. "No one can work in here except you." He paused. "What do you think?"

Joe was stunned. "I don't know what to say," he said. "But what about the others?"

"What others?"

"I mean the other writers," Joe said.

Greenwood frowned. "What about them?"

"I imagine they're not going to be very happy about this."

"You let me worry about that," Greenwood said. "I've sent out a memo telling everyone that this is your office and you're not to be bothered. I consider this script our most important endeavor and I don't want it compromised. This place is off limits for the duration of work on the *Hamlet* script."

"You mean, the others—"

"I mean the others aren't to bother you," Greenwood interjected. "If they do, there will be hell to pay."

It seemed a little odd to Joe that he'd have the place to himself, but before he could say anything Greenwood intervened, frowning. "Jesus Christ, man, do you want it or not?"

"Yes, of course. It's a very generous offer."

"Excellent, excellent," Greenwood said, slapping Joe on the shoulder. He rubbed his hands together and gestured at his secretary. "Ms. Hayden will give you the key."

Joe nodded.

Greenwood headed for the door but stopped abruptly and turned around. "One final thing before I leave," he said. There was something in his voice that made Joe look up.

"Yes?"

"Since I've been incredibly generous by offering you the sole use of this cottage, I frankly expect something in return."

Joe raised an eyebrow.

Greenwood gave Joe a piercing look. "I expect you to work your ass off," he said. "And I expect you to be at my beck and call. If I snap my fingers, I want you to jump, got it?"

Joe almost chuckled. Greenwood's demands had nearly succeeded in wiping away all the positive things he had said over the last twenty minutes. Still, Joe knew the man was completely serious.

"You got that?" Greenwood repeated.

Joe nodded. "Yes, sir, absolutely."

"Good, because my generosity only extends so far." He paused and glanced at his wristwatch. "All right, then, I'll be off." He spun back around and sauntered through the door.

When he was out of earshot, Joe turned to Marjorie, who was studiously examining her nails, and said, "How come C.J.'s in such a good mood today?"

"Haven't you heard?" Marjorie said, looking up. She was gazing at him with her typically expressionless eyes.

Joe shook his head.

"Hal Levinsky over at Palm Studios died of a heart attack last night."

"I'll be damned," Joe said, realizing the long-standing feud between the two men was over. "No wonder."

Marjorie reached into her pocket and pulled out the key. She held it out with her thumb and forefinger.

Joe extended his hand and Marjorie dropped it into his palm.

"Good luck on *Hamlet*," she said. With that, she turned and headed for the door, her heels clicking smartly against the floor.

Joe slipped the key into his pocket. Out of the corner of his eye, he suddenly noticed a figure at the far end of the room. It was Shakespeare. Startled, he jumped.

The Bard had materialized out of thin air and was casually leaning against the far wall with his arms folded across his chest and his legs crossed.

"Oh, it's you," Joe said.

"Good morrow," Shakespeare said. "Thou art ready for another day of work?"

"Yes, I think so," Joe said hesitantly.

Shakespeare uncrossed his arms and pushed away from the wall. He came forward, his expression concerned. "Thou art well?"

"Yes, I'm fine. Last night was like a dream. When I woke up this morning, I wasn't sure it had even happened." He paused. "Sorry, it's just that I'm still getting used to you."

Shakespeare grinned softly. "Indeed so. My apologies if I hath startled thee."

"Have you been here the whole time?"

Shakespeare nodded.

"Well," Joe said, "what do you think? Isn't this place amazing?"

Shakespeare surveyed the room, his eyes narrowed. His expression was somewhat less than admiring.

"What's wrong?" Joe asked, noticing the look on his face.

"An upper loft it is not," he answered.

"Well, judging by my dream, that upper loft looked pretty miserable. It was cramped, dim, and drafty."

"Ah, but Thomas," Shakespeare countered, "hast thou forgotten? Austerity focuses the mind and sharpens the wit. 'Tis not to be scoffed at."

"But why deprive ourselves if we don't have to?" Joe went on. "Look at this place. It's comfortable, well-lighted. It has all the modern conveniences one could ever want."

"'Tis precisely what I mean," Shakespeare said. He was silent for a moment as he stroked his beard. "Still, I suppose it might ultimately prove providential to our goal."

Joe pointed at the Silex coffee maker. "And look at that! Isn't that amazing? We can brew coffee in record time."

"'Tis a wonderment of nature, to be sure," he said, his eyes twinkling with gentle irony. "But, alas, I am a spirit and thus sustenance of whatever kind is not required."

"What about your pipe?" Joe pointed out.

"That is entirely different, my dear boy."

"How so?"

"My good friend Kit Marlowe didst once say that tobacco is one of life's great delectations. 'Tis hardly mere sustenance."

Joe arranged the Remington on a desk. Rolling up his sleeves, he sat down. He still felt uneasy about working on *The Apple*

Orchard when he was supposed to be sweating over *Hamlet*, especially now that he'd been granted the sole proprietorship of the cottage. But as soon as they got going—as soon as they lost themselves in the story—his uneasiness vanished. It was replaced by the simple joy of creation, the simple joy of telling a straightforward yet compelling tale. They worked as they had the previous night; Joe typed away while Shakespeare paced the room. But it was a full and equal collaboration. They bounced storylines off each other, experimented with different scenarios, and argued about the dialogue.

As the story unfolded, Joe began to feel a strange familiarity with it. It was something he hadn't expected. When they first started working on it, Joe had felt it was just a frivolous, sentimental tale with not much substance. It was amusing but he hadn't felt any particular connection with it. But now, as they delved deeper into the guts of the story, it began to resonate. There was an unexpected depth to it that surprised him. It dealt with a number of issues he found fascinating, such as the purpose of art in society, what defines masculinity, erotic desire versus love, and what it means to follow your dreams when everyone seems against you.

———————

Joe was so engrossed in *The Apple Orchard* he almost didn't hear the patter of hurried footsteps behind him. He turned to see Betsy, who had entered the cottage. She was breathless with excitement, her face flushed and hair in slight disarray.

"Is he here?" she asked, scanning the room. "Is the ghost here?"

Joe darted a glance at Shakespeare, who returned his glance with arched eyebrows. Then he turned back to Betsy. "Yes, he's here," he replied. Her failure to perceive Shakespeare, who was standing right next to him, was another reminder to Joe that his ability—to see and communicate with spirits—was unique and special.

"So, who is it? Who is he?"

"You may want to sit down," Joe suggested.

Betsy stared at him. "Why?"

"Trust me," Joe said, motioning for her to sit. "Just trust me."

She dutifully sat down and fixed her gaze on him, her eyes burning with curiosity.

Joe cleared his throat. "The ghost is William Shakespeare."

Betsy was silent for a few seconds. Then she cocked her head to one side, as if she hadn't heard correctly, and her brow furrowed. "Wait, you mean—"

Joe nodded. "That's exactly who I mean."

All at once, she broke into a huge grin. "Of course!" she said excitedly. "It makes perfect sense. The book and all your Elizabethan-era dreams."

"I guess it kind of does, yeah."

"This is so exciting! Tell him I'm so excited."

"He hears you," Joe said, amused.

"What's he doing?" she asked.

Joe chuckled. "He's standing right here listening to you."

"Right now?"

Joe nodded.

"Tell him—"

"He hears you, Betsy."

"Just tell him I'm a great admirer."

Joe looked at Shakespeare.

"Please convey to the excitable young maiden that I am flattered by her praise and attention," the Bard said.

Joe turned to Betsy. "He says he's flattered by your attention."

"That's so neat," she said. She fell silent for a moment. "What are you guys doing?"

Joe gestured at the typewriter. "We're working."

"Of course, I mean I know you're working but I thought—" She hesitated, looking at him.

"You thought what?"

The expression on her face was one of incredulity. "Aren't you excited?"

"What do you mean?"

"I mean you're working with William Shakespeare, for crying out loud! The greatest writer in the history of the world!"

"Yes, I know."

"Doesn't that excite you? I mean, doesn't that make you feel special?"

"Of course it does," Joe said. "But we're busy. Will and I have a lot to do."

"Listen to you," Betsy said. Her face took on a look of mock gravity and importance. "It's 'Will and I' now, is it?"

"Betsy, please, we're busy. We need to work. And, anyway, if Greenwood catches you in here—"

"Okay, okay," Betsy said. "I'm leaving. If 'Mr. High-and-Mighty Screenwriter' doesn't want to talk to his girlfriend—"

"Come on, Betsy," Joe said. "That's not what I meant."

"I'm teasing you," Betsy said, heading for the door. "Don't be so sensitive. I'll see you later tonight."

Once she had left, Joe turned back to Shakespeare. He noticed that the Bard was gazing wistfully out the door through which Betsy had exited. It was a look of reminiscence, as if reveling in a pleasant memory. There was a moment of silence, and then Shakespeare turned to Joe.

"A comely maiden, indeed," he said, nodding. "As comely as a budding flower."

Joe chuckled. "Remind you of someone?"

There was a brief pause before Shakespeare answered. "Aye, in a way."

"Who?"

"A maiden I once knew in Stratford. 'Twas ere the time I met Anne. She was the daughter of a brewer. Like thy Betsy, she was headstrong and gamesome with the first blush of maidenhood."

"What happened to her?" Joe asked, intrigued.

Shakespeare sighed. "It doth not matter," he said. He was silent for a few moments more, as if lost in thought. "Prithee forgive me, I do prattle like an old hen." He smiled gently and gestured at the play. "Come, let us continue."

———————

Joe sat listening to the soft cooing of doves in the eucalyptus tree above the cottage as he smoked a cigarette. Shakespeare was lounging in a chair next to him, his boots propped up on the desk. His long-stemmed clay pipe stuck out the side of his mouth, a cloud of gray smoke floating above him like a halo. It filled the room with the sweet aroma of vanilla and cherries.

It was late afternoon, and they were now taking a much needed break after writing all day.

The silence between them was pleasant and relaxed, the atmosphere unhurried and full of promise. It was an atmosphere that two old friends might have cultivated after having spent a lifetime together, so secure in each other's company that talk was not needed.

Soon, however, Joe felt the old uneasiness he'd earlier experienced come flooding back. He lowered his cigarette and turned to look at Shakespeare. The Bard was puffing on his pipe, his countenance serene and body language content. Joe was about to say something, but he stopped.

Shakespeare took his pipe from his mouth and looked over, concern etching his features. "How now, Thomas? What ails thee?"

"It's nothing," Joe said.

"Come now, Thomas, thy manner is discomfited."

Joe sighed and stubbed out his cigarette, grinding it hard against the ashtray. "It's just that I've been thinking," he said.

"Indeed?"

"I guess I'm just uncomfortable," Joe explained, trying to arrange his thoughts. He paused to draw a deep breath. "I feel like I'm taking advantage of the studio. I know you told me not to worry, but I suppose I can't help it."

Shakespeare smiled gently. "That's because thou art a fellow of moral rectitude, with a conscience as pure as Phoebus Apollo himself," he said. "Thou were always so. Thou were always concerned with questions of a moral dimension. But trust me, good Thomas. Trust that all will be well, or as you wouldst say, 'that all will work out.'"

"I want to, of course. But—"

There was a sudden knock at the door.

Joe stopped talking and glanced over his shoulder. He called out, "Come in!"

The door swung open to reveal Clark Gable. The broad-shouldered actor was attired in a single-breasted pinstripe suit, a bright green waistcoat, and cravat—courtesy of the wardrobe department. He was working on a film version of Jack London's *Martin Eden*, which was set during the turn of the century and had apparently just come from the set. He strode forward a few steps and then stopped, glancing around. The room had the same effect on him as it had had on Joe. He thrust his hands in his pockets and rocked back on his heels, letting out a sharp whistle.

"I'll be damned," he said, "nice digs. I heard C.J. went all out in here, but I didn't believe it."

"What do you think now?" Joe asked.

"I think maybe he's not as much of a skinflint as I thought he was."

"Let's not go that far," Joe said.

Gable laughed. "How you doing, kid?" He looked at the type-writer. "Deep in the throes of *Hamlet?*"

Joe stole a quick glance at Shakespeare who was watching the proceedings with interest, his keen eyes flicking back and forth between the two men. Joe cleared his throat and nodded, though it wasn't a convincing nod.

But Gable didn't seem to notice. "I came by because I thought we might meet tomorrow night."

"To go over *Hamlet?*"

Gable nodded. "You up for it?"

"Sure," Joe said. "You want to meet here?"

Gable grinned and winked. "Actually, I was thinking of a

different venue. I know a little place on Melrose and Vine. It's a little more—" He paused, frowning. "Hell, what's the word?"

"A little more informal?" Joe offered.

"That's it. That's exactly it."

They chatted for a while longer until Gable said he had to get back to the set. As he strode through the door, Joe noticed Shakespeare studying the actor's departing back. When he was gone, Shakespeare turned to Joe and said, "Not an altogether unpleasing visage. Reminds me somewhat of Dick Burbage. The fellow hath bearing. Can he act?"

"In the right role, yes."

Shakespeare was silent, carefully fingering his beard, a slight crease in his forehead. "And yet methinks there is a tragic aspect about him that doth give me pause."

"Tell me more about your childhood," Betsy said.

Joe let out a breath through his teeth. "Where to start?"

"Did you always have this ability? To see ghosts."

Joe nodded. "Ever since I was young."

It was night and they were seated in wicker chairs on the small patio that fronted Joe's beach cottage. The air was laced with the smell of salt and, in the distance, they could hear the monotonous thump of breaking waves. Betsy was wrapped up in a blanket against the chill.

"How did it start?" Betsy asked. "Did you have some sort of strange childhood experience?"

"What do you mean?"

She shrugged. "I don't know, maybe you fell into a witch's cauldron or something." She laughed.

"No, nothing like that," he chuckled along with her. "I think it was just always there. At least as far back as I can remember."

"But your parents made you suppress it?"

Joe nodded.

"Why?"

"Because to them it was bizarre. They were Methodists and that sort of thing, talking to ghosts, is definitely not part of their belief system."

"But isn't that what little kids do? I mean, every kid has an imaginary friend."

"That's what they thought at first. But I guess it became obvious that this was something more. I think they were concerned about my sanity. At one point, they took me to a specialist."

"A specialist?"

"A psychologist, I mean."

"What happened?"

"The less said the better," Joe said, shuddering. "It was a pretty horrible experience. I went through two years of therapy aimed at convincing myself I was a liar. That I was making everything up to seek attention."

Betsy gave him a sympathetic look. "That's horrible!"

Joe didn't say anything.

"What do you remember about the ghosts?" Betsy asked, changing the subject.

"They were my friends. In fact, I didn't think of them as ghosts at all. At that age, I didn't even know what a ghost was. They were simply very special members of the family who used to appear now and then."

"They would just suddenly appear out of the blue?"

"Yes, though only I could see them. At first, I thought everyone could see them, but I learned pretty quickly that that wasn't the case. So, I had to be secretive about it."

"And they would talk to you?"

Joe nodded. "All the time. We used to have the most wonderful conversations."

"About what?"

"Anything and everything. You name it. I don't really remember the details, but we used to talk for hours. Mostly, I think, they were there as companions. To encourage me in whatever I was doing. I was an only child so maybe they were there for that. My parents used to ignore me a lot when I was growing up."

Betsy paused, looking at him wide-eyed. "I still can't believe you haven't told me any of this."

Joe shrugged. "Like I said, there are parts of it that are painful. And when I got older, I began to question the whole experience. Maybe that shrink had been right, I told myself. Maybe I imagined the whole thing."

"You believed that?"

"For a little while. But the experiences were too real to pretend they never happened. By the same token, I didn't want to repeat any of it. So, I made sure I never saw a ghost again."

"How?"

"I told them they had to go and then just shut myself off. I mentally refused to acknowledge them and they never returned."

"Until now."

Joe nodded. "Until now."

"Tell me more about the ghosts," Betsy said, wrapping the blanket tighter around her. "Did they have names?"

He nodded. "There was a Viking warrior I called Roland. He was big and hearty, with this big, booming voice. He was fatherly and protective. Sometimes he carried a lamb around."

"A lamb?"

"A little white lamb that he draped across his shoulders. And there was an Indian brave I called Falling Leaf. He was very stoic, but gentle, too. He didn't speak much but when he did, he was always very thoughtful. The Buddhist monk was named Ching Su. He was calm and rational, always full of advice. He used to calm me down when I was angry or sad. There was also Uncle Jim."

"Who was your favorite?"

Joe chuckled, remembering. "They were all pretty great. But my closest companion was Uncle Jim. He always used to appear as a very dapper gentleman. Someone straight out of the nineteenth century. He had this pinstripe suit and a green waistcoat with a gold watch chain. And he wore a bowler. He even had spats, as I recall. He was a wonderful man. Always so encouraging."

"Why did you call him Uncle Jim?"

"I don't remember why. Maybe he told me at one point, I can't remember. Anyway, we used to talk about everything. He was my childhood confidante."

"It sounds like he was a great friend to you."

Joe nodded, remembering. "He was." His mind drifted back as he spoke.

"The world is your oyster," Uncle Jim said.

Joe scrunched up his face. "Oyster? Isn't that a fish?"

Uncle Jim chuckled. "A kind of fish, I suppose. But it's really a shellfish."

"What's a shellfish?"

They were in Joe's room. It was late afternoon and they were seated on the floor. Around Joe were scattered all his little toy soldiers. Some were standing at attention while others had fallen over. He had been playing with them when Uncle Jim had appeared. They had been spending the last several minutes talking.

"It doesn't matter," Uncle Jim said. "The point is, you can do whatever you want to do in this life, Joseph. Remember that. You have the ability to accomplish anything you put your mind to. Do you understand?"

"I think so," Joe said, nodding. He picked up one of the soldiers that had fallen over and stood it up. Then he picked up another and stood it up next to the first, setting up a little battalion.

"Is there anything you particularly want to do?" Uncle Jim asked. "Is there anything you're particularly interested in?"

Joe looked up at his companion and thought for a long moment. Then he shrugged. "I don't know."

"Well," said Uncle Jim with a soft smile, "you needn't worry about it now. You have lots of time to figure it out."

"How much time?"

"As much time as you want."

Joe paused for a moment. "Will you be there to help me?"

"Of course. As long as you want me to be there."

"I want you to be there."

Uncle Jim smiled and nodded. "Then I'll be there."

Joe paused and looked down at all the soldiers scattered around him. He stared at them for a moment and then looked back up, his brow furrowed. "How come no one else can see you?"

"Does it matter to you that others see me?"

"It's just that no one believes me," Joe said. "I tell them about you, but they don't believe me."

"But you can see me, right?"

Joe nodded.

"That's all that matters."

"But no one else believes you're real."

"That's okay," Uncle Jim said. "They're free not to believe in me. But you believe in me, right?"

Joe nodded. "Yes, because you're my friend."

"I'm glad," Uncle Jim said, nodding. "I am your friend, Joseph, and I always will be."

CHAPTER 12

THE FOLLOWING EVENING, NEAR dusk, Joe approached the entrance to The Watering Hole, the dive bar at which Clark Gable had suggested they meet. It was a low-roofed building with a red neon sign perched crookedly above the entrance. The sign buzzed and flickered, throwing hard red light into the evening. A few people loitered around the entrance, talking and smoking cigarettes.

Joe pushed through the malingerers and walked into the bar, glancing around. It was dimly lit, and the air was warm and thick with the smell of cigarette smoke. The pungent odor of alcohol and sweat hung heavily. It looked like a hangout for truck drivers, cabbies, and assorted blue-collar types. Patrons, most of whom were men, sat on bar stools or at tables near the darkened corners of the room drinking silently and looking around with beady, glazed eyes that dared anyone to come too close. Others sat engrossed in a beer-guzzling contest, matching each other drink for drink. From an ancient jukebox throbbed "Pennies from Heaven" by Bing Crosby.

Joe continued to peer around, looking for Gable, but he didn't see the actor anywhere.

"Kid!" a voice rang out behind him. "Hey, kid!"

Joe glanced over his shoulder and saw Gable seated at the far end of the bar. The actor motioned for Joe to come over.

The two men shook hands.

"Thanks for coming, kid," Gable said. He gestured at the empty stool next to him. "What'll you have?"

"A scotch sounds just about right," Joe answered.

Gable slapped him on the back. "Now you're talking!" He gestured at the bartender. "Hey, Scotty, bring my friend a double scotch, will you?"

"Sure thing, Mr. Gable," Scotty said.

Gable scowled. "Christ, Scotty, how many times do I have to tell you? It's Clark."

"Sorry, Mr.—" He stopped, correcting himself. "I mean Clark."

Gable turned back to Joe. "Busy day of writing?"

Joe nodded. "Yeah, I just came from the studio."

Gable shook his head. "I don't know how you fellas do it."

"Do what?"

"Write all day. I'd go stir crazy."

Joe shrugged. "It's my job."

"So," Gable said, settling himself more comfortably on his stool, "tell me about Shakespeare."

"What do you want to know?"

"Why is he so damned famous? What's so great about him? It's been, what, three hundred years and we're still reading his works—why?"

Before Joe answered, he suddenly noticed Shakespeare standing next to him. He cast a surreptitious glance at the famous playwright and gave a slight nod in greeting. Shakespeare acknowledged him with a friendly but wry grin; he cleared his throat.

"'Tis a most excellent question," he said. "I hath often pondered the query myself."

"You okay, chief?" Gable asked, looking at Joe in puzzlement.

"Yeah, sorry," Joe responded. "I was just thinking." Ignoring Shakespeare, he concentrated back on Gable and paused for a moment, considering the man's question. "Well, if I had to characterize his work, I'd say he's great because he's timeless. I really believe his work captures what it means to be human. What did Samuel Johnson say, 'he's the one writer who faithfully represents reality by holding up a mirror to ourselves.' His characters aren't just cutouts. They could be you or me. They have the same wants and desires, the same hopes and dreams, the same foibles, imperfections, and strivings. Sometimes they succeed and sometimes they fail. But that's how life is. We're imperfect creatures struggling to find our place in an imperfect world."

Joe paused for a moment. "But where I really think Shakespeare's genius lies is not in his plots or characters, but in his ability to make the reader feel."

"What do you mean?" Gable asked.

"The emotion he evokes in his prose and poetry. He's unlike anybody else in his ability to make the reader feel a range of emotions—sadness, joy, pain, compassion. And it's purely his use of words that does that."

"I see you've really studied this stuff," Gable said. "But I can't seem to get past his sentences. Half the time I don't know what the hell he's talking about."

"I wish I could get you to see them differently," Joe said. "I agree that his writing can sometimes sound strange to our modern ears. There are a lot of allusions and archaic verbiage. But you can get past all that. All it takes is a little effort. And when you do, you'll be rewarded. Because, really, like I said, he has a way of saying things—" he paused, trying to articulate his thoughts.

Gable was listening.

Joe finally just threw up his hands. "Well, it's so beautiful, it simply takes one's breath away."

Gable chuckled and shook his head. "I guess I'm not there yet. To me it's incomprehensible."

The bartender brought Joe his scotch, placing the glass down on the bar in front of him. Joe lifted the drink and took a sip, then put the glass on the table and gazed squarely at Gable. "I think you understand his work better than you think."

Gable looked at him. "You think so, huh?"

"I do." He paused to take another sip of scotch. "In fact, I have an idea."

"What?"

"Let's try this: I'll rattle off a Shakespeare quote and we'll discuss it. See how much you really do know."

"Challenge accepted," Gable said. His eyes were suddenly lit by a roguish twinkle. "But why don't we make it a little more interesting?"

"What do you mean?"

"Care to put a wager on it?"

"You mean if I can prove you really do understand Shakespeare I win, and if not, you do?"

Gable nodded and winked. "Exactly."

Joe took a moment to swirl the contents of his glass. "Okay," he said. "But I warn you, if you win you might have a hard time collecting. I'm a writer, remember? I don't make squat."

Gable grinned. "Do you have any collateral?"

"Just my Remington."

"Christ, I don't want to take away your livelihood."

They both laughed.

"Here's one of Shakespeare's most famous soliloquies," Joe said. He cleared his throat. "'To be or not to be. That is the question. Whether 'tis nobler in the mind to suffer the slings and arrows of outrageous fortune, or to take arms against a sea of troubles, and by opposing end them?'"

Gable scratched his chin, pondering.

"Just take the first sentence," Joe said. "'To be or not to be.' What do you think he's talking about?"

"Seems to me he's talking about his own existence," Gable said after a moment. "Whether to be alive or dead."

Joe nodded. "Go on."

Gable shifted on his stool. "I think he's trying to figure out what he should do. Whether he should do nothing, just go along with all of life's outrages, or actively do something about it."

"Bingo!" Joe said.

"Damn," Gable said, frowning. "Does this mean I owe you?"

"Well, we never did actually agree on a price, so I guess you're off the hook."

"Too bad for you," Gable said, chuckling. "Okay, hit me with another."

"'There are more things in heaven and earth—'"

"Hey!" a belligerent voice suddenly broke in on them.

The voice came from behind them and they both looked around. A large, broad-shouldered man was standing a few feet away, glaring at Gable. He was dressed in blue overalls and a shirt open at the collar. He was holding a half-drunk bottle of beer in his left hand.

"You Gable the actor?" the man grunted, squinting at Gable through bloodshot eyes.

Gable looked him up and down. "No, I'm Gable the car parts salesman," he said.

"Wise guy, huh?"

"What's it to you, pal?" Gable said.

"You a tough guy, huh?"

"Come on," Gable said, "give me a break."

"You ain't so tough."

"Yeah, you're right, pal, I ain't so tough. Now scram, I'm busy." He turned his back toward the man.

"I said you ain't so tough!"

"I heard you the first time," Gable said, spinning back around. "What do you want?"

"I think you're a phony," the man said.

"So, I'm a phony. You done?"

Joe watched this back-and-forth with growing alarm. The man was becoming increasingly agitated and angry, a vein on his forehead beginning to throb. Joe saw that the man's right hand kept clenching and unclenching.

"You ain't worth the spit on my shoe," the man said.

Joe put his hand on Gable's shoulder. "Clark," he said, "maybe we should—"

Gable shrugged him off and stared hard at the drunk. "I told you to scram. You deaf?"

The man licked his lips, smirking, and returning Gable's stare with an equally hard gaze. For a moment there was a tense silence. Then, all at once, the man tossed his beer in Gable's face.

The actor's eyes widened in surprise. But then they narrowed with cold menace. He was quiet for a moment, and Joe suddenly felt like he was witnessing a brief calm before the storm. Gable slowly and deliberately wiped the liquid away from his face. Then, suddenly, like a spring uncoiling, he jumped to his feet and swung a solid right. It connected hard with the man's jaw. Joe heard a sickening thud, saw spittle and blood fly, as the man was sent sprawling into a nearby table with a crash. Drinks went flying. The men around the table cursed, and they turned to glare at Gable. A bottle whistled past Joe's ear, shattering against the wall behind him, throwing shards of glass everywhere like shrapnel.

In seconds, the bar erupted into pandemonium. Beer bottles sailed through the air, people cursed and screamed, tables over-turned, and punches were thrown. The sound of breaking glass and the sickening thud of fists pounding against flesh filled the air.

"C'mon, chief!" Gable shouted. He grabbed Joe by the arm and pulled him around impulsively, dragging him toward the front door. They waded into the crowd, fending off elbows, biceps, and hands. A man stepped in front of Gable and swung at the actor. Gable let go of Joe and ducked. The man's fist *swooshed* harm-lessly overhead. Then the actor stepped up and, like an expert boxer, slammed a solid jab into his attacker's face. The man went down, sprawling on the floor, groaning, his nose gushing blood.

Another beer bottle whistled through the air. Joe ducked and heard it sail over his head. He was right behind Gable as the actor made for the door, pushing and shoving patrons out of the way. A man stumbled in front of Gable. Cursing, Gable gave him a fierce shove, sending the man slamming into the wall.

Joe heard the whistling sound of another bottle. He couldn't avoid it this time; it smashed into his head, hitting him above the right eye. Wincing, he felt warm liquid pour down his face. He clamped a hand to his wound as Gable grabbed him by the scruff of the neck.

"C'mon!" Gable shouted.

Two patrons stood in front of the door, trading punches like enraged hockey players, raining blows on one another with a flurry of elbows. Joe and Gable pushed past them and sprang for the exit.

They burst through the door in a stumbling run and, regaining their balance, sprinted across the street like a pair of Olympic runners. The shrill blast of police whistles sounded behind them, but they didn't look back. With adrenaline pumping through their veins, they dashed between two buildings, skidded around a corner and sprinted down a narrow back alley, their feet pounding hard against the ground.

They had run several hundred yards before they came to a stop. Gasping for breath, Gable bent forward with his hands on his knees. Joe leaned his back against a wall and took several ragged breaths. When he recovered, he unclamped his forehead. He stared at his palm, which was covered in blood.

"Christ," Gable said, staring at the gash. "Looks like you got walloped pretty good."

"A bottle hit me," Joe said.

"You gonna live?"

"Yeah, I'll live," Joe grunted. He clamped his hand back on the wound to staunch the blood.

———

"What on earth were you thinking?" Betsy asked, exasperated. She was bandaging Joe's head with a fresh piece of gauze. He was sitting in a chair by the kitchen table with Betsy standing over him. Morning light spilled into the cottage through a window.

"It wasn't our fault," he said defensively.

"You just said Clark threw the first punch."

"He did, but that guy had it coming."

"Oh, for Pete's sake," Betsy said, rolling her eyes. "Why can't you guys just…" Her voice trailed off and she shook her head.

Joe glanced up at her. "Just what?"

"Hold still," she said, pressing down on the gauze with her palm. "I'm not finished."

"Sorry," Joe said, wincing.

She taped the gauze down with a piece of plaster. "I don't understand why guys have to act like guys. You're all so stupid."

"Boy," Joe said, "you're full of piss and vinegar this morning."

"Don't swear," she snapped at him.

"I wasn't swearing. I—"

"I told you to hold still, damn it!"

"Who's swearing now?"

Betsy let out an exasperated sigh. Once she'd made sure the plaster was holding, she stepped back and, appraising her handiwork, said, "There, you're done." Her voice was tinged with irritation.

Joe lifted a hand to the bandage and probed it gently. He looked at her. "What's wrong, hon? Why are you so agitated this morning?"

"I just have a busy day ahead of me. I have my elocution class and then I have to get to the studio for rehearsal. If I don't leave now, I'm going to be late."

"I'm sorry," Joe said, "I wouldn't have called you if I'd known."

"No, it's all right," she said, waving him off. "But I have to get going." She grabbed her sweater and hat and made for the door. "See you later."

When she was gone, Joe stood up with a grimace, clamping a hand to his bandage, and went over to the sink. He began to fill a coffee pot with tap water.

The sudden presence of Shakespeare made him jump. The Bard was leaning against the wall, his arms folded. He was smiling wryly.

Joe glared at him. "Some help you were last night."

"Wouldst thou hath had me draw my rapier and enter the fray?" Shakespeare asked.

"That might've helped."

"Alas, good Thomas, as an apparition, there are certain things I can and cannot do."

"What can't you do?"

"Joining the fray wouldst have constituted gross interference. And that is something I cannot do." He looked at Joe keenly. "And, verily, did thee not hath suspicions upon first entering yon establishment?"

"What do you mean?"

"Come now, Thomas, there is no need to be coy. Surely, thou didst foresee the possibility of such an unfortunate event occurring when thee first did enter. That inn was hardly a setting for the recitation of Psalms or the singing of hymns. 'Twas, in truth, an alehouse of most dubious repute."

"Yeah, I guess you're right," Joe said, conceding the point. He finished filling the pot and set it down on the stove, turning on the burner. "Still, it would've been nice if you had had my back."

Shakespeare raised an eyebrow. "'Had had my back.' 'Tis a most curious phrase. Thy colloquialisms never cease to amaze me."

Joe thought for a second. "Do you have one, by the way?" he asked.

"Doth I have what?"

"A rapier."

Shakespeare grinned and nodded. "Indeed," he said. "But I hath found my poniard to be most advantageous."

"Really?" Joe was surprised. "You carry a knife?"

Shakespeare nodded. "Aye, such an accoutrement is essential. Doth that surprise you?"

"Yeah, it kind of does. It paints a slightly different picture of you."

"Wherefore?"

"Well, for one, you're known as perhaps the world's greatest love poet. I don't think most people can imagine you carried a sword or knife."

"The times were most violent and dangerous. A gentleman needed to protect himself. 'Twere cutthroats and pickpockets around every turn."

Joe paused. "Did you ever have to use it?"

Shakespeare didn't answer right away; he grinned self-consciously for a moment but then nodded. "Once or twice 'twas most useful."

Joe shook his head with amazement. "I'll be damned. There hangs a tale, I'll bet."

Shakespeare chuckled softly.

The two men, one a ghost and the other flesh and blood, stood in silence for a moment, gazing at one another. And then Shakespeare's face grew thoughtful and when he spoke again his voice was soft and without irony. "By the by," he said, "I must confess I was deeply touched and flattered by thy opinion of my work. Thou spoke from the heart and I was most humbled."

"I meant every word," Joe said.

CHAPTER 13

"KID! HEY, KID!"

Joe had just unlocked the door of the writer's cottage when he heard Gable's voice. He glanced over his shoulder and saw the actor striding toward him from across the grass.

"Glad I caught you," Gable said, walking up and coming to a stop. "How're you doing?"

"I'm all right. How about you?"

"Woke up with a headache," Gable said, grinning. "But I'm guessing it's not quite the same as yours." He pointed at Joe's forehead. "How is it, by the way?"

Joe touched the bandage lightly and shrugged. "It's not nearly as bad as it looks. A little sore, but I'll live."

"Sorry about that whole damned fiasco," Gable said. "Sorry I lost my temper. But there always seems to be some Tom, Dick, or Harry who wants to take a poke at me. Tell his buddies he broke Clark Gable's jaw."

"There's no need to apologize," Joe said. "If you hadn't socked that guy when you did, he would've socked you."

"C.J. is furious, and he's working hard to keep the whole thing out of the papers." He grimaced as though he'd stuck himself with a needle. "And the worst thing is, now I owe the bastard."

"We all have our crosses to bear."

"Some heavier than others," Gable said. "Anyway, I hope we're still square."

"Of course we are," Joe said. "I just wish I'd been better backup.

I'm afraid I'm not much good in a fight."

"Hell, kid," Gable said, chuckling. "You were fine. But remind me to give you some pointers one of these days."

"Pointers?"

"Yeah," Gable nodded, "about how to box."

"You box?"

"Damn right," Gable said. "My old man taught me when I was a kid. He was a mean old bastard but at least he taught me something useful."

"He taught you pretty well," Joe said. "You really flattened that guy."

"It's all in the shoulder."

"The shoulder?"

Gable nodded. He assumed the stance of a boxer, his knees bent and hands raised. "When you throw a punch, you gotta follow through. Really step into the punch and put your whole shoulder into it."

"I'll remember that," Joe said.

———————

"Action!" Leighton shouted through his bullhorn, his voice amplified by the acoustics of the stage.

As the cameras rolled, Roger Powell, dressed in the uniform of a French cavalier, drew his rapier from its scabbard with a hiss of steel. The blade gleamed under the bright studio lights as he whisked it through the air in a grand flourish. "Now Monsieur LeGrande," he said, "you will receive your punishment!"

The other actor—the evil villain LeGrande—sneered and drew his own weapon. He was dressed all in black and sported a black eye patch. "You might try," he said. "But you will surely fail!"

The two men faced one other, each assuming a fighting stance.

"*En garde!*" Roger shouted.

The two antagonists rushed at each other. Their swords clanged.

"Cut!"

The actors lowered their weapons. The actor who was playing LeGrande—a man named Vic Taylor—shook his sword hand. He lifted his eyepatch and glared at Powell. "Damn it, Roger, careful with that sword. You nearly sliced my hand."

"It's not my fault you can't handle your own weapon," Roger shot back at him.

"What the hell's that supposed to mean?"

"Exactly what I said. Cower behind your stunt double if you can't stand the heat."

"What the hell's your problem?" Vic Taylor said. "You've been acting like an ass all day, and I'm getting sick of it."

"My problem is your ugly mug."

"You can go to hell, Powell!"

Roger stepped up, his shoulders stiff, his jaw thrust out pugnaciously. "You man enough to send me there?"

Vic Taylor scowled. "Look, you son of a—"

"That's enough!" Leighton intervened, stepping in between them. "Knock it off you two."

"Powell started it!" Vic Taylor said.

"I don't care who started it!" Leighton said. "I want you two to cool off and stop acting like juveniles."

Roger slammed his sword back into its sheath, spun on his heel, and stalked off the set. Vic Taylor glared at him.

"Okay, people," Leighton said, clapping his hands, "let's take a fifteen minute break."

Roger strode over to a table that had been set up for coffee and other refreshments and stood next to it. He lifted the pot and poured himself a cup, and then stood back, gazing around the set with narrowed eyes. He radiated a surliness that the cast and crew members couldn't help noticing, and everyone gave him his space.

At the opposite end of the studio, Betsy and Elsa stood next to each other, underneath one of the large studio lights.

"Holy mackerel!" Elsa exclaimed. "Did you see that? I thought they were going to really go at it."

"Roger's still angry about *Hamlet*," Betsy said.

"Speaking of," Elsa said, "how's that boyfriend of yours? Isn't he working on the script?"

"He is."

"Is he making any headway?"

"He says he is." Betsy suddenly noticed Roger gazing at her from across the room. She gazed back and their eyes met. Betsy looked away quickly and turned to Elsa. "Do you see how he always looks at me?"

"Who?"

"Roger."

"That's because he's infatuated with you."

"It's getting creepy."

"Tell him you're not interested," Elsa said.

"I have! A million times."

Elsa gazed across the studio at Roger. She feigned a look of sadness and sympathy. "Must be hard for the poor guy."

"Poor guy?" Betsy glared at her friend. "What do you mean?"

"A woman turning him down is probably something he's never experienced. I'll bet most of the women he propositions are only too glad to lie back and—"

"Elsa!"

Elsa laughed. "Oh, don't be such a prude!"

"I'm not," Betsy said. "But I'm not going to lie back for him. Ever."

"That's the point I'm making. You're not that kind of gal. You have integrity." Elsa paused and, in spite of herself, cast a wistful glance in Roger's direction. "Still, they definitely broke the mold when they made that one."

"Then you date him!"

"He won't so much as look at me when you're around."

"Well," Betsy said, "the next time he talks to me—which is likely to be soon—I'll introduce you."

————————

The clattering sound of typing filled the writer's cottage. Joe sat hunched over his Remington, pounding away at the keys. Shakespeare stood looking over his shoulder. A small stack of loose, type written pages lay on the desk beside them.

Joe stopped suddenly and leaned forward, squinting at the last few sentences he'd written. He picked up his half-smoked cigarette, which was perched on the edge of his ashtray, and leaned back. He sighed.

"Pray, what is the matter?" Shakespeare said, turning to look at him.

Joe took a long drag and nodded at the typed page with his chin. "I'm just not crazy about this scene," he said.

"'Not crazy about this scene.' Another marvelously eccentric idiom."

"What I mean is—"

"Pray, I know what thou meant." Shakespeare gazed at the page. "How wouldst thou change yon scene, then?"

Joe scratched the side of his cheek and thought for a moment. "Well, for starters, I'd make Nicholas react in a very different way. Remember, he wants to be a poet and he's rather sensitive. I'd have him react with a little more understanding."

Shakespeare stroked his bearded chin. "It hath possibilities, I suppose. But he likewise hath little years, and, like many a callow youth, is oft given to passionate outbursts. This is one such time."

"I don't agree. This is a time when I believe he should react with restraint and sympathy."

Shakespeare slowly shook his head. "Ah, Thomas thou hast forgotten much."

"What do you mean?"

"This equating the poet with a 'sensitive soul' is but a modern conceit."

"But poetry is all about feeling and sentiment. A poet is someone who is in tune with this sentiment. He's someone who—"

"But where is it written that the poet must subscribe to mawkishness? Thou wouldst make him into—what is thy modern term? 'A milquetoast.'" Shakespeare paused and his eyes lit up. "If thou couldst but remember the poets of our day, Thomas. I knew them all. Men like Jonson and Webster, Fletcher and Marlowe. Hardly men given to a surfeit of cloying sentiment."

"Look," Joe said, "I'm just saying—"

There was a sudden knock at the door. Shakespeare immediately stepped into the background.

Joe frowned. So much for Greenwood's vaunted edict about the cottage being off limits, he thought. People were marching in and interrupting him all the time. Irritated, he glanced over his shoulder and called out, "Come in!"

The door creaked open and Joe was surprised to see Archie Duncan-Jones standing at the threshold. The red-haired Englishman was smiling toothily and looking as disheveled as ever with his tie askew and his hair mussed.

"Sorry to intrude, old chap," he said, continuing to stand at the threshold. "Was passing by and I'm afraid my curiosity got the better of me. I wanted to see how the script is coming along. I hope you don't mind."

Joe felt a stab of trepidation that Duncan-Jones might discover the true nature of what he was doing, but he quelled it. "No, not at all," he said. "Come in."

Duncan-Jones stepped inside and closed the door behind him. He advanced a few steps but stopped when he noticed the bandage on Joe's head. "Oh, dear," he said. "I see you've injured yourself. Nothing serious, I trust?"

"No, I'll be okay. It's just a scratch."

"Ah, good." He gazed around the room for a moment. "Quite palatial, this," he said. Shifting gears, he rubbed his hands together, his eyes twinkling. "The script is coming along nicely, then?"

"Yes," Joe nodded. He felt like he should add something else but couldn't think of anything to say.

"Good, good." Duncan-Jones pointed at the pages stacked by the Remington. "Is that the script?"

"These?" Joe forced himself to think quickly. "No, these are just, uh, some notes I'm typing up. One of the other writers is taking a look at the script at the moment. Just doing some basic copy editing for me."

"I see."

Duncan-Jones perched himself on the edge of the desk. "I must say, I enjoyed our little chinwag the other day. I rarely get the chance to discuss Shakespeare with such a well-informed person." He paused, eyeing Joe with a keen gaze. "Have you done any more thinking about this alleged 'Man from Stratford?'"

"About the controversy, you mean?"

Duncan-Jones nodded.

"Actually, I have a little bit, yes." Joe cast a surreptitious glance at Shakespeare and winked. In response, the Bard raised a suspicious eyebrow, looking from Joe to Duncan-Jones and back again.

"So, what do you think?" Duncan-Jones asked. "Have you revised your opinion? Do you still think he was a real person?"

"God in Heaven!" Joe heard Shakespeare exclaim. "'A real person?' Who is this insufferable toad? This vainglorious coxcomb?!"

Joe ignored Shakespeare's outburst. "I think he probably was, yes," he said.

Shakespeare smacked his forehead with the flat of his hand. "Probably? Ye gods…!"

"I'll grant you that he was likely a real person," Duncan-Jones said. "But I very much doubt he wrote any of the plays attributed to him. How could a man from the country—a glover's son, no less—have acquired such an extensive and classical education? And how on earth could one man possibly know so much about politics and medicine and law and agriculture, to name just a few? It's simply not conceivable."

"Well, he did have collaborators. He wasn't always working by himself. At least that's the view of some scholars."

"Hmmm," Duncan-Jones mused. "I think it's more likely that someone well-educated and well-connected in higher political circles wrote the plays. Most likely a nobleman."

"Why do you think that?"

"It's rather obvious, isn't it?"

Joe looked at him. "Is it?"

"Indeed, yes. A man from the country simply could not have managed it. Only a nobleman could possibly have the where-withal to pull off such intricate language and storylines."

"Like the Earl of Oxford, you mean? Or Francis Bacon?"

"Yes, it makes eminently more sense, don't you think? I happen to think Edward de Vere was likely the true author. He was well educated, a poet, and a playwright. As I said, it hardly seems plausible that a country bumpkin from Warwickshire like Shake-speare, a man of limited imagination and intelligence, would be able to write *Othello*, for example, let alone any of the sonnets."

"Country bumpkin!" Shakespeare fumed. "Limited imagina-tion!" His face grew red. "Edward de Vere was a knave, a prodigal, and a scapegrace. The very name blisters my tongue! To bestow upon him the title of poet is an insult to all true poets! The fellow could scarce keep his nose out of scandal for nigh two minutes to write a decent sonnet."

"At any rate," Duncan-Jones said, obviously enjoying himself, "those are my two cents, as you Yanks say."

Joe chuckled. "I'll put you down, then, as a Shakespeare skeptic."

"Don't misunderstand," Duncan-Jones said, raising an index finger to emphasize his point, "whoever ultimately wrote the plays was a genius. I'm just not sure it was this fellow Shakespeare." He nodded at the stack of pages next to the Remington. "Anyway," he said, "I know you're busy, so I won't keep you any longer."

When he had left, Joe turned to Shakespeare.

The Bard was beside himself. "By my troth, I was mere moments from tossing that impudent churl—that ale-soused apple John—out on his ear!" he fumed.

"I thought you had a non-interference rule."

"Aye, 'twas the only thing that stayed my hand. I can withstand an assault on my education, but I cannot abide an assault on my pedigree. A glove-maker's son, indeed! I'll have that festering carbuncle know my father was for a time the mayor of Stratford. Appointed by royal commission. And my mother's family couldst trace their ancestry to before the Norman Conquest. One of her ancestors fought against William the Conqueror at Hastings. Stout Saxon yeomen, all."

"Just relax," Joe said, "he was only expressing his opinion. There was no way he could've known you were standing right there listening."

"The opinion of an ass!" Shakespeare said. "The opinion of an ill-informed cabbage-head! A pox on the knave!"

Joe broke into a chuckle.

Shakespeare stopped and gazed at his companion, his eyebrows raised. "Methinks, Thomas, thou art enjoying this too much."

Joe grinned. "Methinks you might be correct."

Shakespeare was quiet for a moment longer, and then his scowl softened. All his anger dissipated at once and he broke into a chuckle, his face growing philosophical. "Still, I suppose even the likes of such has a role to play in this drama."

Joe looked at him. "This drama?"

Shakespeare didn't answer; instead, he turned his attention back to the typewriter, nodding at it with his chin. "Come, pray let us continue our work."

Joe took a final drag on his cigarette and then stubbed it out. "Once more unto the breach?"

Shakespeare smiled. "Indeed."

———————

"Okay, people," Leighton shouted. "That's a wrap for today. See everyone tomorrow."

Betsy let out a long sigh of relief. It had been a hectic day of shooting and she was tired. Drained, in fact, was the better word. Roger hadn't been the only one in a sour mood. The entire cast and crew, everyone from the lowly technicians up, had been on edge. Even Leighton, who was usually pretty even-keeled, had been ill-tempered and had chewed out several actors for flubbing lines or missing their cues. The only thing she wanted to do now was get out of these clothes and wig, get something to eat, and kick up her feet.

Roger materialized at her side as she headed for the door.

"Good God, Roger," Betsy said, coming to a stop and rolling her eyes in exasperation. "What now? Didn't I tell you to keep away from me?"

"I wanted to apologize."

"I'm not falling for that again," she said, turning away from him.

"Please," he said, "just hear me out."

She stopped and turned. "Why should I?"

"Look," he said, "I know you're mad at me and you have good reason. I was a complete ass."

She put her hands on her hips and glared at him. "I'll say you were."

"Anyway, I want to apologize for my deplorable behavior," he went on, assuming a look of remorse. "I should've never grabbed your arm, and I promise you it will never happen again."

"It better not," Betsy said. There was no mistaking the tone of her voice.

"I also wanted to say that from now on it'll be strictly business between us. Strictly professionalism."

She continued to glare at him. "I'm not sure I believe you."

"You have every right not to," he said, nodding contritely. "I completely understand. I can only hope my future actions will change your mind." He paused, looking at her directly. "By the way, I meant what I said. About you being a natural actress. I truly believe that."

"Are you finished?"

Roger nodded.

Betsy looked him up and down, her eyes narrowed. Then she turned and left the sound stage.

CHAPTER 14

JOE LOCKED THE DOOR to the writer's cottage, pocketed the key, and proceeded across the studio lot. His shoes crunched against brittle eucalyptus leaves.

It was late afternoon and the sun was low in the west, washing everything with a golden glow. The few clouds that hung above the horizon were just now beginning to acquire a rosy tint.

Shakespeare walked beside him.

"'Twas a fine day of work," he said. "We didst accomplish much."

Joe was quiet. He walked with his hands in his pockets, his eyes directed down at his shoes. Although he had heard Shakespeare's words—and agreed with them, because they had indeed done a good day's writing—he was still trying to understand how all this was going to work out. How on earth did he possibly think he could pretend to write *Hamlet* while working on something else? Somehow he'd managed to evade detection but eventually he'd be found out. Eventually Greenwood—and everyone else—would discover what he was really doing. And then what? How on earth could he ever explain the logic of it?

Shakespeare stopped suddenly. He reached over and lightly touched Joe's arm. "Thou art distressed?"

Joe stopped. He sighed and, continuing to gaze at the ground, nodded his head. "I just don't know how things are going to work out," he said. "I'm nervous."

"I wish I might convince thee that all will ultimately be well," Shakespeare said. "But alas, 'tis not something I can do."

"I'm sorry I feel this way."

"Nay, good friend," Shakespeare said gently. "There is no need for such apologies." He paused for a moment. "But come, there is something I wouldst show thee." He turned and headed in the opposite direction.

Joe raised his eyebrows, surprised. For a moment he just stood there but soon followed, hastening his steps to catch up.

Shakespeare led him to a little traveled part of the studio, the area out behind the buildings where the lighting and props were kept. Here there was a prominent knoll, from the top of which one could look down on the city of Los Angeles. They both ascended and stood on the top. It was quiet and peaceful. The city was spread out before them, and they could see the towering edifice of City Hall, the tallest building in Los Angeles, stark against the skyline. To the west, beyond the city, the great swollen sun had begun its descent and was sinking into the horizon, glowing ever more the color of burnt sienna.

"'Tis beautiful, is it not?" Shakespeare said.

Joe nodded, his eyes never wavering from the majestic scene spread out before him. They stood silently for several minutes, watching the sky and hearing the faint sounds of the city below.

Joe felt himself calming as he gazed at the sunset. The soft colors of the sky and the play of light on the clouds began to dissipate his moodiness. He took a deep breath, filling his lungs with the dry air.

A feeling of quiet serenity descended upon him as he continued to gaze out at the scene. It was as if, for the moment at least, all his cares, worries, and stresses had simply melted away. He felt a wonderful, peaceful acceptance, and he found himself totally engrossed in the moment. He lost all sense of time and place and was suddenly aware of sounds he hadn't heard—or paid attention to—swirling about in the air. There was the call of an owl, the twitter of fading birdsong, and the sound of crickets. He absorbed all of it like a sponge.

Strangely, as he stood there watching and listening, he felt an overwhelming sense of gratitude. He felt privileged to be experiencing this marvelous moment, this little, exquisite slice of time—gathered from the sea of eternity—that seemed to fill up all his senses. What had Walt Whitman once wrote? *"Happiness, not in another place but in this place...not for another hour, but this hour."*

But then, as quickly as it had descended, the feeling was gone. In seconds, everything came flooding back, and he found himself standing on the knoll next to Shakespeare. The sun had sunk so deep now that only a thin orange sliver appeared over the horizon. In seconds even that was gone, and the sky was cast in twilight.

"I hath long been moved to write a sonnet," Shakespeare said, "an ode to the setting sun." He shook his head as if overwhelmed by the thought. "But 'tis a fool's errand. Yon celestial orb surpasses in grandeur and beauty all that I might ever put down on parchment."

Joe turned to look at him. "I don't know about that," he said, shaking his head and grinning, "you of all people might be able to pull it off."

Shakespeare smiled. "In this modern world of thine," he said, "'tis said there are no more mysteries. That all hath been solved. That all might be explained by pondering cause and effect." He paused to stroke his beard. "And yet methinks the emotion such a scene evokes is mystery enough to last a thousand lives."

———————

In the extras' dressing room, Betsy shimmied out of her dress. It fell to the ground with a light thump, and she stepped over it. Dressed in her slip, she sat down in front of a large mirror and scrutinized her face in the reflection, looking at one side and then the other. A bowl with cotton balls sat on the table in front of her. She picked one up with her thumb and forefinger and began to scrub off her makeup, dabbing roughly at her cheeks and chin.

The door opened and Elsa stepped into the room.

Betsy looked over her shoulder. "Where have you been?"

Elsa took off her dress and sat down next to Betsy. She picked up a cotton ball and, like Betsy, began to clean her face of the makeup.

"I saw you talking to Roger earlier," Elsa said.

"Hardly talking," Betsy said, making a face. "It was more like he was talking, and I was trying my best to ignore him."

"What did he say to you?" Elsa asked.

"Nothing of importance," Betsy said with a frown. She continued dabbing at her makeup.

"He sure seemed apologetic about something."

"He should be," Betsy said.

They were both quiet. Betsy continued vigorously scrubbing her face with the cotton ball.

"You're not going to tell me, are you?" Elsa said.

"Why do you want to know so much?"

"I don't," Elsa said, shrugging. "I was just curious."

"Like I said, it doesn't matter. He was just being his normal asinine self."

Elsa was silent for a moment and lowered her cotton ball. She bit her lower lip. "Maybe you should give him a break. Maybe you should—"

"Maybe I should what?" Betsy stopped dabbing her face and had swiveled around in her chair.

"Don't you think you're being a little hard on him?"

"I'm being hard on *him*?" Betsy gazed at her friend in amazement. "You're joking, right?"

"Well, come on, Betsy, he's just trying to help you. You don't want to be an extra the rest of your life, do you?"

Betsy narrowed her eyes. "You sound just like him. What, are you two in cahoots, or something?"

Elsa gave a self-conscious grin. "Don't be silly. But he's obviously taken an interest in you, and—"

"His 'interest,' as you call it, has nothing to do with me as an actress. It has everything to do with me as a potential conquest."

"Don't be so cynical, Betsy. Maybe he really wants to help you."

"I'm the least cynical person alive," Betsy retorted. "But I'm not stupid. And I trust Roger about as far as I can throw him."

"I just don't understand why you have to be so stubborn. He's been in this business for a while. He knows the ropes."

Betsy glared as her. "Why on earth are you taking his side? You saw how he acted today. He was a complete ass. Vic didn't deserve any of that."

"I'm just saying maybe you should listen to what he has to say."

"If he ever had anything intelligent to say, I might." Betsy paused, gazing at Elsa with a quizzical expression. "Seriously, Els, what's gotten into you? Why are you defending him? A few hours ago, you were saying I should tell him to drop dead."

"I never said that."

"Yes, you did! You told me to tell him I'm 'not interested.' And now you're saying I should 'listen to what he has to say.' Why the sudden change?"

"I'm just saying that if things don't work out, you'll only have yourself to blame."

"What are you talking about? What do you mean if things don't work out?"

Elsa was quiet for a moment. "Do you remember when we first met? We were both poor, but we had dreams. You remember?"

Betsy nodded.

"And do you remember what we told ourselves?"

Betsy nodded again. "I remember. That we'd both succeed no matter what. That we'd both become actresses."

"Don't you see? This is your chance. This is your big opportunity." She paused, and her voice suddenly took on the tone of a wise matron. "Sometimes in life we have to do things that aren't always pretty in order to achieve what we want. So what if you have to sleep with him. Big deal. Is it really going to hurt you? Think of what he can do for you."

"I love Joe and I'm not going to betray him," Betsy hurled back, her voice angry. "And I'm going to succeed on my own terms. I'm not going to be Roger's concubine, or whatever you want to call it."

"Good God," Elsa said. "Are you really that stubborn? This is a chance to advance your career. Can't you see that?"

"I'm not going to be a notch in Roger's belt. Like I said, I'm going to do this on my own terms."

Elsa stared at her for a long moment. "Then you're an idiot." With that, she stood up and left the room, slamming the door behind her.

———

"I'm sorry you had such a lousy day," Joe said, handing Betsy a martini.

She took the proffered drink and smiled wanly. "Thanks." She sank back into the couch with a long sigh. "It was just one of those days, I guess."

"We all have them."

She paused. "Elsa and I got into an argument."

"I'm sorry," Joe said. "What was it about?"

"It doesn't matter. It was stupid, anyway."

It was night and they were sitting in the living room of Joe's cottage. Joe went back into the kitchen where he'd been mixing the drinks and began to prepare his own. He poured a healthy slug of gin into a shaker and swirled in some vermouth. He gave the container a vigorous shake and then poured the contents into a frosted glass. As the final *piéce de résistance*, he took a plump olive and speared it with a toothpick, which he dropped into the glass.

"But that wasn't the worst of it," Betsy called out from the living room. "Roger Powell nearly got into a fistfight with Vic Taylor."

Joe looked over his shoulder, surprised. "What brought that on?"

"Roger was just in a foul mood. He's sore that Gable got the part of Hamlet and he didn't."

Joe nodded but didn't say anything. He carried his own drink into the living room and joined her on the couch, scooting in beside her. "Well," he said, "it's over now. You can relax."

She took a sip and sat quietly for a moment, a slight frown on her face. "I just don't understand why people have to be so selfish," she said. "We're all working for the same goal, aren't we? We all want to make the best picture possible, right?"

"I'm not sure all your cast mates would agree."

She looked at him. "What do you mean?"

"If you haven't noticed by now, Betsy, actors have huge egos."

"I know that," Betsy said. She paused. "But that's so silly. If we all work together, it'll be so much better. Why can't people just control themselves?"

"People are people," Joe said, shrugging. "They're competitive, and they like to argue and squabble. And any time you get a number of egos together, especially actors, there's bound to be friction with everyone jockeying for position."

"It's just so frustrating."

"Anyway," Joe said, "there's no point in rehashing it."

Betsy sighed. "I guess you're right." She took another sip and then lowered her glass. "By the way," she said, "everybody keeps asking about *Hamlet*. They want to know how it's coming along."

Joe hesitated. He looked down at his martini glass as if studying it. For a moment he thought about telling her everything. He looked up and opened his mouth to speak but clamped it shut instead. He wasn't ready to reveal what was really going on. He took a sip to calm himself.

"Are you all right?" Betsy asked, noticing his silence and looking at him.

"Yes, I'm fine," he said. "The script is coming along, I guess."

"You guess?"

He scratched the back of his head. "It's just that it's a little complicated."

She looked at him, not knowing what he meant. "You mean the writing's proving more difficult than you anticipated?"

"Yes, that's right," he lied. He felt a twinge of conscience shoot through him like a sharp pain. It distressed him to lie to her.

Finally, she turned away and gazed around the room, wrinkling her nose. "Do you smell that?" she said.

He nodded. In fact, he'd noticed it for at least the last several minutes. Shakespeare was sitting in a nearby chair, smoking his clay pipe, a cloud of thick smoke encircling his head.

"You should really get your couches cleaned," Betsy said. "That tobacco smell is really strong."

"It isn't the couches," Joe said. He broke into a chuckle.

She was surprised by his laughter and looked at him suspiciously. But then her expression changed. "Wait a second." She gazed around the room wide-eyed and with growing excitement. "Is he here?"

Joe nodded. "He is."

She set her drink down on the table and continued looking around. "Where?"

Joe pointed at the empty chair. "There."

She stared at it for several moments, blinked her eyes, and continued to stare at it, even harder. "What's he doing?"

Joe suppressed a laugh. "Besides smoking his pipe, you mean?"

"Is he listening to us?" she asked. "Has he heard what we've been saying?"

"I suppose he has, yes."

As if that was his cue, Shakespeare removed his pipe and said, "Prithee, tell the young maiden that I am once again grateful to be in her most excellent company. Her cheerful countenance and dulcet tones are the highlights of my evening."

"He says your dulcet tones are the highlight of his evening," Joe told her.

"My dulcet tones!" She giggled happily and blushed. "Did he actually say that?"

"He did."

Shakespeare continued. "Tell Mistress Betsy that the music of her voice is a rapturous dream that melts the day and night into one eternal bliss."

Joe relayed this to Betsy.

"'One eternal bliss'! That's so poetic!"

Shakespeare looked at Joe and gave a knowing wink. "I am aggrieved to hear that the maiden's day was a most distressing one," he added.

"He's sorry to hear you had a bad day," Joe told her.

"Really? Tell him that talking to him has brightened my day," Betsy said.

They continued this back and forth for a while, each complimenting the other until Betsy finally had to leave.

When she had gone, Shakespeare said, "Verily, she is an ethereal creature. A Rosalind in the flesh."

Joe raised an eyebrow and gave him a sidelong look. "I believe you were flirting with her."

"Flirting? Nay, good Thomas, I was merely complimenting."

"I don't believe you," Joe said. "But if that's how you want to spin it. There's a fine line between complimenting and flirting."

Shakespeare's mouth curved into a tight smile. "Thou art, as thou wouldst say, a lucky man."

Joe chuckled and nodded. "Yes, I am."

"But be not lulled by her sanguine disposition. There is a wrinkle in her brow as deep as philosophy."

"Deep waters reside there, you mean?"

Shakespeare nodded. "There is much to her. Much of significance. She is young in body and spirit, but her soul is old and wise."

"I'm learning that," Joe said. He sipped his martini.

The two men were quiet for a time.

"So, tell me more about Thomas Middleton," Joe said at length.

Shakespeare paused to draw on his pipe, his cheeks sucking in from the effort. Tilting his head upward, he presently blew out a perfect smoke ring. "Thou wouldst know more?"

Joe nodded. "I have a million questions." He scratched his chin. "It's such a bizarre concept. To think I was another person. A whole different life that I know absolutely nothing about. I'm still having trouble believing it. It boggles the mind."

"That is because we doth come into each life having forgotten the previous."

"But why?" Joe asked. "Wouldn't it be easier if we knew something about our past lives so we wouldn't make the same mistakes over again?"

Shakespeare shook his head. "Nay, my friend. Such memories wouldst but interfere with the goals we hath set for ourselves in this life."

Joe nodded. "So, during each life we work on specific goals?"

"Aye."

"And each life has a different goal?"

"Nay, not necessarily so," Shakespeare said. "We oft work on the same goal over and over again."

"Because we may not accomplish it during a certain life?"

Shakespeare nodded. "'Tis so."

Joe paused. "So that means sometimes we fail?"

"Aye." After a brief silence, Shakespeare grinned and said, "But 'tis glorious when we succeed. At such times, the very cosmos rejoices with us."

"What type of goals do we work on?"

"They are legion. But our most important lesson is the giving and receiving of love."

"I see." Joe reflected on that for a long moment. "Why is love so important?"

"Love is the Alpha and the Omega," Shakespeare said. "'Tis the essence of the universe. The essence that binds all together."

Joe sat quietly, pondering Shakespeare's words.

"Tell me about Middleton's life," he said at length.

"He was London born and bred," Shakespeare said. "His father was a bricklayer, a member of a successful London guild. A prosperous gentleman. His mother was a rather formidable woman, one Anne Middleton, née Snow. When Thomas was eight his father died. 'Twas traumatic, but Anne soon remarried. 'Tis unfortunate that she didst not choose wisely. The gentleman in question was one Thomas Harvey, a scoundrel, knave, and rake.

He was interested in one thing and one thing only: To get his hands on thy inheritance."

"My inheritance?"

"Indeed so."

"Bastard," Joe muttered.

"I cannot comment upon his parentage but only on his character, which was low and venal."

"What was Anne—I mean my mother—thinking?"

"Do not cast too much aspersion on the poor woman. Thou must think of her position. Her husband had died, and she was responsible for the lives of two children. A woman of the time had few legal recourses. 'Twas a harsh time, especially for a woman. Still, once Harvey's true intentions were known, she was a veritable wildcat in defense of her brood."

"What do you mean?"

"The knave was not allowed one red farthing. Thy mother made certain of that."

"Good to know he didn't get any."

"Nay, indeed, he didst not. But, alas, the lawyers did. Much of thy estate was drained as a result."

"So I grew up poor?"

"Nay, I wouldst not say poor. But 'twere days of privation."

Joe paused a moment longer. "Was my childhood happy?"

Shakespeare grew silent for a brief time. "Thy mother loved thee, but verily, times were difficult. Her burdens were great. And your childhood, well…" he paused. "'Twas at times toilsome."

"I see."

"Nonetheless, in 1598, thou matriculated at Oxford. Thou wanted to pursue the life of a scholar, but such was not your lot."

"Why not?"

Shakespeare grinned. "Something intervened."

"What?"

"Poetry," Shakespeare said, "that lickerish delight, that sweet-honeyed poison that swells a supple scholar with unprofitable sweetness and delicious false conceits." He nodded. "I know the thing well."

Joe chuckled. "You make it sound like a vice."

"Forsooth, poetry has led many a young lad astray." He continued to grin. "But, as Providence would have it, thou were rescued."

"Why? What happened?"

"Thy savior appeared in the form of the theater."

"That's when I started writing plays?"

"Indeed. Thou began as an apprentice but soon rose by force of talent."

"Is that where we met? At the playhouse?"

"Aye, indeed," Shakespeare said, nodding. "I saw that thee had talent and were so eager to write that thou wouldst work for, as thou wouldst say now, 'mere peanuts.'"

"Wait a minute," Joe said, feigning umbrage, "you exploited me?"

Shakespeare grinned again. "Perhaps," he said, "the better phrase might be that I was able successfully to, shall we say, leverage thy talents toward certain ends."

"'Leverage my talents?' That simply means you exploited me."

Shakespeare sucked on his pipe, blew out smoke, and continued. "At any rate, thou did indeed, by crook or by hook, rise to prominence as a formidable playwright."

"When did we work on *Timon of Athens* together?"

"'Twas early in thy career, I recall. The idea for the play was yours. Thou had read of the man's travails in the works of Plutarch and wanted to explore the topic of overzealous liberality. Methought the idea a goodly one and thus we embarked."

"But we didn't finish it?"

"Alas, no," Shakespeare said, shaking his head. "We finished a draft but 'twas not complete to our satisfaction. I wanted to start over from the beginning, but another project intervened and then another. Before long, we had both, as you modern fellows now say, 'moved on to other things.'"

"We never collaborated again, I mean except for *The Apple Orchard*?"

"Indeed no," Shakespeare was quick to answer. "We did

collaborate. On *All's Well that Ends Well* and *Measure for Measure*. And after my death, thou worked on *Macbeth*."

"Really?" Joe was surprised and couldn't control the excitement in his voice. "On *Macbeth*?"

Shakespeare grinned back at him. "Really."

"That's amazing," Joe said. "I mean, I had no idea." A thought struck him like a thunderbolt, and he looked eagerly at Shakespeare. "And the line in Act Five, Scene Five. The line that goes, 'Tomorrow, and tomorrow—'"

"I knoweth what thou art thinking," Shakespeare said, intervening, "but I must sadly disabuse thee of such a thought. 'Twas my hand that wrote that line."

"I see," Joe nodded. He suddenly felt embarrassed he'd brought up the idea. "Of course."

"But fear not," Shakespeare said, continuing to smile, "'twas thee who gave me such a notion."

Joe looked up in surprise. "Me? But how?"

"Thou once, when we were musing upon the inherent brevity of human life, didst liken the lives of men to actors in a larger, cosmic drama. 'Cavorting upon a stage until the final act' as thou put it. And the idea didst stay with me."

CHAPTER 15

THE NEXT MORNING, JOE made his way across the studio lot. The day was bright and warm, with the sun glinting off the buildings and sound stages. The scent of budding flowers hung heavy in the air and butterflies flitted about the manicured lawn and garden, their wings flashes of iridescence.

Near the writer's cottages, he saw David Levy and another Apex writer, a man named Sidney Maxwell, who was the current president of the Screen Writer's Union. Joe had never been friendly with Maxwell, finding him prickly and opinionated to a fault.

Both men were loitering under the eucalyptus tree, smoking cigarettes and chatting. David was wearing a sleeveless sweater over an open-collared shirt. Sidney, meanwhile, was dressed as if he was a representative of the People, or some facsimile thereof. He was wearing an old tweed coat, worn at the elbows, baggy corduroy trousers, and scuffed brown shoes.

Joe waved as he approached, and David waved back. But Sidney just stared, silently smoking his cigarette.

"Gentlemen," Joe said, striding up. "Ready for another day of toil in the Greenwood sweatshop?"

"I don't think jokes about sweatshops are at all funny," Sidney snapped. He dropped his cigarette, stepped on it, and strode off without another word.

"What's wrong with him?" Joe asked, watching the man's back.

"It's nothing," David replied. "You know how he is, he's always sore at something. If he couldn't rail against some injustice *du jour*, he wouldn't be happy."

"And what injustice have I perpetrated?"

"Well,…" David mumbled, his voice petering out. He shrugged and looked away.

"Wait a second," Joe said. "What's going on?"

David turned back around. His jocular expression had faded. "I'm surprised you haven't figured it out."

"Figured what out, for Christ's sake?"

David was silent for a moment. He looked at Joe evenly. "Doesn't it bother you that you have sole use of the new cottage?"

Joe stopped as the question sank in. For a moment he didn't know what to say. "Yeah, I mean, I guess it is a little odd."

"Only a little odd?"

"It was a little strange at first. But it's only temporary. Until we finish the screenplay. I wouldn't begrudge another writer from doing the same if he needed to get a script done lickety-split."

"The fact of the matter is, the union doesn't like it," David said. "Frankly, they think it's unfair. No single writer should be given such a privilege above and beyond everyone else. And especially not a whole building."

"I didn't make the rules," Joe said, irritated.

"That's just the point," David said. "There are no rules. It's simply Greenwood ruling by fiat. The 'rules' as you put it, were made solely by Greenwood, to benefit Greenwood. He may be the head of this studio, but he can't just trample on the other writers."

"Come on, David, this is hardly trampling on anyone's rights."

"Maybe you don't see it that way, but the union does."

"Seriously," Joe said, "what was I supposed to do? Refuse his offer because some of the other writers were jealous?"

"Is that what you think this is all about, jealousy?"

"Sure sounds like it. And for Christ's sake, it's not like the place is really off limits. I don't know how many times I've gotten interrupted when I was trying to write. People are traipsing in there all the time."

David shook his head. "Look, Joe, perhaps if you had voiced a tiny bit of apprehension about the whole thing it wouldn't have blown up into this. You yourself said you felt a little strange about it at first. Why didn't you say anything to Greenwood?"

Joe was silent. He had to admit, he'd liked the idea of having sole access to the cottage more than he was admitting.

"You've never been much of a team player," David continued. "And this just confirms it in Sidney's mind."

"You know Sidney has never liked me. He'd find any excuse to skewer me, one way or another." He paused. "And anyway, you haven't been much of a team player, either."

"True, but at least I know when to toe the line every now and then. And, anyway, I'm not the one in hot water."

"How much hot water can I be in? I always pay my Union dues on time." With sarcasm, Joe added, "Not that I've ever gotten any benefit in return."

"That's not true and you know it," David said testily. "Would you rather we not have a union? Would you rather we all competed for space on Greenwood's plantation?"

"You're joking, right? You make it sound as if we work in some soul-depleting factory. We're screenwriters, for crying out loud. Sure, I bitch and moan every once in a while, but frankly, we're pretty damned privileged."

"You're the one who called it a sweatshop."

"That's because I was joking!" Joe said, exasperated. "Something you used to engage in. You used to be pretty good at it, as I recall."

"I don't find the world to be much of a funny place anymore," David said with a shrug.

"Look," Joe said, "I have no issue with the union if they did their job. But all they seem to be interested in is passing some resolution that has nothing to do with anything. Certainly nothing to do with the studio."

"These are dangerous times," David said. "I think it's good that the union take a position on world events. Don't you?"

"I notice they only pass a resolution when it has something to do with denouncing fascism."

David stared at him. "And, what, you think that's a bad thing?"

"I just wish they'd muster the same amount of moral indig-nation when the communists slaughter people they don't like. When that thug Stalin was starving his own people did the union lift a finger in protest?"

"You're going to bring that up again? That whole thing is a fabrication of Hearst's right-wing paranoia."

"Really? Photos of starving children are fabrications?"

David was silent. "Look, there's no point in rehashing that. The point is the cottage. And your—"

"My what?"

"Your complicity."

"You make it sound as if I'm abetting some unspeakable crime."

David just shrugged. With that, he turned and strode back to the opposite cottage.

Joe unlocked the door and went inside. He switched on the lights and stood for a moment, still bristling from the conver-sation. He took a deep breath to calm himself and then crossed the room to where the coffee machine had been set up. As he was fiddling with the machine, he felt Shakespeare beside him.

"Did you hear all that?" Joe asked, without looking over.

Shakespeare nodded. After a moment, he said, "In truth, my friend, it doth not matter where we write yon play. The venue is immaterial."

"It apparently matters to them," Joe said.

Shakespeare smiled, one of his soft, gentle smiles. "A very wise man once said, 'remember, my child, thou alone canst choose what matters and what doth not. The meaning of everything in thy life hath precisely the meaning thou giveth it.'"

Luau Lou's Tiki Bar and Grill on the beach in Santa Monica was a hive of activity. The sun had set and the dinner crowd, loud and boisterous, was arriving to swell an already crowded dining room. The air was filled with talk and laughter, and the room echoed with the clink of glasses and the scrape and rattle of utensils. Waiters bustled back and forth between the kitchen and the dining room, carrying platters of food and drinks of all varieties.

Though no one could prove it, it was rumored that "Luau Lou" Lipscomb, one of Los Angeles' most successful restaurateurs, had made a bundle bootlegging gin during Prohibition. He'd used the money from that to finance his restaurant business. A savvy businessman, he'd marketed it as an "authentic South Sea Island" eatery and decorated it with all manner of kitschy paraphernalia.

Joe and Betsy were seated at a table near the big bay window. The table was made of koa wood, at least it was rumored to be, and they sat in rattan chairs, which creaked with every little movement.

Their entrees hadn't arrived yet, though both had drinks. Betsy sipped hers slowly as she eyed Joe. His drink untouched, he gazed out the window into the gathering night, drawing on his cigarette until the end glowed redly. A slight crease marked his forehead.

"Are you all right?" she asked him.

He didn't look over, simply nodded and blew out a ring of smoke, continuing to stare out into the night.

"You seem distracted," Betsy said.

"No, I'm okay," he replied. He still hadn't looked at her.

She gazed at him a moment longer, before saying, "I just read a book about reincarnation."

This time he turned to look at her, but it was clear from the blank expression on his face he hadn't been paying attention. "A book?"

"Yes, aren't you listening? I just said I read a book about reincarnation."

"Oh, I see." He took another drag and turned again to gaze out the window.

"It's an amazing concept. I happen to think—" she stopped talking and studied him with a frown, tired of his inattention. "Are you listening to me?"

He lowered the cigarette and turned to look at her, blinking. "I'm sorry, what?"

"Are you listening to me?" she repeated. The irritation in her voice was unconcealed.

He nodded. "Yeah, you said you were reading a book."

"About what?" she quizzed him.

He sighed. "I'm sorry, I guess I wasn't listening."

She glared at him a moment longer but then her gaze softened. "What's wrong? Are you sure you're okay?"

"Yeah, just a little distracted, I guess." He paused to stub out his cigarette. "Tell me about your book."

"It was about reincarnation."

"Who's the author?" he asked. This time he tried to pay attention.

"This fella Paramahansa Yogananda."

"Parama...who?"

"Paramahansa Yogananda," she repeated.

"That's a mouthful," Joe said. "Who's he?"

"He's an East Indian. He's very learned. Very wise and spiritual."

"Never heard of him."

"That's not a surprise," Betsy said, looking at him askance. "Anyway, I believe in it."

"Reincarnation?"

She nodded. "Yes. I believe in it firmly."

He nodded but didn't say anything. For the first time he picked up his drink and took a sip.

The silence was telling, and she cocked her head to one side, studying him. "You don't?"

He set his drink back down on the table and shrugged. "I don't know."

"What do you mean? How is that possible?" Her gaze was probing. "Shakespeare even told you about one of your past lives. Don't you believe him?"

He shrugged again. "I don't know. Maybe."

She stared at him for a moment. "You're a strange one, Mr. Holliday," she said, shaking her head.

"Just because I see ghosts doesn't mean I necessarily believe in reincarnation," Joe said.

Betsy was incredulous. "But Shakespeare even told you about one of your lives!"

Joe was quiet for a moment; he didn't respond to her statement. After a pause, he looked over at her. "So, what did he say?"

"Who?"

"That East Indian guy. What did you say his name was again?"

"Paramahansa Yogananda."

Joe nodded. "What did he say about reincarnation?"

She sat up, suddenly animated. "He says that reincarnation is the law of spiritual evolution. It's the process by which all souls work out their karma. We come down to learn different lessons so that we can progress."

"Progress toward what?"

"Individual spiritual perfection."

"What does that mean?"

"Enlightenment, I suppose."

"Those are all just words," Joe said, frowning, fixing his gaze on the moon as it hovered over the ocean. It was full and bright, casting its light on the surface of the water. "People throw them out, but do we really know what they mean? What is spiritual perfection? What is enlightenment?"

"Perhaps we won't know until we experience them. Perhaps they're not anything that can be described in words, only experienced."

"That's an unsatisfying answer," Joe said.

"But maybe it's true. Haven't you ever had an experience that you couldn't really describe?"

Joe was silent for a time. "What does all this mean, anyway?" Joe said.

"What do you mean 'all this'?"

"Everything," Joe said, waving his hand in the air as if the answer was obvious. "The universe. Our lives. Existence. What do they all mean?"

"I never said I had an answer to any of those questions. I'm just telling you what I read about reincarnation."

"But you believe in it?"

"Yes, very much so."

"I just don't know how you can be so sure."

"I don't either," she said. "But I am. I wonder what lives I've lived?"

After another moment of silence, Joe asked, "What else did he say?"

"About reincarnation?"

Joe nodded.

Surprise flickered in her eyes and she gave him a wry grin. "So, you are interested after all, huh?"

He grinned back and shrugged nonchalantly. "I might be."

She thought for a moment. "Well, he said that we all have a larger spiritual self, which is the sum total of all our separate lives. Eventually, this larger self learns that his true nature is spirit. And spirit is present in everything."

"Everything? What do you mean, 'everything'?"

"I think it means we're all connected."

"How so?"

She stopped her train of thought and frowned. "Are you going to ask a question after everything I say?"

"I'm just curious. I want to find out what all this means."

"It's more like you're being deliberately disagreeable. Like I said, I don't necessarily have answers to any of this. I'm just telling you what he said."

"Okay, sorry," Joe said. "Go on."

Betsy continued her explanation and when she was done, Joe sat quietly, mulling over her words. He suddenly sensed Shakespeare next to him, standing at his shoulder. He glanced up.

The Bard acknowledged his gaze and smiled, nodding slowly.

Joe stopped typing and glanced at his watch. It was a little after five o'clock. He yawned and rubbed his eyes, and then glanced over his shoulder. Shakespeare was standing behind him, arms folded.

"Burbage approaches," Shakespeare announced.

"Who—?"

There was a knock at the door.

"Come in!"

Clark Gable entered the cottage. He was dressed in a light cotton shirt open at the collar and gabardine pants. "Hiya, kid."

"Hi, Clark. What's new?"

"Thought I'd swing by and relieve you of your drudgery."

"Perfect timing."

"You finished for the day?" Gable asked.

Joe nodded and yawned again.

"You look tired," Gable observed.

"I'm okay," Joe said. "Just been a long day and now I need to unwind."

"What you need is a drink," Gable said. "What say we grab one?"

Joe put up his hand in mock defense. "I'm not so sure that's such a good idea, especially after last time."

Gable grinned. "Don't worry," he said. "I thought we could head up to the farm if you're up for it."

"The farm?"

"Yeah, my place in Encino."

"But that's out in the Valley. That's kind of a drive, isn't it?"

"Hell, no," Gable said. "It ain't far. We can make it before night-fall. Whattaya say?"

Joe shrugged. He was quiet for a moment, but then he nodded. "All right."

"Great! This'll give us a chance to discuss *Hamlet*. Did I tell you I started reading it again?"

Joe was surprised. "Really? What do you think this time around?"

Gable grinned self-consciously. "Hell," he said, "you were right, it ain't so bad."

Joe suddenly had a thought. "I have to do one thing before we go," he said.

"What?"

"I've got to stop by my place and feed Desdemona."

"Who?"

"My cat."

Gable just stared at him.

"Sorry," Joe said, his tone defensive, "but I can't leave her without any food."

"All right, all right," Gable conceded, "we'll swing by your place first. Feed your damn cat."

They made for the door, but Gable stopped suddenly and gazed around the room, as if looking for something—or someone.

"What's wrong?" Joe asked.

Gable continued to gaze around but then looked back at Joe. "I just had the strangest feeling."

"What?"

Gable was silent. His brow was creased. "For a moment it almost felt as if—"

Joe was quiet, just listening.

"Ah, it's nothing," the actor replied after a moment, swiping at the air with his hand. "I'm just imagining things."

"What things?"

"You'll think I've gone loony."

"No, I won't. I promise."

Gable scratched his chin. He looked slowly around the room again and then back at Joe. "It almost felt like someone was watching us," he said.

Joe glanced at Shakespeare. The Bard was listening intently.

"Who's watching us?"

"I don't know. It's hard to explain, but it almost felt as if there was a third person here. It was like they were listening to our conversation."

Joe gave a subtle grin. "Why do you think that?"

"Aw, hell," Gable said. "I'm talking nonsense. Let's go."

They left the writer's cottage and made their way across the lot.

Chapter 16

Joe unlocked the door of his cottage and stepped inside. He flicked on the lights and motioned Gable to follow him.

"C'mon in," he said.

Gable sauntered forward several steps, came to a stop and looked around. "Cozy little place you got here," he said, nodding approvingly.

"Thanks." Joe headed into the kitchen while Gable lingered in the living room. "Be back in a second."

Desdemona was sitting on the kitchen windowsill. When she saw Joe, she meowed and hopped down. Her tail shot up and she padded across the floor.

"Hi Dez," Joe said, reaching down to pet her as she began to twine herself about his legs. "You gonna be all right by yourself tonight?"

Joe fixed her a plate of sardines and set it out for her. She pounced on the food and made little grunting noises as she devoured the fish, which Joe knew to be a sign of contentment. He filled a small bowl with water and set it down next to the plate of food. "There," he said. "That should tide you over 'till I get back."

When Joe returned to the living room, Gable was standing by the bookshelf, flipping through a small, thin volume, his brow furrowed. The actor looked up and nodded with his chin at the bookshelf. "You read all these books?"

"Most of them."

"Must've taken you forever," Gable said.

Joe shrugged. "Not really. I'm a pretty voracious reader. But several are from my college days. I haven't opened them in ages."

"Quite a collection. I can't even pronounce some of the titles." Joe chuckled.

"Carole says I should read more," Gable said with sudden irritation in his voice.

"You don't like to read?"

"No, it ain't that. I just can't seem to sit still for that long." He paused, frowning. "And sometimes the words get all mixed up in my head."

"Mixed up?"

"Yeah, it's like the words get all jumbled around and turned backwards. It doesn't happen all the time, but it happens enough. Makes it difficult to read sometimes."

Before Joe could comment, Gable asked, "So who's this guy Marcus Aurelius?"

Joe noticed that Gable was holding a copy of Marcus Aurelius' *The Meditations.*

"He was a Roman emperor," Joe explained. "He was famous for his philosophical speculations."

Gable nodded and scanned the text. He flipped back a few pages and then forward several more and stopped. He read out loud: "If you are distressed by anything external, the pain is not due to the thing itself, but to your estimate of it; and this you have the power to revoke at any moment." He paused for a second, nodding. "Yeah, I guess that makes some sense. Sounds pretty erudite for an emperor, though. It's funny, I always pictured Roman emperors as crazy bastards, like that guy who played his fiddle while Rome burned. What was his name again?"

"That was the emperor Nero," Joe said. "Marcus Aurelius was different. He was considered one of the 'good' emperors. He was a Stoic philosopher."

"A what philosopher?"

"Stoic philosopher," Joe repeated.

"What did they believe?"

"Well," Joe said, "at its core, it's a philosophy that stresses that life should be lived in accordance with nature. And that we must use reason, not our emotions, to understand the world."

"Oh," Gable said. He seemed surprised.

"What were you expecting?"

"I don't know," Gable shrugged. "I guess I thought it had something to do with enduring hardship or something like that."

"That's part of the philosophy, too. But it has more to do with controlling one's own thoughts."

"How so?"

"The Stoics believed that we can only ultimately control our own thoughts and attitudes. Just like that quote you read. There are a lot of things we can't control in life, but we can control how we think about things. And it's how we think about things that creates our reality."

Gable scratched his chin, pondering.

Joe grabbed a jacket from his coat rack. "You ready?"

Gable slipped the book back into the shelf. "Yeah, let's go."

The light turned green and Gable stepped down hard on the accelerator. His eight-cylinder roadster—a 1933 Packard De Luxe Eight—roared its engine and tore down the street, its tires squealing. Joe was pressed back against the seat as they accelerated.

"I think I've figured it out," Gable raised his voice over the noise of the engine. "I know there's a lot of death in *Hamlet*, but it's really about life, isn't it?"

Joe raised an eyebrow. They were cruising west down Sunset Boulevard, heading toward the distant Santa Monica Mountains. The evening sky flared a burnt sienna in the waning light and the clouds were tinged in orange.

"What I mean is," Gable went on, "it's about the meaning of life." He stopped for a moment and looked over at Joe, as if for confirmation.

"Go on," Joe said.

Gable cleared his throat. "Well, it's like this, Hamlet is trying to figure out what it all means. Not just the murder of his father, but all of it. Does life have any meaning at all? Is there a point to our existence? To our suffering?" He stopped again to see if Joe was following.

"I'm listening," Joe said, nodding. "Go on."

"If life doesn't have any meaning, then why seek revenge? What would be the point? But if life does have meaning, is seeking revenge the best thing to do? What about the whole Christian thing?

"You mean Christian charity and forgiveness?"

"Yeah," Gable nodded.

"And yet Hamlet finally resolves to undertake his revenge. What do you make of that?"

Gable thought for a moment. "That's a tough one," he said. "I'm not sure." He paused and tapped his fingers on the steering wheel. "What do you think?"

Joe gave a subtle grin. "I thought I was supposed to be asking the questions here."

"You are, but that one's got me stumped."

"Think about it for a moment," Joe said. "Try to come up with an answer. I'm not saying there's any right answer, I'm just saying it might be interesting to speculate."

Gable stared off into the distance, his brow furrowed. They turned right onto Laurel Canyon Road and, as they began to ascend into the mountains, Gable shifted gears. The Packard took the ascent with ease, its powerful engine churning along smoothly. After several minutes, Gable glanced back over at Joe. "Sorry, I'm still stumped."

"Nothing?"

"Not a thing." He shook his head. "And I ain't gonna come up with anything any time soon. Might as well tell me what you think."

"Well," Joe began, scratching his chin, "maybe at the end he is simply compelled. Maybe action is demanded of him."

"What do you mean demanded? Who demands it? The ghost?"

"The ghost certainly—but maybe, even more importantly, the society in which he's a member. The cultural values and mores. Think about it. Maybe those forces around us—society, family, the law, even our morality, whatever it is—compel us to act even though we can never be sure whether it's the right course of action. We may be told it's right, but do we really know, on an existential level, that it is?"

They were both silent for a moment, and the words seemed to linger in the air.

Finally, Gable shook his head. "I gotta tell ya, kid," he said, "I know you're a screenwriter, but I think you would've made one hell of a literature professor."

"It's just speculation," Joe said, shrugging, "I'm not necessarily saying I know what I'm talking about."

"Could've fooled me."

As evening fell, they pulled into the long, winding driveway of Gable's sprawling ranch-style home. The tires crunched against gravel as the vehicle rolled to a stop near the front door. Joe gazed up at the house.

It was in the style of a Spanish *hacienda*, one of those stately homes that might have graced a sleepy pueblo town in Old California—if at least in the imagination. Although shaded by tall oak trees, its white plaster walls shown in the fading light. A short flight of steps led up to a covered porch which was capped by a red-tiled roof. On this purple bougainvillea sprawled in a lazy riot.

"Welcome to the old farm," Gable said with a wink. Immediately he opened the door and bounded out.

Joe followed. "This place is really a farm?"

"Damn right," Gable said. "I got some chickens and horses right now. Eventually, I want to get some cows."

They went up the stairs to the front door, which Gable unlocked and flung open. The actor filed inside, with Joe following. Gable took off his jacket, tossed it casually on the back of a chair, and switched on the lights.

"Carole won't be back until tomorrow morning," he said. By "Carole" Joe knew Gable was referring to Carole Lombard, the leggy, wise-cracking blonde actress with whom he had been living for the past year. She, like Gable, was beginning to make a name for herself, mostly in screwball comedies.

Joe gazed around. The living room was sunken and there were several couches situated around a brick-lined fireplace. It was smartly decorated yet casual, with a homey feel despite the expensive-looking furnishings. The floor was composed of sienna-colored squares of Mexican tile overthrown here and there by brightly colored rugs. There were several large mahogany china cabinets with glass fronts and filled with all sorts of dishware—dishes, cups and plates. A hunting rifle hung over the fireplace mantle. At the opposite end was a hallway that led to another part of the house.

It was rumored that Gable had purchased the house from the director Raoul Walsh. The other rumor was that he had used Carole's money to pay for it.

"Okay, chief," Gable said, rubbing his hands together. "What'll it be?"

"Be?" For a moment Joe was confused.

"Yeah, kid, what do you want to drink?"

"Oh, right. What are you having?"

"Thought I'd have a beer," Gable said. "Been thinking about a cold brew ever since we left the studio."

"That sounds good," Joe said. "I'll have the same."

"Make yourself comfortable," Gable said, turning down the hallway and lumbering off. "I'll be back in a minute."

Joe suddenly felt Shakespeare standing beside him.

"Reminds me somewhat of Charlecote," the Bard said, gazing around the room with an appraising eye.

"Charlecote?"

"A manor house in Warwick. It hath the same mood and character."

The name jogged Joe's memory. "Wait a second," he said,

"wasn't that the place you poached that nobleman's deer?"

Shakespeare made a face. "What doth thou imply?"

"Didn't you get in trouble for stealing some nobleman's deer? And that's why you left Stratford and went to London?"

"Sir Thomas Lucy was a knave despite his pedigree. And, nay, I did not poach the fellow's deer."

"But what about that story?" Joe said. "It's said you were caught red-handed."

"Lies and calumny!" Shakespeare cried. "It had naught to do with a deer." He looked away and took a moment to flick a piece of lint from his sleeve. "It involved a pheasant. And the lamentable bird was not even on Sir Lucy's property."

"So you did—"

"So I did what?" Gable's voice sounded behind Joe.

Joe spun around. Gable was standing with two bottles of beer and two glasses, a questioning look on his face.

Joe had to think quickly. "I just meant…that you did some nice decorating in here."

"Thanks, but Carole did most of it," Gable said, cracking open the beers with a bottle opener. As he poured out the liquid, he nodded with his chin at the rifle on the mantel. "But at least she let me keep the gun."

"Is that a hunting rifle?"

Gable looked up and nodded. "That's a Mannlicher. Austrian made. One of the best hunting rifles around." He paused and looked at Joe curiously. "I thought you said you hunted."

"I didn't say that," Joe corrected him. "I said I liked to fish once in a while."

"Oh, right." He handed Joe a glass of beer.

"Thanks."

Gable sat down on one of the couches and sighed heavily. "This is much better than being in a bar with a bunch of jackasses spoiling for a fight." He took a sip and focused his attention back on Joe. "So, you've never hunted before?"

Joe sat down on the couch opposite. "No, I'm afraid I haven't."

"Have you ever fired a gun?"

"I'm afraid I haven't done that either. My family was…" He paused. "Let's just say my father didn't go in for that sort of thing."

"I know how that goes," Gable said. "My old man was a rat bastard." He was quiet for a moment and took another sip of beer, staring off into space. Finally, he cracked a smile. "Well, I won't hold the fact that you haven't shot a gun against you, but it does need to be remedied."

Joe chuckled.

"Now," Gable continued, "let's get to it. You said Hamlet was basically forced into seeking revenge, right?"

Joe chuckled, amused at Gable's sudden enthusiasm for *Hamlet*. "I did, but remember, I was merely speculating. Throwing that out there for conversation's sake."

"But I think you got something there. I've been thinking about that ever since you said it."

"Oh?" Joe was surprised.

"Yeah, it makes a lot of sense," Gable said. "It sounds like he really just wants to flush the whole thing. What's that line near the beginning? Something about melting flesh?"

"'Oh, that this too sullied flesh would melt, thaw, and resolve itself into a dew,'" Joe quoted.

"That's it!" Gable said. "That's the line. Seems to me he just wants to say 'screw this whole thing, I'm not doing it!' What do you think?"

"That passage suggests he seems to prefer suicide to carrying out his filial duty."

"His what duty?"

"Filial duty. What sons are supposed to do for their fathers," Joe explained.

"That's the 'self-slaughter' thing, right?"

Joe nodded. He quoted the passage, "Or that the Everlasting had not fixed His canon 'gainst self-slaughter. O, God, God! How weary, stale, flat, and unprofitable seem to me all the uses of this world!"

"That's the line," Gable said. "He considers suicide but knows it goes against his religion."

"Exactly."

"Damn," Gable said, grinning, "I'm really getting this stuff, aren't I?"

"You are," Joe said, nodding agreement. He took a big gulp of beer, enjoying the conversation, buoyed by Gable's enthusiasm.

Gable put his beer down, jumped to his feet, and began to pace the room. "So that's why your suggestion—about being forced to seek revenge—makes sense. He doesn't want to go through with it, but he feels he must. His duty—and the ghost—are forcing him."

"We could now, of course, flip the question completely around."

Gable stopped pacing and looked at him. "What do you mean?"

"We've established, or at least agree, that Hamlet doesn't want to seek revenge, but he does so anyway because of his sense of duty to the values of his society. They are, in effect, forcing him to do so. But we've never established why he doesn't want to act in the first place. Why doesn't he want to go through with it? Why doesn't he just act like a dutiful son and seek to avenge his father? Isn't that what is expected of loyal sons? Especially princes? Why would he prefer suicide to carrying out his 'duty'? Isn't that extreme?"

Gable remained standing. His brow was furrowed, and then all at once his shoulders slumped. "Damn, now I'm stumped again."

"Look at so many of the heroes in literature prior to Hamlet," Joe continued. "Take Orestes, for example—"

"Who?"

"He was the hero of a trilogy of plays by the Greek playwright Aeschylus," Joe said. "His father was murdered, too. And he sought revenge. He was even lauded by the other Greeks for doing so and held up as an exemplar. In fact, it's the god Apollo who urges him to do it."

"Who killed his father?" Gable asked.

"His mother and her lover."

"Who? Orestes' mother killed her husband?"

"That's right," Joe nodded.

"Wait a second," Gable said, "let me get this straight, you're telling me this Orestes guy killed his own mother?"

Joe nodded again. "He also killed his mother's lover."

"Christ on a stick!" Gable said. "Sounds like a bloodbath. So, he doesn't hesitate at all, unlike Hamlet?"

"He hesitates, but only for a moment before the actual act, as any sane person would. Otherwise, he has no qualms. He never agonizes over the decision like Hamlet does."

"Sounds like a cold bastard."

Joe chuckled. "But that's the point I'm making. In *Hamlet*, Shakespeare seems to be doing something very different. He's exploring new territory. Aeschylus implies that seeking revenge is the right thing to do. It's the proper thing to do because it's ultimately sanctioned by the gods. Immoral acts, especially murder, must be avenged. That is a fundamental value. But in *Hamlet*, nothing is clear cut. Life is more ambiguous. Morality is more ambiguous. In fact, you could argue that the entire play is a debate about the essence of morality. Hamlet is constantly questioning himself. 'Am I doing the right thing?' 'Is the ghost telling me the truth?' Is revenge ever justified? He's looking for an answer from the heavens but never receives it."

Gable sat back down. He lifted his beer glass and took a long drink. He stared across the room, squinting, obviously pondering what Joe had told him. "So," he said, "what you're really saying is that he's questioning, what, his own life?"

"In a sense, yes. But more accurately, he's questioning the values of his society. And those values have always given his life meaning. Until now. When you told me that he's searching for meaning, you touched on something I think is quite profound to the story."

"You do?"

"Yes, absolutely," Joe said. "He's questioning the very basis of what he's been taught all his life. He's questioning those foundational values about what's right and wrong, what's proper and what's not."

"'Foundational values,' damn," Gable said. "We're really getting into some serious stuff here, aren't we?"

Joe chuckled. "Yeah, I guess we are."

"I never knew this stuff could be so interesting. I always thought Shakespeare was just about high-falutin', fancy language. I never dreamed it could be so damned fascinating."

The two men were silent for a moment. Gable drained his beer and then jumped to his feet. "I'm going to get another beer. You want one?"

CHAPTER 17

JOE AWOKE TO THE sound of a rooster crowing. He had a mild headache and the sound reverberated in his skull. He lay there for a moment before coming fully awake. When he did, he remembered where he was—in Gable's guestroom. They had talked long into the night—and drank a lot of beer. It was sometime well after midnight when Gable had shown him to the guestroom and Joe had tumbled into bed, his mind a swirling mix of alcohol and classic literature.

With a groan, he rolled over onto his back and opened his eyes, blinking them against the early morning glare. He rubbed his temples and lay in that position for several minutes before sitting up and staring at the far wall, trying to focus his vision. Reaching over, he fumbled with a pack of Lucky Strikes on the nightstand beside the bed. He extracted a cigarette and was about to light it when he noticed Shakespeare sitting in a chair at the end of the room. The Bard was reading a book but looked up when Joe noticed him.

"There you are," Joe said. "I was beginning to wonder. What happened to you? Once Clark and I started talking last night you disappeared."

Shakespeare put the book face down on his thigh. "I merely diminished some of mine energy so that thou might not detect my presence."

"Why?"

"I didst not want to interfere," Shakespeare said. "But I was exceedingly intrigued by thy discussion. 'Twas most illuminating."

"But I'm sure it was all wrong," Joe said with a chuckle. "Right?"

"Nay indeed," Shakespeare was quick to reply. "Not wholly so. Thou were correct in bringing Orestes into thy discussion. Aeschylus, whom I know well, was indeed an inspiration."

"Really? I always thought that might have been the case. Good to know. What about the rest?"

Shakespeare paused for a moment, looking thoughtful. "I must answer, perhaps evasively, with both a yea and a nay."

"You're going to have to explain that," Joe said.

Shakespeare grinned. "I thought as much. And I will attempt to do so." He paused to cross his legs neatly and methodically. "When I embarked upon yon play, 'twas solely an attempt to write a revenger's story. Such plays were, as you say now, 'all the rage' at the time. Thomas Kyd's *The Spanish Tragedy* had been supremely successful, and I thought I might emulate his success. I thus sat and wrote a version." He shook his head. "But I was never satisfied with it."

"Why not?"

"'Twas in every way quite conventional and derivative. I thus embarked upon a second version."

"And it was completely different?"

"Aye," Shakespeare nodded. "Very different indeed. The story was in essentials the same, but I began to explore the characters in greater detail." He grinned. "And truth be told, I indulged some of mine own whims."

"What do you mean?"

"Certain philosophical concepts that had long intrigued me. I sprinkled yon play with a liberal dose of these. Perhaps too liberal a dose, some might argue." He shrugged, giving a slight smile. "But 'twas my play. If one canst not indulge one's whims, then what is such a thing good for?"

"I agree."

"Thereupon, I—" Shakespeare deliberately paused, his words hanging in the air.

There was a sudden knock on the door.

"Kid!" Gable's voice bellowed. "You in there, kid?"

"Yeah, I'm here."

"You awake?"

"Yes, I'm awake."

"You decent?"

Joe glanced at his boxer shorts. "Sort of."

"Well, get dressed for Christ's sake and come out for breakfast! Carole's making flapjacks. The coffee's hot, too."

"Be out in a sec," Joe called out. He turned and whispered to Shakespeare. "You're not off the hook. We'll have to discuss this later."

Shakespeare nodded and then vanished.

Joe dressed and headed down the hallway, following the smell of freshly brewed coffee as if heeding the commands of a Svengali, the scent lingering pleasantly in his nostrils. When he found the kitchen, he saw Gable seated at the table reading the newspaper. In front of the stove, with her back to the hallway, was Carole Lombard. She was pouring batter onto the griddle. He stared at her for a moment. She was tall and blond, and dressed casually, in blue jeans and a plaid shirt, over which she had an apron. Joe had seen her on the lot before but never in such relaxed attire. The shirt she was wearing was much too large on her, even with the sleeves rolled up. Joe guessed it was one of Gable's shirts. The contradiction of seeing such a glamorous star in a circumstance of humble domesticity was a bit jarring and Joe took a moment to adjust.

"Morning, chief!" Gable said, looking up from the paper.

"Sorry I'm late," Joe said. "I didn't realize everyone was up."

"Hell, you're not late," Gable said. He folded the paper and slapped it down on the table, then gestured at the chair opposite. "Sit down, sit down."

Carole glanced over her shoulder and smiled. Her face was devoid of makeup but still very pretty with perfectly even white teeth and deep-set blue eyes that seemed to sparkle with an inner vibrancy. "I hope you're hungry."

"I am, yes," Joe lied. His stomach still felt a little unsettled, but he didn't want to be rude. What he really wanted, above anything else, was a cup of coffee—black coffee. As he sat down, Gable seemed to read his mind and poured him a cup.

"Good," Carole said. "Because we have lots of food." She paused. "I'm Carole, by the way."

"Nice to meet you." Joe took a sip of coffee and sighed in satisfaction.

"Nice to meet you, too. Clark's told me a lot about you. He says you're quite the intellectual. A regular Isaiah Berlin."

"I'm not so sure about that," Joe said with a grin. "I like to think of myself more in the vein of a Socrates or Montaigne. Only certain about one thing: my ignorance."

Carole laughed. "He says you're modest, too." Her laugh was surprisingly deep, almost masculine, which seemed an odd juxtaposition coming as it did from an otherwise feminine package.

"Clark's told me a lot about you as well," Joe said. "All good things."

"Enough with the mutual admiration society," Gable said with mock irritability. "Let's eat. I'm starving!"

"Coming up, Pappy," Carole said. She brought a platter with a tall stack of pancakes to the table and set it down with a thump. "Dig in, boys."

"You've outdone yourself, Ma," Gable said, picking up his knife and fork. Joe watched as the actor helped himself, heaping a mound on his plate and smothering it with butter and syrup.

After a moment, Gable looked up, his mouth stuffed with pancakes. "What are you waiting for, kid, a sealed invitation?" He gestured at the stack of pancakes with his fork. "Help yourself."

Joe took a small stack and piled it on his plate. While he ate slowly, Gable devoured his pancakes like a hungry wolf, stopping periodically to slather on more butter and drizzle more syrup. This was accompanied by a cacophony of satisfied grunts, lip-smacking, and high-blown praise of Carole's culinary skills. When the two men were finished, Gable sat back and patted his stomach.

"Nothing better than flap-jacks," he said, "to squelch the hunger pangs."

"When have your hunger pangs ever been squelched?" Carole chimed in with a wry smile. "You're a bottomless pit. You could eat pancakes all morning."

"That's because I'm a growing boy," Gable said, grinning at her.

"Well, you got the 'boy' part right," Carole retorted.

Gable threw his head back and roared with laughter as if it was the funniest thing he'd ever heard.

Joe grinned at their easy, playful banter. Watching their interaction, he knew that the rumors were true: Gable was obviously crazy about her. He might grumble about her occasionally, but it was obvious he was altogether smitten. They seemed like kindred spirits in the truest sense of the term.

Gable turned to Joe and gazed at him with narrowed eyes. "You weren't yanking my chain when you said you liked to fish, right?"

"Not at all," Joe said. "I do like to fish. I just don't get out very often."

"How about next weekend?" Gable said.

"You want to fish next weekend?"

"Yeah, Carole and I were thinking of taking *Tar Baby* out for a spin."

"*Tar Baby?*"

"My yacht," Gable explained. "Thought we'd head out to Catalina and spend the night. Head back Sunday. What do you think?"

"Sounds like fun, but—"

Gable put up his hand. "Don't say you're going to be busy with the script, for Christ's sake. I know you're going to be busy. That's the very reason you need to take a break. Greenwood can't rule your life. And he certainly can't rule your weekends. Screw him!"

Joe considered the invitation for a moment.

"And bring along that girlfriend of yours," Gable added. "The actress. What was her name again?"

"Betsy."

"Bring her."

"Okay," Joe said, nodding. A sudden determination seized him. "I will."

"That a yes?"

Joe nodded again.

"Great!" Gable clapped Joe on the shoulder and jumped to his feet. "Wait here a sec, chief, I want to show you something." With that, he ambled off down the hallway.

"I'm glad you decided to go fishing with us," Carole said. "He was hoping you would."

"I just hope I don't disappoint him. I like to fish but I'm no great champion angler."

"Don't worry about that," Carole said, waving him off. "He'll just be happy to have someone to pal around with."

Joe chuckled. "I'm sure that's never been a problem for him. He's a pretty gregarious guy."

"You'd be surprised," Carole said, rolling her eyes.

"Really? You mean—"

"What I mean is, he actually has very few 'real' friends."

"That is a surprise," Joe said. "I would've thought he had a million friends."

"All his so-called friends always want something from him," Carole said, her voice suddenly scornful. "Most of them are just a bunch of 'hangers-on.' And he's too good natured to refuse them." She looked at Joe and her voice softened. "You're not like that. That's one of the reasons he likes you. He says you're a 'swell egg.'"

Joe chuckled.

She paused for a moment. "And thanks for helping him out, by the way."

Joe looked at her. "You mean about *Hamlet?*"

"Yes," she said, "he would never tell you himself, but when they offered him the part, he was terrified."

"Really?" Joe was surprised.

"Oh, yes," she nodded. "He was absolutely petrified. He didn't think he had a Chinaman's chance of pulling it off. He didn't think he was a good enough actor."

"I thought he didn't want to play Hamlet because he thought

Shakespeare was, well, a little on the swishy side."

"That's just a smokescreen," Carole said. "Truth be told, he thought the part was way beyond him. But he didn't want to admit *that*. Frankly, he was in a bind."

"I see," Joe said. He took a sip of coffee.

"Please don't tell him I told you that."

"No, of course not."

"Anyway," she said, "you've given him a lot of confidence. And heck, from what I can tell, it sounds like he's actually beginning to like the play."

"Yeah, we talked about it all last night. His comments were pretty insightful."

"I'm glad to hear it," Carole said.

"What are you two gabbing about," Gable said, clomping into the kitchen.

"We're gabbing about how you like to blunder in and interrupt conversations," Carole said with mock irritation.

Gable seated himself and thrust a framed photograph into Joe's hands. It was a black-and-white photo of a sleek-looking yacht.

"That's *Tar Baby*," Gable said. "Isn't she a beaut?"

Joe scrutinized the picture. "Yeah, she's a real beaut," he replied, nodding.

The morning air reverberated with the blast of a gunshot. The clay pigeon that had been careening through the sky exploded in a perfect cloud of dust. A shower of debris floated downward.

Gable lowered the shotgun and cracked open the breech. The spent shells flew up and over his shoulder. He turned to look at Joe. "Nothing to it," he said, grinning. "Wanna give it a try?"

"Sure."

Gable inserted two cartridges into the double-barreled shotgun and snapped the weapon back together. "Okay, chief," he said, handing the gun over. "It's all yours."

Joe accepted the shotgun and held it for a moment. It was lighter than he would have expected. The metalwork displayed an intricately carved surface that flashed in the late morning sun. He looked over at Gable. "So, I just aim and pull the trigger?"

"That's pretty much all there is to it," Gable said.

They were standing on the edge of a flat, level lawn that stretched for about two hundred yards toward a copse of oak trees. Joe lifted the rifle to his shoulder and spread his feet slightly apart, as Gable had shown him. He aimed the barrel at the sky and squinted.

"The safety off?" Gable asked him.

Joe scrutinized the small lever near the trigger that Gable had earlier pointed out. It was in the "off" position. "Yes."

"Tell me when," Gable said.

"Pull!"

Gable yanked the cord that was attached to the spring-loaded pigeon trap. The trap sprang into action with a *zing!*, flinging the clay pigeon sailing into the air.

Joe shadowed the ascending pigeon for a moment and then squeezed the trigger. The shotgun blast reverberated through the air and Joe felt the weapon recoil against his shoulder.

Untouched, the pigeon continued to sail away until dropping out of sight beyond the trees.

"Damn," Gable said. "Missed it."

Joe lowered the smoking gun with a disgruntled shrug. "I'm afraid I'm not any good at this."

"Buck up, chief," Gable said. "No one hits it the first time. You just have to be patient and take careful aim. Don't rush it. Go ahead and load another shell."

Joe cracked open the breech as Gable had shown him and extracted the shells. He selected two more cartridges from a box on the ground and levered them into the chamber. Slamming the breech shut, he lifted the gun into firing position again, cradling the butt against his shoulder.

"Ready?" Gable asked.

Joe nodded. He closed one eye and squinted through the other, trying to hold the gun as steady as possible.

"Pull!" he called out.

Gable jerked the cord. The pigeon went whistling into the sky.

Joe drew a bead on it and squeezed the trigger. Again, the blast recoiled against his shoulder. But, again, the pigeon sailed away, unscathed. It fell and disappeared into the trees.

Joe lowered the gun with a disgusted sigh. "Damn it, missed again."

"You gotta keep trying," Gable said.

Shakespeare appeared next to Joe. "I hath been told the archers at Agincourt took their time to pick their targets. I wouldst advise likewise. Do not rush thy shot." With that, he vanished.

"Want me to load another pigeon?" Gable asked.

Buoyed by Shakespeare's words, Joe nodded. "Yeah," he said.

"That's the spirit," Gable grinned. "Okay, get ready. I'll count to three."

Joe loaded two more cartridges into the gun and lifted it up to his shoulder. He took a deep breath.

"Ready?" Gable asked.

Joe nodded.

"One, two…three!"

The clay pigeon flew in an ascending arc, spinning like a whirligig. Joe drew a bead on it but took his time before firing, making sure it was in his sights. Just as the pigeon began to drop, Joe squeezed the trigger. The pigeon exploded in a cloud of dust and debris. The blast echoed over the trees.

"Good shot!" Gable exclaimed.

Joe lowered the gun. In the distance, standing in front of the oak trees, was a man—a spirit—wearing an iron helmet and a quilted doublet with a large red cross emblazoned across the chest. Over his back was slung a longbow, the top of which extended beyond his shoulder for a good foot or more. He lifted an arm as if in a salute and then vanished.

———

That evening back at his cottage, Joe scooped sardines into Dez's bowl. He set it down on the kitchen floor and watched as the cat rushed over.

"Sorry, Dez," he told the cat. "Sorry I'm late."

The cat was oblivious, focused solely on her food. He reached down and stroked her fur, but she barely reacted, only arched her back a little. Joe went to a cabinet and took down a tumbler. He put some ice in the glass and poured in a splash of scotch.

Joe returned to the living room and sat down on the couch. He sipped his drink slowly, feeling the liquid warm his chest as it went down. He listened to the sounds of the ocean. The monotonous murmur of the waves rising and falling against the beach put him in a reflective mood.

He had to admit, he had had a good weekend. It had been more enjoyable than he had expected. He and Gable had hit it off. Although they were different, Joe had genuinely enjoyed the actor's company.

"Thou didst have a most felicitous outing?" Shakespeare appeared on the couch opposite. He took his tobacco pouch from a pocket in his doublet and began filling his long-stemmed pipe.

"Now that's a word that isn't used very often nowadays," Joe said.

Shakespeare raised an eyebrow.

"Felicitous," Joe explained.

"Ah," Shakespeare nodded. "From the Latin, *felix*. Happy or fortunate."

"Yes, I know what it derives from," Joe said. "I'm just saying it's a word you rarely hear today."

"Ben Jonson was wrong about me," Shakespeare said. "My Latin and Greek were always adequate to the task. True, I was no scholar, but I knew the essentials. Though, truth be told, he was not incorrect regarding my Greek. My Latin far exceeded my Greek."

"From what I've read of Jonson," Joe said, "he liked to provoke. Sounds like he was a bit of a blowhard."

Shakespeare nodded. "Jonson was of a most turbulent

character. He ate too much and drank too much. Pity the poor maid who stood nearby."

"Why am I not surprised?" Joe said.

Shakespeare chuckled, a gleam of amusement in his eyes as he regarded Joe. "'Tis indeed true what the sages say."

Joe looked at him.

"The more the world changes, the more things stay the same," Shakespeare said. "Thou didst not care for the irascible Jonson then and 'tis apparent thy feelings have little changed."

"You're saying we didn't get along?"

Shakespeare nodded. "There was little love lost between thou and him."

Joe scratched his chin. "That's funny," he said. "I've always had a dislike of his plays when I read them in college. Something about them always rubbed me the wrong way."

Shakespeare chuckled again.

Joe laughed along with him. "By the way, when you use 'outing,' you make it sound like I was on a picnic or something."

"Verily?"

Joe grinned. "Verily."

"Wouldst have preferred I used jaunt or junket?"

"I guess 'outing' is better," he said after considering the alternatives. "But, yes, to answer your question, I did enjoy it."

"Thy outing?"

Joe nodded.

"'Tis well." Shakespeare tamped down the tobacco and lit the pipe. He sucked gently and soon clouds of smoke surrounded his head and obscured his features.

"You were going to tell me more about *Hamlet*," Joe said.

Shakespeare nodded, continuing to smoke his pipe. "Indeed, I was." He lifted his head and, cocking it to one side, glanced up at the ceiling. "Where were we?"

"I believe you were telling me about the second version of *Hamlet* you wrote. You said you did a certain amount of philosophizing in it."

"Ah, that is indeed so," Shakespeare said, nodding.

"So why does Hamlet hesitate so long?" Joe asked.

Shakespeare chuckled. He drew on his pipe and blew out a perfect ring of smoke. "'Tis most curious that such hath entertained the minds of so many. But think upon it for a moment, my friend. I couldst not have Hamlet rush to take his revenge."

"Why not?"

"Then the play wouldst have been very short, and not at all satisfactory."

CHAPTER 18

JOE STARED DOWN AT the memo that had just been delivered. For a moment his expression was blank. But gradually, as he read it and the full meaning became clear, his expression changed. His face dropped and he felt his heart begin to race. He stared at the memo once more, as if truly seeing it for the first time.

March 21, 1936

Mr. Joseph Holliday:

Mr. Greenwood requests that you come to his office at once. Bring a copy of Hamlet.

Marjorie Hayden

All at once, Joe's hand began to tremble. He crumpled up the memo and tossed it in a wastebasket. He took a deep breath to calm himself but that only half helped. He gazed about the room. Where was Shakespeare? He suddenly couldn't sense him at all. He had been here a minute ago—they had been working on *The Apple Orchard* together—but now he had vanished.

Panic seized him. This was it, he told himself; this was what he had most feared. It was a reckoning. There was no way he could possibly talk himself out of this. For a moment he thought about leaving. Simply leaving and never coming back. But that was cowardly. No, he had to face the music. He had no other option but to show Greenwood *The Apple Orchard*—and throw himself on the man's sense of mercy. Of course, Greenwood had no sense of mercy. Joe knew that when Greenwood found out what he had been doing this whole time, the producer would go ballistic.

And the truth of it was, the producer would have a point. In fact, he would be absolutely justified. Joe had to admit that. He had been deliberately lying about what he was doing. He had been deliberately deceitful. He had told the producer he had been working on *Hamlet* when he hadn't. There was only one thing to do: come clean.

Joe gathered up *The Apple Orchard* and thrust it under his arm. He marched out of the writer's cottage and locked the door behind him. The day was warm and pleasant with blue skies and barely a hint of cloud. But all that didn't register as he set out. It might as well have been a cloudy, overcast day. In fact, he felt like a condemned prisoner as he trudged across the lawn.

He still couldn't sense Shakespeare. Had the Bard abandoned him?

Soon the executive offices loomed in the distance, stark against the sky. Joe was reminded of the Tower of London—a place of punishment. As he neared, Joe felt as if he were walking through thick mud.

Reaching the entrance, he came to a stop. He took a deep breath, as if to buoy his confidence. Then he squared his shoulders and went inside. The building was surprisingly quiet despite it being midday; the only sounds he heard were his footsteps. Usually at this time the offices were bustling with activity. But now, for whatever reason, it was quiet—as quiet as a mausoleum. Only a few people passed by him in the lobby. He took the elevator to the top floor and when the doors rolled open, he walked slowly down the hallway. His heart hammered in his chest as he approached Greenwood's office. It took everything in his power not to turn and run away.

He knocked on the door.

"Come in." Marjorie's voice was crisp and formal, as ever.

Joe stood for a brief moment with his hand on the knob. Then, mustering his courage, he turned it and stepped inside. His footsteps sounded inordinately loud in the momentary silence that ensued.

Marjorie, who was sitting at her desk, looked up. "Oh, it's you," she said. She was dressed in a steel gray business suit over a red blouse. Her reading glasses were perched halfway down her nose.

Joe nodded, feeling tension in his throat. He swallowed. "I got the memo," he said. He tried his best to keep anxiety out of his voice. He held up *The Apple Orchard*. "And I brought—"

"I'm afraid we'll have to cancel," Marjorie interjected quickly, holding up her hand. "I sent another memo, but I guess you didn't get it in time. Sorry you had to come all the way across the studio."

"Cancel?" The word didn't sound real, and for a moment he thought he had misheard her. "Did you say cancel?"

"Yes, I'm afraid so," Marjorie reiterated. "Mr. Greenwood came down sick. He canceled all appointments and went straight home."

Joe was stunned and for a moment he didn't say anything. He just stood there, staring at her dumbly. His mind was still trying to process what she had told him. He gradually regained his composure and found his voice. "I'm sorry to hear it." He paused. "Did he...did he want to reschedule?"

"He didn't mention anything like that," she said. "He was suddenly feeling very poor and, like I said, canceled everything."

"I see."

"He'll get back to you at some later date," Marjorie said.

"Okay," Joe replied. He remained standing, still stunned.

Marjorie adjusted her glasses, squinting at him. "Are you all right, Mr. Holliday?"

Joe nodded. "Yes, I'm fine." He turned to leave the office but paused. "I hope Mr. Greenwood feels better," he said over his shoulder.

———————

Outside the building, Joe lit up a much needed cigarette as he felt an involuntary shiver run through him. He inhaled deeply, filling his lungs and forcing himself to breathe out slowly. His blood pressure dropped to more normal levels and he relaxed. He stared out over the studio lot, studying the sky through a cloud of smoke.

He was still shaken by the whole episode. It had been an emotional whirlwind. First there had been the inescapable panic and the desire to flee, and then the flood of guilt that made him resolved to confess everything—and accept his punishment. And finally, the complete reversal of fortune. It left his head spinning.

He finished his cigarette, dropped the butt on the ground, and started across the lawn. He suddenly felt Shakespeare striding alongside him.

Joe stopped and glared. "Where the hell have you been?"

"With thee the entire time," Shakespeare said.

"Impossible," Joe fumed. "I didn't sense you at all." He felt a surprising wave of anger well up. "You deserted me!"

"Nay indeed, my friend. I was with thee, 'pon my word. Thou were, as you might say, 'blocked.'"

"Blocked?"

"Aye. Fear does such. 'Tis the primary barrier to one's communication."

Joe was quiet for a moment. He stared at the Bard. "You mean I blocked myself?"

Shakespeare nodded.

"But how on earth did everything else happen? I mean, Greenwood gets sick right after asking for the script. That's not a coincidence." He stared suspiciously at Shakespeare. "What happened? What did you do?"

Shakespeare just grinned.

"You keep telling me you have a non-interference rule, but if you got him sick—"

"Nay, my friend, I didst not 'get him sick' as you say. That wouldst indeed be gross interference. The undercooked meat he ate for his midday repast didst get him sick, not me. I merely orchestrated his sickness to, shall we say, coincide with his demand to see *Hamlet*. That is all."

"Well, however you did it you sure saved my bacon." He paused. "But what about next time?"

"Next time?"

"I mean he's bound to ask for the script again. We can't keep avoiding him."

Shakespeare paused. "A while ago thou said thou trusted me. Is such still the case?"

Joe paused. He scratched the back of his neck. "Yes, but—"

Shakespeare was silent, listening.

Joe continued. "What I mean is, I do, but it's difficult."

"'Tis true," Shakespeare said, giving a sympathetic nod and a gentle smile. "'Tis most difficult. I understand."

———————

"What do you mean my scene was cut?" Betsy asked, incredulous.

"Exactly that," Elsa said. "They're not going to use it."

"Why not?"

Elsa shrugged. "Scenes get cut all the time."

They were seated at a table in the studio commissary. Betsy had been seated alone drinking coffee and reading *Variety* when Elsa had joined her and asked to sit down. At first, Betsy had been surprised, given the tenor of their prior meeting. But Elsa had seemed sincere. Now, however, as this revelation dropped like a lead weight, Betsy wondered what would come next.

Betsy frowned at her. "Who told you this?"

"Does it matter? The point is, it was cut."

Betsy's eyes narrowed as she had a thought. "I'll bet it was all Roger's doing."

"Don't be silly," Elsa said. "He's an actor, not an editor. He didn't have anything to do with this. He doesn't make decisions like that."

"Come on, Elsa, you're kidding yourself if you think he doesn't have that influence. I think it's his way of getting back at me."

"What I do think is that you're obsessed."

"What?"

"You keep saying Roger's obsessed with you, but I think it's exactly the opposite. You're obsessed with him."

Betsy stared at her. She couldn't believe what she was hearing. "You're joking, right?"

"I'm not joking at all," Elsa said.

"If you think I'm obsessed with him then you've got bats in your belfry."

"Deny it all you want but it's written all over your face. You're the one who's always talking about him."

"I only talk about him because he won't leave me alone." She paused and stared at Elsa. "Whose side are you on, anyway? I thought we were friends."

"I'm not on anyone's side," Elsa said.

"Well, you're not on my side. That's for sure."

"I'm only telling you your scene was cut because I thought you should know. I didn't want you to be blindsided."

"Yeah, right, you're just the messenger," Betsy said sarcastically.

"That's right, I am just the messenger."

Betsy glared at her. "You want to know something? I think you're enjoying this," she said. "I think you secretly like the fact that my scene got cut."

"Don't be crazy," Elsa said dismissively. "I'm actually trying to help you."

"How? By suggesting I sleep with Roger to advance my career? Some advice…"

"Go ahead and pretend you can make it on your own, but you're only fooling yourself."

"I will make it on my own!" Betsy retorted.

"Wake up and smell the coffee, Betsy," Elsa said. "No one makes it on their own. In this town, the only way you get your back scratched is if you rub someone else's."

"I'm done with this conversation," Betsy said, irritated. She began to get up.

"Save your breath," Elsa said, "I'm leaving." She stood up and began to walk off but turned around. "If you want to sabotage your own career, be my guest. But don't say I didn't try to warn you."

———————

A burst of laughter broke from the radio followed by the sound of clapping. Immediately, the familiar *Amos 'n' Andy* theme music filled the living room of Joe's cottage, signaling the end of the broadcast.

Joe slid off the couch and switched off the radio. He looked over at Shakespeare, who was leaning against the wall.

"What did you think?" Joe asked.

Shakespeare stroked his beard for a moment. "'Tis a most innovative medium," he said. "There is much to say in its favor." He paused. "As for the content, well, methinks your modern saying best encapsulates my feelings, 'to each his own.'"

"You didn't like it?"

"To use another of your modern proverbs, 'twas not my cup of tea.'"

"Oh well," Joe said, shrugging. "You can't please everybody."

"Spoken most truly. My own comedy, *Two Gentlemen of Verona*, was much maligned in its day."

Joe paused and said with a wink. "Well, to be honest, that wasn't one of your best."

Shakespeare looked at him for a moment then broke into a broad smile. "Indeed, 'twas not. I was young and still learning my craft." He grinned wryly. "But have a care my friend, I well remember your initial efforts."

"My first writings were bad?" Joe asked.

"Nay, not 'bad.' Not bad at all. Simply…unpolished."

Joe chuckled. "We all have to learn to walk before we can run."

"'Tis true," Shakespeare said. "We all have our idiosyncrasies. Things we must needs work upon."

"What were mine? I mean, what were Middleton's?"

"Faults, thou meanest?"

"Yes."

Shakespeare thought for a moment, stroking his beard. He grinned suddenly. "Punctuality was not one of thy strong suits."

"Really?"

Shakespeare nodded. "Thou wouldst oft arrive late for engagements. Thy fellows wouldst oft comment upon thy lack of promptness with sardonic amusement. Forsooth, thou were at times, as Jonson relished in saying, a bit 'muddle-headed.'"

Joe laughed. "Let's hope I've progressed since then." He settled down on the couch and thought for a moment. "You said we met at the theater? What were the circumstances?"

"Thou had submitted a play to our company."

"What was it called?"

"'Twas called *A Yorkshire Tragedy*. Thou had written a few plays prior to this but 'twas this that caught my attention. 'Twas a one-act play. Full of pathos and desperation. The thing appealed to me."

"So, what happened? You liked it and accepted me as an apprentice?"

Shakespeare was silent for a moment. "Methinks rather than tell thee, I might show thee."

"Show me?" Joe was puzzled. "How so?"

A slow smile spread across Shakespeare's face.

———————

Joe felt as if he were watching a movie, but a movie of a very peculiar sort. It was all around him, in vivid color, vivid detail, and vivid three-dimensions. In fact, it felt as if he had stepped into the movie, become part of the scene, and yet was unable to affect the actors or anything else. They moved and spoke as if he wasn't there, and in one sense that was correct. Shakespeare had told him that when viewing these scenes—scenes of the past—he would be unable to interfere. He would be observing the proceedings as they had happened. He would be observing but not participating.

195

He found himself standing inside a tavern, a swirl of activity around him. Crowded and noisy, it rang with the shouts and laughter of young men, the clink of ale tankards, and the bawdy catcalls of whores. Games of cards, dice, and dominoes went on amid the incessant chatter. The air was thick with tobacco smoke and smelled of spilled beer.

Shakespeare stood next to him—the Virgil to Joe's Dante in this surreal experience. He drew Joe's attention to two men at the far end of the tavern. One was seated at a table, a tankard of ale before him, while the second paced back and forth in front of the fireplace. The first man was blond and ruddy with curly hair and a thick beard. The man pacing was the same fellow Joe had seen in his dreams. The young man with the wispy Van Dyke beard. Thomas Middleton.

Shakespeare pointed at the seated man. "That worthy is John Fletcher, playwright for the King's Men. Thou art discussing thy play, *A Yorkshire Tragedy*."

"What year is this?"

"The year of our Lord, 1603."

"And what is—"

"Quiet now," Shakespeare said, gently touching Joe's arm, "let us observe."

Joe watched as the scene unfolded before him.

"God's blood!" Fletcher growled. "Cease thy infernal pacing!"

Thomas glanced around. "Wouldst that I might," he said. "But my heart is all aflutter with the anticipation."

"Persist and thou wilt anon need an appointment with the cobbler for thou wilt wear out thy boots." His voice took on a more soothing tone as he patted the tabletop with the flat of his hand. "Come, sit, and have a drink."

Thomas stopped pacing. He let out a sigh and came over to Fletcher's table and slumped down on the opposite stool. He looked at his companion with an earnest expression.

"And, pray, what if 'tis not accepted?" he said. "I shall have to return

to writing pamphlets for a ha'penny. Writing pamphlets and starving."
He shook his head gravely. "I do not relish the prospect."

"Do not fret my friend, it will be accepted. Mark my words. Master Shakespeare knows a good tale when he sees it. Trust in his judgment. And thy own."

"I wish I could convince myself of such. And yet I doubt."

"The curse of humanity since Adam," Fletcher said. "'Doubt.' Do not dwell upon it. Come, drink thy ale and let us discuss more sanguine topics."

Thomas sighed deeply and gazed into his ale for a moment before taking a perfunctory sip. The two men were silent until Fletcher spoke up.

"I have seen thee recently in the company of Mary Marbeck," he said, giving his companion a knowing wink. "A fetching woman, indeed."

Thomas waved a dismissive hand and raised his head slightly, registering only a weak smile. "We are but friends."

Fletcher laughed caustically. "Come now, Thomas, don't play the blushing schoolboy. I am well pleased. If it is a wife thou seekest, then thou will be hard-pressed to find a more suitable match. Mistress Marbeck is both comely and possessed of a rarefied intellect. She both reads and writes and is accomplished on the virginal. She is truly a marvel."

Thomas put out his hands in a gesture of acquiescence. "And yet I have no prospects. I am a lowly scribbler. What might I offer her?" He dropped his head and stared down again at the tabletop.

Fletcher's eyes twinkled with sardonic humor as he contemplated his companion's hangdog expression. "If thy current mood is any indication, then thou wilt offer her only a morose and self-pitying fool."

Thomas's head came up sharply and he stared at Fletcher with a look of surprise. All at once, he burst into laughter. "By my troth, thou art right. I act and sound a right fool. A right jackass."

Fletcher grinned. "Come now, no more such talk. Let us make merry tonight." He took a long drink.

Thomas shrugged and took a drink of his own ale.

"Now," Fletcher said, setting his flagon down on the table with an air of decisiveness. He eyed Thomas keenly. "Art thou or art thou not interested in this woman, Mistress Marbeck?"

"I am."

"Then do not tarry, my friend. Make thy sentiments plain. 'Tis not a time for dilly-dallying. Be a leopard not a sheep. The good lady's charms hath not gone unnoticed by others."

"Well I know it," Thomas sighed. "And yet her father stands as a bulwark to our affections."

"Wherefore?" Fletcher asked.

"Her father doth think I am unworthy of her. He would that I were not a scribbler of words but an official of the law or a clergyman."

Fletcher nodded sagely. "All fathers are concerned about the welfare of their daughters. 'Tis as natural as the sun rising and setting each day. What thou must do is prove thy worthiness to him."

"How so?"

"'Tis a simple thing. We will become conspirators, like Brutus and Cassius. We will be conspirators against unyielding fathers but use our wits instead of daggers." He paused, lifting his index finger. "Here is what thou must do—"

There was a sudden commotion at the other end of the tavern and both men turned to look. The door burst open and several men clomped noisily inside, spilling into the room. They were boisterous and loud, their boots pounding against the floorboards. Flush-faced and grinning, they scanned the room for a moment. When their eyes alighted on Fletcher and Thomas, they immediately made a beeline and crowded around Thomas. One of the men, a tall, rangy fellow with a prominent nose, grabbed Thomas's shoulder.

"Master Shakespeare bade us to tell thee he hast accepted thy play!" he shouted.

"God in Heaven!" Fletcher roared, rolling his eyes up to the ceiling and effecting a look of great reverence. He turned to Thomas and clapped him on the shoulder. "There! Didst I not tell thee? Now, no more fretting! Let us celebrate!"

"Aye," the tall fellow said, "'tis an occasion for a round!"

Joe opened his eyes. He was back in his cottage, sitting on his couch in the living room. The transition had been so abrupt that it made his head spin. One moment he had been in an Elizabethan tavern and now he was home. He blinked several times to make sure he really was home, rubbing his eyes and glancing around the room.

Shakespeare was standing quietly, gazing at Joe.

"That was incredible," Joe said. "How were we able to do that? It was like stepping into a motion picture but much more vivid."

"'Tis called the Akashic Record. 'Tis a compendium of all that hath occurred to each individual on this planet."

"What do you mean? Everything?"

Shakespeare nodded. "Aye, all events that hath ever occurred art recorded. Every deed and thought and word. The history of every soul since the beginning. Recorded forever."

"What is it?" Joe said. "I mean, how is that possible?"

Shakespeare paused to think for a moment. "'Tis, I suppose, much akin to thy modern phonograph. Like that device, it records and can play back what it hath recorded. Yet thy phonograph is but a crude device in comparison. The Akashic Record records all things as they actually happened. Not just sound."

"How is it accessed? How were we able to view it?"

"'Tis a matter of vibrations," Shakespeare said. "One must attune to the correct vibration. 'Tis not unlike thy modern radio in that respect."

"You mean like tuning into a particular station?"

"Aye, just so."

Joe scrunched up his forehead. "I still don't understand. How did it come into being? I mean, who created it?"

"'Twas never created. It hath always been and will always be. Like the universe."

"But…" Joe paused. "That doesn't make any sense. How can something have no beginning?"

Shakespeare grinned. "Some things, my young friend, are beyond the ken of even heaven."

CHAPTER 19

THE *TAR BABY*'s BOW sliced through the ultramarine water like a knife, leaving a white, foamy wake. In the distance, the brown mass of Santa Catalina Island loomed on the horizon, rising and falling with the swells.

Joe took a deep breath, filling his lungs with the sea air and trying to keep his footing on the pitching, rolling deck. He was standing near the bow, getting the full force of the breeze against his face.

Above him, the blue sky was nearly devoid of clouds, only a few wispy traces scudded past. Behind him, the southern California coastline grew fainter and fainter until it appeared only as a thin brown line.

"Want some company?"

Joe turned to see Betsy making her way toward him. She was gripping the railing, moving hand over hand. Her dark hair whipped about her face.

"Of course," he said, grinning. "Where have you been?"

"Topside," she said. "At least I think that's the right word."

"Sounds very nautical," Joe said.

She came up and stood beside him, her hands continuing to grip the railing.

"Getting your sea legs?" he asked.

"I think so. Carole gave me some saltines earlier. That helped settle my stomach."

Joe looked out at the island. It appeared like a craggy mountain emerging from a blue medium. He distinguished the rounded peak of Mount Orizaba, the highest point on the island. "Well, we don't have long until we get there. Clark said we're about an hour or so away."

Releasing her grip on the railing, she snuggled up next to him and he put his arm around her.

"Thanks for bringing me along," she said.

Joe looked down at her. "I wasn't about to leave my best girl behind, was I?"

"Better not," she said. She looked up at him with playful eyes. "But I don't want to be your best girl."

He looked at her, surprised. "What do you—"

"I want to be your *only* girl," she said firmly.

He chuckled and nodded. "You are." He leaned down and kissed the top of her head.

They held each other as the sea breeze whistled about them.

Betsy suddenly pointed off the starboard bow.

"Hey, look!" she shouted.

Joe turned and saw a dorsal fin break the surface of the water. It was followed by several more fins. A pod of dolphins had surfaced parallel to the boat and were cruising in unison, their sleek bodies glistening in the sun. There must have been a dozen animals, all swimming rapidly, riding the boat's wake.

Joe and Betsy rushed to lean over the starboard side.

"Just look at them!" Betsy squealed excitedly. Her eyes were as big as saucers as she watched the animals.

The dolphins raced alongside, keeping pace with the yacht. They looked streamlined and powerful up close, creatures well inured to aquatic life.

Suddenly, for no apparent reason either Joe or Betsy could fathom, one of the dolphins broke the surface and launched itself into the air. It arched its body and somersaulted back with a splash. It seemed to Joe an act motivated out of sheer exuberance or joy.

"Did you see that?" Betsy shouted.

Joe nodded.

The dolphins followed the boat for a while longer before veering off to the northwest, disappearing as quickly as they had appeared.

An hour later, just as Gable had predicted, the *Tar Baby* cruised into Avalon Harbor. About fifty boats bobbed gently up and down at anchor. The harbor was crescent shaped and fronted by a small sandy beach from which jutted a long pier. On the far edge of the beach, the little town of Avalon sat placidly, set in front of steep cliffs. On the north end was Avalon's most famous landmark, the Catalina Casino, which had been built by William Wrigley—the chewing gum baron—in 1929. Reputed to have cost two million dollars, it was a round building with a ballroom and a state-of-the-art movie theater. In height, it was the equivalent of a twelve-story structure and was topped by a bright red dome-like roof that reminded Joe of the Duomo in Florence.

Joe and Betsy made their way back to the wheelhouse where Gable was behind the wheel, guiding the *Tar Baby* to its final destination, an anchorage just to the north of the pier. His face wore a serious expression but when he saw Joe and Betsy he grinned, flashing them that infectious Gable smile.

"Enjoying yourselves?" he asked. He was dressed in white Bermuda shorts, a white shirt open at the collar, and deck shoes. Carole was seated on the bench that encircled the wheelhouse. She was wearing a wide-brimmed hat and a pair of dark sunglasses.

"We saw some dolphins!" Betsy exclaimed.

Joe sat down on the bench across from Carole as Betsy excitedly described the encounter.

"What kind were they?" Gable asked.

"Kind?" Betsy said. She wrinkled her forehead. "There are different kinds?"

"We get all kinds in the channel," Gable said. "White-sided, bottlenose, Risso's."

Betsy sat down next to Joe. "I'm not sure," she said. "But they were gray."

"And big," Joe added with a chuckle.

"Sounds like bottlenose," Gable said.

"Whatever they were," Betsy said, "they were adorable."

With a well-practiced motion, Gable cast his line out into the water. The baited hook struck the surface with an audible *thwump!* and sank down into the depths. He let the line run out a ways, before reeling in the slack.

Joe reached into the bucket Gable had provided and pulled out a pulpy looking squid. He baited his hook, impaling the creature on the sharpened point. Stepping over to the side, he cast his line out, too. It hissed as it uncoiled before striking the water.

"Good cast," Gable said.

"Thanks."

Gable sank down on his deckchair with a sigh. "Hell," he said, gazing out over the calm water, "I could spend the rest of my life doing exactly this."

"Fishing?"

Gable nodded. They were seated on the deck of the *Tar Baby*. After a short stay in Avalon Harbor, where they had eaten lunch at one of the local eateries, they had motored around to the south-western part of the island and anchored at a deserted cove Gable had been to on a previous occasion. In fact, he said he'd been there during the filming of *The Mutiny on the Bounty* with Charles Laughton. He said the fishing was especially good in the cove and there was a picturesque little sandy beach.

"No doubt about it," Gable went on, a touch of wistfulness in his voice, "this is the life. Beats the hell out of any goddamn gala the studio ever hosted." He paused. "Still, I'll admit it's pretty hard to give up the whole acting thing when they keep throwing ridiculous amounts of money at me. Know what I mean?"

"Yeah, I understand what you're saying," Joe said, "though I can't say I've experienced anything even remotely similar."

Gable laughed. "Yeah, I guess not. What about you? Want to write screenplays the rest of your life?"

"All in all, it's a pretty good gig," Joe admitted, "but what I'd really like to do is write novels."

Gable looked at him. "I'm surprised you haven't already."

"Actually, I have," Joe said. "I wrote a novel a few years back, but I haven't been able to get it published."

"Really?" Gable was surprised. "Why not? You're one hell of a writer."

"Any number of reasons, I suppose," Joe shrugged. "But I'm guessing the main reason might have something to do with the fact that it's over six hundred pages long. Nearly seven hundred."

"Damn, that is long. What's it called?"

"*All That Glitters.*"

"What's it about?"

"A man's spiritual journey."

Gable nodded. A slight breeze kicked up and blew across the surface of the water, raising small ripples. Both men were silent for a brief time and Gable checked his line.

"That all?" Gable asked. He had turned and was looking at Joe expectantly.

Joe cast the actor a surprised look. "You want to know more?"

Gable nodded. "Why so surprised?"

"It's just that I can't seem to interest anybody in it," Joe said. "Once I start talking about it most people's eyes glaze over."

"Well, hell," Gable said, "I'm interested. I'd like to hear it."

"You want the long version or the short version?" Joe asked.

"Looks like you already gave me the short version, why don't you give me the long. We're certainly not going anywhere."

Joe started slowly and hesitantly. He wasn't convinced Gable wanted to hear him talk about it. He figured the actor might simply be humoring him.

"Well," he began, "it's about a veteran of the Great War who returns home after experiencing the horrors of the trenches. He's particularly haunted by his involvement in the killing of a young German soldier during a battle."

"How'd he kill him?" Gable asked.

"With his bayonet. Stabbed him right through the heart. Like I said, he has trouble adjusting to civilian life as a result of his experiences. He can't seem to find meaning in anything he does. He works in his father's business but finds it tedious and unfulfilling. Soon he falls into a deep depression and begins to ask himself questions of an existential nature."

"You mean like questions about God?" Gable asked.

"That's right," Joe nodded. "But also about good and evil, right and wrong; those sorts of things. Have you ever heard the German word *weltschmerz*?"

Gable shook his head.

"It means 'world-weariness.' Basically, it's a feeling of anxiety that stems from dwelling on all the horrible ills of the world. In a nutshell, I guess, this is what the protagonist is suffering from."

"*Weltschmerz*," Gable said to himself. "Funny sounding word. Sounds like a type of sausage."

"Anyway," Joe continued, "he's unable to find answers to his questions so he sets out to discover the answers for himself. He goes to Paris where he falls in with the bohemian crowd, thinking that they might be able to help him with answers. But he soon realizes they don't have any answers either, they're just dedicated to hedonistic pursuits. Eventually, he ends up in India."

"He goes from Paris all the way to India? What happens there?"

"He joins an ashram."

Gable looked at him blankly. "What's that?"

"It's like a monastery," Joe said. He paused. "Keep in mind I'm condensing things, of course. There are a number of things that happen to him in Paris. For example, he falls in and out of love with a beautiful painter. But this is the basic story outline so I'm going to skip over those. So, anyway, the main character—his name is Alan, by the way—becomes a monk and begins to train with the abbot. He tells the abbot about his experiences in the war, especially his killing of the German soldier. The abbot urges Alan to seek out a poor peasant family and make a difference in their lives. So, this is what Alan does, except he meets a poor 'untouchable' and her son who are living in squalid conditions on the streets. He helps them out in myriad ways, and soon, over time, Alan begins to have feelings for the woman and her son."

"He falls in love with her?"

"It's a deep affection that eventually develops into love, yes. Though it's a love that is never acted upon. Only from afar and only through acts of kindness. But Alan is truly inspired by Samira's—that's her name—quiet dignity, her perseverance in the face of crushing poverty, and her absolute dedication to her son. It's through her that he begins to pull himself out of his depression and ennui. You might say she breathes new life into him. Unfortunately, a horrible cholera epidemic sweeps through the community, claiming her son's life. Distraught, she commits suicide. Alan, of course, is devastated. He leaves the monastery and heads off into the mountains."

"Is that how it ends? He disappears in the mountains? Does he die?"

"No, he doesn't die. He gets caught in a snowstorm and nearly dies but is saved by a goatherd."

"Then what?"

"The goatherd's family nurses him back to health. This poor family with little to offer him nonetheless saves his life, without asking for anything in return. When he recovers, he decides not to return to the monastery but to return home. To America."

Gable was quiet for a moment. "That's quite a story," he said. He scratched his chin, pondering.

"You look confused," Joe said.

"No," Gable said. "Just thinking." He scrunched up his brow and gazed off toward the island before turning to look back at Joe. "The ending seems kind of unsatisfying given everything the guy's been through."

"You're right," Joe said, conceding Gable's point with a nod. "I've never been happy with it. In fact, I'd like to rework it some-time. Tinker with it and make it better. But that's where the novel basically ends."

Suddenly Gable's pole nearly bent double. He sprang from his chair and grabbed it. With the effort of a seasoned pro, he gripped the rod and played out some line so the fish could get a good bite into the hook. Then he gave a sharp tug. About twenty yards out, the fish broke the surface with a furious splash and Joe caught the flash of a red tail. It was unmistakably a large fish and it was putting up a fierce struggle to free itself.

"This one's a fighter," Gable said, gritting his teeth. He began to reel in the line furiously, pausing every so often to tug on the pole, then reeling again.

Joe leaned over the side, watching the battle.

"Get the net!" Gable called out.

Joe propped his pole against the railing and scrambled back to the wheelhouse, frantically searching for a net. He didn't see one right away and began tossing the covers off the seats as Gable called out again for the net.

"I can't find it," Joe called back.

"It's under the seat!" Gable shouted, glancing over his shoulder.

"What seat?"

"The captain's seat, for Christ's sake!"

Joe noticed a wooden box with a clasp under the seat in front of the wheel. He tore off the top and saw a large fish net. He grabbed it and ran over to Gable's side. "What do you want me to do?" he asked breathlessly.

"When I pull him up," Gable said, "get the net under him."

Joe nodded.

Gable strained at the pole, frantically reeling in the fish. It broke the surface of the water again with a loud splash as Gable brought it skillfully alongside the boat. Joe leaned down with the net and positioned it under the fish, then scooped upward, ensnaring the creature. Together, they hauled the catch over the railing and dropped it onto the deck with an audible thud. It flopped and thrashed about, further entangling itself in the net.

"Damn," Gable exclaimed. "It's a big one!"

Joe saw that it was a good two feet in length and bright red in color. It had sharp, needle-like teeth and a large mouth that kept opening and closing as it gasped for breath. "What is it?" he asked.

"It's a red."

"A red?"

"A red snapper," Gable said.

"That's good eating, right?"

Gable nodded, grinning from ear to ear. "One of the best."

Joe went back to his pole and, before long, he felt something pull on the end of his line. He gave a sharp tug in response.

"Got something!" he called out excitedly.

Gable looked over at him and grinned. "Now you're talking!"

———————

The smell of roasting fish drifted in the air. Joe felt his mouth water in anticipation as he watched Gable prepare the day's catch. The actor had laid the two plump fish side by side on the grill and was now basting them with a concoction of butter and garlic. They sizzled and periodically melted butter would drip and fall through the grill onto the bed of hot coals that were glowing red underneath.

"That's got to be the most heavenly smell imaginable," Joe said.

"Can't go wrong with butter," Gable said, looking over his shoulder and winking. "And lots of it."

Joe noticed that Shakespeare was leaning against the starboard railing, his arms folded across his doublet, watching and listening to the proceedings with an amused aloofness. Joe hadn't seen the Bard all day and was surprised that he had suddenly materialized.

"What do you want in your martini?" Carole's voice drifted up from the cabin where she was mixing drinks. "An olive or an onion?"

"An olive," Joe called back.

"I'd like an olive, too, please," Betsy said. She was seated on a deckchair near the railing.

"Olives it is!" Carole said cheerily.

Gable flipped the fish over, frying them on the other side. The grill sizzled and popped. "Been thinking about your novel," Gable said without turning around.

"Have you read it?" Betsy chimed in.

This time Gable turned around. "No, but Joe was telling me the story earlier today."

Betsy affected a pouty look. "Joe won't let me read it."

"It's not that," Joe said. "It just needs more work. I'm still editing it."

"Joe's a perfectionist," Betsy said.

"I think it'd make a hell of a picture," Gable said.

"You think so?" Joe said. "I mean it's pretty damn long. They'd have to shorten it."

"Yeah, but that's okay."

Carole emerged from the cabin carefully balancing two full martini glasses. She was wearing slacks and a white blouse over which she'd draped a light sweater. "I come bearing libations," she said.

"Oh, goody!" Betsy squealed.

Carole passed out the drinks and then sat down in one of the unoccupied deckchairs. She crossed her legs and glanced around the deck at everyone. "So, what were you saying? What would make a good picture?"

"Joe's novel," Gable said.

Carole looked at Joe with interest. "You've written a novel?"

"He has," Gable said. "But he's still editing it."

"It's a first draft," Joe explained. He moved the speared olive to one side and took a sip of his martini.

"Who's your publisher?" Carole asked.

"I don't have one," Joe said.

"Really? Why not?"

"Can't seem to get anyone interested in it."

"What's it about?" Carole asked, settling herself more comfortably into her seat.

Joe spent the next several minutes telling her the story. When he had finished, Carole sat quietly, nodding her head slowly, ruminating on the story. "That's quite a tale," she said at length.

Gable erupted into laughter. "That's exactly what I said!"

"It's ultimately sad, though, isn't it?" Carole continued. "And tragic."

"It is, yes," Joe conceded.

"I know who could play Samira," Carole said. "Merle Oberon. She'd be great. She's so pretty."

"I like that idea," Gable chimed in, perking up, his eyes twinkling. "In that case, I'd like to play Alan."

Carole glared at him. She lit a cigarette and, leaning back, directed her gaze at Betsy. "So, Joe tells me you're an actress. How come I haven't seen you on the lot?"

"Well," she said, "that's because I'm actually just an extra."

"She's a damn good actress," Joe intervened. "She just needs a chance."

The hint of a smile crossed Carole's face as she studied Joe for a moment. She turned her attention back on Betsy. "Well, then," she said, "I hope to see more of you."

"I had a speaking part in *The Queen's Cavalier*," Betsy said, "but it was cut."

Carole turned her head and blew out smoke. "That's Phil Leighton's latest picture, isn't it?"

Betsy nodded. "We wrap up shooting in a week."

"Why'd they cut your scene?"

"I don't know," Betsy said, shrugging. "I guess they were trying to save screen time."

"How are you getting along with Phil?" Carole asked.

"He's all right," Betsy said. "But he sometimes has trouble keeping order on set."

"That's Phil," Carole said, nodding. "A decent director but not the world's greatest disciplinarian. He's one of those guys who tolerates a lot but then suddenly blows up. His shoots can be pretty chaotic."

"I'll say," Betsy said. "We almost had a fight on set a while back."

"A fight? Good heavens!" Carole said.

When the fish were ready, they all sat down to the feast. In addition to the day's catch, the spread included potato salad, bread and butter, and a green salad.

Everyone sat on deck after dinner, chatting, smoking cigarettes, and sipping cocktails. The sun had set and the black canvas of night with its sprinkling of stars had descended. Gable set up a lantern so they could have some light.

Carole leaned forward in her seat. "Anyone know a good ghost story?"

"Good God," Gable said, rolling his eyes. "Here we go again with the ghost stories!"

Carole waved a dismissive hand at him. "Aw, don't listen to him. He doesn't know anything."

"Ask Joe," Betsy said quickly. "He has a lot of ghost stories." She turned and gave her boyfriend a mischievous wink.

Joe didn't return the gesture. Instead, he turned to Carole and, perhaps emboldened by all the alcohol he'd consumed, said, "Well, it just so happens I do have a few."

"That's swell," Carole said, pulling her sweater tighter around her shoulders, "I love a good ghost story." Her eyes focused on Joe intently.

Joe cast a quick glance at Shakespeare who was still leaning against the railing. His form was partly obscured by shadows and Joe couldn't see his expression. But he sensed that he was listening and fully engaged in the conversation. He turned back to his assembled audience. "This happened when I was very young," Joe said. "I was in my room one afternoon—"

"Wait a second," Carole interrupted. "Is this a true story?"

"I'll leave that for you to decide," Joe said. He paused and then continued. "Anyway, I had just been scolded and sent to my room for something I'd done. I don't remember what it was exactly, but my father had cuffed me and unceremoniously sent me to my room. I was lying on the bed crying when I suddenly felt something beside me. I looked over and noticed a white cat."

"A cat?" Carole said, puzzled.

Joe nodded. "It was a beautiful white cat with soft, silky fur and a fluffy tail. I had no idea how it had gotten into my room because the door and window were closed. But there it was. Rubbing its head against me and purring. So, I began to pet it. And I began to feel better. Soon I wasn't upset anymore."

"What happened next?" Carole asked.

"It wasn't long after that that my mother came in. She wanted to see how I was doing. When she opened the door, the cat disappeared."

"What do you mean disappeared?" Carole asked, looking at him skeptically.

"It vanished into thin air. One moment it was there and the next it was gone."

"You saw it disappear?" she said.

"That's right."

She continued to stare at him for a moment longer, her eyes narrowed. "Are you sure it didn't scurry across the floor and run out the door when your mother came in?"

"I'm sure."

Carole was quiet for a moment. "That wasn't scary at all," she said, shaking her head.

"Oops, did I not adhere to proper ghost story protocol?" Joe said facetiously.

"Not scary at all," Carole repeated. Then she grinned. "But a good story nonetheless."

"Come on, chief," Gable said, leaning back in his chair and sipping his drink, "you're telling me that actually happened?"

Joe just took a sip of his martini.

Chapter 20

THE TOP OF THE ridge loomed above, emerging from the morning mist.

"C'mon, old man!" Betsy called out, breezing past Joe. She was wearing a wide-brimmed sun hat and a good pair of walking shoes Carole had given her.

Wheezing and sweating, Joe came to a stop. He placed his hands on his hips and gasped for breath. This hike demonstrated how out of shape Joe was. His life had been far too sedentary of late and filled with too many cigarettes and glasses of scotch. He shook his head in disgust, silently cursing himself, but soon followed, the pleasing sway of Betsy's hips giving him incentive.

They had left the *Tar Baby* earlier that morning and were now more than half-way up a trail that switch-backed up the side of a mountain. Clumps of prickly pear cactus and coastal sage lined the path; every so often they passed a Toyon tree or were confronted by a sprawling patch of giant coreopsis in full, brilliant bloom.

Although the mist was dissipating, a few patches clung stubbornly to low hollows. All in all, the day was promising to be warm and sunny.

Eventually they reached the top and drew to a halt. A large clump of cactus occupied nearly the entire ridgeline. They stood next to it, careful to avoid the wicked-looking spines. From their vantage, they had a panoramic view of the surrounding area. Far below, the Pacific Ocean stretched out in all directions, like a rippled blue carpet.

Betsy swept her gaze in an all-encompassing arc, her eyes wide and unblinking. "Isn't it beautiful?" she said.

Joe stood next to her, still breathing hard. After he had recovered and wiped sweat from his eyes, he gazed back at the mainland. The distant mountains of southern California framed the horizon like a row of jagged teeth. He swung his gaze to the south where he could see San Clemente Island, the southernmost of the Channel Islands in the distance.

"Did you ever think you'd be standing at a place like this?" Betsy asked.

"It is nice up here," Joe said, nodding. He continued to gaze at the water. Far out he spied what looked like a puff of smoke. It appeared briefly but then dissipated, carried away on the breeze. He squinted and brought up a hand to shade his eyes. In moments he saw another puff and realized it was the mist rising from a whale's blowhole. He pointed it out to Betsy.

"Where?" she said, scanning the water excitedly.

Joe waited until another spout broke the surface. "There!" he called out.

"I see it! I see it!" Betsy shouted.

The whale's back appeared as a small black dot. They watched as it slid out of the water, rolled ponderously forward, and then sank, disappearing into the depths.

"First dolphins and now whales." Betsy shook her head in amazement. "Never in a million years did I think I'd see anything like this!" She turned to Joe and smiled at him. "Thanks for this, Joe. It's like a dream."

"Thank Clark and Carole," Joe said. "They arranged everything."

"I know, but I wouldn't be here without you."

A breeze sprang up. It blew in from the ocean and rustled the surrounding shrubs. It felt pleasingly cool in the day's gathering warmth.

Eventually, they headed down the switchback. They followed a well-trodden trail that led back to the little cove where *Tar Baby* was anchored. Betsy led the way while Joe followed in her wake.

He was surprised at her energetic pace.

Joe suddenly felt Shakespeare walking beside him. He stopped.

"There you are," Joe said, turning toward the Bard. "I was wondering where you were."

"I hath been exploring this most excellent island," Shakespeare said.

Betsy overheard Joe's voice and she turned around. "You coming?"

"Go ahead," he said. "I'll catch up with you at the cove."

She looked at him. "You sure?"

"Yeah, I'll catch up."

Betsy shrugged and headed off skipping down the trail. When she had disappeared around a bend, Joe said, "What do you think of the island?"

"A rare treasure set amidst the sparkling brine," Shakespeare said. "A precious stone set in the silver sea."

"And good fishing," Joe added.

"Aye, indeed," he said. "A veritable angler's paradise. My good friend Izaak Walton—an angler beyond compare—wouldst find this island most amenable."

"You've been sightseeing this whole time?"

Shakespeare nodded. "And I hath discovered something that might be of interest."

"To me?"

Shakespeare nodded.

"What is it?"

"A place of rare and delicate beauty. Wouldst thou care to accompany me?"

Joe glanced at the trail that led to the cove and then at Shakespeare. He grinned wryly. "Is it worth it?"

"Methinks it might," Shakespeare said.

The Bard led him away from the trail. They meandered for a few minutes, skirting dense underbrush and tromping through the knee-high coastal shrub. As they wandered farther away from the trail, the trees grew denser and the foliage thicker. Oak trees cast dappled shadows on the ground and the air was suffused with the scent of sage. Joe picked his way among the trees, trying his best to keep up and wondering where Shakespeare was leading him. Eventually they came to a small clearing perfectly encircled by trees. Joe stepped between two trees and entered the clearing but stopped cold.

Three individuals stood in the middle of the clearing—like phantoms from his past. They included the Viking, the Indian, and the Buddhist monk. Joe looked at each one in turn, moving his eyes deliberately from one to the other, as if to make sure they were real. All three stared back at him with prominent smiles. They looked the same as the last time he had seen them—nearly thirty years ago. Roland was wearing his chainmail armor, Falling Leaf his war paint, and Ching Su his saffron robe.

The monk clasped his hands together in front of him and bowed reverently. The Viking nodded and, his hand on his sword hilt, grinned from ear-to-ear. The Indian brave stood quietly but Joe could see that his eyes were filled with emotion.

Despite his best efforts, Joe felt his own eyes water. He was stunned and at a loss for words. "I don't know what to say. It's great to see all of you."

The monk, Ching Su, stepped forward. "We are once again most pleased to be in your company."

"It's...I'm overwhelmed," Joe stammered. "I've thought about you all a lot." He wiped away tears with the back of his hand. "I didn't think I'd ever see any of you again."

"Rest assured," Ching Su said, "we have been with you all these long years. We are very proud of the man you have become."

The ice broken, they all started talking at once. They chattered incessantly for the next several minutes, like old friends who have a lot of catching up. Even Falling Leaf uttered a word here and there. When things quieted down, Joe turned to Shakespeare. "Where's Uncle Jim?" he asked. "I was hoping he'd be here, too."

"He is," Shakespeare said.

Joe looked around the clearing excitedly, expecting to see Uncle Jim emerge from the foliage or step from behind a tree.

But he didn't see the dapper ghost anywhere. He turned back, puzzled. "Where is he?"

Shakespeare smiled softly. "Here," he said, gesturing at himself. With that, he suddenly began to morph. His form blurred and he began to take on a different aspect. Joe stared, thinking his eyes were playing tricks on him. But they weren't. Gradually, Shakespeare changed into a different person. His hose and doublet disappeared, replaced by a pinstripe suit. A bowler hat. Spats. And green waistcoat with a gold chain.

Soon Uncle Jim was standing before him, grinning jauntily, his blue eyes sparkling. "Hello, Master Joseph," he said, his voice as familiar as if he'd just spoken the day before. "It's good to see you again."

Joe stared in amazement, speechless. Finally, he regained his voice. "Uncle Jim! Is it really you? What just happened?"

"Yes, it's really me," Uncle Jim said.

"I don't understand," Joe went on, completely mystified. "What happened to—" He stopped in mid-sentence as the explanation suddenly dawned on him. His jaw dropped open in utter amazement as his brain processed this new revelation. The whole thing was suddenly, overwhelmingly, inescapably obvious. Shakespeare and Uncle Jim were one and the same. They had always been the same. Different incarnations of the same soul.

As if to confirm what Joe was thinking, Uncle Jim nodded sagely and said, "Yes, it is true what you're thinking. We are the same."

When Joe got back to the little cove, he saw Betsy sitting on the beach. Her knees were drawn up to her chest, her arms wrapped around her legs. She was humming a tune and rocking gently back and forth. When she heard his footsteps, she looked around. "Where have you been?" Her tone held a note of teasing mockery. "I was beginning to worry. Thought you might have twisted an ankle."

Joe didn't say anything, just strode across the sand toward her, his shoes crunching on dried seaweed.

Alarmed by his silence and the dazed look on his face, Betsy scrambled to her feet, holding the brim of her hat against the breeze. She looked at him curiously.

Joe came over and stood next to her. "I think I need to sit down," he said.

"Are you all right?" Betsy asked.

Joe nodded and lowered himself onto the sand. Betsy sat down beside him. Concern etched her features. "What's wrong?"

He scratched his head, bewildered. "I think I just got the revelation of my life."

She furrowed her brow and looked at him. "What do you mean?"

He took a deep breath and then explained what had happened. When he finished, he saw that Betsy was just as stunned as he was.

"He's both Shakespeare *and* Uncle Jim?" She was amazed. "How is that possible? I mean—"

"Both are different incarnations of the same soul. He's both Shakespeare and Uncle Jim. And he can choose whichever form he wants. He can flit back and forth between the two. He told me he was Uncle Jim during his last life when he lived in New York City and was a businessman. He died of a heart attack in the financial panic of 1896."

"He died of a heart attack?"

"He said it was exacerbated by stress, too much alcohol, and too rich of a diet."

"That doesn't sound at all…romantic," Betsy said. "Hardly the ending for a famous poet."

"That's just the point," Joe said. "He wasn't a famous poet in that life. He was just an ordinary man. A businessman with a family."

Betsy frowned. "But why did he choose such a drab life?"

"He told me it wasn't a bad life at all. He had a loving family and two fine children whom he loved dearly. He said the point of that life was to learn love within a family setting, a theme that had eluded him during his life as Shakespeare."

"But you said he died of stress, so his life couldn't have been all that happy."

"He told me that near the end of his life he let his financial worries get the better of him, but that the majority of his life was a happy one."

Betsy nodded. She was quiet for a moment. "And you had no idea they were the same person?" she asked at length.

"None," he said. "None whatsoever. It was a complete surprise."

She thought for a moment. "So, this means he's been with you your entire life, right?"

Joe nodded. "I guess so."

"That's incredible." Betsy reached out and touched his arm. "He must really care about you."

"He explained that our lives are intertwined. We've known each other for a long time. Apparently, I've looked after him during some of his incarnations just as he is looking after me now."

"Really? That's amazing," Betsy said, and then suddenly broke into a chuckle.

Joe was surprised by her sudden outburst. "What's so funny?"

"It's just that I'm having trouble picturing you caring for somebody—anybody—like that."

"What do you mean?" Joe said, somewhat taken aback. "I'm not that much of a callous bastard, am I?"

"I don't mean that," Betsy said with a grin, reaching out to touch his arm, "but, come on Joe, you have to admit you're not the most sensitive guy in the world. I mean, you love your cat and everything but you're hardly the nursemaid type. You're pretty self-absorbed and in your head a lot."

"Am I?"

Betsy nodded. "But it's okay," she said, giving him another grin, "I still love you." She paused and readjusted herself on the sand. "Tell me more. What else did he say? Why did he appear to you as Uncle Jim when you were a child and Shakespeare when you were an adult?"

"I asked him that," Joe said, "he told me that when I was a child it was important that he appear to me in a fatherly guise. Because my real father was so distant. And now that I'm a writer, well," he shrugged, "I guess that's pretty self-explanatory."

Betsy chuckled. "Yeah, I guess so."

———————

Catalina Island grew smaller and smaller as the *Tar Baby* plowed through the channel, heading for the mainland. Joe and Betsy stood at the bow as the breeze blew stiff against them, fluttering their clothes and hair.

Betsy shivered.

"You cold?" Joe asked.

She nodded.

Joe put his arm around her shoulders. She smiled up at him and lifted her face to be kissed. He obliged. Her lips were moist and soft.

"Disappointed to be going back?" Joe asked.

She nodded again and sighed. "Back to the mundane. Me to a movie set where they won't let me say even four words and you to *Hamlet*. At least yours is interesting." She paused. "How's it going by the way?"

The question was like a gut punch, and Joe was quiet for a moment. He gazed out toward the mainland through narrowed eyes, his chin set. The breeze whipped at the water, raising whitecaps. He had to tell her. He simply couldn't keep it a secret any longer—at least from her. Now was the time.

Betsy noticed Joe's lingering silence. "You all right?" she asked.

He paused a moment longer before answering her. "I have a confession to make."

Betsy looked up, mildly surprised, studying his face and waiting for him to continue.

Joe took a deep breath and then spoke. "I'm not writing *Hamlet*," he said. His voice was even and measured.

Her eyes widened in surprise. "What do you mean you're not writing *Hamlet*?"

"I'm writing something else," he replied.

"What?"

"A play. *The Apple Orchard.* Remember I told you about it?"

"Yes, of course," she said.

"I haven't been writing *Hamlet* at all."

"What do you mean?" She blinked. "This whole time?"

He nodded. "I've been lying to Greenwood," he said. "And you."

She shrugged out of his arm and stepped back, staring at him. Her hair was tossed about her face by the breeze and she tried to corral it with a hand. "I don't understand," she said. She was looking at him intensely, her large brown eyes staring with an unblinking focus.

"Shakespeare and I have been working on *The Apple Orchard,* not *Hamlet.* Remember when you told me you thought *The Apple Orchard* was the writing project I was supposed to be working on?"

"Yes, but you said you couldn't do it because you were busy with *Hamlet.*"

"I know, but—"

"You haven't been working on *Hamlet* at all?"

He nodded.

She looked at him as if he'd gone mad. "Are you trying to put your whole career in jeopardy?" Her voice carried a note of anger.

"It's complicated," he said. He wished he had a better answer for her. But he didn't. The whole thing *was* complicated. He didn't even understand all of it.

"What are you going to tell Greenwood? He's bound to find out."

"I know," he said, nodding again. "I guess when the time comes, I'll tell him."

"And then what?" Betsy asked. "He's going to fire you. Have you considered that?"

"Look, Betsy," Joe said, "I know all this. I've considered all of it."

"Then why on earth are you doing it?" Betsy was incredulous; she stared at him in utter disbelief and shook her head vehemently. "It doesn't make any sense. You said you were going to work on *The Apple Orchard* once you finished *Hamlet.*"

"Like I said, it's complicated."

"That's all you're going to say?" Betsy said, glaring at him. "'It's complicated.' You of all people should have a better answer than that!"

Joe shrugged. "I'm sorry, that's the best I can do right now."

She stared at him for a long moment. "I don't understand this at all." She turned and made her way back to the cabin.

When the *Tar Baby* docked at Marina Del Rey, Betsy exited without a word and took a taxi back to the boarding house. Joe stood on the dock, his hands in his pockets, and watched as the vehicle sped away in a cloud of exhaust.

He stood quietly, let out a sigh, and stared down at his shoes.

Gable strode up and stood next to him. Joe noted his approach but said nothing.

The actor was quiet for a moment and he put his hands on his hips. "None of my business, but you two have a fight or something?" he asked finally.

Joe looked up and nodded. "Yeah, I'm afraid so."

"I know how that goes," Gable said, shaking his head. "Women are creatures I will never fully understand."

CHAPTER 21

THAT EVENING, JOE SAT in a quiet and still house, staring blankly at the walls.

Desdemona was curled up on his lap, purring. He ran a hand through her fur as his mind replayed his conversation with Betsy over and over again. He knew that Betsy's outburst today had been prompted by fear—her fear of what all this meant for Joe's career and livelihood. But Joe had hoped she might have been more sympathetic. He needed sympathy rather than judgment. He already knew the possible consequences of his actions; he knew what the potential ramifications would be once Greenwood found out. He simply had to trust Shakespeare's words: that it was all going to work out. He was already in far too deep to change course now.

Carefully picking up Desdemona and placing her on the couch beside him, he stood up. He reached over and turned on the radio, seeking distraction from his thoughts. Tommy Dorsey's "Alone" burst from the radio. It was a fitting song for his current circumstances.

He crossed the room and stood in front of the window, staring out into the night as a trumpet solo drifted in the air. The moon, a huge white orb, hovered over the ocean, casting a silvery glow on the surface of the water. He rubbed his chin thoughtfully as he gazed at it. The reflection danced with the rippled movements of the water.

"'Tis truly beautiful, is it not?"

Joe turned to see Shakespeare standing by the bookshelf. The Bard was wearing a different doublet from the one he had worn before. This one was bright red with a high, stiff neck and a row of brass buttons newly polished and gleaming in the light of the living room. Delicate white lace protruded from his cuffs.

"What is?" Joe asked.

"The play of moonlight upon the water. It doth strike a pleasing chord in me. And yet, at the same time, it evokes a piercing melancholy. I hath observed it often and yet I ask how such a tableau canst stir feelings of such opposite and opposed sentiments. 'Tis wondrous strange."

"Spoken like a poet," Joe said. He crossed back to the radio and turned down the volume just as Jo Stafford began to croon "Manhattan Serenade."

Shakespeare gave a dismissive shrug. "Nay, 'tis more like a man fumbling to express that which cannot adequately be expressed in mere words."

"What would Uncle Jim say?"

Shakespeare raised an eyebrow. "About yon moon?"

Joe nodded.

Shakespeare chuckled and gently stroked his goatee. "Much the same sentiment, I fathom. Yet the words wouldst be different. The man was attuned more to numbers than words."

"You speak of him in the third person," Joe observed. "Isn't that a little odd?"

"In faith, it must indeed sound so," Shakespeare agreed. "But 'tis a thing in which one may easily fall. When I assume the guise of Jim, I find myself speaking of Will in much the same terms."

"But they're both you," Joe said. "Or you're both of them." He hesitated and gave a muddled shake of his head. "I'm not sure how to say it. It's confusing."

"Aye, indeed. I am them and they are me. They wilt always be a part of me. As I wilt always be a part of them."

Joe looked at Shakespeare with a clear and direct gaze. "Then... who are you?"

"Both of them, and more."

"We're an amalgam of all our lives?"

Shakespeare nodded. "'Tis so," he said. "We hath all had many faces." He paused, thinking. "Imagine a string of pearls. Each pearl is a life, yet yon string connects each pearl. We are, ultimately, that string."

"And all those pearls?"

Shakespeare nodded. "Each pearl is a particular vibration—with particular memories and experiences. If we choose, we canst step into that vibration and experience those memories yet again."

Joe thought for a moment. "How many lives have I had?"

"Thou hast lived nearly forty lives."

"Forty?"

Shakespeare nodded. "Thou art surprised?"

"It seems like a lot," he said.

"'Tis around the same amount as the lives I hath lived."

"What was I? In some of my lives, I mean."

Shakespeare smiled. "I hath been waiting for thee to ask." He paused. "Thou were an Athenian hoplite at the battle of Marathon."

"Really? Did I survive?"

He shook his head. "Nay, sadly, thou died that day defending thy city thou loved."

"I see." Joe nodded. "What else was I?"

"Many things. A Sumerian scribe. A member of the Jewish Sanhedrin. A Jesuit. And thou were also a Chinese soldier during the Tang dynasty."

Joe sat back down on the couch. He softly stroked Desdemona. The two men were silent for several long minutes as Joe considered Shakespeare's analogy of the string of pearls. After a time, they fell into a comfortable, lingering silence, simply listening to the radio. Gradually, however, the day's events slowly crept back into Joe's consciousness.

"I see that thou art distressed," Shakespeare said.

Joe sighed. "I assume you heard Betsy's reaction today."

"Aye," Shakespeare said, nodding. "And I advise patience and tolerance if thou wilt accept such advice."

Joe continued to stroke the cat. "I knew she was going to be upset once I told her, but—"

Shakespeare was silent, watching Joe with a rueful smile, waiting for him to finish.

Joe sighed again and shook his head sadly. "I guess I was hoping she'd be more understanding." After that, he fell silent as the music continued to play.

———————

At the studio the next day, Joe had trouble concentrating. He and Shakespeare worked on *The Apple Orchard* but weren't making much headway. Joe found himself easily distracted, restless, morose, and irritable. To cap things off, Joe had heard through the grapevine that Greenwood was on a tear; apparently, the producer had recovered from his bout of food poisoning and returned to a studio rife with rumors of dissatisfaction among the Carpenter's Union. They were angry that several members had allegedly been forced to repair a set, and that the repairs had constituted an overtime issue for which they hadn't been paid. The "strike" word hadn't been uttered yet, but tensions were high. Greenwood had been involved in a long meeting early that morning with the union's representatives, which apparently hadn't gone well.

By mid-day, Joe's restlessness had become all-consuming. He was about to grab his jacket and go for a walk when, to his surprise, the cottage phone began to ring. For a moment, he stared at it, thinking about simply letting it ring. But curiosity got the better of him.

"Writer's cottage," Joe said, answering, "Holliday speaking."

"Hi, Joe." There was considerable static on the line, but Joe immediately recognized Betsy's voice.

"Hi, Betsy." Joe paused for an awkward moment. "How are you?"

"I'm sorry I ran out on you like that yesterday," she said. "That was rude. You didn't deserve it."

"It's okay," Joe said. "I understand why you were upset. I don't blame you. It was a lot to take in. I'm afraid I dumped a lot on your lap."

"I've thought about it all day," Betsy went on, "and I want you to know I support you. I don't quite understand what you're doing, but I love you and support you. I want you to know that. You're a good man and I know you wouldn't be doing this without some type of reason."

"Thanks, I appreciate it," Joe said. "I don't exactly know where all this is headed myself, but I have to trust that Shakespeare isn't leading me astray." He paused. "He can't be."

"Have you asked him about any of this?"

"Yes, of course."

"What has he told you?"

"To trust him," Joe explained. "To trust that everything will work out."

"God, when you first told me you weren't actually writing *Hamlet* but that other play, I couldn't believe it. And then when you said you were lying to Greenwood, I nearly hit the roof. I couldn't believe you were actually telling me that." She paused. "But I'm over it. I have to trust there's some reason for all this. Some overarching plan."

"I hope so, too," Joe said. "By the way, where are you calling me from?"

"The commissary phone," Betsy replied. "Why?"

"Horrible static."

"Yeah, I know. But that's life in the fiefdom of Greenwood. Low budget."

"Anyway," Joe said, "will you be around tonight? Maybe we could grab a malt at Duke's?"

"You've got a date, buster," Betsy said.

———————

Betsy hung up the phone. She turned and nearly bumped into

Elsa. For a moment she stared at the blond actress, wondering how long she'd been standing there, and if she'd heard anything. But before Betsy could say anything Elsa spoke up.

"Can we talk, Betsy?"

"About what?"

"I want to apologize," Elsa said. "I was jealous, and I let my jealousy get the better of me."

Betsy was silent. She gazed at her friend with skeptical eyes.

"I was an idiot," Elsa went on, "and I'm sorry."

Betsy remained silent. As she stared at her former friend, she suddenly had the feeling that Elsa's apology was insincere, that it was all an act. She felt it in her gut. Finally, she spoke up. "Look, Els, I appreciate the apology, I really do, but maybe we should both stay out of each other's business for a while."

"I understand why you feel that way," Elsa said, "and maybe you're right, but I still wanted to apologize."

"Apology accepted." Betsy turned and strode away. When she had covered nearly the entire length of the commissary, she allowed herself a glance back over her shoulder. She saw that Elsa had picked up the phone and was dialing it.

————

Joe felt immeasurably better after talking to Betsy. It had buoyed his confidence and set his mind at ease. After hanging up the phone, instead of taking a walk, he fired up the Silex machine. Soon the cottage was filled with the savory aroma of brewing coffee.

He and Shakespeare spent the rest of the afternoon working on *The Apple Orchard*. At five o'clock, just when Joe was packing up to leave for the day, he heard a knock at the door. Before he could answer, the door creaked opened on its hinges. Joe was surprised to see Roger Powell standing on the threshold.

"Sorry to bother you," the actor said, smiling pleasantly. "But I've been meaning to see the new digs. Hope you don't mind."

Joe stared at the actor for a moment. "No, of course not," he answered at length.

Roger strode forward, his hand outstretched. "I'm Roger Powell, by the way. I don't believe we've met. But I must confess, I do know who you are. You're Joe Holliday, the illustrious writer of *Hamlet*."

"Adapter," Joe corrected him.

"Of course," Roger said with a lop-sided grin. "My mistake. There is only one writer of that great masterpiece."

"I'm afraid I was just about to leave," Joe said. As he spoke, he stole a quick glance at Shakespeare who was standing to one side, his arms crossed. The Bard's face was inscrutable.

"I won't be a minute," Roger replied, "just wanted to look around." He whistled a jaunty tune and surveyed the inside, gazing about the room with a discerning eye. "This is some place you got here. 'Ole Greenwood didn't spare any expense, did he?"

"Yes, it's quite nice."

Roger's gaze fell back on Joe. "I understand you've got this place to yourself." He grinned. "Must be nice."

"Just until I finish *Hamlet*. Then it'll be open to all the writers."

"I see." Roger's gaze continued to roam around the room, eventually coming to the Remington and alighting on the neatly stacked pages of *The Apple Orchard* that was lying next to the machine. Luckily, the manuscript was lying face down.

Roger nodded at it with his chin. "That must be *Hamlet*, right?"

A twinge of uneasiness coursed through Joe, but he brushed it off. "Yes, that's it."

"Looks like you've got quite a bit done. I'm impressed."

Joe nodded. "It's coming along."

Roger stared at the manuscript for a moment longer. Then he looked up. "All of us have great hopes for *Hamlet*. I think it's the most creative thing Greenwood's done in a long while. It'll be good for Apex. A win-win situation, I think. But I'm a little surprised he wanted to do it, aren't you? I mean, he's never been interested in real art."

Joe shrugged. "Sometimes people surprise you."

"You're certainly right about that." Roger stole another glance around the room as he spoke. "I'll admit I was sorely disappointed when Gable got the part of Hamlet and I didn't. I was really hoping to stretch myself as an actor. I'm told Barrymore spent six months rehearsing the part. Can you believe it? Six months." He shook his head in seeming amazement. "But you can't win 'em all, can you? What's that French phrase? 'Such is life.'"

"*C'est la vie.*"

"My sentiments exactly," Roger said.

Joe grabbed his jacket. He checked his pockets to make sure he had his keys and looked at his watch.

Roger plopped down in one of the chairs and propped his feet up on a desk. "I must say," he said. "I admire you writers."

"Oh?"

"Yes," he nodded, "I admire you writers very much. Must be difficult thinking of stories all day. How do you do it?"

"How do I think up stories?"

Roger nodded.

"Well, when they pay you to think up stories it adds a bit of incentive."

Roger laughed. "I imagine that it would. Still, it can't be easy." He paused to scratch his chin. "Didn't someone once say there were only four true plots or something like that? And that all stories originate from those."

"That was Jung," Joe said.

"Ah, yes, Sigmund Jung."

"Carl Jung," Joe corrected him. "He derived the idea from his concept of the archetype. Schopenhauer had a similar concept. Except he called it a prototype."

Roger's eyes grew large and he chuckled. "Well, I see you've studied this stuff."

Joe nodded but didn't say anything.

"Don't you think it's strange we've never worked together?" Roger said.

"We have worked together," Joe replied. Roger had starred in one of Joe's early scripts, a picture called *Buccaneer Vengeance*, a story about swashbucklers of the Spanish Main. But Joe doubted Roger remembered. The actor had talked to only two people during the entire shoot, his ravishing red-haired co-star, Gloria Sullivan, and the director. He had treated everyone else with disdain.

"Did we?" Roger was surprised.

Joe jangled his keys. He tried not to seem too impatient.

"Oh, that's right," Roger said, springing to his feet. "You said you had to go, didn't you?"

"Yes, I'm afraid so."

Roger extended his hand. "Well, it was nice to meet you."

Joe shook it. "Nice to meet you, too."

Roger made for the door but stopped and turned back around. His eyes fell on *The Apple Orchard* once again. He stared at it for a long moment and looked like he was about to say something but apparently decided against it and left. When he was gone, Joe locked the cottage door and started out across the lot. Ten minutes later, he passed through the arch-like front gate and left the studio. Turning north, he walked a few blocks until he came to Duke's.

———

"What on earth was Roger doing there?" Betsy asked, her tone suspicious.

"I don't know," Joe shrugged. He took a sip of his Coke. "But it was a little strange."

"More than a little." She frowned and her eyes narrowed as she gazed across the room. "What's he up to?"

"He was pretty chatty. Acted like I was an old college buddy or something."

"If you ask me, it sounds like he wanted something," Betsy said.

"He never asked me for anything. Like I said, sounded like he just wanted to chat."

"Roger never 'just wants to chat.' There's always some ulterior motive."

"Well," Joe said, "if there was, he hid it pretty well."

The sound of Artie Shaw's clarinet broke from the jukebox and filled the room, cutting through all the chatter. A few couples got up to dance.

"Anyway," Betsy said, "I'm really sorry I jumped down your throat yesterday."

"Like I said, you're forgiven. I did drop a lot on your plate."

"I'm still concerned," she said. "I mean, I still think it's crazy, but I trust you when you say it'll all work out."

Joe took another sip of Coke. He had no clue how the whole thing was going to work out. He was simply putting his trust in Shakespeare.

"Hey, I just had a thought," Betsy said, brightening.

"What?"

"What if it turns out that Greenwood likes *The Apple Orchard* so much he decides to scrap *Hamlet* and make a picture out of it instead?" She grinned. "Wouldn't that be something?"

"Yeah, that would be something," Joe said, chuckling.

"You never know," Betsy said. "Stranger things can happen."

Joe nodded. "Stranger things can—and do—happen. My life has certainly been a testimony to that."

———————

Later that evening, sometime after midnight, the figure of a man dressed all in black furtively made his way across the Apex Studio lot. Carrying a crowbar and wearing a mask that looked like it had come from the set of a *Zorro* movie, he darted from building to building, trying to stay out of the moonlight. He stopped several yards away from the writer's cottage and glanced around, making sure no one was nearby. Then, crouching low, he moved silently across the lawn and sidled up to the front door. Carefully he ran his hand along the crease between the door and the doorframe.

He inserted the crowbar into the crease, wedging it in good and tight. He looked around again, scanning the area. When he was satisfied that he was alone, he took a firm grip of the crowbar and yanked. The door buckled but didn't budge. Gritting his teeth, he readjusted his grip and gave a tremendous yank on the crowbar.

This time there was a loud crack and the door swung open.

Chapter 22

Morning dawned bright and early. Joe left his cottage, took the Red Car up Santa Monica Boulevard, and arrived at Apex Studios around nine o'clock. But he was surprised to find Woody barring his way.

"I'm sorry, Mr. Holliday," Woody said, his voice firm, "but I can't let you in."

Joe was surprised. "What do you mean? Why not?"

"Greenwood's orders, sir. I'm sorry."

"What's this all about?" Joe demanded.

"I don't know, sir. But like I said, I can't let you in."

"What am I supposed to do? Just stand here?"

"Please stay here for a moment, sir," Woody said. "I was told to give the executive offices a call the moment you arrived."

Joe gave an irritated sigh and nodded.

Woody bustled into the kiosk, closed the door behind him, and dialed the phone. Because the door was closed, Joe couldn't hear what was said. In a moment, Woody came back out. "They're sending someone out right away, sir."

"Someone? Who?"

"An escort, sir."

"What do I need an escort for?" Joe asked. He stared hard at Woody. "Do you know what this is all about?"

"I'm afraid I don't, sir. I'm sorry."

After that, Joe was quiet. He stood with his hands in his pockets, his expression glum. He wondered whether Greenwood had somehow discovered *The Apple Orchard.* Immediately Betsy's suggestion that Greenwood might, in fact, be enamored by the play flashed through his mind. Perhaps it wasn't as absurd as it had sounded. Maybe that was what Shakespeare had meant by everything eventually working out.

Ten minutes later, a man arrived whom Joe had never seen before. He told Joe in no uncertain terms he was going to accompany him to the executive offices. From the way the man looked—like a scarred ex-prizefighter—Joe figured he wouldn't be very communicative, so he didn't try to ask why he was being escorted.

The two men started off across the lot, walking side by side. Joe felt his initial bloom of optimism fade and wilt to nothing. It was absurd to think Greenwood would react with anything except anger when he found out about *The Apple Orchard.* Still, Shakespeare's words about "everything working out" resounded in his mind. But as they neared the executive offices, Joe increasingly felt like a prisoner being escorted to a prison cell block.

They soon arrived and took the elevator up, proceeding to Greenwood's office. Without a word, Joe's escort opened the door and let him inside.

Marjorie Hayden was sitting behind her desk. She looked up at Joe's arrival and adjusted her glasses, staring at him with narrowed eyes.

"Hello, Ms. Hayden," Joe said. He tried to put a positive spin on the situation and said, somewhat flippantly, "I was wondering what all the fuss—"

"Mr. Greenwood will see you right away," Marjorie said, cutting him off. Her voice, as always, was matter-of-fact, though this time Joe detected a hint of hostility. "Please go in."

Feeling his stomach tightening, Joe entered Greenwood's inner sanctum. The room was dimly lit, the only source of light coming from a lamp on Greenwood's table.

The movie mogul was behind his desk. He was sitting very still, his elbows on the arms of his chair and his fingertips steepled together, gazing at Joe through his thick spectacles. At first, Joe wasn't sure how to read Greenwood. But then his eyes alighted on a manuscript sitting on the middle of the producer's desk. Joe recognized it immediately as *The Apple Orchard.*

"Well, well, well," Greenwood said, breaking the silence. His voice carried a pale, cold menace. "Who knew I had a Benedict Arnold in my midst."

Joe's heart sank.

"You lying son-of-a-bitch!" Greenwood spat out, standing up, his face crimson. "Who the hell do you think you are? Think you can pull one over on me?"

"Listen, I know this looks bad Mr. Greenwood, but—"

"Where the hell is my *Hamlet!*" the mogul thundered. He stabbed a finger at the manuscript. "And what the hell is this?"

"It's called *The Apple Orchard,* sir. It's—"

"I know what it says, you idiot. I can read! I want to know why it doesn't say *Hamlet.*"

"Please, if you'll just calm down for a moment."

"Calm down!" Greenwood's face grew even more crimson and the veins on his forehead trembled. "You have the nerve to tell me to calm down!" His voice spilled forth with fathomless contempt. "You lying, traitorous piece of shit!"

Joe felt his face stiffen. He did his best to quell the anger that was beginning to overtake him at Greenwood's constant abuse. He needed to stay as rational as possible.

"What do you have to say for yourself?" Greenwood demanded. "You never had any intention of working on *Hamlet,* did you?"

"No, sir, I didn't," Joe said. "You're right, I lied to you."

Greenwood was stunned by Joe's admission. "You admit it?"

"Yes, I admit it."

Greenwood snorted. "And, what, you're proud of that? Proud of pulling the wool over the boss's eyes?"

"No, sir, I'm not proud of lying to you," Joe said, shaking his head. "But, yes, I did lie."

"So, what do you have to say for yourself?" Greenwood

repeated. Surprisingly, he had calmed somewhat. His face was less red, but his eyes were still blazing.

Joe cleared his throat. "Nothing."

"Nothing?" Greenwood looked at him, incredulous. His glasses slid down his nose and he pushed them back up. "What do you mean, nothing?"

"There's not much point in trying to defend myself," Joe said. "I'm guilty as charged."

Greenwood glared at him. "Let me get this straight," he said, continuing in a condescending manner. "Did I, or did I not, contract you to write a revised *Hamlet?*"

"Yes, you did."

"But you wrote this instead," Greenwood said, jabbing a finger at the manuscript again. "What the hell is this, anyway? I can't even tell if it's a screenplay or a play. I don't understand a god-damned word of it."

"It's a play," Joe said.

"So, you spent your time working on this 'play' rather than what you were contracted to write? Is that correct?"

"Yes, that's correct."

Greenwood paused for a moment, his eyes hard. "So, you're saying you deliberately lied to me. You deceived me into thinking you were writing my screenplay when all the time you were writing this?"

"Yes," Joe said. He was rapidly tiring of Greenwood's condescension. "We've already established that I lied to you."

Greenwood burst into white-hot anger once more. "You're fired, Holliday!" he bellowed. "You're through! Canned! Kaput!! You'll never work as a screenwriter again. By God, I'll see to that!"

Although Joe was angry, he was surprisingly calm. "Is that all?"

Greenwood seethed with rage, spittle flying from his lips. "You want more? I'll give you more! Since you were well paid last month while you were supposed to be working on *Hamlet*, I consider this *Apple Tree* thing, or whatever the hell you call it, the property of the studio. It's mine." He smiled smugly. "In fact,

I always needed a good doorstop."

It was a long moment before Joe said anything. "I probably should've said this a long time ago, Mr. Greenwood, but I'll say it now: You can go to hell."

Without waiting for a response, Joe left the office amid a hail of curses, deprecations, and threats.

———————

A warm Santa Ana breeze was blowing as Joe made his way down the sidewalk. It swirled along the street and kicked up trash and debris about his ankles.

With his hands in his pockets, he walked rapidly, with the intention of getting as far away from the studio as possible. Cars passed back and forth on the street, but he didn't notice. His mind was still focused on his argument with Greenwood. He could still hear the angry words resounding in his head, lingering in the ether like a bad dream.

He would be the first to admit what he'd done was wrong, but he'd put his faith in Shakespeare. He'd trusted the Bard, believed the ghost when he'd said that everything would eventually "work out."

But it was obvious everything hadn't worked out. He felt like a dupe, and he wondered if he'd been played. He wondered if he was the butt of some giant cosmic joke. But that was absurd. Utterly absurd. He couldn't imagine Shakespeare was capable of such a thing. Rationally, he knew there had to be some other reason. But he was at a loss to think what that other reason might be. Still, his irrational side was immensely annoyed at Shakespeare—angry even. Why hadn't Shakespeare warned him? What was the whole point of this exercise, anyway? What about Shakespeare's strict adherence to the law of non-interference? To Joe, this seemed like interference on a massive scale.

In the meantime, he had more practical matters to juggle. He was out of a job. And he wondered whether Greenwood's threat—about ever finding work as a screenwriter—was credible. There were other movie studios in Hollywood, of course, and Joe knew Greenwood wasn't too well liked in the industry. So, it was possible that Greenwood's threat was ultimately hollow. By the same token, Greenwood wasn't someone to be trifled with; the man did have influence. He did wield a certain amount of power. Despite the string of B pictures the studio cranked out, Greenwood generated a lot of money. And, as everyone knew, "money talked."

Joe came to a newsstand and glanced at the headlines. He saw that parliamentary elections had been held in Germany and that the Nazi Party had won ninety-nine percent of the vote. He also noticed that no opposition parties had been allowed. On a lighter note, he read that baseball season had begun with a bang: the Cleveland Indians had trounced the Detroit Tigers in a one-sided victory, eleven to one.

Joe continued walking, eventually coming to a streetcar stop where he hopped on the Red Car. He rode it all the way to Santa Monica, got off, and walked the rest of the way to his cottage.

He unlocked the door and let himself inside. Desdemona was asleep atop a cabinet. When she heard him enter the living room she hopped down from her perch, stretched languidly, and padded over.

"Hi Dez," he said, reaching down to pet her. "You're probably wondering why I'm here early."

The cat meowed and rubbed against his ankles, purring loudly.

Joe went over to a cabinet and took down a bottle of scotch. He poured himself a splash and went over to the window. He sipped the drink slowly and looked out at the water. The sun sparkled on the surface of a sea rippled by the Santa Ana breeze.

He sighed and glanced at the clock on the wall. It was fifteen minutes before noon. He was never at home at this time of day during the work week and it felt strange. Like he was violating some unwritten rule. Or transgressing some Calvinist-inspired injunction against loafing at home during a workday. In fact, the whole day felt surreal, like he was living in a bad dream.

He decided he needed to take a walk on the beach. He'd found that a stroll on the sand was a great way to clear his head and restore some semblance of normalcy. He'd always been able to do just about anything better—writing or thinking—after a beach walk.

After downing the rest of the scotch in one gulp, he went outside. The breeze was blowing through the coastal canyons and out toward the water, carrying with it the scent of sage. He lingered outside the door for a moment, and closed his eyes, breathing deeply. The air felt pleasingly dry in his lungs. He opened his eyes and stared out at the water. The sea glittered in the mid-day light, and gentle waves were rolling up and down the beach.

He strode onto the sand, which was hot from the direct sun. He veered down toward the water's edge and, rolling up his pant cuffs, strolled through damp sand, which was cool under his bare feet. He walked for a ways, leaving deep impressions behind him. There was something about sand between his toes that was invigorating. Right now, it helped him forget the awful scene in Greenwood's office.

Up ahead was a flock of seagulls. They took to the air as he approached, wings flapping frantically. He stopped and looked up, squinting against the glare. Squawking and screeching, they circled out over the blue water and made toward the horizon.

Continuing along, he came across the carcass of a dead sea lion. It lay bloated and rotting, tangled in seaweed, half in the sand and half in the water. Waves rolled in and thumped against it, moving it around in a haphazard fashion, pushing it this way and that. The animal's eyes, protruding and dark, stared up at him, vacuous of life.

———————

When he got back to the cottage hours later, he was surprised to see Betsy at the front door. She was dressed in a blouse and light sweater and carrying a paper shopping bag as if she'd just come from the grocery store. She looked up at the sound of his footsteps. "I was just about to leave," she said. "I didn't think you were in."

"What are you doing here?" Joe asked.

"I came to make you supper."

"You didn't have to do that."

"I know I didn't have to," Betsy said. "I wanted to."

"Anyway," Joe said glumly, "I'm sorry, Betsy, I'm just not really hungry."

"Yes, you are," she said, "you just don't know it yet."

There was no sense in arguing with her, Joe figured. He unlocked the door and allowed her to enter. She breezed into the kitchen and put the bag of groceries down on the counter. Wrinkling her nose, she cast a disapproving glance at the dirty dishes that lay in a haphazard pile in the sink. She came back out as Joe was sitting down on the couch.

"There's no point in pretending you don't know why I'm here," Betsy said, looking squarely at him. "It's all over the studio. No one's ever seen Greenwood so angry. And that's saying something."

"It's funny," Joe said, settling himself. "I've never actually been fired. It's a bit sobering. When I lost my job at Troy Studios it wasn't because of anything I'd done. It was because the studio went bankrupt. They let go of everyone."

"Do you want to know why I think Greenwood was so mad?" Betsy said.

"Why?"

"Because deep down, I think he actually liked you."

"I don't think he likes anyone," Joe said.

"No, I'm serious," Betsy insisted. "You were his 'golden boy.'"

"Hard to believe. He always struck me as an equal opportunity insulter."

Betsy sat down on the couch next to him. "Sure, he insulted you like he did everyone else. But it was obvious he considered you his most talented screenwriter." She paused. "That's why I think it hurt so much when you—"

"When I betrayed him?"

Betsy frowned. "I wouldn't exactly use that word."

"I would," Joe said, "because that's kind of what happened."

They were both quiet. Joe stared across the room.

"What are you going to do now?" Betsy asked at length.

Joe scratched his cheek and shrugged. "I don't know," he said. "I really don't know."

Betsy stared at him for a moment and then stood up. "Well, in the meantime, I'm going to make dinner." She bustled off into the kitchen, leaving Joe alone with his thoughts. He stared at the opposite wall. Except for the noises coming from the kitchen as Betsy prepared dinner, the cottage was quiet. His psychic senses detected a presence standing next to the bookshelf. Immediately he shook his head as if to clear it. If the presence was Shakespeare, he wasn't in the mood to hear what the Bard had to say. He was still angry and didn't want to engage the ghost in conversation. Gradually, he noticed, the presence faded into nothingness.

Betsy poked her head out of the kitchen. "Dinner's ready," she announced.

That night, Joe tossed and turned in bed, unable to sleep. A million thoughts, worries, and fears raced around in his head, each vying for his attention. All of these seemed to pile one on top of the other so that it seemed as if a huge weight was bearing down on him. What was he going to do now that he'd been fired? Would be able to find work? More pointedly, would he be able to work as a screen-writer again? Would he be able to pay his rent? Would he be able to feed himself? It was as if the cozy little world he'd created for himself had suddenly been pulled out from under him. Gradually, despite all these thoughts, he drifted off. As he slipped into dreams, he felt the presence of someone standing at the foot of his bed.

Joe found himself walking alongside Shakespeare down a long corridor. The floor was marble and on either side were evenly spaced Greek columns. There were no walls between the columns so that Joe could look out and catch glimpses of green, rolling hills and vivid blue skies.

242

He stopped. "Where are we?" he asked.

"Come," Shakespeare said, gently taking Joe's arm and leading him forward.

They continued walking in silence, the only sound was their footsteps echoing hollowly on the marble. They came to the end of the corridor, which contained a door. Shakespeare opened it and bade Joe step inside.

He entered a great hall with a high vaulted ceiling. It angled up to form a rectangular skylight through which golden sunlight streamed down in a single illuminating column. The column fell on a massive fountain, the centerpiece of which contained two Olympian gods carved out of marble and standing side-by-side. On the left was Apollo, the god of poetry, art, and music. Standing next to him, wearing her plumed helmet, was Athena, the goddess of wisdom, inspiration, knowledge, law, and justice. On either side of the hall were massive, reinforced bookcases divided into separate levels or stories that ran from the floor to the ceiling. Each level contained its own outthrust balcony so that one could browse. Access to the higher levels, Joe noticed, was through a series of staircases that led from one level to the next. The bookshelves were crammed with books and scrolls so numerous it was overwhelming. There seemed to be every conceivable piece of literature—books, manuscripts, scrolls, codices, papyri, tablets, everything. Joe had never seen anything like it.

Joe felt Shakespeare come up and stand next to him.

"What is this place?" Joe asked. His voice was marked with unconcealed wonder and awe.

"Doth it feel familiar to thee?" Shakespeare asked.

Joe was silent for a moment, searching his memory. Although he didn't think he'd ever been here before, there was nonetheless a strange feeling of familiarity. It seemed to emanate from his gut. It was almost instinctual.

"Yes," he nodded, "but I don't know why."

Shakespeare smiled.

"How many books are here?" Joe said, his gaze traveling from floor to ceiling.

"Verily, my friend," Shakespeare said, "that number is countless."

Joe took several more steps into the room. The place reminded him of a massive cathedral, except it was filled with books. He turned to Shakespeare again. "I still don't understand. What is this place? Why am I here?"

"'Tis a library," Shakespeare said. "Though thou doth not remember, thou hath been here many times." The Bard nodded as if to reinforce his statement. "Indeed, many times."

"I have?"

"Aye. Between lives we doth come here often. 'Tis what thou might call 'our sanctuary.'"

Joe was simply speechless as he continued to look around. "It's amazing," he said.

CHAPTER 23

IT HAD BEEN A week since Joe had gotten the boot from Apex Studios, and he had spent most of it simply loafing. He'd slept in late most mornings and stayed up late most evenings. During the day, he'd either taken long beach walks or read. The only productive thing he'd done was draft a few half-hearted letters to the various studios in town inquiring after work. But he hadn't yet sent them out because his typewriter—his beloved Remington—was still at the studio.

Betsy had been by almost every night, bringing him food, admonishing him about drinking too much scotch, or just trying to cheer him up. He was grateful for her visits because he knew she genuinely cared about his welfare and wanted to help. Nothing seemed to rattle her, or if it did, she camouflaged it well. They had discussed his future a few times, but Joe wasn't in the mood to go into any great detail. Frankly, at least for the time being, he didn't have the energy to map out his future. Truth be told, he wasn't sure what he wanted to do; he wasn't certain he wanted to go back to screenwriting. It had satisfied him in the past, but now he wasn't so sure it would satisfy him in the future.

He hadn't spoken to Shakespeare the entire time. He was still angry with the Bard and had effectively banished him from his life, though he'd shown up in Joe's dreams here and there. Strangely, in his dreams Joe wasn't angry with Shakespeare at all; it was only when he awoke that he remembered his situation and his anger—like a reignited flame—would flare up again.

On Saturday morning he arose late, made himself a cup of coffee, and checked his mail from the previous day, which lay in a pile on his kitchen table. He'd collected it but hadn't yet looked through it. He saw that he had a letter from the Screen Writer's Union. He carefully slit the envelope open with a knife and extracted the letter. He unfolded it and began to read:

Dear Mr. Holliday,

We regret to inform you that we have decided to terminate your membership with the Screen Writer's Union. This was not a decision we took lightly nor was it made in haste. Considerable thought has gone into it, and all appropriate protocols, as per the union's guidelines, were followed. All members voted on the action and a majority decided the outcome. Given your complete disregard for your contract with Apex Studios, we believe our decision is justified. However, if you wish to appeal the decision you have that right. To do so, you must send a letter to the union formally requesting reinstatement.

In the meantime, please turn over your membership card and all sundry documents acquired during your time as a Union member.

Sincerely,
Sidney Maxwell
Acting President, SWU

That didn't take long, Joe thought sourly. Sidney must have been chomping at the bit to write that letter. "Considerable thought." "Appropriate protocols." What a crock! Angrily, Joe crumpled up the letter, kneaded it into a tight ball, and tossed it into a trashcan next to the sink.

He paced the room, trying to control his anger, his fists clenched. In his mind's eye, he could picture Sidney's sanctimonious face grinning at him.

Still angry, he wandered out to the patio and sat down in one of the wicker chairs, which squeaked under his weight. He stared out at the water. The waves matched his mood this morning; they thundered against the beach in a riot of whitewater.

To his surprise, he felt an entity around him. But it wasn't Shakespeare. When he tuned in, he saw that it was a young boy, maybe nine or ten years old with a mop of unruly blond hair, freckles, and a pair of denim overalls over a stained white shirt. His face was smudged and grubby and he had dirt under his fingernails. Joe was reminded of Huckleberry Finn; the only thing he lacked was the corncob pipe.

"Hello," Joe said.

The boy grinned at him, showing a gap between his two front teeth. "Howdy," he said.

"I've never seen you before," Joe continued. "Where did you come from?"

"From?" the entity said. He looked confused. "I ain't come from nowhere."

"How did you get here?"

"Was just passing by," the boy said.

"But you came to see me."

"Oh, that," the boy said, "that's just 'cause you can see me. Most people can't."

"I see," Joe nodded.

"Ya know," the entity said, "when I get angry, I count to ten."

"Does it help?"

"Works every time," he said, nodding his head in an exaggerated gesture. "Then, heck, I ain't angry no more."

"I'll have to try that," Joe said, grinning at the boy. "But I have to admit, just talking to you has calmed me down."

The boy grinned back. "Knew it would."

"You knew, eh?" Joe scratched his chin in mock contemplation. "I have a feeling you weren't just passing by."

The ghost didn't say anything; he continued to grin toothily. "Know what?"

"What?"

"I can make butterflies."

"You can *make* them?"

He nodded. "Wanna see?"

"Sure," Joe said.

The boy raised his arm over his head, his fingers closed and making a fist. When he opened his hand, several beautifully colored butterflies flew out, as if conjured by magic. They flitted about his head, dancing in the air, iridescent wings fluttering gently. Joe watched as they lifted higher and, caught by the breeze, began to drift away. Mesmerized, Joe followed their ascent. To his surprise, they gradually began to dissipate, leaving only a trail of color against the sky, like a rainbow. But that faded, too.

Impressed, Joe turned back to the boy. "Wow, that was—" He stopped, flabbergasted.

The boy was no longer a boy. It was Ching Su. As always, the monk was clad in his saffron robe and a pair of open-toed sandals. He smiled, clasped his hands together and bowed reverently so that Joe saw the top of his shaved head. In seconds, he, too, was gone—faded into nothingness like the butterflies.

Later that afternoon, as Joe lounged on the couch smoking a cigarette, a folded newspaper across his chest, he heard the rumble of a car engine outside. He listened as it grew louder, drawing near, its engine clattering. He heard the squeak of tires and then the engine idle briefly before shutting off. Soon there was a knock at the door. Joe tossed the newspaper aside and stubbed out his cigarette in an already overflowing ashtray. He heaved himself up from the couch and went to the door. When he opened it, he was surprised to see Gable. Behind him, parked on the curb, was the actor's Packard De Luxe Eight, shining brilliantly in the afternoon sun.

"Hey, chief," Gable said.

Joe recovered from his surprise. "Clark, what are you doing here?"

"Was in the neighborhood," the actor grinned, "and thought I'd swing by."

"It's good to see you," Joe said. "Come in." He stepped back and held open the door.

Gable angled his broad shoulders through the doorway and stepped inside. He looked around, noticing the clutter: the clothes draped on chairs, plates and cups scattered about the furniture, and ashtrays filled to the brim with cigarette butts. "Definitely looks lived in."

"Sorry about the mess," Joe said. "I guess I've just been loafing around recently."

Both men were quiet for a moment.

"Look," Joe said, "I want to apologize. I'm really sorry I lied to you. I never meant—"

"Don't apologize," Gable said, holding up a hand. "There's no need. Hell, I don't pretend to know why you did it, but I figure you had your reasons." He shrugged. "And anyway, I'm not sure I was right for the role."

"I don't know if I agree," Joe said. "I think you might have surprised yourself."

Gable gave a self-conscious grin. "Anyway, I heard about how you stuck it to Greenwood. That makes everything all right in my book. Wish I'd been there. I don't think anyone's ever told him to go to hell before. Heck, you're my hero." He paused. "By the way, that's the real reason I swung by."

Joe gave the actor a curious look. "To praise me for sticking it to Greenwood?"

"No," Gable said, "to tell you I'm through with him, too."

Joe looked at him. "What do you mean?"

"I tendered my resignation, you might say. MGM's been hounding me for months. So, I finally jumped ship."

"You're with MGM now?"

"That's right. Just signed the contract yesterday. Ink's barely dry."

"Poor Greenwood," Joe said, shaking his head. "Two setbacks in one week."

"He's a big boy, he'll get over it. Anyway, I'd been thinking about getting out of there for months. I guess when you made your move, it spurred me to make mine."

"That's great, but my move was far from calculated," Joe said. "It just kind of happened. Still, I'm glad it gave you some incentive. It always seemed to me you weren't very happy at Apex."

"I wasn't," Gable admitted. He paused. "Remember when we talked about that Roman emperor?"

"Marcus Aurelius?" Joe nodded. "Yes, of course."

"That helped, too."

"How so?"

"Remember when you said we create our own reality about how we think about things? Well, I realized I needed to really think about my life; I needed to make a decision about my career. No one was gonna make it for me. The jump to MGM was something I really wanted to do—so, damn it, I did it. And damn the torpedoes."

Joe grinned. "Then we've both been freed, I suppose. At least yours was voluntary. I'm still debating the wisdom of mine. Anyway, to celebrate our emancipation proclamation why don't we have a beer? You want one?" he asked. "We can drink a toast to Marcus Aurelius."

"That sounds just about right," Gable said, chuckling.

Ten minutes later, they were seated outside on the patio and were discussing Gable's move to MGM.

"I'm going to work with Selznick," Gable said, taking a sip of beer. "You know him?"

"David O. Selznick?"

Gable nodded.

"Not personally," Joe said. "But I know of him. He made *A Tale of Two Cities* last year, didn't he?"

"That's right. He's got a new project. He's been trying to buy the rights to some Civil War novel."

"What novel?"

"Hell, I can't think of the name," Gable said. "It's by that Southern woman. Can't think of her name, either. But it came out earlier this year. Was a big seller."

Joe suddenly remembered what Gable was talking about because he'd recently read a review of the book in the *Atlantic Monthly*. "Oh, you mean *Gone with the Wind* by Margaret Mitchell?"

"Yeah, that's the one," Gable said. He waved his hand in the air. "But I doubt the whole thing will come off."

"Why's that?"

"Rumor has it that Mitchell woman drives a hard bargain." Gable paused and looked at Joe. "But enough about me. What about you? What are you going to do now that you're out of a job? If you want, I could put a good word in for you at MGM. I understand they have a full stable of writers, but you never know."

"Thanks. I'll take all the help I can get because I'm not sure what I'm going to do. But I'm not exactly sure I want to go back to screenwriting."

"What do you want to do instead?"

"I'm not sure," Joe shrugged. "I know I still want to write, but—"

"What about finishing your novel," Gable suggested, taking another sip of beer. "You finally got some time on your hands. Hell, might as well make the most of it and finish the damn thing."

"Not a bad idea. Wish I could muster up some inspiration, though." Joe lifted his beer to take a sip.

"'Where art thou, Muse, that thou forget'st so long,'" Gable recited.

Joe lowered his beer and turned to stare at Gable, surprised. "You realize that's Shakespeare, right?"

Gable nodded. "Sonnet one hundred."

"No kidding," Joe said, still surprised. "When did you—"

"I know it probably comes as a shock, but I've been reading the sonnets. Carole bought me a copy." He paused and broke into a grin. "And I'll be damned—they're not half bad!"

———————

Joe spent the next several hours that night lying awake in bed, staring up at the ceiling and listening to the sound of the waves against the beach.

He realized he wasn't going to sleep any time soon, so he pushed off the covers and sat up. Shivering, he rubbed his shoulders vigorously. The room was chilly from the damp air that drifted in from the open window. He hopped off the bed and closed the window. The sounds of the waves were muted, and the room fell into silence. Joe put on a shirt and left the bedroom.

He walked into the living room and up to the cabinet that contained *All That Glitters*. Opening the drawer, he took out the battered old manuscript box and set it down on his writing table. He took off the cover and gazed at the pages. Once again, he thumbed through them, like reconnecting with an old, slightly wayward friend. He spent a long time looking at each page, spot reading a few sentences here and there and then setting the page aside and grabbing the next one. He was so engrossed in what he was doing, a good hour had passed by the time he turned to the final page. There was still a lot of work to do—a lot of "polishing"—but it was a decent novel. Or at least he thought so. The editors who had seen it had all told him the same thing: it was too long. Cut this passage out. Shorten this chapter. Don't dwell on this episode. With a mordant sense of irony, he remembered almost verbatim the criticisms various editors had tossed at him.

"Only established writers can get away with a novel that long. And you're not an established writer!"

"Christ almighty! You don't really expect me to sit down and read all this, do you?"

"If you can't say what you're going to say in 75,000 words, it isn't worth saying!"

"Utterly too long. What are you trying to write here, *War and Peace*? You're hardly Tolstoy."

But he hadn't taken any of their advice. In fact, if anything, since his initial go-around with publishers, the novel had actually expanded as he had fleshed-out some scenes, added a few more, and enlarged the role of certain characters.

He pondered Gable's advice as he stood over the manuscript. The actor was right. He did indeed have ample time on his hands, at least for now. Instead of moping around the house and feeling sorry for himself he might as well be productive. He might as well try to finish his novel once and for all—work on those last few chapters and finish the "damn thing," as Gable has said.

He glanced at the clock and noticed the time—it was a little after four o'clock. Although he didn't have his Remington—it was at the studio—he could still do some writing.

Setting a pot of coffee to brewing, he sat down at his writing table, picked up a fountain pen and took out a clean sheet of typing paper. He sat with pen poised over the paper for several minutes, thinking about the last few chapters, trying to work out in his mind a satisfying ending. He had read somewhere that the first chapter of a novel was always the hardest to compose. In his case, the most difficult chapter was proving to be the last few. Nonetheless, as the hours dragged on, he jotted down several promising ideas.

Later that morning, sometime after nine o'clock, Joe dressed and left the house. He trudged the half-mile to the pay phone outside the liquor store and deposited a few coins. He wanted to bypass anyone in the executive offices, so he dialed the writer's cottage directly. A female voice he didn't recognize answered.

"May I ask who's calling please?" she asked.

Joe gave his name and asked for David Levy.

At first the woman seemed reluctant to accommodate him but eventually agreed. "All right," she said, "I'll get him."

David came on the line after a few moments. "This is Levy."

"David, it's me, Joe."

"Yeah, I know. I'm surprised you're calling. I wasn't expecting to hear from you."

David's diffident response rankled Joe. "Typically, I wouldn't be, but you have some of my property, and, frankly, I want it back."

"I don't have anything of yours," David said.

"Not you personally," Joe replied. "Apex. You have my Remington. I may not be a member of the union anymore but that doesn't give you the right to abscond with my property."

"No one's absconding with your stuff, Joe."

"That's good to hear. So, when do I get it back?"

"When do you want it?"

"Preferably today," Joe said. "How about this morning?"

"Yeah, all right," David sighed.

"I can meet you outside the gate in an hour."

———————

Joe stood outside the arched gates and waited for David. He smoked a cigarette and gazed through the gates into a familiar scene—one that he had viewed nearly every day for the last four years. It felt surreal that now he was denied entry.

David soon arrived, lugging Joe's Remington. He exited the gate and strode up to Joe, placing the typewriter on the ground with a grunt. "This thing weighs a ton," he said.

"Thanks for bringing it," Joe said. His voice was flat and monotone.

David nodded and straightened back up, rubbing his sore arms and catching his breath.

Joe dropped his cigarette and stamped it out. Without a further word, he leaned down and picked up the Remington.

"So, how have you been?" David asked.

Joe cradled the typewriter in his arms. "Look, David," he said, "there's little point in us trying to pretend everything's back to normal. I got fired. Sidney found a great excuse to dump me, so let's just leave it at that."

"I wasn't pretending," David said. "I was just asking how you were doing."

"I'm doing peachy," Joe said sarcastically. "I've joined the ranks of the unemployed. If I play my cards right, I might even lead another Coxey's army."

"It might surprise you to know I was the only one who spoke up for you."

"What do you mean?"

"I voted against revoking your membership."

"I appreciate it," Joe said. "Too bad the others didn't see it your way. I'm surprised Sidney even put it up for a vote."

"Actually," David said, "he didn't want to. He thought he could just make an executive decision. But I convinced him he had to."

The two men were silent. Joe turned to leave.

"Aw, hell," David said, letting out a long sigh. "We used to be friends. What happened?"

Joe looked at David. He saw that the man was sincere, and he felt his own anger dissolving. It seemed ludicrous to keep going back and forth like this, sniping at one another. "We let humorless putzes like Sidney get in the way of our friendship. That's what happened."

David chuckled. "Yeah, he is a humorless putz, isn't he?"

"And a smug, sanctimonious bastard. Pretty bad combination."

"He's that, too."

"On the bright side," Joe said, "at least I'm rid of him. You still have to suffer through his sanctimonious pronouncements."

David winked. "Don't worry," he said. "I'm a Jew. I know all about suffering."

Joe shifted the typewriter to his left arm and put out his right hand.

David grasped it. "Take care, old man."

"You, too."

"By the way," David said, "the word 'putz' is Yiddish. It means penis."

Joe grinned. "And I can see you're proud of that."

CHAPTER 24

Joe took a long drag of his cigarette, blew out smoke and leaned back in his chair. Strewn about his feet and scattered over his writing table were crumpled up sheets of paper. They lay like fist-sized snowballs, the detritus of several fits and starts. At the same time, lying next to the Remington was a neat stack of clean copy—several finished pages of *All That Glitters*.

For the last two days, Joe had spent all his waking hours working on his novel. It had become his sole reason for living and he was determined to finish it.

But, right now, he needed to take a break. He'd been writing non-stop with little thought for anything else—like food or basic hygiene. Stubbing out his cigarette, he stood up and rubbed his eyes. They were sore and tired from squinting all day at small type. His lower back was sore as well. He knew that sitting hunched over for hours was bad for his posture. He placed his hands on his hips and leaned backward, stretching his lower back. He heard several pops and cracks.

Straightening, he walked into the kitchen and glanced at the clock. It was a few minutes after five o'clock. Through the window the sun hung low on the horizon, hovering over the ocean. His mind flashed back to the time—seemingly ages ago—when he and Shakespeare had enjoyed the sunset together, viewing it from the top of the knoll. The memory lingered pleasantly in his consciousness, and, despite himself, he wished such times would return. A part of him missed his companionship with Shakespeare.

But he quickly squashed any such thoughts. He was still angry; he was still mad that Shakespeare hadn't warned him that all this would lead to losing his job—and possibly his livelihood. He couldn't bring himself to get over that.

He poured himself a glass of water from the tap and drank it down. He turned and walked back to the living room. He saw that Desdemona was below the desk, batting around one of the crumpled pieces of paper.

———————

Betsy arrived later that evening. As she had been doing for several nights now, she carried a bag of groceries and set about preparing dinner in the kitchen. Joe had never thought of her in domestic terms—he had never seen her so much as boil an egg—but as he watched her chop vegetables and potatoes for a pot of soup, he couldn't help thinking that another side of her was being exhibited. Another layer of her complex personality was on display. Not only that, but she seemed to enjoy it. She whistled as she set the pot to boiling and carefully dropped in the ingredients.

Joe turned on the radio and made drinks. Benny Goodman's clarinet soon filled the cottage.

While the soup was simmering, Joe and Betsy sat down in the living room.

"How's life at the studio?" Joe asked.

"We finally finished *The Queen's Cavalier*," Betsy said. "Tomorrow I'm going in to see what my next assignment is. There's a picture in pre-production called *The North Star*. Something about the gold rush in Alaska. Leighton said he wanted me as an extra."

"What about a speaking part?"

"There's a good chance," Betsy said. "Leighton hinted at that a while back."

"That's great! I'm happy for you."

"I didn't want to tell you, though."

Joe was surprised. "Why not?"

Betsy shrugged. "Well, I figured with everything you just went through at Apex, the last thing you wanted to hear about was another Apex success story. "

"That's not true at all," Joe said. "I'm proud of you. I'm happy about your success. My experience with Apex has nothing to do with yours. I think it's great you're pursuing your dream of becoming an actress."

"But what about you?" Betsy asked. "How's the novel? Looks like you've made a lot of headway in the last two days."

"I have," Joe said.

"Think you'll finish it soon?"

Joe nodded. "Yes, I think I will. I'm nearly done now."

"I can't wait to read it."

Joe chuckled at her enthusiasm. "This time you will, I promise. I won't use the excuse that it needs 'more editing.'"

Benny Goodman transitioned to Ella Fitzgerald singing "A Foggy Day." The singer's famously strong, clear voice drifted about the room.

"So," Betsy said at length, "have you heard from—" She caught herself and broke off discreetly.

Joe looked at her. "Have I heard from whom?"

"Oh, never mind," Betsy said, waving a dismissive hand. "It was nothing."

Joe was silent for a moment. He took a sip of his drink and frowned. "No, I haven't heard from him and I'm not planning to."

Betsy didn't respond.

When the soup was ready, they both sat down at the kitchen table. Betsy ladled out two bowls and handed one to Joe.

"I forgot to tell you," Betsy said suddenly. "Remember when we talked about Paramahansa Yogananda?"

"That Indian swami guy?" Joe nodded. He picked up a spoon and blew at the rising tendrils of steam. "Yes."

"He's coming to LA on his lecture tour. He's going to speak at the Civic Auditorium next weekend. I want to hear him."

"Then you should go."

"I was hoping we could go together."

"You want me to go?"

"Yes, I think you'd enjoy it. He's really amazing."

"I'll think about it," Joe said. "What's he going to talk about?"

"His lecture's called 'Spirituality and Reincarnation.' I have the flyer in my bag."

They finished dinner and sat back down in the living room. Betsy dug into her purse and pulled out the flyer. He looked it over.

Free Lecture!
A great opportunity to hear the distinguished
Hindu master from India. He comes a stranger.
He will depart a friend.
Swami Yogananda, A.B.
Will speak on
"Spirituality and Reincarnation."
Sunday, April 10, at 6:00 pm at the Los Angeles
Civic Auditorium

They chatted for another hour, with Betsy discoursing on her admiration for Paramahansa Yogananda and explaining some of his philosophy. When nine o'clock rolled around, Betsy took a taxi back to the boarding house.

As Joe switched off the lights in preparation for bed, he detected a presence by the bookshelf, exactly where he had felt it before. But he turned away, doing everything in his power to shut down his psychic awareness.

———

The next morning, Betsy went to the office of Elaine McKay, the perpetually harried and overworked assistant director of Central Casting who was in charge of coordinating the "supernumerary" players—the extras, bit players, and stand-ins. The studio had finished shooting *The Queen's Cavalier* and *The Story of John Cabot* and the hall outside her office was filled with eager hopefuls. Betsy dutifully took a number, which was the correct protocol to see Elaine, and waited. There was nowhere to sit so she stood up against the wall and surreptitiously gazed at all the aspiring actors and actresses. There were so many attractive faces, handsome young men and nubile young women, that Betsy began to feel a little discouraged. Every year it was always the same: an army of youthful wannabe actors camped outside Elaine's office.

As she stood among the crowd, clutching her number as if it was a lifeline, she felt like she hadn't progressed at all. She had worked so hard and yet she found herself here once again—just a number waiting outside Elaine's office. It felt like she was back at square one.

An hour later, Betsy's number was called. She pushed away from the wall, straightened her dress, patted her hair, and marched dutifully into Elaine's office, her heels clicking against the floor.

The assistant casting director was wearing her trademark wire-chained glasses and sitting behind her desk, which was stacked high with papers, manila folders, and memos. She was smoking a cigarette—her eighth cigarette of the day—and reading through a document.

"Any experience?" she asked without looking up. Her voice was monotone.

"Hi, Elaine," Betsy said, as cheerfully as she could muster, holding up her chin and trying to smile.

Elaine looked up, surprised. "Oh, hi Betsy," she said, taking her cigarette from her lips. For a moment there was a look of astonishment on her face as if Betsy was the last person she had expected to walk through the door.

"Got anything for me?" Betsy asked, trying not to sound too eager, though she was ready to move on to her next assignment. "Leighton told me I had a good shot at *The North Star*. He even mentioned a small speaking part."

"That's strange," Elaine said. "I looked over *The North Star* list just yesterday and your name wasn't on it."

"Really?" Betsy's eyes widened in surprise. "Are you sure? I mean, that's hard to believe. Leighton was pretty sure that I would at least get a part as an extra."

"I suppose I can double-check," Elaine said.

"Would you?"

Elaine stood up and went over to the big metal filing cabinet that stood up against the far wall. She opened one of the drawers and took out a thick manila folder. Opening it, she flipped through the loose pages for several long minutes. She finally looked up and adjusted her glasses. "Nope," she said, shaking her head and closing the manila folder. "You're not on the list, I'm afraid." She returned the folder and closed the drawer with a clang.

"That can't be right," Betsy said, flummoxed. "I distinctly remember Leighton telling me he had a part for me. He said the speaking part was less certain but that he definitely wanted me as an extra."

"When was this?" Elaine asked.

"Weeks ago."

"Well, you know how Leighton is. He's pretty absent-minded."

"He's not that absent-minded," Betsy said. "Not for things like that."

"I don't know what to tell you," Elaine said, sitting back down at her desk. "I can't authorize you because you're not on the list."

Betsy let out an irritated sigh. "Well, what about anything else?"

"There are only three other pictures currently in production," Elaine said. "I've already seen those lists and you're not on any of them."

"How can you be so sure? Can you please look for me?"

"I know because I've been dealing with the extras lists all morning. I've seen the lists at least a dozen times already."

"Just can you please look?"

"Oh, all right," Elaine sighed. There were three manila folders on her desk, forming a small stack. She perused the contents of each one in turn by running her finger down the list of names. When she had finished, she looked up. "Like I said, you're not on any of these."

The sudden realization dawned on Betsy and her face dropped. "You mean I have no work whatsoever?"

"That's what it appears."

Betsy stood still for a moment as if struck immobile. Then she blazed with sudden anger. "What's going on here, Elaine?"

The older woman looked up, surprised by the young actress's tone. "What do you mean?"

"When I first walked in here, you gave me an odd look. Like you were surprised to see me."

Elaine wrinkled her brow. "Don't be ridiculous," she said. "No, I didn't."

"Did someone tell you something?" Betsy demanded.

"Tell me what? I don't know what you're talking about."

"I think you do."

"Look, Ms. Parker," Elaine said defensively but with rising anger. "It's not my fault you're not on the list. I don't make these decisions."

"I've been blackballed, haven't I?"

"I have no idea what you're talking about," Elaine repeated.

"Who was it?" Betsy demanded. "Who blackballed me?"

"No one blackballed you, for crying out loud. And if you keep this up, I'm going to ask you to leave."

"It was Roger Powell, wasn't it?"

Elaine just looked at her.

"Why don't you tell me the truth?"

Elaine glared at the young actress. "I think you should leave, Ms. Parker."

"Why don't you just tell me who is behind—"

"I said I think you should leave," Elaine repeated. "You want me to call security?"

Betsy felt her face burn with a combination of anger, hurt, and frustration. She bit her lip, turned, and rushed out of the office. She hurried down the hallway as tears sprang to her eyes so that by the time she burst through the doors and staggered outside, tears were tumbling down her cheeks. She ran down the concrete path that led away from the building. She felt dizzy and numb as she stumbled down the path, her body racked by sobs.

Her world had suddenly been upended. For two years now she had had steady if not lucrative work as an extra. It was something she had been able to count on. And each job had led to a better opportunity. Each job expanded her connection with other actors and actresses, and she got to know the directors—and, importantly, they got to know her. She had slowly climbed the ladder up to a speaking part in *The Queen's Cavalier*. And now this! She suddenly wondered whether Roger had anything to do with this. Was this his revenge for her refusing to sleep with him? As one of the studio's leading actors, he certainly had the power to throw his weight around. Had he influenced Leighton? Had he poisoned the director against her? She was already convinced he had orchestrated her speaking scenes being cut.

She came to a stop and gulped the air as if gasping for breath. Calming, she reached into her handbag and brought out a handkerchief. She wiped her eyes and tried to pull herself together. She blew into it and wiped her nose, and then stuffed it back into her handbag. Taking a deep breath and thrusting her shoulders back, she continued down the path.

As she walked along, hurt and frustration gave way to rising anger. She grew more and more furious with each step so that the emotion finally overwhelmed her, reaching a crescendo. She came to a stop, her hands clenched, her blood boiling.

She wasn't going to let that son-of-a-bitch get away with it. How many other actresses had he done this to? How many lives had he ruined? The injustice of it rankled her.

She started walking again, but instead of leaving the studio she made an about turn and took the path that led to the actors' cottages. She walked slowly but determinedly, her jaw set. Up ahead was the largest of the cottages, a Spanish-style affair that everyone knew was Roger Powell's dressing room.

Betsy heard a strange sound emanating from inside the cottage as she neared. It sounded like a high-pitched squeal. She got to the door but saw it was closed. As she put her hand on the doorknob, however, she was surprised to find it unlocked. The squealing continued and for a moment Betsy wasn't sure what to make of it. Furrowing her brow, she turned the doorknob and pushed open the door.

Immediately she was confronted with the indelible image of two naked bodies entwined and deep in the throes of vigorous lovemaking. The squealing came from the woman, who was straddling her partner, and bouncing up and down, her arms around his neck. Her back was arched, her lips parted in desire. The man, whom Betsy recognized as Roger, was seated on a chair, holding the woman's hips and guiding her, his own head thrown back, his eyes closed and mouth open. Their bodies glistened with a sheen of sweat as they thrust and ground against each other, grunting and panting, oblivious to everything except their own carnal urges.

Betsy stared at the couple, completely shocked. It suddenly dawned on her that the woman was none other than Elsa.

At that exact moment of recognition, Elsa glanced over. Betsy and Elsa's eyes locked. Elsa immediately stopped bouncing up and down, a surprised expression on her face. For several milliseconds, the two women just stared at each other.

Roger, noticing that Elsa had stopped, opened his eyes. He cast a questioning glance at her but saw that she was looking toward the door. Following her gaze, he swung his head around, his eyes wide with surprise.

"What the hell?" he exclaimed, blinking, a scowl on his face.

Betsy stepped back and slammed the door. Mortified, she spun around and hurried away as fast as her legs could carry her. She heard the door of the cottage bang open behind her. She looked over her shoulder. Elsa, clad in a bathrobe, came marching toward her. The woman's face was twisted by rage and her fists clenched at her sides.

"How dare you barge in on us like that!" Elsa screamed.

"I didn't—" Betsy stumbled over her words, still flustered. "I mean—"

"Who do you think you are?" Elsa demanded. "What the hell do you think you're doing?"

As Betsy stood there, receiving the full brunt of Elsa's ire, the sheer absurdity and utter predictability of the situation dawned on her. The whole thing was ridiculous and pathetic. Of course Elsa was sleeping with Roger. Of course the two of them had gotten together. When Roger couldn't get Betsy into bed he moved on to the next ripe fruit, but only after ruining Betsy's career. Roger was a "player" and Elsa was willing to do anything to get ahead, to further her career. Betsy should've figured that out weeks ago. She also realized that Elsa had been Roger's spy and party to all his machinations. If she wasn't already upset about losing her acting job, she might even have laughed.

"Do you make a habit of sticking your nose into places it doesn't belong?" Elsa continued.

Betsy had had enough. "Oh, put a cork in it," she said sharply, regaining her composure. "Spare me your self-righteousness."

Elsa stopped and blinked, surprised by Betsy's sudden change.

"I should've known," Betsy said, shaking her head. "I should've known all along."

"Should've known what?"

"About you two."

"What do you mean?"

"About you two," Betsy repeated. "You two have been in cahoots a long time, haven't you?"

"I just seized an opportunity you were too stupid to seize," Elsa said.

"If that's how you want to rationalize it go ahead."

"What do you mean?"

"It's simple," Betsy said. "You're willing to prostitute yourself for your career and I'm not."

Elsa flew into a rage again, her eyes blazing. "You don't know what you're talking about! Roger loves me!"

"Go ahead and believe that," Betsy said, throwing up a hand. "I don't care." She turned to walk away.

"Don't walk away from me!"

Betsy stopped and turned back around. "This is pointless," she said. "You've made your decision and I've made mine. There's no point in discussing it."

"I'm going to be a great actress," Elsa spat out. "And you're going to be a nothing! A zero! You're going to stay what you always were: a Minnesota hick from the backwoods! You'll never amount to anything!"

"Once Roger tires of you, he'll move on to someone else. He's done it a million times."

"You're just jealous!"

"Good God," Betsy said, shaking her head in amazement. "You *are* deluded." She turned and strode away.

"Oh, by the way," Elsa called out after her, "how's your boyfriend? Enjoying his 'early retirement'?"

Elsa's barb hit its mark. Betsy spun around angrily.

"Roger fixed his hash," Elsa said. "He'll never set foot on a picture studio again." Her lips curled in a contemptuous sneer. "Shouldn't leave your scripts lying around. Or in this case, scripts you're working on while pretending to work on something else."

Betsy glared at her. "You are a miserable bitch, aren't you?"

"You're the miserable bitch!" Elsa screamed back at her. "And an out-of-work miserable bitch, to boot. You and your hack boyfriend can enjoy retirement together. I hope you both like park benches and cat food."

Anger coursed through Betsy like hot flame and she wanted to smack Elsa right in the face. But she quelled the desire, turned, and walked off.

CHAPTER 25

JOE PACED BACK AND forth across the floor of his cottage. The final chapter of *All That Glitters* was proving difficult to finish. After all his recent work on the last few chapters, he still couldn't seem to come up with a satisfying denouement, something that would gather all the loose ends while simultaneously providing a telling conclusion to one man's long personal journey.

Seeking inspiration, he wandered over to the bookshelf and stood looking at all his books. Next to *The Meditations* was his dog-eared copy of Aristotle's *Poetics*, a book he hadn't opened since college. And next to that, reading from left to right, was an eclectic group, including Virgil's *The Aeneid*, Dante's *The Divine Comedy*, Henry James's *The Wings of a Dove*, Carl Jung's *Modern Man in Search of a Soul*, Friedrich Nietzsche's *The Birth of Tragedy*, Lucretius' *On the Nature of Things*, and a collection of plays by Henrik Ibsen.

So much inspiration was there, in those books, crammed into those pages. Joe wondered if any of these authors had ever grappled with writer's block. They must have, he thought. Every writer does. In his mind's eye he pictured Dante Alighieri, dressed in his red cassock and skull cap, sitting at his writing desk, twiddling his thumbs and staring off into space, an empty manuscript on the table in front of him, a half-burned candle providing light.

Joe glanced at the wall clock. It was already nearly half past eight o'clock. He wondered why Betsy was so late. Where on earth was she? She usually arrived at six o'clock or seven at the latest. He rubbed his chin and wondered whether he should worry because she hadn't actually told him she'd be over tonight. He had gotten used to their nights together over the last week and assumed she would be over again tonight.

There was a sudden knock at the door. He spun around and bounded across the room. When he opened the door, he was relieved to see Betsy.

"Betsy," he said, "I was just wondering where—" His words trailed off as he saw that her eyes were red and puffy, her cheeks glistening from tears.

"What's wrong?" he said.

Betsy stood completely still for a moment, not saying anything, her arms at her sides. She stared at him, trying her best to keep her composure. But then her jaw began to tremble, and, with a sudden sob, she stumbled across the threshold and fell into his arms. He cradled her as she put her face against his chest and squeezed him tightly. He guided her the rest of the way into the room and closed the door behind her.

"What's wrong?" he repeated, looking down at her.

She shook her head and clung to him, her body convulsed by heaving sobs.

"I'm really sorry," Joe told her. He handed her a handkerchief.

Betsy used it to wipe her eyes and let out an exhausted sigh.

They were sitting across from each other in the living room. Joe leaned forward and put his forearms on his knees, looking at her sympathetically. "How come you didn't tell me about Roger? That he was harassing you like that?"

Betsy lowered the handkerchief. "There was nothing you could've done."

"I could've punched him in the face," Joe said angrily.

"That wouldn't have solved anything," Betsy said.

"Certainly would've made me feel better."

"Then you would've been fired."

Joe shrugged. "I got fired anyway, so I guess it wouldn't have mattered."

Betsy blew her nose.

"And you think he was the one who stole *The Apple Orchard*?" Joe said. "To get back at you?"

Betsy nodded. "Elsa basically admitted as much."

Joe shot to his feet, his fists clenched. "That lousy son-of-a-bitch."

"Sit down, Joe," Betsy said. "There's no point in getting angry about it now. What's done is done."

Joe sat back down with a disgruntled sigh. "I guess you're right," he said. "I'm not mad so much at the fact he stole my script. I mean, Greenwood would've found out sooner or later. I'm mostly mad at the fact that all of this was really aimed at you. To hurt you."

"Let's not discuss it anymore tonight, Joe," Betsy said. "I'm sorry, I just want it all to go away."

Joe nodded. He knew when a subject had been flogged to death.

Betsy yawned. "God, I'm so sleepy. Do you mind if I sleep here tonight?"

"No, not at all," Joe said. "But what about your boarding house? Won't Mrs. Kendall be worried?"

"I don't think I'll be able to pay rent anymore, anyway."

"Then you can stay here," Joe said. "As long as you want."

"I don't want to be a burden."

"You won't be." Joe gave her a grin. "In fact, what this place needs—"

Before Joe could finish, Betsy had lain down on the couch with her hands folded under her cheek and her legs drawn up in a fetal position. Soon she was fast asleep, breathing softly and evenly.

Joe took a blanket from a cabinet and covered her with it. She barely moved as he tucked the sides of the blanket underneath her so she wouldn't get cold. He stood over her for a moment, watching her sleep. Then he turned, switched off the lights, and retired to his bedroom. Desdemona followed in his wake, her tail raised and paws padding silently against the floor.

———————

Joe awoke later that night seized by a thought. He sat bolt upright in bed and gazed around the darkness. Desdemona was fast asleep next to him, curled up in a tight ball.

He had an idea for the novel's ending, and he wanted to get it on paper. Gingerly moving Desdemona aside, he pushed off the covers and stood up, his bare feet against the cold hardwood floor. Outside he could hear the ocean, the monotonous rise and fall of the waves.

He threw on some clothes and slipped silently into the living room, trying to be as quiet as possible. Betsy was fast asleep on the couch, still wrapped in the blanket. She had changed position and was now facing the couch, her back to the center of the living room.

Joe crept over to his writing desk and switched on a lamp. Sitting down, he inserted a clean sheet into the typewriter and rolled it into position. He started typing almost immediately.

At the sound, Betsy rolled over and cast a bleary eye on him. "What're you doing?" she asked groggily.

"Sorry about the noise," Joe said, "but I had an idea and I wanted to get it on paper."

Betsy rolled back over, yawned, and fell asleep again, despite the clattering of the typewriter.

Joe spent the next several hours writing. The world dissolved around him as he was swept up in his own imagination. He wrote in a frenzy of fierce, concentrated effort, and when dawn broke, he had several typewritten pages.

Leaning back in his chair, he let out a yawn and scratched his scalp. He pulled the sheet out of the typewriter and read back through what he had written. He stared at the words and it was as if he had suddenly awakened from a trance. By the light of morning, what he thought was a brilliant idea was in fact not very good. It didn't jibe with the rest of the story. With a frown, he thrust the page aside and began to read back through the other pages he had written. This unsettling realization was only strengthened as he read through each page so that by the time he reached the last page, he recognized that his late night writing marathon had been a complete waste—a complete failure. He crumpled up each page and tossed it into the wastebasket.

Disgruntled, he gazed across the room. Betsy was sound asleep, her shoulders gently rising and falling.

He stood up and went over to the window, opening it. The air was cool and moist, and Joe filled his lungs. A hazy, overcast sky sat over the water, its color matching Joe's mood. He heard the squawk of gulls, their plaintive cries echoing along the shore.

"What time is it?"

Joe turned at the sound of Betsy's voice. She had awakened and was sitting up, her hair disheveled and face puffy from sleep.

"Good morning," he said. "How'd you sleep?"

"Like a baby." She rubbed a bleary eye with the palm of her hand.

"My typing didn't bother you?"

"At first, I guess. But then I didn't notice a thing. I slept pretty deeply." She paused. "Did you write all night?"

Joe nodded.

"You must've gotten a lot done."

Joe just shrugged.

She noticed the glum look on his face. "What's wrong?"

"I can't use what I wrote."

"Any of it?"

He nodded.

"Why not?" she asked.

"It's just not any good. I thought it was when I started, but it just isn't. I already tossed it out."

"I'm sorry," she said.

He gave a disgruntled shrug. "I just have to keep working, I guess."

———————

The following week crept by with glacial slowness. Betsy spent her time trudging from movie studio to movie studio, looking for work. But the answers she received were always the same. "Nothing today, sister. Come back tomorrow." Each time she came back, eager that today would be the day, she heard the same answer, "Nothing today, sister. Come back tomorrow." The only job she was offered was seamstress at Warner Brothers Studio, but she had to turn it down because she didn't have any skill as a seamstress. Each night she came home frustrated and in tears.

Joe continued to work on his novel, but his progress was slow and frustrating. Most of the time he simply paced the house, a perambulating victim of writer's block. At the same time, he tried his best to buoy Betsy's spirits and offer encouragement where he could. As the week wore on, he found himself increasingly anxious about his own job prospects. Luckily, he had some money in the bank that was keeping him in rent and food, but he knew the funds wouldn't last forever. If he was frugal, he could make it stretch but eventually it was going to run out.

He knew he had to take seriously the task of hunting for a job. And he would. On Monday, he planned personally to deliver some letters to several different movie studios. By the same token, he began to think about other career possibilities. With his degree and his writing experience, he might find work as a teacher. Or he might go back to journalism.

Betsy came home late on Thursday night. The expression on her face as she stood in the doorway was unmistakable: It had been another long day of failure. She had been to five separate studios that day but had come up empty. The studios weren't interested in hiring extras. The only thing she had to show for her efforts were blistered feet. She winced as she walked into the living room.

Kicking off her shoes, she dropped onto the sofa with a heavy sigh. She propped her feet up on the coffee table and wriggled her toes with a sigh of satisfaction. "On the way home, I saw a sign at a diner on Santa Monica that was looking for a waitress," Betsy said.

"You don't want to do that, do you?" Joe replied.

"No, but I may have to if I can't find any acting gigs," she said. "And I can't keep mooching off you."

"You're not mooching," Joe insisted. "You're my girlfriend, for Christ's sake. And have you ever waitressed? If you think you're tired now, you definitely will be after ten hours on your feet serving food all day."

"It's the only job opening I've seen all week," Betsy said. "If I don't act soon it may go to someone else." She gave him a surly look. "And, anyway, I have waitressed before. I did some in St. Paul. It was the first job I had after I left the farm."

"Look," Joe said, "I'm sure you'll find an acting gig eventually. You just have to keep looking."

"I've looked all week!" Betsy snapped at him. "No one's hiring."

Joe rarely saw her in a bad mood, but it was obvious the stress of all the week's failures had gotten to her.

"I'm sorry," he said, "I didn't mean to upset you."

She looked at him and sighed. "I'm sorry, too. I'm just tired and my feet are killing me." She wrapped her arms around herself, sank deeper into the sofa, and let out a frustrated sigh.

The following evening, Betsy went to see Madam Petrova. She had convinced Joe to come along, though he had been reluctant. He wasn't in the mood to commune with spirits. In fact, he was coming to the conclusion that his "ability" had caused him only trouble.

As usual, the séance was held in Madam Petrova's kitchen. Joe and Betsy seated themselves as Madam Petrova lit the candle. She gathered her shawl around her and sat down. Like the previous time, she closed her eyes and took a deep breath. Despite his misgivings, Joe followed suit, allowing himself to tune in and immediately saw two entities standing at either side of the medium's shoulders. One was a dressed as a Sikh, with a bright yellow turban and a thick bushy beard. He was tall, broad-shouldered, and stood ramrod straight. Joe wondered if he had ever been a soldier.

The ghost acknowledged Joe, nodding his head in greeting, his eyes friendly but formal. Next to him was a tall, slender and attractive woman, dressed in the attire—a free-flowing chiton held in place across her shoulders with an ornamental clasp—of a wealthy matron from ancient Greece. Her dark, wavy hair was bound up with purple ribbons and she wore a jeweled necklace that sparkled in the candlelight. She also nodded at Joe, a soft smile breaking across her attractive, regal features.

Joe nodded back with a grin, captivated by the spirit's dignified bearing and beauty. There was something about her—not only her beauty but the way she carried herself—that he found immensely appealing.

Madam Petrova turned her attention first to Betsy. "The spirits want you to know that there is a light at the end of the tunnel."

"Does that mean I'll find a job?" Betsy asked, leaning forward over the table. Her body language was expectant and eager.

Joe watched as the Sikh leaned down and whispered in Madam Petrova's ear. The medium listened for a moment, nodded, and then addressed Betsy. "I am told that you must expect something to come from a very unexpected corner."

"What does that mean?" Betsy asked.

"That is the extent of the message."

Betsy sat back and frowned, her lips pursing into a slight pout.

Joe suddenly heard the Greek woman say distinctly, "Please tell Mistress Betsy that this unexpected opportunity will be accompanied by a major life change."

Madam Petrova conveyed the message to Betsy.

"Really? What's going to happen?" she asked.

Both entities were silent, and Joe knew they weren't going to say any more on the subject.

Madam Petrova next turned to Joe, but before she said anything, she gave him a long, clear-eyed look. "You really don't need me, do you?" she said at length. "You can hear all this, can't you?"

Joe nodded. "I can see all of it, too."

Madam Petrova gave a knowing grin and nodded. "I suspected as much."

"Still," Joe said, "I wouldn't mind getting a message."

She continued to grin. "I think we might be able to arrange that."

The Greek woman took this as her cue and looked directly at Joe. Her gaze was a mixture of benevolence and serious intent. "You must decide whether to wade into the stream and be carried by the swiftly flowing current, or remain on the shore and watch," she said. "The choice is yours." She paused and nodded her head. "Bless you, my child."

Chapter 26

Joe and Betsy hopped off the Red Car at Olympic Boulevard and proceeded along the sidewalk toward downtown Los Angeles. Betsy walked quickly so that Joe hastened his steps to keep up with her. The evening was warm, but a light breeze was blowing. The sun was nearly down, prompting the streetlights to begin to flare to life.

"I think you'll really like his lecture," Betsy said.

"We'll see," Joe said with a wink. "If I don't, I'm holding you personally responsible."

"You will," she laughed. "I can't wait. It's the only thing I've looked forward to over the past week."

They continued walking. The ornate neo-classical facade of the Civic Auditorium loomed at the end of the street. They saw that a line was just now forming at the entrance of the Auditorium.

"I've been thinking," Betsy said suddenly.

"Yes?"

"I've decided," she said with an air of finality in her voice. "I want to be an actress no matter what. I want to pursue that life. It's all I've ever wanted to do."

"Then you must do that," Joe said.

"I don't care how long it takes me to achieve. And I don't care whether it's on a movie set or on the stage." She added, "Though the movie set is seeming less and less likely."

"What was the message Madam Petrova gave you?" Joe said. "Something about a 'light at the end of the tunnel?'"

She nodded. "And I've been thinking about that a lot. She also said to expect something from an 'unexpected corner.'"

"Yes, I remember."

"Well, I'm done speculating about it. I'm simply going to let it happen." She paused to let out a sigh. "It's so easy to get in the way of yourself, isn't it?"

Joe chuckled. "Yes, it is."

"Does that ever happen to you?" Betsy asked. "You getting in your own way?"

Joe nodded. "All the time. I call it the Hamlet-syndrome. 'Thinking too precisely on the event.'"

"You would," she said with a light laugh. "Anyway, that's what I'm going to do. I'm not going to get in my own way. I'm going to expect good things to happen—and they will."

"Just like that?"

She nodded. "Just like that."

They walked on, eventually joining the line that was forming at the entrance.

"Do you believe in fate?" Betsy asked.

"I'm not sure I'd use that word exactly," Joe said, "because I don't think things are set in stone. Our lives, I mean. But I do believe that our lives are aimed at something. A lot of the time, though, we don't even know what that something is."

"Did Shakespeare tell you that?"

Joe nodded. "He said we come into each life with a definite goal or set of goals. These goals are lessons that we need to learn."

"Did he tell you what yours is?"

"No," Joe said, shaking his head. "I get the impression we don't know until after the fact."

"That doesn't seem very helpful, does it?"

"What do you mean?"

"I mean, wouldn't it be better if we knew what the goal was so we could plan for it?"

Joe laughed. "I had the same thought," he said. "But apparently it doesn't work that way."

"Why not?"

"Well, what if the experience you had to go through to learn a particular lesson wasn't so pleasant? What if you had to lose your legs or your eyesight, or something? You'd do everything in your power to avoid it, don't you think?"

Betsy thought for a moment and looked up at the evening sky, her brow furrowed. "I wonder what my goal is?"

"What do you think it might be?"

She shrugged. "I don't know. I've always wanted to be happy, but I'm not sure that's it. In all honesty, I haven't had a chance to think about anything like that."

"What do you mean?"

She shrugged again. "I guess because I feel like I'm always running. First it was away from my father and Minnesota. And then it was toward acting."

"And now?"

"I feel like I'm simply running in place," she said. "Running but getting nowhere." She sighed and let out a frown. "Why does life have to be so difficult? Wouldn't it be easier, if—"

"If what?"

She shook her head and waved her hand dismissively. "I'm being silly."

"What?"

"Why can't people just be nice to one another? Why do people have to be so vile toward one another?"

Joe, of course, didn't have an answer. No one did. "'The web of our life is of a mingled yarn, good and ill together,'" he said.

"Is that Shakespeare?"

Joe nodded. "From *All's Well that End's Well.*"

"That's what I hope happens."

He looked at her, confused.

"That everything ends well," she explained. She suddenly reached over and put her hand on his arm. "Hey," she said, smiling, "tonight's the first time I've heard you talk about him in ages."

Joe nodded and cracked a little smile despite himself. "Yes, I suppose you're right."

Betsy snuggled up next to him. "We've been through a lot of ill recently but tonight is part of the good. The good yarn of our life."

———————

The Civic Auditorium was filling up rapidly. Joe swiveled his head, looking around. He had never seen such a large crowd. Luckily, he and Betsy had arrived early for Paramahansa Yogananda's lecture so had been able to find a seat close to the stage.

He stared up at the long, high-ceilinged auditorium and then dropped his gaze, looking around again. He was surprised by the appearance of the crowd. Not exactly sure what he had been expecting, he was nonetheless surprised by the overarching normality of everyone. There were couples, families, and individuals—all moderately prosperous and, by the look, solidly middle class. Most of the men wore suits and ties and the women unpretentious, conservative dresses as if they were outfitted for a Sunday morning church service.

As he shifted to a more comfortable position in his seat, he wondered what had brought all these normal-looking—*painfully* normal-looking—people out to hear the words of a short, long-haired, orange-robed and dark-skinned Indian swami. What about the man's words were so electrifying? What was he saying that was so different from the other spiritual teachers—the priests and ministers and rabbis?

Soon nearly every seat in the auditorium was taken. People crowded the back of the room, jostling each other for space and craning their necks over the shoulder of the person in front. The murmur of talk drifted about, accompanied by the scrape of chairs and an occasional cough as audience members settled themselves.

A hushed silenced suddenly fell as a short, stocky man with long dark hair and a dark complexion walked slowly across the stage toward the lectern. He was dressed in an orange robe that fell all the way to his ankles and swished back and forth as he walked. Despite his bulk, he moved lithely, with a gracefulness that belied his appearance.

Paramahansa Yogananda settled himself behind the lectern and gazed out at the assembled crowd. He smiled broadly, flashing white teeth and animated eyes.

Joe studied the man's face. His cheekbones were high and wide and his nose somewhat broad but well-shaped. His eyes were a deep shade of brown and his eyebrows thick and black.

"Greetings brothers and sisters," Yogananda said. His voice was flavored with a distinctive Indian accent so that his English, while precise, carried a sing-song quality. "I am once again very happy to be back in this marvelous city with so many of my friends. I wish this morning to discuss two topics: Spirituality and reincarnation. Hopefully, by weaving the two together, you will understand how one cannot be understood without the other."

Joe stole a quick glance at Betsy. Her eyes were riveted on the Indian swami, her hands folded on her lap.

"We are all on a spiritual journey," Yogananda began, "whether we are aware of this fact or not. We are all striving to understand ourselves, to progress as spiritual beings. For that is ultimately what we are, spiritual beings. Here in the West, you would call these souls or Children of God. There are many names. In India, we call a spiritual being the atman. But it is the same. We all come from different cultures, yes, but we are all children of God, we are all atman." He paused, seemingly to gather his thoughts. "A moment ago, I used the word 'striving.' I now wish to clarify that. The word 'strive' implies toil and sweat. To struggle. I do not want to leave the impression that this spiritual journey is a long, unceasing struggle, and that we can only achieve it with the sweat of our brow. Now, it is true that many of us have placed deliberate obstacles in our lives during this incarnation so that we might learn a valuable lesson. And such obstacles will indeed require much sweat and sacrifice to overcome. But I want to emphasize that ultimate reality—call it God if you like—is love, and that our greatest lesson is love. In the giving and receiving of love. In India, we often like to use the word 'harmony' in place of love. But it does not really matter. They are the same. Love ties all the threads of the universe together."

Yogananda went on to explain the four types of love, as understood in Hindu philosophy. He described these as progressively complex levels or stages through which the individual climbs towards greater awareness. At the lowest level is erotic desire. Although it occupies the lowest rung, Yogananda said, it is not to be dismissed because it has its own lessons to teach. Erotic love is followed by the love between two committed individuals, which is characterized by great intimacy and sharing. Next is a love for humanity, which compels one to undertake acts of kindness and compassion. The highest level, Yogananda explained, is called "bhakti."

"It is a love that is difficult to describe because it cannot adequately be captured in words," he said. "The sages describe it as a mixture of wonder, joy, and compassion. They describe it as a deep gratitude for the simple act of being alive. It is the realization that love is reflected in all aspects of creation. It is the realization that love can move mountains and change destinies."

This idea—that love was "reflected in all aspects of creation, that it could move mountains and change destinies"— resonated with Joe. But before he could ponder it too deeply, Yogananda continued.

"Reincarnation is the vehicle by which we progress along this spiritual journey toward ultimate love. In India, we consider it a law of the universe. But I will not try to convince you of that. I will simply say that, as spiritual beings, it is the way in which we experience the physical world. The spirit incarnates into different bodies in order to have experiences and learn important lessons. In this way, we gradually progress as spiritual beings. Reincarnation is an evolution. It is a spiritual evolution, a journey of the soul."

Yogananda paused for a moment, looking around the auditorium, his eyes sparkling with an inner fire. The audience had fallen into a deep silence. Joe could tell by the bated breath of those around him that everyone was listening intently.

"Think about what it would be like if we only had a single life to learn and progress," he continued. "We would invariably fail to learn anything. Indeed, such an idea goes against the very grain of the universe—which is about change and evolution. Just as material objects change and morph, so does spiritual energy. Nothing is ever the same. As the poet Ovid said, 'All things change, nothing is extinguished. There is nothing in the whole world which is permanent. Everything flows onward; all things are brought into being with a changing nature.' So it is with us."

Yogananda went on to discuss reincarnation in greater detail, explaining how the soul migrates from one body to the next, from one life to the next. The experiences the soul gains in each life are like the pieces of a jigsaw puzzle. Gradually, over time, the puzzle is assembled, and the individual comes to know himself and know that he, ultimately, is love. Yogananda also explained how the concept is not as alien to a Western audience as many have supposed, citing the examples of Pythagoras, Plato, and the Medieval Christian mystic Origen.

"I have explained the concept of reincarnation," Yogananda went on. "I will now attempt to explain spirituality. What does the concept mean? What does it mean to live a spiritual life? Over the millennia, there have been many definitions. And the future will no doubt add more. But I happen to think the concept is a simple one. It's about love; our capacity to love. Living a spiritual life means having a great capacity for compassion, for nurturing, and for forgiveness and understanding. It does not mean knowing the correct rituals or the most appropriate way to kneel while praying. All that is immaterial. Your great spiritual teacher Jesus admonished the Scribes and Pharisees for their dogmatic emphasis on ritual, piety, and the Law—on their desire to present the outward appearance of devoutness. The 'Sabbath was made for man, not man for the Sabbath.' Recall that Jesus' greatest commandment—the core of his teachings—is about love."

Yogananda concluded his lecture, quoting a passage from the *Bhagavad Gita*, the renowned Hindu treatise that contained the famous dialogue between Lord Krishna and the hero Arjuna. "'But of all I could name, verily love is the highest. Love and devotion that make one forgetful of everything else, love that unites the lover with me.'"

Joe and Betsy followed the line of people leaving the auditorium.

"What did you think?" Betsy asked, putting her arm through his and leaning against him. "Wasn't he marvelous?"

Joe nodded but remained silent. They walked out onto the street and proceeded along the sidewalk.

Betsy looked up at him. "Didn't you enjoy it?"

"I did. Very much. He was a very eloquent and engaging speaker."

"But you're so quiet. Is anything the matter?"

"I'm just thinking about the last stage of love he talked about," Joe said. "He called it bhakti. I'm trying to figure out what he meant by it. It's still a little unclear."

Betsy thought for a moment. She walked several paces before she spoke up. "Maybe it's the love that transcends the sense of self," she said. "Maybe bhakti is what it means to become love."

"Become love?"

She nodded. "The earlier stages of love were all focused on something outside."

"Outside? You mean, like a lover?"

"Or a spouse, or even humanity. But it's always something outside of oneself." Betsy paused and furrowed her brow, indicating she was thinking deeply about the subject. "It seems to me Yogananda was trying to say that bhakti is the experience of love itself. Maybe at that stage, someone is no longer themselves. Maybe they are love itself. Maybe bhakti provides a glimpse into what we truly are—love. Maybe love isn't just an emotion, or an abstract thought. Maybe love is a real thing."

They walked several more paces until Betsy spoke up again. "And maybe there's this great capacity in each of us for love. And it's the end goal of our spiritual journey. To really know what love is, to have experienced all its aspects, and to become a being of pure and enduring love. Maybe that's what he meant by bhakti. Maybe that's everyone's ultimate destiny."

Joe walked along, contemplating Betsy's words.

CHAPTER 27

WHEN JOE GOT BACK to the cottage, he felt a burning desire to write. The lecture and his subsequent talk with Betsy had inspired him. And he knew exactly what he wanted to say. Yogananda's concept of the different stages of love had provided him a framework with which to understand his novel. He realized that these stages were exactly what his protagonist had gone through. From the ex-soldier's Paris experience among the hedonists, when all he cared about was satisfying his erotic desires, to his monogamous relationship with the painter to, ultimately, his Platonic yet deeply felt love for the untouchable woman and her son. These mirrored what Yogananda had talked about as the stages of love—from sensual desire to a compassionate, impersonal devotion. All he needed to do was describe the protagonist's immersion in this final aspect of love. The love that Yogananda had described as having the ability "…to move mountains and change destinies," and that Betsy had so adroitly explained.

He had a sudden thought and immediately went over to his bookshelf and took down his copy of Dante's *The Divine Comedy*. He flipped to the last section, Canto 33, and read the final words written by the famous poet:

> But already my desire and my will
> were being turned like a wheel, all at one speed,
> by the Love which moves the sun and the other stars.

Joe sat down at his writing desk and inserted a clean sheet into the typewriter. He was quiet for a moment, gathering his thoughts; but soon he started typing. The world dissolved around him as he was swept up in his own imagination. He wrote in a frenzy of fierce, concentrated effort for the next several hours, oblivious to everything around him. He wrote all afternoon and late into the night. He discovered, to his amazement, that the actual writing came surprisingly easy; the words seemed to flow with a facility he rarely experienced and a small stack of pages formed at his elbow as if conjured by magic. Eventually, Joe reached the final few pages of his novel. He began to write:

The morning air was clear but bitter cold.

Alan adjusted his rucksack to a better position on his shoulders and started off down the trail, leaving the small, dilapidated goatherd shack behind. His boots crunched on a thin veneer of newly fallen snow, leaving deep impressions behind. His breath, visible in the air, swirled around him as he trudged along.

The countryside through which he passed was rugged and sparse. Stark granite peaks towered above, their snow-capped tops set beneath a dazzling blue sky and wispy patches of gauzy cloud. But the land was hardly devoid of life. Every so often Alan came across a small reminder—a tiny wildflower or a blade of grass struggling up from the earth, seeking the sun.

The trail began to descend, and he followed it for a long time, passing from the high mountain altitudes to a more subalpine zone. Trees, though small and stunted, began to appear with greater regularity and patches of snow gave way to green grass materializing in scattered clumps. The gurgle of running water could be heard rushing along small streams.

Though the day was still, the air was filled with a multitude of noises—noises indicative of teeming life. From the trees came the twitter of birdsong. He heard the buzz of insects and far above, in the realm of cloud, echoed the screech of an eagle. He passed a small, furry rodent perched atop a rock pile, gazing at him as he passed. Its high-pitched warning squeak resounded in his ears.

In the distance, nestled in a meadow and hemmed in by mountains, was a patch of bright wildflowers. They lay spread out like a multi-colored carpet, fulgent in the morning light. He stopped to survey the arresting contrast of colors—purples, pinks, and yellows—marveling at the brilliant hues. They filled his vision, drowning out everything else, garnering all his attention.

He was soon walking through the meadow. Butterflies flitted about his ankles. In the middle of the field, he came to a stop and breathed deeply. The flowers' scent filled his nostrils like an intoxicating fragrance. He looked up at the mountaintops, watching wisps of cloud drift in the currents, like puffs of white paint on a blue palette. Their movements seemed specially choreographed for his eye. Alan felt overtaken by a sudden surge of emotion.

He reached into a pocket and felt for the lock of hair Samira had given him—the only thing she could've given him. He brought it out and held it in his palm. Its slick blackness contrasted sharply with the ruddy color of his skin. He knelt and placed it next to the flowers. Beautiful things needed to lie next to beautiful things, he mused.

Standing back up, he continued to look around. The scene he beheld was so beautiful, so vivid, that it took his breath away. Colors were sharp-edged and vibrant. But it wasn't only the flowers. As he gazed around, he saw that everything seemed bathed in an aura of crystalline purity. It felt as if he was seeing things for the first time—really seeing them, discerning the essence of each thing.

He took a deep breath, feeling an intense kinship with the earth and sky, with the flowers, trees, insects, and birds. He wanted to reach out and embrace everything. Gradually, but with building momentum, the feeling intensified; it was as if he were expanding—becoming something greater than himself. It was as if his physical body had begun to dissipate and merge with his surroundings. He became a part of each flower, of each butterfly, of each living thing. Everything became a single, unitary whole. He drifted with the clouds. He mingled with the breeze as it rustled the tree branches. He swayed back and forth with the grasses. And it all happened simultaneously so that he was experiencing all these things at once, without time. He realized that binding *everything together was love—a love so intense, so overwhelming, it was all that mattered. It was the reality of the universe—a tangible essence beyond time and space.*

This realization struck him to the core, unleashing a feeling of indescribable joy. Love coursed through him like a raging torrent, sweeping everything along with it. It filled up all aspects of life, of the world, of the universe. It flowed like a mighty river, forming an infinite ocean that covered all of existence.

Then, as quickly as it had come, it was gone. He was Alan again.

He was standing in the field of flowers, his shoulders sore from his rucksack straps, his brow sticky from dried sweat. Tears began to fill his eyes. So overcome with emotion he dropped to his knees. But his tears were not of sadness or pain. They were tears of gratitude. The cosmos had given him a brief glimpse of its true nature. And he knew he was a part of that nature.

He was love.

After a time, though he didn't know how many minutes—or, indeed, hours—had elapsed, he picked himself up. He wiped his tears and looked around. He sensed something different about the world, something he had never experienced before. Yet he couldn't adequately describe it; he could only feel it. It was like coming out of a fog—a fog that had been with him his entire life but now was gone, never to return, dissipated like an insubstantial cloud scattered by the breeze. It was a deep sense of being in the world, of being an integral part of it. He was still an individual, yes, but he was also, paradoxically, a part of all that existed.

And the beauty he saw now as he gazed around was overwhelming. How come he hadn't seen it before? Had he not been paying attention? He realized it had always been there, but he had simply been blind to its existence. But those blinders had finally been removed.

He remained standing for a moment, reveling in the feeling, gazing at the world with new eyes—with loving, compassionate eyes that encompassed everything and left nothing out. Then, like a traveler anticipating a long but pleasant journey, he adjusted his rucksack to a better fit and started off down the trail again. His strides were long and purposeful, his soul exultant.

When dawn broke, Joe had finished his novel.

He unrolled the final page from the typewriter and placed it face down on his manuscript. The gesture was done without fanfare but with a sense of deep satisfaction. He sat quietly for several minutes, just listening.

The cottage was quiet. The air seemed suffused with a great sense of accomplishment, as if something planned had finally been achieved, a goal had been met, a hurdle surmounted.

He yawned, rubbed his eyes with the palm of his hand, suddenly realizing how tired he was.

"Thou hath finished thy novel, I see."

Joe turned toward the sound of the voice. Shakespeare was seated in the chair near the lamp, his long-stemmed pipe protruding from a corner of his mouth, smoke drifting lazily over his head.

Joe stared at the Bard for several long minutes, saying nothing. As his eyes focused on the apparition, Joe felt a sudden great change overtake him. It was as if a great weight had suddenly been lifted from his shoulders. His anger toward the Bard completely dissipated, like water cascading off a roof. In fact, it felt as if it had never existed. Joe knew in a sudden flash of insight that Shakespeare had never abandoned him. There had been no betrayal, no deliberate attempt to derail Joe's hopes and dreams. It was exactly the opposite. These turn of events were meant to be. They had played out—indeed, they were still playing out—as they should. As painful as they had been, they were meant to propel him forward, to move him from one stage of life to another. Joe felt this realization in his gut. It was as if the very cosmos had ordained it.

"I understand now," Joe said. "I see the bigger picture. It was supposed to be like this."

Shakespeare took his pipe from his mouth and nodded, his eyes glistening with emotion. It was a nod that spoke volumes. In it, Joe knew Shakespeare was telling him that not only were things supposed to unfold like this but that these things were meant to disclose an important lesson.

"When thou didst agree to trust the process as it unfolded," Shakespeare said, "I was asking thee, in reality, to trust thyself. To believe in thyself. Thou were doing something that was against thy nature."

"I felt like I was betraying my employer. And others."

Shakespeare nodded in understanding. "Loyalty is indeed a worthy trait. An admirable trait. In many situations 'tis the correct way to proceed. But even such an admirable trait hath limits. We must not live our lives for others. We must be the person 'tis our nature to become, not the person others want us to be. We must needs pursue our own dreams and desires—our own pathway. Sometimes thy pathway conflicts with what others want thee to do. There is oft no easy resolution. And sometimes thy pursuit of this pathway causes pain in others. But such is life. A human life incorporates both good and ill—it hath always been and will ever be. Sometimes thou must simply follow thy own heart and, as hath oft been said, 'let the chips fall where they may.'"

Joe grinned. "'To thine own self be true?'"

Shakespeare grinned back and nodded. "I knew not the full import of the words when I wrote them."

Joe paused for a moment and glanced around the room. His eyes came back and rested on Shakespeare. "It's kind of funny, though, isn't it?"

Shakespeare looked at him.

"I mean, I'm one of the lucky ones, aren't I? It's like I've been given a second chance. A phoenix from the ashes." He paused again and shook his head, amazed. "Strange thing to say from a guy who just lost his job and doesn't have any prospects, isn't it? I may be unemployed, poor, and just a lowly writer, but I feel I have everything."

Shakespeare let out a small grin but didn't say anything.

"What now?" Joe asked.

"'Tis as we hath just discussed," Shakespeare said. "Follow thy heart, my friend. 'Twill not leadeth thee astray."

Joe nodded. For a moment he didn't say anything, but there was a question that was burning within him—it was a question with which he'd long been grappling. "What I don't understand," he said at last, "is why you've done this for me. Why are you here to help me? You said our lives are intertwined and that we've long been friends. But how long have we known each other? What brought us together? Why do we have this bond? Was it forged in Elizabethan England?"

"Nay," Shakespeare said, shaking his head. "'Tis a bond that goes back farther. Indeed, much farther."

"How far?"

"By thy modern reckoning, our souls hath known one another for two thousand five hundred years."

Joe was stunned and all he could do was stare, his mouth agape.

"Long ago, though thou doth not now remember, we met as young men—as young Athenians. The year was 490 B.C., and the place was the dusty plains of Marathon, twenty-five miles east of Athens, as the crow doth fly. We were not dissimilar, thou and I—both young men fired with enthusiasm for our city and for the fledgling young democracy we had taken a sacred oath to defend with our lives. The Persians—over twenty thousand strong—had invaded our homeland and were intent upon destroying the city. But at Marathon they stood against ten thousand heavily armed Athenian hoplites. We were among them."

Joe listened, captivated by Shakespeare's tale.

"Though our forces were outnumbered," Shakespeare continued, "we were determined. The night ere battle, as our generals debated whether to join the fray, we hoplites pledged before Athena that we wouldst never leave the field. We wouldst prevail or die in the trying. When battle was joined on the morrow, we were in the front lines of the shield wall that met the Persian foe face to face. Though we hailed from different tribes—different Athenian clans—we were thrown together in the confusion and fog of battle. A Persian axe had sundered my shield, shattered my helmet, and cast me to the ground. The death blow was imminent.

But I didst not die that day. Though blood poured down into mine eyes and obscured my vision, I beheld a young hoplite rush to my aid. I didst not know him but he bore the image of an owl—the symbol of Athena—on his shield. With the Athenian war cry on his lips, he thrust his spear into the attacker's breast, killing him outright. The Persian fell backward, whereupon the young hoplite lost his spear. 'Twas then a host of Persians converged, and that young hoplite fell, pierced in several places, mortally wounded. But his brave actions allowed me to scramble to safety and I thus survived the battle."

Joe barely dared to breathe, listening intently, his throat dry from Shakespeare's dramatic telling of the tale.

"'Twas after the battle I learned who had saved me," Shakespeare continued. "His name was Aristarchus of the Leontis Tribe, the son of Aegisthenes, a shipwright by trade. His body was cremated, and his ashes buried in the great mound along with the other brave warriors who fell that day. When I returned to Athens, I presented the father with his son's armor and spoke of the young man's great bravery. I thereafter honored the memory and deed of Aristarchus, son of Aegisthenes, unto the end of my day."

Joe hesitated, swallowing. "Was that hoplite—"

"Aye," Shakespeare said, nodding. "'Tis as thou hath surmised. Thou were that owl hoplite. Thy sacrifice allowed me to live and prosper. Indeed, I lived a long life, sired many children, and became a playwright." He grinned self-consciously. "Albeit a minor one, though I didst apprentice myself to the great Aeschylus. My plays are now lost but 'twere performed at the major Athenian festivals and at the theater of Dionysus. But 'twas that life in which I began to write plays—to put pen to parchment for the first time." He looked at Joe with great emotion, his eyes glistening. "And thee had made such a thing possible by sacrificing thy life that I might live."

Joe remained quiet; the story had affected him deeply. Although his ears had never heard the story, he felt it resonate in his gut, as though a long-lost memory had resurfaced.

"What finally happened to you?" Joe asked.

"Like many, I perished in the terrible plague that swept through Athens in 430 B.C.," Shakespeare said. "But by then I was an old man. 'Twas my time. I had no regrets. Mine life had been a charmed one—ever since that fateful day at Marathon."

Joe heard footsteps and looked over his shoulder. Betsy had entered the room, having come from the bedroom where she had been asleep. She rubbed a bleary eye and looked around, her gaze falling on the neat stack of copy near the typewriter. She looked back up at him, her expression suddenly bright and cheery.

"Looks like you got a lot of writing done last night," she said.

Joe nodded. He tried to regain his composure after the emotional jolt he'd gotten from Shakespeare's story. He lit up a cigarette.

Betsy looked at him. "Are you all right?"

He nodded again and blew out a long plume of smoke. "Yes, I'm all right. And, yes, I did get a lot of writing done last night." He paused and added with a wry smile, "In fact, I finished it."

Her eyes widened in astonishment. "You finished it? You mean you're done?"

He nodded again.

"That's wonderful!"

He paused to draw a breath. "Of course, now the hard part begins."

She gave a puzzled frown.

"I have to get it published."

CHAPTER 28

ANOTHER WEEK PASSED. ALTHOUGH Joe hadn't expected to hear anything so soon after sending out his manuscript to various publishers, he was nonetheless anxious and excited. The process had begun, he told himself. And this time he would see it through to the end. He didn't know how but he knew that he'd eventually get his book published—he'd be a published novelist.

Closer at hand, he hadn't been able to secure a screenwriting job, despite his canvassing efforts. Gable had sent a telegram saying he hadn't found any openings at MGM at the moment, but that he would keep looking.

On Friday afternoon, as Joe was returning from visiting Paramount Studios, he noticed a car parked on the curb outside his cottage. But it wasn't just any car. It was a Duesenberg Model J roadster in immaculate condition. The car was unattended now, but Joe figured the owner couldn't be too far away. He wouldn't want to be too far away with a car like that.

Joe stopped to admire it, marveling at its exquisite craftsmanship, its sleek lines and glistening metalwork. It had white-walled tires, a convertible top, and an elaborate hood ornament depicting a winged goddess. The inside seats were upholstered in rich red leather. He wondered if Clark had traded in his Packard De Luxe Eight for the Duesenberg. If he had, the actor must've signed a hefty contract with MGM.

"Ah, there you are, old bean."

Joe turned at the sound of the voice. To his surprise, Archie

Duncan-Jones came bounding toward him, his shoes squeaking against the pavement. The Englishman looked as rumpled and untidy as ever, despite the white suit and black tie he wore. He gave a subtle grin as he approached. "I must say, you are a difficult man to find."

"Hello, Mr. Duncan-Jones," Joe said. "Is this your car?"

"It is indeed."

"Quite a vehicle," Joe said.

"Please, call me Archie. No need for formalities."

"Of course." Joe grinned, putting out his hand. "How are you, Archie?"

"Excellent," Duncan-Jones replied, taking Joe's hand.

"Have you been looking for me?"

"Yes, as a matter of fact."

"Oh? I figured you probably never wanted to see my face again."

"Quite the opposite, I assure you," Duncan-Jones said. He broke into a chuckle. "I'll admit I was a bit perturbed when I found out about the whole *Hamlet* debacle. Not as perturbed as your Mr. Greenwood, however. The man was positively livid."

Joe looked down at his shoes. "I'm sorry about that. It's a bit complicated but—"

"Fear not, old chap, that's not why I came to see you."

Joe looked up, surprised.

"I wanted to make you an offer, as you Yanks say," Duncan-Jones said.

"An offer?" Joe raised an eyebrow.

For a moment Joe was speechless. When he finally broke out of his immobility, he said, "You bought it from him? You bought *The Apple Orchard?*" He stared at the ruddy Englishman, mystified.

"Yes, indeed," he said. "Mr. Greenwood drove a hard bargain, but I saw the significance of the thing right away and had to have it. As it so happens, I'm a bit of a keen negotiator myself. And I must say, all told, I think I came out on top." He had just explained to Joe how he had, during a meeting with Greenwood concerning the fallout from the *Hamlet* debacle, come across the copy of *The Apple Orchard*. Greenwood had indeed been using it as a doorstop.

The two men were seated in Joe's living room. Desdemona had taken an immediate liking to the Englishman as soon as he walked into the cottage and had planted herself on Duncan-Jones' lap soon after he had sat down. The Englishman now stroked the cat as he spoke.

"As I said, I saw the significance of the thing right away. It is quite marvelous. A masterful piece of work."

"I'm glad you think so," Joe said.

"So, my good man," Duncan-Jones said, "it appears you have been involved in finishing one of Shakespeare's unfinished plays."

"Yes, that was what I was doing," Joe admitted.

"And yet it appears the unfinished play remains unfinished," Duncan-Jones said.

Joe nodded. "Yes, we——, I mean, I didn't have a chance to finish it. Greenwood seized it before I could finish."

"Well, that is where my offer comes in."

"What offer is that?"

"Would you be willing to finish it? Because I want to produce it."

Joe was confused. "What do you mean, produce it?"

"My dear man," Duncan-Jones said, noting Joe's expression with amusement. "I'd like to make it into a picture. I believe I once told you I was interested in purchasing a movie studio." He grinned toothily and tapped his chest. "Well, I have. I acquired one outside London. And I want to make *The Apple Orchard* my first production. Bill it as 'Shakespeare's Unfinished Play, Now Finished.' What do you think?"

Joe was stunned.

"But that means, of course, it needs to be finished," Duncan-Jones added. "What do you say?"

Joe remained silent, still stunned. "I don't know what to say," he replied finally, his thoughts running in all directions.

"I will, of course, compensate you for the effort," Duncan-Jones said, nodding vigorously. "You may rest assured on that account. The artist should always be duly compensated."

"That's wonderful, of course," Joe said. He paused, utterly dumbfounded by the rapid turn of events. It was hard for him to grasp the full extent of what Duncan-Jones was telling him, especially after so much recent disappointment. He just stood for a long moment, saying nothing.

"If it's so wonderful," Duncan-Jones said, observing him with a frown, "why are you deliberating? Hang it all, man, don't you want to finish it? What are you waiting for?"

Joe's face finally broke into a grin and he said, "I'm testing the waters, trying to decide whether to wade in or stand on the shore and watch."

Duncan-Jones stared at him, puzzled.

Before the Englishman could respond, however, Joe thrust out his hand. "It's a deal," he said.

Duncan-Jones grinned and shook Joe's hand. "So, this means you'll be coming to England, then?"

Joe was surprised. "What do you mean?"

"I can't possibly have you here working on the script," Duncan-Jones said, shaking his head. "That would hardly be economical. And anyway, a movie studio needs a screenwriter. You'd be my first. What do you say?"

"Are you offering me a job?" Joe asked.

Duncan-Jones chuckled and nodded. "In my roundabout way, I suppose I am, yes."

This time Joe did not hesitate. "I accept."

"Smashing," Duncan-Jones said.

Again, they shook hands.

They spent the next half hour talking about the studio, including what Duncan-Jones had planned, what he expected from a screenwriter, and some of the movies he wanted to make. "If you don't mind, I'll swing by tomorrow with all the requisite paperwork," Duncan-Jones said. "And I'll bring along *The Apple*

Orchard so you can get started."

Duncan-Jones discretely put Desdemona aside and got to his feet. He turned to leave but noticed the *All That Glitters* manuscript lying on the table. He stopped and lingered over it.

"I say, you are productive." He gestured at it. "What is this?"

"That's my novel," Joe said.

"A novelist, a screenwriter, and a playwright? Good God, man, you are versatile. Is there anything you can't write?"

Joe just shrugged.

"Rather a hefty tome, isn't it?" Duncan-Jones gazed at the title page. "What's it about?" he asked.

Joe told him.

Duncan-Jones was quiet for several long moments. "Have you a publisher?"

"No," Joe shook his head. "But I'm trying to find one."

Duncan-Jones thought for a moment, scratching his chin. "I have a friend. A chum of mine from university. He owns a large publishing firm in London. Quite the prestigious firm. It just so happens he spent several years in India and has an interest in all things Hindu. Bit of a fanatic about it, you might say. Has his own little Hindu shrine in his office. He might find your novel of some interest."

Joe couldn't believe what he was hearing. He blinked. "Really?"

"Oh, yes," Duncan-Jones said, nodding. "Sounds like this would exactly be his cup of tea."

"Do you think he could look at it?"

"I'll make sure he does, if you like."

Joe's heart pounded and he felt flush with excitement. "Yes," he said, "I'd like that very much."

Duncan-Jones smiled. "It's settled then. I'll arrange a meeting once you're in London. No point in wasting time."

Joe chuckled and winked at the stout Englishman. "That's your motto, isn't it?"

"What is?"

"'No point in wasting time,'" Joe said. "I notice you like to get things done with very little lag time."

Duncan-Jones smiled. "It would indeed make a good motto. I shall have to think about that."

Joe saw Duncan-Jones to the door. They shook hands a final time. In his enthusiasm, Joe squeezed the Englishman's fleshy hand a little harder than usual. But Duncan-Jones didn't notice— or if he did, he didn't say anything.

The Englishman started off toward his car but stopped and swung back around with sudden determination. "Tell me something," he said, eyeing Joe keenly. "We're both men of the world. I've read a lot of Shakespeare in my life, and I must say *The Apple Orchard* is the closest thing to anything I'd say was authentic. How did you manage to do it?"

"I thought you didn't believe in Shakespeare," Joe said, grinning at him.

"Yes, well, let me rephrase that," Duncan-Jones replied, grinning back, "I've read a lot of work attributed to this so-called 'Stratford chap,' and I must say, this is quite remarkable in its similarity."

Joe shrugged and let out a wry grin. "Got lucky, I guess."

Duncan-Jones eyed him a moment longer. He opened his mouth as if to say something but clamped it shut and broke into his own version of a wry grin. "Tomorrow it is, then. Cheerio." He slid behind the wheel of the Duesenberg and drove off.

"That's amazing, Joe," Betsy said excitedly. "And you're going to take the job?"

Joe nodded.

She paused and her expression faltered. "Does that mean you're going to live in England, then?"

"It might," he said. "We'll have to see. In the meantime, I'll be over there for at least a few months, maybe longer. Once I finish *The Apple Orchard* Archie wants to go into pre-production."

"And he wants you there for that?"

Joe nodded.

Betsy looked around the living room. "What about the cottage?"

"I'll rent it out. Or sell it."

Betsy was silent for several long moments. "Maybe I could stay here," she ventured. "I mean while you're gone."

Joe grinned. "I have a better idea."

Betsy looked at him.

Joe reached across and put his hand on her knee, giving her a gentle squeeze. "I want you to come with me," he said.

A look of astonishment lit up her face. But then she shook her head quickly. "But he hired you, Joe, not me."

"I'll make sure he hires you, too."

"I can't ask you to do that," Betsy said, shaking her head again, this time with even stronger conviction.

"You're not asking me. I'm suggesting it," Joe said. "He's going to need actresses, right? Why not you?"

"But what if he says no?"

Joe paused; he shrugged. "Then I won't take the job."

"But you've already accepted."

"Not yet," he said. "I haven't signed any contract. I only gave him a verbal agreement. I can still back out."

"Oh, Joe," she said, her voice agitated. "Don't say that! This is your big chance. Don't mess it up on my account."

"You always said you wanted to go to England. Come with me. And anyway, my 'big chance' includes you."

Betsy looked at him. Her eyes began to well up with tears, and her voice was tremulous with emotion. "Do you really believe that?"

"I do." He stopped for a moment and dropped his eyes to the floor. He took a deep breath and when he looked back up, he stared directly into her eyes. "You've been my rock from the beginning. You've always believed in me and never wavered." He paused, feeling his own emotions build as he lifted his hand and tenderly touched her cheek with his fingertips. "And I love you for it."

She leaned over and kissed him. "But I really don't want you to lose this opportunity because of me."

"I'm not going to," he said. His voice was firm and confident.

"How can you be so sure?"

"Because I've already stepped into the river. The current's strong. There's no going back now."

———————

Joe and Betsy hurried across the tarmac toward the big Boeing 307 Stratoliner. It had taxied out and was now sitting like a giant silver behemoth, bright and shiny in the sun, its blunt nose aimed down the runway.

"I can't believe I'm actually going," Betsy said excitedly, struggling along with a heavy and bulging leather portmanteau. "Can we see a castle?"

Joe was hauling his own suitcase, which, though smaller than Betsy's, was nearly as overloaded with clothes and materials for a stay of several months. "On our first day off, we'll go see the biggest castle in the entire country."

"Which one is that?"

"I have no idea," Joe said, "but we'll find it."

They ascended the mobile stairs that had been set up. Betsy went first, tugging with both hands on the overstretched leather handle of her portmanteau so that it banged against each step as she struggled upward.

"Sure you don't want me to carry that?" Joe asked.

"No, I've got it," Betsy insisted. She half-carried, half-dragged her luggage up the stairs.

Joe shrugged and followed.

They entered the plane and went down the aisle, finding their seats near the back of the plane. The leather seats were surprisingly plush and comfortable, and Joe settled into his with a long, relieved sigh. He closed his eyes and sat without moving for several long minutes, simply enjoying the sensation.

Betsy's elbow suddenly nudged him. "Look at this," she said.

He opened his eyes and looked over. Betsy was holding a copy of the latest *Variety*. She pointed at the headlines.

Selznick Acquires the Rights
to Mitchell's *Gone with the Wind*

Joe moved his eyes down to the fine print.

> In a move many in the industry are considering a coup, David O. Selznick recently acquired the cinematic rights to Margaret Mitchell's sprawling bestseller *Gone with the Wind*. After a lengthy negotiation, the two parties reached a settlement reported to be in the neighborhood of $60,000. Pre-production is set for the fall, though sources say the sheer volume of work in recreating sets reflecting the old American South will likely push any serious production into the new year.
>
> *Gone with the Wind* is set in the tumultuous period of the American Civil War and tells the story of spoiled Southern Belle Scarlett O'Hara and the rakish Rhett Butler. Spanning several years, it begins in the halcyon days just before the war, in an American South character-ized by hoop skirts, mint juleps, and drooping elm trees…

Joe finished the article and looked up. "I'll be damned," he said, shaking his head in amazement.

"Wasn't that the picture Clark was telling you about?" Betsy asked.

Joe nodded. "But he said he didn't think it was ever going to get made."

"Looks like it is now. Think Clark will be in it?"

"He's going to be working with Selznick, so I would guess there's a good chance."

The plane's engines kicked into life with a roar, its propellers churning. With a lurch, it started off, rumbling down the runway, slowly gaining momentum. Soon the plane was blasting down the tarmac and with a sudden heave lifted skyward.

Joe felt himself plastered against the seat as the plane ascended. He turned and looked out the window, watching the ground recede rapidly. Soon Los Angeles lay spread out below, everything in miniature. Betsy continued to flip through *Variety*. Joe turned from the window and sat back, relaxing. He closed his eyes again.

"'Tis glorious, is it not?"

Joe's eyes snapped open.

Shakespeare was sitting next to him in the unoccupied seat near the aisle. He glowed with a vibrancy that almost hurt Joe's eyes. He was wearing his bright red doublet with the polished brass buttons, which shined brilliantly. There was a faint whiff of rosewater in the air and the Bard's beard and mustache were neatly trimmed. When he looked at Joe his eyes twinkled with an inner light.

"What is?" Joe whispered, inclining toward his ghostly companion.

Betsy cocked her head slightly but didn't look up from her reading. "Hmmm?"

"Nothing," Joe said, "just mumbling to myself."

Betsy nodded, rattled the paper, and went on reading.

"New beginnings," the Bard answered. "Such are always times for rejoicing."

Joe nodded, agreeing. He leaned in close and lowered his voice to the faintest of whispers. "So, are you ready to finish *The Apple Orchard?*"

Shakespeare nodded. "After three hundred years," he said, grinning, "aye, methinks this 'Stratford chap' is ready."

The plane rose quickly through a layer of clouds and ascended into a magnificent cobalt sky as if seeking the sun.

AFTERWORD

I HAVE ALWAYS WANTED to write a ghost story. But not one filled with graveyards, gothic buildings, and things that go bump in the night. My ghost story, when I first conceived the idea, would be different; the ghost in my story wouldn't be some pale spirit intent on creating fear, havoc, and misfortune among the living. Nor would it be some malevolent demon summoned from the depths of Hades. My ghost, by contrast, would be a helper and a mentor, an entity with the goal of assisting humans through difficult times or major life changes. This idea, of course, is not new. The ancient Greeks used the term daimon, also spelled daemon, to indicate a spirit who, through a sense of benevolence, was dedicated to helping and serving the living. This is a tutelary spirit who watches over a person. Socrates' famous daimon—who made itself known to the great philosopher as a disembodied voice—is perhaps the most well-known daimon of antiquity. In some versions, a daimon is associated with an individual from birth and guides him or her throughout life. The Greek drama-tist Menander once remarked, "A *daimon* stands by every man, straightway from his birth, a beneficent guide initiating him into the mysteries of life..."

While the idea of evil ghosts has been a mainstay in literature for centuries, the idea of a helper spirit or guide has also been used in literature, albeit less often. The 1945 novel *The Ghost and Mrs. Muir*, which was made into a movie in 1947, is one example. Writ-ten by Irish writer Josephine Leslie (who used the pseudonym

R.A. Dick), it tells the story of recently widowed Lucy Muir who moves into a cottage by the sea in coastal England that is haunted by the ghost of a sea captain. The sea captain, cantankerous but ultimately wise and kind hearted, helps Lucy navigate life's turbulent waters. Going farther back, one is also reminded of Oscar Wilde's comedy *The Canterville Ghost* about a family that moves into a manor house haunted by the ghost of a nobleman. The family learns about life through their interaction with the ghost, but the ghost also learns valuable lessons from the family.

I'd like to think my novel, *Such Stuff as Dreams*, follows in the footsteps of stories like those of Leslie and Wilde's.

www.ingramcontent.com/pod-product-compliance
Lightning Source LLC
Chambersburg PA
CBHW030644020726
47493CB00006B/1865